I

'Dr O'Brien. Wouldn't it be fair to say that if Mr Boyle had taken the advice of the paramedics to go by ambulance to Beaumont Hospital, he would still be alive? And my client would not be sitting in this court?' The defence counsel swept his arm towards a rather puny-looking man in his early twenties, sitting in the dock of Court 17 of the Central Criminal Court, a stricken look etched across his pale face. The eminent barrister's gown flapped in the air before settling again around the heft of his bulky body.

Dr Terry O'Brien was not fazed by the counsel's theatrics. She had given evidence in the High Court in Glasgow, and that was a much tougher crowd to crack.

Terry felt all eyes in the court on her. You could hear a pin drop. The defence counsel's question was an important one and deserved careful consideration. Of course, she had anticipated it and was well prepared. In fact, she had asked herself the same question the day Robbo Boyle ended up on her mortuary table.

Before she could speak, a keening sound came from the back of the court, and she peered around the barrister to establish the source of the plaintive lament. In the back row of the spectators' benches a woman in an ill-fitting black blazer was rocking back and forth, her face contorted with grief. Terry recognised her as Robbo's mother. A flustered female garda, most likely the family liaison officer, had her arm around the devastated woman's shoulders, gently trying to calm her.

Defence counsel turned his head and tutted. Terry looked towards the judge, expecting him to offer a sympathetic word, but he was scowling and gesticulating towards the gardaí standing at the back of the courtroom. He wanted this distraction removed. Even the prosecution team looked embarrassed at the display of raw emotion, shuffling papers and keeping their eyes down. She shook her head – where was the empathy? This poor woman had lost her son. Sure, wasn't that why they were all here? Terry sighed. She knew that the function of a court was to mete out justice, but did it have to be so cold and clinical?

While Robbo's mother was guided out by the FLO, Terry noticed a younger woman seated on the bench behind the defence team. She sat motionless, but the distress on her face was visible to see. The partner of the accused, Terry guessed.

Same old, same old, she thought. *Two families devastated by a single punch*. Her dad always said, 'When the drink's in, the wit's out'. A scuffle outside a pub had ended with the bouncer being knocked to the ground and a drunken eejit on a stag night accused of manslaughter.

The door to the court thudded closed and the room fell silent once again. The barrister repeated the question. Terry sat up straight and kept her eyes focused on the jury. 'I am neither clairvoyant nor God. There is no way to predict the outcome of a head injury, even if Mr Boyle had gone to hospital. But what I can say is that if he had, his chances of survival would have greatly increased.'

'No further questions, Judge.' The defence barrister swished his gown back and sat down, the bench quivering under his weight.

Pretentious twat, Terry thought.

The prosecution counsel looked up, but remained seated. Always a good sign. 'I have no further questions for Dr O'Brien, Judge.'

Terry nodded – court speak for 'thank you'.

The judge inclined his head towards her, dismissing her. 'Thank you, Doctor. You are free to go.'

She avoided looking at the accused as she walked past him. The next witness had been called and Terry smiled at the toxicologist heading for the witness box, the seat still warm. 'Good luck,' she whispered as he walked by.

God knows what the jury would make of what they were about to hear. Robbo Boyle had been a muscle-bound hulk, born of a gym obsession and large doses of steroids. She knew the defence would seize on that information suggest that Robbo's 'roid rage' had led to an aggressive attack on his client, who'd had no option but to retaliate in self-defence. She could imagine the defence counsel casting a sympathetic glance towards the feeble figure of the accused, dwarfed by the officers sitting either side of him. The clear implication being: what possible threat could he pose? The unspoken reference to David versus

Goliath would not be lost on the jurors. He would stop short of saying that the bouncer was instrumental in his own death. *Justice!* she thought as the court door slammed shut behind her.

As Terry walked out onto the concourse she rummaged in her bag and pulled out her phone. She saw that there were three missed calls from the Office of the State Pathologist, where, today, Friday, 3 January, she would be starting in her new part-time role.

Terry had been employed as a state pathologist the previous year on a temporary contract while Dr Paul Hannah was on compassionate leave. Much to her surprise she had loved it, feeling instantly at home in Dublin. In Glasgow, she'd always been an outsider, never fitting in with the team there. But here she had formed strong relationships with everyone she worked with. Well, almost everyone. She had thought that Professor Charlie Boyd, chief state pathologist, would be delighted to get rid of her when Paul returned to work, so she had been surprised when he contacted her with the job offer. It seemed that the Prof wanted to take a step back – more time for golf, she guessed.

The person who really wielded the power behind Charlie's throne, however, was Mrs Carey, the office manager of the OSP. She was not to be ignored. The fact that Mrs Carey had called repeatedly meant she had her knickers in a twist over something. Terry had hoped today would be easy and drama-free. She smiled to herself. Who was she kidding? All the same, it was good to be back.

Placing her file on the marble bench outside the courtroom, she dropped her bag next to it and stood facing the wall to discourage anyone from approaching her. She had forgotten how stressful giving evidence in court was. In Glasgow, she would have headed straight to Babbity Bowser's, a ten-minute walk from the High Court, for a stiff drink. But that was then.

She stretched and arched her back. Her shoulder ached from holding herself upright in the witness box. It had taken intensive physiotherapy to get full movement back in her upper body after the brutal attack she'd been subjected to just a few months before. She had honestly thought she might never get back to wielding her scalpel in the mortuary. While the physical injuries had healed, the mental scars were taking that bit longer.

Terry took a deep breath, trying to remember her breathing exercises. She needed a few minutes to ground herself. She was determined to show her team that Rupert Hunt, the serial killer responsible for the attack, had failed not just to kill her, but also to kill her spirit. She had trusted Hunt, a forensic archaeologist, to help in an investigation into the murder of popular true crime podcaster Rachel Reece. But instead, he had manipulated Terry in a game of cat and mouse with the sole intention of luring her to her death. It hadn't worked out as he had planned though. She had managed to fend him off, resulting in the fight for her life, one that had almost killed her and that had left Hunt with a severed spinal cord. Both had survived the ordeal, but both were changed by it. Hunt was awaiting trial for the brutal murders Terry had uncovered, but it wouldn't be over until he was jailed for life.

When she was discharged from hospital, she had retreated to her dad and stepmum's house in Glasgow to lick her wounds and reconsider her future. Charlie Boyd's job offer had come not a moment too soon. When she realised that the highlight of her days had become watching *Countdown* – her dad was always better at the words but she thrashed him with the numbers – she knew she was ready to go back to work.

She had swithered about returning to Dublin, concerned that everyone would treat her with kid gloves, but a terse phone call from Mrs Carey made it clear that a near-death experience was no excuse for tardiness and she was expected to finalise outstanding post-mortem reports in a timely manner. That had sealed the deal.

Now, feeling ready for whatever this day would bring, Terry sat down on the marble bench, ready to return Mrs C's calls. Looking about, she realised that the concourse was strangely empty. Two hours earlier it had been buzzing: counsel taking instructions from solicitors, solicitors chatting with clients, huddles of anxious family members, expert witnesses consulting notes, as well as members of An Garda Síochána milling around. Maybe it was just the pre-lunchtime lull.

Then she heard some sort of commotion drifting up below. Above the ground floor of the Criminal Courts of Justice were three tiers of courts, like three doughnuts perched atop the grand circular atrium. She leaned over the parapet to try to see what was going on. It looked chaotic from what little she could glimpse. Gardaí were shouting into their radios and running towards the stairs. She could see people hurrying towards the exit. Mrs Carey would have to wait. She slipped her phone back into her bag and, slinging it over her shoulder, started towards the glass elevators, hoping to sneak out of the building and not get caught up in whatever madness was unfolding.

When she got out of the lift on the ground floor, she kept her head down and quickly made for the security area and the exit turnstiles. Just as she hit the metal spar with her hip her arm was roughly grabbed from behind. She immediately froze and held her breath.

'Terry. Wait. You're needed.'

Recognising the voice of Detective Sergeant Mary Healy, Terry relaxed.

But when she turned around she saw the panic on Mary's face. 'Have you not heard? A guard's been shot. He's dead!'

2

Terry's heart skipped a beat, but she quickly regained her composure.

'It's not anyone you know,' Mary reassured her.

Relief washed over Terry. She had gotten close to the Dublin gardaí she had worked with, one in particular.

'But it is one of Fraser's team,' Mary explained. 'You know he's now heading a team in the Garda National Bureau of Criminal Investigation, investigating gang-related crime?'

'Mmm,' murmured Terry non-committally. She didn't want to appear too interested in the activities of Detective Inspector John Fraser.

Mary didn't seem to notice. 'He thinks this might be some form of retaliation from a gang he's got his eyes on. It could be the Hayeses, the new old family on the block. Donal Hayes was a big player back in the day and it looks like he could have resurfaced. Fraser's on his way to the scene and asked me to get hold of you – Mrs Carey told him you were on call. I'm under strict orders to take you straight to the crime scene.'

'Did he say anything else?'

'Not a lot, just to get you there ASAP.'

Terry looked away, annoyed at herself for asking. Mary would think that she cared about Fraser.

Mary punched her arm. 'Oh! Don't tell me you two aren't talking? Or anything else for that matter!' She gave her a sideways glance, eyebrows raised, then registered the scowl on Terry's face and put her hands up. 'Okay, none of my business!'

Then, seeming to suddenly remember the urgency of the matter, Mary pushed through the turnstile and strode out through the massive glass doors.

Terry hurried after her, her stiletto heels clicking across the marble floor. The white garda van was abandoned haphazardly on the pavement between the entrance to the Phoenix Park and the courts building. Terry had barely had time to fasten her seatbelt before, they sped off up Arbour Hill, lights flashing. She grabbed the handhold above the door. 'For Christ's sake, slow down.' She saw the look of shock on some old boy's face as the van careered over to the wrong side of the road, narrowly missing his car.

'Calm down, Doc. I know what I'm doing. More than can be said for these wankers.' Mary pressed her left hand firmly on the horn and swung right into the oncoming traffic and onto Montpelier Hill. 'Just up here. New builds in Delaney Gardens.'

Mary pulled in sharply behind a line of garda vehicles. 'Guess we're late to the party, Doc. Mind those good shoes – it's still pretty much a building site around here and we don't want you falling on your arse.'

Terry ignored her as she struggled to get out of the van without flashing her knickers. When she'd dressed this morning, she was thinking of the impression she wanted to make for her comeback: serious, professional, an air of sophistication – all of which the suit and heels were meant to convey. She had thought she looked pretty good, but she had to admit she would be better in trackies and runners in her current surroundings.

She took stock of the terrain, hoping to be able to navigate her way through the building debris without twisting her ankle. Up ahead was a block of ugly-looking flats, and a large group of garda personnel, some in white suits, were gathered about the bin area. Terry tried to pick out DI John Fraser. As she and Mary passed the Technical Bureau's van, the door slid open and Detective Garda Vincent Green stepped out. He was in full protective gear and had his camera slung around his neck. Vinnie was a garda photographer and seemed to turn up at all the crime scenes Terry had worked, which suited her just fine as he was the best of the bunch.

'Good timing, Mary. Welcome back, Doc. Get in there.' He nodded towards the van's interior. 'I managed to save a large suit for you. There was no chance I was letting those fat buggers rob it.'

Terry smiled at Vinnie's thoughtfulness. It was a bone of contention that the powers that be decided it was more cost-effective to order extra-large or extra-extra-large Tyvek suits. Anything smaller was coveted by the female members of the team.

'Grab some gloves too,' he instructed.

Terry ducked inside the van and emerged moments later in the protective white suit, hood up, mask on and with a fist full of gloves.

'Bet you didn't think you'd get something as exciting as this on your first day back?' He gave her arm a quick squeeze. 'It's good to see you. We missed you. Come on, the body's round the back of the building.'

Mary stayed put, letting Terry know she would wait for her to give her a lift afterwards.

'Do you have a name for him?' Terry asked, as she and Vinnie made their way across the concrete wasteland, strewn with broken glass and rubbish.

'Detective Garda Martin Higgins.'

'Doesn't ring a bell with me.'

'He is – he was – on Fraser's team. He was in Pearse Street and Galway before that. I don't think Fraser was too happy getting landed with him. By all accounts he was a bit of a lad. And he was friendly with Bob Paterson.'

'I remember Bob from the Reece case. Between you and me, I wouldn't be a fan. He seemed a bit … boorish.'

'A real gentleman in comparison with Martin Higgins, apparently.' Vinnie shrugged. 'But I guess the big brass thought Higgins spoke the same language as our gangland friends and was a good fit for Fraser's team.'

'Hmm … Anyway, who found him?'

'Anonymous call earlier this morning, as far as I know.' They fell silent as they approached the tape marking the crime scene.

Four white-clad figures were standing beside three colossal wheelie bins on the periphery of the tarmacked area behind the block. 'Doc's here!' Vinnie shouted over and one turned around. Terry recognised Detective Inspector Alan Ahern, a ballistics expert from the Technical Bureau.

'Alan's crime scene manager,' Vinnie said, and waved as Alan started making his way over to them.

'Hi, Doc.' Alan smiled at Terry. 'Good to see you. Nasty one this. Not great when it's one of our own. We haven't touched anything yet. He's on his side and I can see a bullet hole in his forehead.'

'Not great, all right.' She grimaced. As they walked towards the bins, she turned to Vinnie. 'Have you finished photographing the body?'

He nodded.

Terry perched on one of the metal plates that had been placed on the ground in front of the body. She looked it up and down. She checked the ground around it, then stood up and surveyed the area, as far as she could see. The body wouldn't be directly visible unless someone walked right over to the bin area. Higgins could have been lying there a while before someone noticed. Crouching down, she bent over the head.

'I can only see one gunshot wound to his face. I'll need to get him cleaned up to be sure there isn't anything else.' She looked over her shoulder to where Ahern was standing. 'What do you think about the blood staining?'

'Not as much blood as I would have expected to see. But if he was already lying there when he was shot in the face, the blood, brains and whatever could have exited the back of the head and all that mess might be underneath. The bullet might even be in the ground.'

'Maybe, but I'm not sure.' She called over to Vinnie. 'Have you taken close-ups of the face?'

Vinnie stepped onto the plate behind her and scrolled through the images he had taken. Once he'd found what he was looking for, he held the screen in front of her.

'Look at this, Alan.' Terry pointed at the image. 'Look at the blood over the top half of the face. Vinnie, can you enlarge that?' She watched as he zoomed in. 'Compare the blood over the forehead with the blood around his mouth and chin.' Ahern took the camera from Vinnie and studied the screen. Terry continued, 'Do you see that the blood over the bottom half of his face is thick and smudged but the blood over the top half, around the gunshot injury, is a light smear and there is textured pattern to it?'

Ahern nodded. 'So what does that mean?' He handed the camera back to Vinnie.

'After he was shot, something was put over the wound to soak up the blood. A towel or something.'

'But why?' Ahern didn't look convinced.

'To prevent blood contaminating someone or something? Maybe he was shot in another location and then his body moved here. He might have been shot a second time in the mouth when the body was dumped here, hence the blood around it. Just to throw us off the scent. But why? And why here?'

She looked around and was surprised to see John Fraser standing behind them. He came closer to their huddled group, keeping his eyes on the body. 'Maybe because we've been keeping an eye on this building,' Fraser said. 'We had intel that the Hayeses were running a brothel from the top flat.' He glanced back at the desolate block. 'But they've all scarpered.'

The RTÉ van was just pulling up as Terry came out onto the road looking for Mary, intending to tell her she was almost ready to leave. She spotted the garda vehicle first, then the young guard who waved her over. When Terry reached her, Mary said, 'Keep that up.' She pointed at the hood of the white coverall Terry was wearing. She was right – it was the perfect disguise. The pathologist would be just one of several anonymous personnel hanging around the Technical Bureau vans.

By the time she had walked to the kerb, Mary was already in the driver's seat. Terry hesitated. This was wrong: the normal protocol was to remove all potentially contaminated protective clothing and leave it at the scene. She stood with her hand on the door handle, reluctant to risk an encounter with the media.

Then door slammed into her, as Mary shoved it open, making the decision for her. 'Get the fuck in!' Mary shouted, leaning across the passenger seat. 'Now!'

Terry looked back over her shoulder and saw a soundman and a cameraman hurrying towards them. She jumped in and the van sped away.

As they hit the quays, Mary slowed and Terry relaxed her grip on the handhold. At the lights, Mary glanced at the time and sighed. 'Is it all right if I take you straight to the mortuary? I need to get back to court. I've got a domestic abuse case that's been dragging on, but we finally got it over the line. Judge

Henderson has made it known he wants it done and dusted today. He's happy to sit a little later this evening, but he'll have a face on him if it tips over to Monday. It'll ruin his court list for next week. Court 18 is brutal. They don't call him Hanging Henderson for nothing.'

'I thought it was assaults and road traffics in there. Not quite hanging offences.'

'And the domestics. I'd say he takes no prisoners, but he does. If they're found guilty, they get the maximum sentence, especially the men.'

Terry leaned back against the headrest and closed her eyes, remembering again how she'd hoped for an easy first day back. She could feel a familiar throbbing at her temples, a clear sign that a headache was imminent. She hoped Mary would take the hint and leave her be. It worked. Nothing further was said until they reached the entrance to the mortuary and the van cleared the security gate.

The Dublin mortuary was situated in the medico-legal complex off Griffith Avenue. Toxicology and Forensic Science were close neighbours. The mortuary occupied the ground floor of the building housing the Office of the State Pathologist. These modern edifices concealed the murky secrets of death and crime in Ireland.

Terry jumped out of the van, shouting her thanks to Mary. She rang the bell on the wall beside the gate opening into the mortuary's vehicular entrance. In truth, the only vehicles entering carried the dead or belonged to the state agencies investigating the deaths, and the mortuary staff would have been watching out for her. Mrs C would have told them a guard had been shot, and, Friday afternoon or not, it would be all hands to the helm.

Within seconds, the gates slowly slid open and she followed the footpath around to the back of the OSP building to the mortuary entrance where the hearses and ambulances pulled up, steeling herself for whatever reception she got. She hadn't seen any of the upstairs or downstairs staff since she'd left hospital and gone back to Glasgow following the 'incident with Hunt', as her dad liked to call it.

Terry needn't have worried. When she rounded the corner, the mortuary door burst open and Tomas came flying out. He was one of the mortuary staff, an anatomical pathology technician. He took the steps two at a time and embraced her in a bear hug. She was taken aback by his exuberant welcome and teetered on the top step. 'Steady on, Tomas. Folk will talk!'

He jumped back, embarrassed, then realised she was grinning at him.

'Will you stop that nonsense and get back in here! You're letting the heat out.'

She recognised the gruff voice and looked over Tomas's shoulder. Jimmy, the mortuary manager, was standing in the doorway. Jimmy was old school – he was probably younger than he looked, with a grumpy demeanour and dishevelled appearance.

'Hi, Jimmy. Good to see you.' She followed them both inside.

Tomas scurried along the corridor, like an excited springer spaniel. 'We've got your room ready, Doc. Mrs Carey even got a gold nameplate for the door.'

The 'Pathologist's Office' was now 'Dr O'Brien's Office'.

Tomas pulled the sleeve of his white lab coat over his hand and gave the sign a little polish before he opened the door with a flourish and stood aside to let her enter. Terry laughed and stepped past him. She knew they were waiting for her reaction and she didn't want to disappoint. 'Wow!' She turned around slowly, taking in the improvements and nodding her head in approval. The old scuffed furniture, rickety hatstand and stacks of chairs had been replaced by a sleek desk, matching bookcase and a humongous black leather chair. She smiled at the two expectant faces. 'It's really fancy. Thanks, boys. You done good.'

Tomas beamed back. Jimmy, true to form, shook his head, brushing off her praise. 'Oh, it wasn't our doing. The prof ordered the desk. Cherrywood or something. Though I thought a bit of Pledge would have brought up the old one a treat.' He turned and left. A flurry of animal hair and the distinct odour of wet dog lingered in his wake as he retreated to the tea room.

Terry watched him go. 'He's in good form. There must be a race meeting on tonight.' Jimmy's real passion was his greyhounds. He wasn't a people person.

Sitting in her new chair, she smoothed her hands across the gleaming wood of the desk. 'And who is responsible for this beautiful floral display?' She pointed to the centre of the desk, where there sat a small plastic plant that she recognised from the waiting room for families coming in to identify their loved ones.

'That was Jimmy,' said Tomas. 'He did run it under the tap to take off the dust.'

Terry stifled a giggle. 'It's a lovely touch, but maybe not practical on the desk. I'll find a better spot for it.'

Then, a thud made Terry and Tomas look towards the door. Jimmy shuffled in, balancing a china teacup on a saucer. 'Leave the doctor in peace, Tomas.' The cup rattled on the saucer as he placed the tea on the desk, spilling some in the process. 'Mrs Carey sent a tea set down from upstairs,' he said by way of explanation for the dainty offering.

Trust Mrs C, Terry thought. She should nip upstairs and say hello to her, but she needed to make sure they were ready for the post-mortem first. At that moment her mobile rang. Michael's name flashed on the screen. She ushered the two men out.

'Hi, Mikey boy,' said Terry cheerfully, delighted to hear another friendly voice.

Michael had been her best friend since their first day at medical school at Glasgow University. But he had dropped out, deciding a doctor's life wasn't for him, and eventually became a forensic scientist. That had piqued her interest and she had pursued a parallel career in forensic pathology, training in Boston which is where she had met Paul Hannah. Later, she'd introduced Paul to Michael, and they both ended up in Dublin. When Paul took compassionate leave and returned to Boston for family reasons, Michael and Paul split up. For a time, it had looked unlikely that he would return to Ireland, but he had, and they were now back together. But their relationship was complicated and exhausting.

'Don't Mikey me. What the hell are you up to, Terry?' Well, maybe not so friendly.

'Nothing.'

'Nothing. That blonde woman on the news just announced that the assistant state pathologist had attended the scene of a garda murder. And then I see you flash up on the screen having the chats with Vinnie and Alan.'

'That's neither here nor there. Anyway, I'm not an assistant, I'm a part-timer.'

'When were you thinking of telling me you were back in town?' he demanded. 'I've got to find out my best friend is back from the dead on RTÉ's breaking news? Class!'

'Well, I would have thought it was obvious,' Terry replied. 'You knew I was due back, I just didn't mention a specific date. And who did you think was covering your boyfriend this weekend while he's off in Cardiff? Didn't he mention it? Charlie's in Madeira. That leaves me. I didn't think I'd get called out on day one. I was planning to give you a ring to meet up this weekend to celebrate my return. I just wanted to come back quietly and not make a fuss.'

'Are you in a mood with me because Paul's back on the scene and I didn't come to Glasgow to visit you over Christmas?' he huffed. 'We've been busy.' Typical Michael. Always on the defensive.

'Michael,' sighed Terry, pushing the plastic plant over to the edge of her desk, 'you're being an arse. I'm delighted Paul has returned from Boston. And so is Charlie. Working in the OSP part-time suits me just fine. For God's sake, how long do you think it would be before Charlie and I came to blows without Paul as a buffer? This way, I parachute in and out, which minimises the risk of me getting on Charlie's nerves, and Niamh gets her eye candy back in her web – I mean, lab. You do know she thinks she can turn Paul?' she teased.

Niamh was the histology technician in the OSP. She

processed the pieces of tissue the pathologists took during post-mortems to confirm their findings or to exclude other pathologies or diseases that might be relevant to the cause of death. Niamh was a bit quirky but she was a damn good technician. Her only fault was her eternal quest for a husband. No man was safe, even Paul, who was in a relationship and gay. She wasn't interested in Michael though, who she thought was 'cute but a short-arse', and there was no way she was giving up her heels.

Unappeased, Michael snapped back. 'There's been no call for a forensic scientist to go to the scene. I would have thought they would want to bring in all the big guns for this one?'

'Ah, well, Alan Ahern is crime scene manager. I'm sure he'll be in touch if he needs you. Will it be a bit awkward, what with you dumping him when Paul came back?'

'There won't be an issue. Alan and I are okay. We're professionals. We can work together.'

'If you say so. I think he'll be glad of your input in this case,' she said, softening her tone, hoping Michael would lose his sarky attitude. 'Look, what about a drink Sunday night when Paul gets back and takes over the on-call? I'll text you.'

Michael agreed and Terry said a quick goodbye when she heard activity in the corridor outside her door. She looked out just in time to see a man and woman being ushered into the waiting room. Tomas closed the door behind them.

When he saw Terry, he whispered, nodding at the door, 'That's Martin Higgins's wife. We weren't expecting her. Were you?'

Terry shook her head.

'I had to get the hearse to wait round the corner until I got her inside. I'll get them to bring the body in now.'

'I didn't expect her to be brought here so soon. I told them I'd be in touch when we were ready for her to do the formal ID. We know who he is, for God's sake,' said Terry, heading back into her office. 'See if she wants a tea or coffee. Is there a family liaison officer with her?'

'Jimmy's got the tea in hand. The guard with her isn't an FLO. He's been here before at post-mortems. I know his face but can't remember his name. He just ignored me when I asked.'

'Rude. Let's not get involved – we'll leave it to DI Ahern. I'll check with him when he's here. You get the body set up in the post-mortem room.'

Ahern and the scene-of-crime officers, or SOCOs as they were more commonly known, arrived ten minutes later, and Tomas escorted the DI into Terry's office. There were no spare chairs, so he perched on her desk.

'I'm sorry that the wife was brought in before the PM but there's really nothing I can do. My hands are tied. The order came from above.'

Terry frowned. 'Alan, you know as well as I do that nobody but myself and the technicians should get near the body until we've harvested all the forensic evidence. We can't risk contamination.'

'I know, I know,' he said apologetically. 'But this time we need to make an exception to the rule. Please just go along with me on this.'

Terry knew that there was no point insisting on delaying formal identification. She wasn't going to win this battle. 'Fine, but she'll have to identify him from the viewing room. I don't care who she is. We can't afford to take any risks on a case this big.'

As a compromise, she asked Vinnie to take some preliminary photographs while she gowned up before heading into the post-mortem room. With assistance from the SOCOs, she took tape lifts from the face and ran a swab over the gunshot entry wound. Paper bags had been put over the hands at the scene, so she draped a sterile sheet over the body, tucking the sides under and leaving only his head exposed before she allowed Tomas to clean up the face and put a dressing over the wound so as not to distress Mrs Higgins too much.

Terry hated when her normal ritual of taking forensic samples from a body was interrupted. Sighing, she dropped her disposable gloves and gown in the bin. She checked her reflection in the glass window above the dissection bench, washed her hands and left the room, kicking off her wellingtons outside the swing door to the changing area and slipping on her clogs. Tomas wheeled the body away to the adjacent viewing room.

Bracing herself, she walked into the waiting room. She tried to conceal her surprise at finding Detective Garda Bob Paterson inside, sitting very close to Mrs Higgins. Vinny had mentioned Paterson and Martin Higgins were friendly, Terry remembered. She had never liked Paterson. There was something about the guard that unsettled her, a sense that barely contained aggression was hidden just below the surface. She decided to ignore him and introduced herself to Mrs Higgins. Terry was constantly surprised by how calm the family of the deceased could be – no screaming or shouting, just a resigned acceptance. This woman sat staring ahead, dry-eyed. Gesturing towards it, Terry asked her to accompany her to the curtained window. Paterson grabbed Mrs Higgins's arm and yanked her to her feet when she didn't immediately stand up. Terry shot him a scathing look, appalled that he should treat a colleague's wife so roughly. She would have a word with Ahern about him.

Terry rapped on the window and the curtain slid back, revealing Martin Higgins lying on the metal table. Mrs Higgins slumped a little. Terry made to steady her but Paterson tightened his grip on her arm and pulled her back. Mrs Higgins wrestled her arm free then and turned to Terry. 'It's him, my husband Martin. Martin Higgins.' She turned to leave and, as she did, Terry was sure she heard her add under her breath, 'May he rot in hell.'

Mrs Higgins blessed herself and walked out the door.

The atmosphere in the post-mortem room was subdued. The viewing gallery was standing room only, with Fraser front and centre, flanked by Mary and Paterson. Tomas had refused to allow anyone other than the crime scene manager, DI Ahern, garda photographer Vinnie Green and two SOCOs from the Technical Bureau – Pete Harkins, the fingerprinter, and Clodagh Rafferty, a member of the ballistics section – into the post-mortem room.

Tomas had everything laid out just as he knew Terry liked,

so she ignored her audience and set to work. She understood that the gardaí were more interested in this post-mortem than usual, the victim being one of their own, but she knew that could lead to cutting corners and making assumptions that in the future could come under attack when, or if, the case came to court. She would not be hurried or harassed.

She started with hair combings and swabs before removing the clothing, handing each item to Clodagh, who laid them out on the adjacent PM table. Each step was photographed by Vinnie. Knowing this often provoked a wince from those observing, Terry concealed a smile as she inserted the rectal thermometer into the anus to take the internal body temperature. 'I'll need the local temperatures over the last twenty-four hours. Even then, don't get your hopes up.' She looked up at the faces anxiously watching her behind the glass partition. 'Best I'll be able to do regarding time of death is a range – a few hours either way. Sorry.' Next, she swabbed the inside of the mouth. As she withdrew the swab, a large blood clot slithered out. Fearing Higgins had had a second shot to the mouth, she prised his teeth apart with a bit of effort, rigor mortis having seized up his small muscles. She reached for the handle of the overhead light as she tilted the head back to get a look inside the mouth.

'Fuck!' She let the head drop back onto the table and took a step back. Startled by the clang of the head against the metal table, Tomas came over. She looked up at the figures behind the glass.

Fraser leaned over and spoke into the microphone. 'What's wrong, Terry?'

'His tongue's missing,' she said quietly, almost in disbelief.

At that precise moment, Clodagh let out a yell. 'There's something in his jacket pocket!'

All eyes turned to the SOCO's table. 'Put the jacket down!' Terry told the stricken guard. 'Tomas, carefully move it over to the dissecting bench. Vinnie, get ready!'

The figures behind the glass surged forward to get a better view as Tomas placed the jacket on the bench. Terry suddenly felt claustrophobic. Carefully laying out the jacket, she signalled to Vinnie and pointed at the bloodstains around the collar and down the centre front. These were directional drips from the entry wound, confirming that Higgins had been upright, standing or even sitting, when shot.

Blood was smeared around the left-hand jacket pocket, but it also appeared to have seeped through the material from inside the pocket. Tomas handed Terry a sturdy pair of surgical scissors and she made two cuts to form a flap and peeled it back to reveal a bloody mass, which she carefully lifted with forceps and placed on the dissection board. Then she dabbed at it with sterile paper towels.

Vinnie followed every movement through his lens, recording each step photograph by photograph. She was aware that Clodagh had moved over beside her and Terry could hear the other SOCO retching. She looked up at Fraser, who was now the only man standing behind the glass, but even he looked perturbed.

Gesturing with the forceps towards the gory lump, Terry said, 'The missing tongue. It's been hacked out.' She pointed at the ragged strands of tissue opposite the tip of the tongue.

'What the fuck's going on?' asked Fraser to nobody in particular.

Mary leaned over his shoulder to get a look. 'Even Higgins didn't deserve that.'

Fraser turned his back to Terry. She could see the tension in the hunch of his shoulders. 'What are you all doing here, gawping?' he shouted at the assembled guards, who had returned their seats to avoid seeing Terry's discovery. 'Get the fuck off your arses and get out there!'

She heard the scraping of chairs as the room emptied. She rapped on the glass to get his attention. 'You don't have to hang about, John. We'll carry on here and I can bring you up to speed later.'

'No need. Alan will fill me in. There's a case conference in the morning, 8 a.m. at Walter Scott House. Can you be there?'

She nodded. Without another word Fraser got up and left.

3

Terry groaned as her phone alarm beeped incessantly at seven the following morning. She hadn't got home until after midnight. The post-mortem had taken a long time – she'd wanted to be sure she missed nothing, outside or in. While Tomas cleaned up, she had gone back to her office to type up her notes. Normally she would dictate her findings and Mrs Carey would produce the post-mortem report, but it had been late and she was exhausted, so she settled for a list of the salient points.

After dragging herself out of bed, she jumped in the shower, hoping it would wake her up, and slapped on some tinted moisturiser and mascara. She decided to throw on her Levi's, a white shirt and a pair of New Balance runners. It was Saturday – no one would be in office wear.

By 7.30 a.m. she was on the road and driving to the swish new garda building of Walter Scott House, or WSH as it was more commonly referred to by its occupants, in Kilmainham.

She crossed her fingers that there would be a free space in the basement car park. Luck was on her side, and she parked quickly and bounded up the stairs, fearful she was late for the conference. Fraser had been curt with her yesterday, which shouldn't have come as a surprise given that she had been the one keeping him at arm's length, refusing to take his calls when she was in Glasgow. The distance had made it easy for her to pretend he didn't exist, but now that she was back and confronted by the reality of him, she wasn't sure how she felt anymore. All she knew was that she didn't want to piss him off even more by swanning into the case conference when he was mid-sentence.

When Terry opened the door to the main conference room, she was taken aback: it was packed. She squeezed between the groups, who were speaking in hushed tones or not at all. She found a small gap where she could see the front table facing the room, where Sandy Stapleton, the assistant commissioner for organised and serious crime, sat flanked by a guard in a flashy uniform and a man Terry recognised. At the right end of the table sat Fraser and a group of chief superintendents, superintendents and detective inspectors from Dublin and beyond.

The troops have rallied, she thought. There were criminals out there who would be only too happy to lob a grenade or two into the room. The tension was palpable and intimidating. They were worried – and she understood why. This didn't have the feel of a random attack – and a gangland shooting was one thing, but the brutality of this killing was something else.

She noticed Monica MacKenzie, Michael's boss and head of Forensic Science Ireland, across the other side of the room, and of course she had bagged a seat. She was talking to the woman who had just taken over the state laboratory, Dr Fionnuala Brady. It was too early to have the toxicology results from the post-mortem, so maybe she had been brought in because they thought there was a possible link with the drug gang Mary mentioned yesterday.

The assistant commissioner got to his feet and cleared his throat. 'Good morning. Thank you all for coming in on a Saturday morning. The death of a member of An Garda Síochána is a tragedy. Detective Garda Martin Higgins was a valued member of the force. I will personally see to it that his wife and family are fully supported.' Stapleton turned to the man sitting to his left. 'Minister Farrelly has come this morning to assure me that I have his full backing.'

The last time Terry had seen the minister had been when he'd visited her in hospital to thank her for her role in bringing his niece Rachel Reece's killer to justice. He had been minister for finance then.

Farrelly nodded to confirm his support. The assistant commissioner continued. 'I know you are all affected by this attack on one of our own. I know I can rely on you to apprehend the perpetrator as swiftly as possible.'

Terry appreciated that this was a call to arms, and those in the room were responding favourably – she almost expected clapping and cheering. After some other words of encouragement, Stapleton took his leave and led his entourage and the minister out, followed by a mass exodus of many of the gardaí who were not directly involved in the investigation. As the numbers dwindled, she felt herself relax.

'Dr O'Brien, come and sit down.' Fraser waved her over. 'I've organised tea and coffee. Once everyone's settled, we'll get on with things.'

After she grabbed a quick coffee, Fraser introduced her to the people who remained, and Terry stood and faced her audience. A hush descended in anticipation of her revelations. Of course, by now it was general knowledge that DG Martin Higgins had been shot and his tongue cut out, but Terry knew that what she was about to tell them would come as something of a surprise.

'Death was due to a contact gunshot injury to the head.' She paused, waiting for the usual smartarse responses to her stating the bleeding obvious. But there was silence, as they all stared straight ahead, transfixed by the image of Martin Higgins that Vinnie had projected onto the giant screen.

'As you can see, the entry wound is just above the left eyebrow.' She turned and pointed to the injury. 'In the centre is a hole about half a centimetre across and the skin margin is split.' Walking over to the screen, she tapped it with the tip of her pen. 'It has a star shape.'

Terry nodded at Vinnie and a closer view appeared. 'See the searing of the skin caused by the flame and hot gases produced as the bullet is fired from the barrel? When I peeled back the skin, soot and unburnt gunpowder were trapped between the skin and the skull.' She realised that a lot of the guards were looking at the ground. 'Don't worry, I'm not going to show you inside shots.'

Eyes flicked back up to the screen. She pointed at her own forehead. 'The bullet penetrated the skull and carried on through the brain and out the back of the head.' The next photographs showed a large, ragged split in the scalp on the right side of the back of the head. 'A through and through wound.' She looked over her shoulder at the photo showing a probe sticking out the front and back of the head. 'The brain was wrecked and no bullet was retrieved at the post-mortem.'

Alan Ahern got to his feet. 'I have reason to believe his own gun was the murder weapon. It had been fired recently and replaced in his holster. I'll be carrying out a full ballistic examination later today.'

Terry continued. 'I've been told Martin Higgins was known to carry a Leatherman. One with the initials MH was retrieved at the scene. It would require a sharp, sturdy blade to hack off the tongue. It's likely his own penknife was used to cut it out.'

'Fucking animals!' Further expletives echoed around the room.

'Settle down!' Fraser shouted. An uneasy silence settled.

A voice burst out from the back. 'Was his tongue cut out before or after?'

Terry craned her neck to see who had posed the question. 'I'll come back to that.'

The next photograph showed the right arm. 'There were linear abrasions encircling the wrists – handcuff marks. But no handcuffs were found at the scene.'

Ahern nodded to confirm. 'Martin's handcuffs are missing. Was he cuffed when he was shot?' Ahern asked Terry.

Terry thought for a second. 'I don't know. I've taken a sample of skin from the wrists for histology. I might be able to age the scratches to give me a better idea. But if he had been cuffed, why remove them and take them away and leave the gun and the knife? That doesn't make any sense.' She looked around the room. 'There were no other significant marks. Nothing to suggest he was assaulted, manually restrained or tried to defend himself. Although I can't rule out a whack to the back of the head due to the damage the bullet did. And of course, toxicology will take some time.'

At this, Dr Brady, the toxicologist, interjected. 'So far, our preliminary analysis of the urine sample Dr O'Brien sent to the state lab shows 35 milligrams of alcohol – the equivalent of one drink. The drug screen will take another few days.'

'So he could have met up with someone for a drink?' It was the same guard who had spoken before.

'That would be pure speculation, Chris.' Fraser dismissed the question and nodded at Terry to go on.

She nodded back. 'To summarise then: He was shot at point-blank range. He may have been restrained with his handcuffs. And to answer a previous question, then his tongue was cut out. The tongue is highly vascular so would have bled like hell if he had still been alive. There wasn't much blood so I reckon it was cut off shortly after he was shot.'

'Is there anything else you can add, Doctor?' Fraser asked.

'Well, then I'd be the one speculating,' she warned.

'Yes, but there would at least be some substance behind it.'

'Okay.' Terry turned back to her rapt audience. 'The pattern of bloodstaining on his clothes and face suggests to me he was upright or seated when shot. But – and it is a big but – this could have happened at a location other than the spot where the body was found. There was an imprint pattern on the blood around the entry wound, so I think something was wrapped around his head to prevent him leaking blood and leaving a blood trail. His body could then have been moved to where he was discovered. Then his tongue was cut out.' She looked over at Monica MacKenzie. 'Of course, FSI haven't had a chance to check out the scene or the body yet. But that's what I think.' She looked around the room, waiting for the penny to drop. She turned back to Fraser. She could sense the room becoming restless and the noise level began to rise.

'So there's possibly another scene,' Fraser said. When she nodded, he slammed his hand on the table. 'You heard the state pathologist. We need to find it now.'

4

Terry had waited to see if Fraser would have a word with her after the conference, but no. He immediately left the room, phone pressed to his ear, a look of intense concentration on his face. Alan Ahern had come over to let her know that there was nothing pending, no deaths needing her expertise. So she had slipped out of the room before anyone else approached her.

Deciding to take advantage of a few hours to herself, she hit the shops. She had let the lease go on her last flat because she didn't know if she still would have a job in Dublin after her run-in with Hunt. It was good to have a change, anyway. New beginnings and all that. Her new flat at Spencer Dock came fully furnished, but it was a bit soulless. If things worked out, Dublin would be home for some time. She stocked up on some classy-looking faux fur cushions and soft throws in varying shades of cream. Hopefully they would lend a cosy feel to the place.

Back at her flat Terry dressed the leather sofa and her bed, delighted with the results. After lighting some candles she put an M&S lasagne in the microwave. A nice red wine would go down a treat, but sadly not when she was on call. Grudgingly she flicked the kettle on. She checked her phone again, but the screen remained frustratingly free of any missed calls or WhatsApp notifications. She had hoped Fraser might get in touch, but she guessed a dead guard took precedence over a dying relationship. She was probably being a bit melodramatic, but that's what Saturday nights alone did to a person, she guessed. Now she was wondering why she pushed him away. Was it simply because she was terrified of getting too close to him? She wasn't good at talking about her feelings and it was looking like she wouldn't get a chance. It was enough to give her indigestion. Or maybe that was just the lasagne.

She was on her third episode of *Married at First Sight Australia* when her mobile buzzed – she could tell from the prefix it was a garda number. She muted the TV. 'Hello.' She waited for the caller to speak.

After a pause, she heard, 'Is that Dr O'Brien?'

'Yes.'

Then the voice at the end of the line hesitated again. She rolled her eyes. Michael said she could be downright rude on the phone, but she could never understand why people couldn't get straight to the point. *Someone is dead, get on with it.* 'I'm just guessing,' she said, breaking the interminable silence, 'but I would suspect you're dealing with a death?'

The guard stuttered out the facts. Two deaths, actually. And two post-mortems for her to carry out on a Sunday morning.

Terry sighed wearily as she switched off the TV and got ready for bed. *Welcome back, indeed.*

'The coroner sent these requests through.' Tomas pointed at the two C71 forms he had left on her desk, the forms prepared by the gardaí when a death is unexpected, or unnatural, and must be reported to the coroner for further investigation regarding the cause and circumstances.

The first form told the tale of a middle-aged man who had been found dead, curled in a ball, as if sleeping peacefully, in his front garden in the Liberties. He was discovered behind the perimeter wall, hidden from view of any passers-by. His house keys had been found in the flower bed at the side of his front door. He'd last been seen stoating back from the Brazen Head, where he had been drinking. There was no evidence he had been attacked or even fallen.

The other death was a twenty-four-year-old man, also found collapsed in his garden, but in contrast, a neighbour had seen him jogging up the path to his home in Glasnevin on his way back from his evening run. He found him on the ground and unresponsive an hour later when he went out to put rubbish in his bin. The young man had been taken to the Mater Hospital, but he was pronounced dead on arrival.

Soon, Terry was looking down at the first body on the mortuary table. The garda report had described him as middle-aged but he looked to be in his sixties. She flicked through the diagrams on her clipboard and pulled out the ones depicting clothing. 'Tomas, is this how he came in? You could spit through that jacket he's got on. It's bloody freezing out there. What is it with these eejits?'

Drink and the elements were a powerful mixture – this guy likely froze to death. It didn't take her long to confirm that. When she opened his stomach, not only did the whiskey fumes just about knock her out, but the tell-tale stomach ulcers were revealed, as well as the so-called leopard-skin appearance of hypothermia. He'd probably dropped his keys when he tried to open his front door and eventually gave up looking for them, lying down to sleep before being overcome by the cold. It was a pity he apparently hadn't a partner, or anyone, really, waiting for him to come home or he might have been found in time. She had no doubt that toxicology would confirm he was too drunk to think clearly.

Terry changed her gloves and plastic apron, picked up a fresh set of diagrams and moved to the other table. *What a contrast to the previous fella*, she thought. This guy looked fit. Okay, he wasn't wearing much more than his buddy on the adjacent table, but he had been out running, the cold not a deterrent to his activities – probably a welcome relief.

Half an hour later she held the answer to his death in her hand – a humungous heart, double the size of a normal one. Hypertrophic cardiomyopathy is a genetic condition, with the heart outgrowing the body. It was literally a ticking timebomb, a hidden danger lurking inside the chest, waiting to take the unlucky individual by surprise. He could never outrun his destiny. Sadly, it was too late for him but there were implications for the family, who would need genetic counselling and thorough medical examinations to identify others at risk.

And they would now live with the constant fear of another family member dropping dead at any time.

This job sucked at times. Well, actually, it sucked all the time. There was never a happy ending.

After work, Terry dropped her car off in the residents' car park under her apartment block. She'd arranged for a drink with Michael and had less than an hour to get showered and changed. Whatever disinfectants the mortuary used, they clung to her hair and Michael was sure to notice. Even Jo Malone couldn't mask it. She jumped on the Luas into the city centre with ten minutes to spare.

Mulholland's on Dame Lane was half empty, which wasn't surprising given that the usual clientele was mainly gardaí and all leave had been suspended during the investigation into the murder of DG Higgins. The place was soulless without their background chatter. It always gave off school canteen vibes, minus the smell of stewed cabbage.

Her friend was leaning against the bar. She smiled, transported back to the day they met at uni. His friendship meant so much to her. They were like bickering siblings – each knew the buttons to push – but they couldn't stay angry with one another for long.

Proving her point, Michael turned towards the door as she walked in, as if he sensed her presence and his face broke out in a wide grin at the sight of her. After giving her a tight hug, he settled her at a table and went to get them both a gin and tonic. The wine here gave her heartburn – gin was a safer bet.

'Cheers, Tez!' he said as they clinked glasses. 'What were you up to today? Anything juicy?'

'Nah, just an old man who froze to death after a night boozing, and a fitness fanatic with hypertrophic cardiomyopathy.'

'Poor buggers.' He screwed up his face and stirred the ice in his glass with his finger.

'Anyway,' Terry continued, desperate to change the subject from work and death, 'you never told me how Christmas went at your sister's.'

'Ah, it was fine, you know, the usual family drama. Nothing interesting, though.'

'Lucky you,' said Terry. 'Mine was full-on. Dad and Aileen had their usual Christmas bash. Invited all their friends and the neighbours. And then there was Aileen's family. They can fairly put it away.'

Michael shook his glass in her face. 'Pot! Kettle! Anyway, how is the new flat? Now you're just along the quays from me.'

'Yes, you and Paul can pop in when you're passing, see for yourself. How's it going with him, by the way?' Terry dared to ask. It was either amazing or awful. There never seemed to be anything in between where Paul and Michael were concerned.

Michael ran his finger up and down his glass, avoiding eye contact.

Obviously, it was coming down on the side of terrible. Terry grabbed his hand 'Okay, what's the story?'

He shifted in his seat and let out a long sigh. 'Paul wants to take it slowly. We're dating, apparently!' There was an edge to his voice.

'Maybe that's a good idea. He was the one to fuck off and

leave you.' But Michael looked so dejected that Terry softened her tone. 'Okay, maybe I'm being a bit harsh. His mum was sick, but she's better and he did come back. It'll work out. You're good together. He's just being ...' She wanted to say 'an arse' but settled on 'cautious'.

Then, she got up abruptly, pushing back her chair. 'Right! Hold that thought. I'll be back.'

Michael was engrossed in his phone when she returned, gingerly lowering two flaming glasses onto the table. 'Shots. No argument.'

'Fuck!' groaned Michael. 'Not sambuca!'

'Don't be such a killjoy,' she chided, raising her glass to her lips. 'Blow and down. One, two, three.'

In unison they lifted the glasses. After downing the shots, they slammed the sticky empties on the table and grimaced, chanting in unison, 'Slange! Here's tae us, wha's like us? Gey few an' they're a' deid!'

A gulp of gin was immediately required to cleanse the palate.

Terry wiped her hand over her mouth. 'No more boyfriend talk. How's your mum? It was good of her to come and visit me at my dad's. She was saying she was having bother with her hip.'

'She's fine! She's never happy unless she's got something wrong. She was in her element down at our Sarah's new place in Kent. It's something else. Living the good life.' Michael added with a wistful sigh, 'Paul loved it too.'

'Maybe we could do a long weekend over there?' Terry suggested hopefully. One weekend back at work and she was already thinking she might need a break.

Michael didn't reply and Terry realised he was checking out something behind her. She turned around and saw Alan Ahern and another man pulling out chairs at a nearby table. She clicked her fingers in her friend's face. 'Michael! Seriously, you're not still mucking around with him?'

He crouched down in his chair, hiding behind her. 'No! I haven't even seen him since Sinnott's retirement do just before Christmas.' Chief Superintendent Archie Sinnott had overseen the investigation into the murder of Rachel Reece. Terry had crossed swords with him on more than one occasion.

'Well, keep it that way if you're serious about Paul.' Really, she tried her best to be supportive, but she had a niggling feeling about their relationship. She always felt that Paul indulged Michael and was a little superior. But then, she was no expert. She had a string of romantic failures behind her. She had been glad when Michael took up with Alan – she really liked the detective inspector and felt comfortable in his company. Anyway, it would work itself out. Michael just had to make up his mind. She stood up. 'I'm off to the toilet. Your round, Romeo. Get them in!'

The drinks were on the table when she returned, but Michael was missing. And there was no sign of him at Alan's table.

A moment later Michael reappeared, sliding his mobile back into his pocket. 'That was Monica. She wants me on the Higgins investigation. Is tomorrow okay? She asked me to check out what forensic evidence the SOCOs took and get a feel for it.'

'I told you they needed a forensic scientist. Are you sure you'll be all right?' Terry flicked her head back towards Alan Ahern. At that moment her mobile bleeped. She pulled it out of her bag and checked the screen. 'The minister for justice has asked to see me in his office tomorrow morning. Guess that means I won't get out to the scene until the afternoon.'

'Get you – the minister! Maybe you're getting the National Bravery Award or freedom of the city!'

'I'll be sure to bring my sheep along to St Stephen's Green,' she quipped, winking.

5

Terry paused for a second to take in the red-brick Georgian grandeur of the Department of Justice building on St Stephen's Green before walking quickly up the granite steps towards the arched doorway. She was eager to make sure she was on time for her 10 a.m. meeting with the newly appointed minister. He was a stickler for timekeeping, and she was loath to get on his wrong side.

After signing in at reception, she sat waiting, checking the time every thirty seconds. After about ten minutes the door to the inner sanctum opened and she looked up expectantly.

'Dr O'Brien.' It was a command, not a question, and she knew she was expected to react immediately. *A typical middle-ranking civil servant*, she thought, wearing a suit more suited to a level above his current pay grade – she could smell the ambition off him. 'Follow me, please.'

Grabbing her bag, she hurried after him.

Edward Farrelly dropped his pen and rose from his seat as Terry was led in through the door of his office. He came around from behind his desk and clasped her right hand, wrapping his left arm around her shoulder in an over-familiar manner that she wasn't entirely comfortable with, then guided her to the small conference table in the corner of the room.

'Dr O'Brien, Terry, thank you so much for coming in this morning. I know you are busy so I don't intend to keep you long.'

She merely smiled, not sure how she should respond. 'Please take a seat.' He remained standing. 'I'll get straight down to it. My family can't thank you enough for finding Rachel's killer. My sister will never get over losing her daughter, but she takes some comfort in the fact that Hunt is no longer a threat to others.'

Terry nodded in acknowledgement, her face reddening, but decided it was best to remain silent.

'When I heard that Dr Hannah had returned to the Office of the State Pathologist and there was no longer a position for you – well, I couldn't countenance this country losing your expertise.'

'That's very kind. When I took the job here I always knew it was likely to be a temporary arrangement, but I was delighted when Professor Boyd offered me the opportunity to return.'

'I think you underestimate the impact of the work you did. You took Rachel's investigative work seriously. She was passionate about seeking justice for murdered women and their families. You managed to finish what she couldn't and the result was closure for the family and friends of those women

44

killed by that evil monster.' Farrelly was getting into his stride. 'Terry, I want you to continue that work. I like to think of it as Rachel's legacy. I am sure there are other cases out there where families feel that the death of their loved one has been overlooked, forgotten, the garda investigation wound down. Justice not done. Since Rachel died, I have been asking myself what I can do to help those families.'

This meeting wasn't going quite the way Terry had thought it would. She tried to keep a neutral expression on her face.

Farrelly continued: 'The commissioner has spoken to me at length about the pressures on the gardaí on a day-to-day basis. They are doing what they can to review cold cases, but staffing issues mean limited resources. We've decided to establish a new unit, the Open Case Review Unit – or OCRU. It's my way of letting the public know that all deaths deserve to be treated equally.' Terry noticed the emphasis on *my*, but kept her poker face. 'In my opinion, you are ideally suited to head the OCRU. In effect, you will have the authority to review any case that has not been officially closed by the investigating gardaí or the coroner.'

There was a brief silence, then she realised he had finished speaking and was waiting for her response. She had no idea what to say. 'That's an amazing opportunity, but I'm not sure I understand what my role would be exactly?' Terry watched his expression change from friendly to wary. He had obviously thought she would be thrilled with his idea. 'It just seems a bit … open? And what about my role in the OSP?'

He moved closer to where she was sitting. She had to tip her head further back to maintain eye contact. Was this some sort of power play?

'I see this as a hybrid role between cold case reviews and current investigations – just as you did when you were looking into Rachel's death. You would split your time between the OSP and OCRU.'

'I don't think the teams investigating a homicide will want me butting in.'

'I see you more as a resource, just like any other state agency.'

Terry considered this. He was giving her carte blanche to get involved in a way she wouldn't be allowed in her role as a state pathologist. 'Who would I be reporting to?'

'Ultimately me.' She looked quizzically at him. In response, Farrelly made a dismissive gesture. 'Well, mainly the assistant commissioner for organised and serious crime, and they would expect you to co-operate with the gardaí involved in whichever case you are investigating. This is a new venture and, to that effect, I have asked for two detectives to be assigned to your team. One will be a full-time member, the other will work part-time, like yourself. At the moment, it is envisaged that they will only be seconded to the OCRU. I have secured funding for six months, and then it will be reviewed. What do you think?'

A handshake sealed the deal.

Terry couldn't believe her luck. This was right up her street. And now no one could complain about her going rogue, especially not DI John Fraser.

That afternoon, security at Walter Scott House directed Terry to the office of the new OCRU on the fourth floor. She decided to take the stairs, get her steps in, and use the time to decide on her approach to her new team members. The immediate start to the position had been a surprise but her head had been buzzing with ideas since her meeting with the minister and she was eager to kick things off. Already she had a rough plan as to how she could make this work, even if she wasn't that sure of the staffing arrangements he had outlined.

She heard her new colleagues before she saw them. As she got nearer the door, she could make out a strident male voice. 'I don't know who she thinks she is. Charlie's fucking angel? Boyd obviously wanted rid of her. She caused nothing but trouble in the Reece case. And now she thinks she can swan in here and tell me how to conduct an investigation.'

Terry's heart sank as she recognised the sneering voice of Detective Garda Bob Paterson. There was something about him that rattled her. He never seemed to miss the chance to make a dig about women. If someone hadn't broken his nose before, she would have been very tempted to do so. Jesus, the man wore brown suits – that said it all.

Taking a deep breath, she pushed the door fully open, just as Bob concluded his monologue. 'Well, she'll get no help from me.'

'Shut up, Bob, you're getting on my tits!' DS Mary Healy had her back to the door and was unpacking a cardboard box filled with thick files. 'Suck it up! Higgins might have been your pal, but Fraser took you off the team for a reason. There's no way you'd have gotten your grubby little hands anywhere near the investigation.'

'Well, now! Isn't this nice?' Mary and Bob spun around to face Terry. When she realised her new boss must have heard what had been said Mary's face turned puce. Meanwhile Bob scowled and clenched his fists.

Terry decided to ignore the obvious tension in the room. 'Hi, Mary. Good to have you on board. You're looking great in your civvies.' As a member of the Technical Bureau, Mary usually wore the unisex uniform of polo shirt and cargo pants, which, to be fair, did no one any favours.

Terry turned to her new adversary. 'Bob. What can I say? Your reputation precedes you. But let's get this straight – I'm no angel, Charlie's or otherwise, and don't try to fuck me over.' She gave him a bright smile, which she knew would piss him off. 'Welcome aboard.'

Bob spun around, walked over to the desk furthest from her and sat down with his back to her. Mary mouthed 'sorry'.

Terry shrugged her shoulders and carried on regardless. 'I'm not interested in whether or not you like me or want to be here, but I do expect you to be professional. Let's lay some ground rules. This is a new venture and eyes will be on us. Fuck up at your peril.'

She looked around the office. It was snug. She turned to Mary. 'DG Paterson seems to have selected his workstation. Choose your desk – I'm not fussed.'

Terry walked over to the filing cabinet in the corner opposite Paterson, reached into the Dunnes carrier bag she had brought with her and pulled out the essentials: a new kettle, four mugs, a jar of Nescafé, a box of Barry's teabags, milk and a two-litre bottle of water, which she used to fill the kettle.

She made a coffee and settled at the free desk. Mary, ever the diplomat, had taken the desk beside Paterson.

'Right. The minister is going to make an announcement about us shortly. We're a new unit within the Garda National Bureau of Criminal Investigation, and will sit alongside the Serious Crime Review Team, but we're not restricted by their parameters. Our remit is wider: unsolved suspicious deaths, unidentified bodies, links with missing person cases and current investigations. Any of the state agencies can ask us for help.'

Paterson was still facing away from her but she saw him sit up and take notice as soon as she mentioned current investigations. She knew he would be keen to get a foothold in the Higgins case. Terry wasn't sure what had transpired between him and Fraser, and she didn't care. She could use it to her advantage though. Carrot and stick. The Higgins investigation would be the carrot – she was sure Bob wouldn't be able to resist an opportunity to keep an eye what was happening with it – as long as he behaved. But she also knew she would have to keep a tight hold of that stick – she would need it.

'We have access to all garda files,' Terry continued, 'but I also want to reach out to the coroners. Are there any deaths where the body remains unidentified or no cause of death was given? Or any case that had an open verdict returned at the inquest, and the coroner thinks the death warrants further investigation? That will be the first task for the team.'

Mary nodded. 'I'll get started on that right away, Doc.'

'Good. Bob!' Terry waited until he swivelled his chair around to face her. 'The elephant in the room is the Martin Higgins murder. It would be helpful if you could dig out all garda murders in the last twenty years, as well as all known, or potential, gangland hits, no matter who the victim was. We need to look at patterns. Okay?'

Paterson gave a curt nod.

Satisfied, Terry got up and grabbed her coat and bag. She was due at the OSP. 'Bob, I've been told you'll be full-time here, but Mary and I have other duties. Are you fine to hold the fort until we meet here on Wednesday? You can call me anytime.'

She knew hell would freeze over before he would. Baby steps. This was a chance for them to make a difference. So she wasn't going to allow a truculent guard to get in the way.

6

Michael leaned against the sink in the tea room of the OSP while he waited for the kettle to boil, watching the others chat around the table. Mrs Carey had invited him to join an impromptu afternoon tea party to officially welcome Terry back. She had baked specially so no one dissented. Even Jimmy and Tomas had been enticed up from the mortuary.

Michael noticed with mild irritation that Niamh was sitting a bit too close to Paul. Maybe Terry was right about her intentions. Paul had often joked about the histology technician's attempts to lure him into her lab, which seemed to happen most days as it was next to the tea room. Michael knew she was on a hiding to nothing, but he couldn't help but feel insecure. Things between him and Paul were still a bit unsteady. Now Paul was laughing at something Tomas said and, not for the first time, Michael was overwhelmed by how handsome his partner was.

With a sigh, he turned as the kettle clicked off. That was the problem – he'd always felt that Paul was way out of his league. He suspected Paul enjoyed his undying adoration, but maybe it had become wearing. By contrast, his relationship with Alan Ahern had been easier, more equal.

The door flew open and Terry stomped in. 'It's like the frigging Marie Celeste out there. There's not a sinner to be seen.' Her voice tailed off as she took in the scene.

'Welcome back, Doc!' Niamh jumped up and came round the table to hug her. Michael smiled. Terry hadn't expected any fuss, and he could sense her embarrassment.

'Thanks,' she said, her cheeks flushing slightly.

'Niamh! Let Dr O'Brien sit down.' Mrs Carey shot Niamh one of her deadly looks but, as usual, Niamh took no notice.

Michael busied himself making Terry a coffee. As he set the steaming mug down on the table in front of her, he saw her gently squeeze Paul's arm. 'How about you, Paul? Good to be back?'

'I feel like I've never been away.' He laughed.

Not quite, Michael thought, *otherwise you'd be back in our flat.* He caught Terry's eye and tapped his watch.

'Michael and I have to go out to the Higgins scene' – it was her turn to glare at Michael – 'but we've got time for a cuppa and some of this amazing-looking cake first. You've done a grand job, Mrs C – best yet.'

'It's just a chocolate cake. Anyone could make it.'

'I guess you haven't tried Terry's baking, Mrs Carey.' Michael harrumphed. 'No rush, Terry. I've a call to make before we go.'

He was glad to get out of the kitchen. He patted Paul's shoulder as he passed.

Alan Ahern was waiting outside the depressing block of flats in Delaney Gardens, so Michael hung back, not sure how the other man would react to seeing him. Terry rolled her eyes, as she often did, and went on ahead. Michael had been so angry at Paul breaking off their relationship and then swanning back into his life, assuming he had been pining for him. It was Alan who'd been the bigger man and persuaded Michael to give Paul another chance. He'd wisely sensed unfinished business and didn't want to be stuck in the middle. They had parted on friendly terms, but hadn't crossed paths since. Michael had managed to avoid any scenes Alan was working – up until now. But he needn't have worried. Once Michael finally made his presence known, Alan merely smiled and fell into step beside him, launching straight into where the enquiry was at from an evidence perspective. And Michael was instantly reminded of how easy it was to be in his company.

As Alan spoke, Michael looked around the desolate complex. He had heard of people describing where they lived as a building site, but this was exactly what this was. It felt like a joyless place.

It was also eerily quiet. Usually at a crime scene like this there would be residents going about their business, many complaining about the continued police presence, and kids pestering the guards. Noticing his reaction, Alan explained that the flats on the upper floor were empty, and the people living on the ground floor were elderly or police shy. 'House-to-house enquiries haven't turned up anything useful,' he said. 'Apparently, no one saw or heard anything.'

While Terry chatted to Clodagh from ballistics, who had just arrived on the scene, Alan showed Michael the spot where the body had been found. Michael stood for a moment, his eyes flicking back and forth over the area, and then began to walk in ever-increasing circles away from the bloodstain on the ground, which identified the position of Higgins's head. It would have been better to see the body in situ, but nothing stood out. There was nothing else he could add. Maybe the body would hold some clues.

When he was done, Terry drove Michael back to the mortuary. She was quiet, no doubt running through possible scenarios in her head. Once they were seated in her office, she got down to business. After riffling through the paperwork on her desk, she handed him the evidence sheets that recorded the forensic samples taken during the post-mortem examination to ensure that nothing was missed.

Michael read through them quickly. 'Very thorough, State Pathologist O'Brien. But ...'

'But what? Don't be a twat, spit it out.' She looked at him anxiously.

'Let's go with your theory. Higgins was shot elsewhere and moved to behind those flats. Let's not get bogged down by the whys: look at the evidence. That's what we live and die by. Pardon the pun. What if he wasn't taken unawares, but there was a confrontation that got out of hand, guns were drawn and fired?' Michael pointed his right index and middle fingers towards her.

Terry rolled her eyes. 'This isn't the wild bloody west. But yes, your ex-boyfriend, DI Ahern, also thought about the possibility that Higgins fired his gun in offence or defence.'

As if she hadn't spoken, Michael continued, miming an explosion with his hands. 'Bang! And a cloud of smoke and particles of soot and unburnt gunpowder appears at the muzzle. While the bullet powers on towards the target, the residue settles onto the shooter's hands and the cuffs of whatever they're wearing. If Higgins fired his gun at someone, I'll find that evidence.'

This was the essence of any forensic investigation, the pathologist, scientist and ballistics expert working together. It wasn't just about counting holes in the victim, or even determining the internal trauma caused by a tiny piece of metal, travelling at speed, tearing the tissues apart as a consequence of its kinetic energy. This was about trace evidence, or the lack of it – the chemical explosion required to propel the bullet along the barrel of the gun and on towards the target, producing microscopic particles, soot and unburnt gunpowder, which are deposited on any surface close to the muzzle of the gun – obviously the hand of the shooter, but also the victim, if close enough.

The experts could use all the information, visible and invisible to the naked eye, to determine the likely scenario: point-blank versus long range, or something in between.

'Well, if he did pull out his gun,' Terry said, 'he wasn't much of a shot if he was the one who ended up dead. But with that in mind, Ahern took gunpowder-residue swabs from Higgins's hands at the scene before they moved the body. I'm sure he'll drop the samples up to you. Didn't he mention that when you were having your cosy little chat at the scene?'

Michael sighed. Terry could never avoid an opportunity to wind him up. He decided to ignore that remark. 'I'll examine the cuffs of the clothing you removed from the body for gunpowder residue. It might help build up the picture.' He looked down at the checklist. 'Tape lifts from the face – was that also for gunpowder residue?'

'Nup,' Terry replied. 'Not necessary – it's definitely point-blank range. It's to do with the textured mark on his face. It looks to me as if some material had been pressed onto the blood on his face and some fibres might have been left behind.'

'If they're there I'll find them. Alan didn't mention anything that could have been used lying about at the scene. Just that he'd found a muckle flashy penknife.'

'That was probably used to cut out Higgins's tongue, but there wasn't anything around his head when he was found.' Terry frowned. 'I've been thinking, though – I heard Alan say to you that no one heard anything. What if putting something over his face wasn't about mopping up blood, but to muffle a gunshot?'

'Could be another theory, all right,' Michael said, as he began pulling his coat on. 'I'll let you know the results once I run the tests. Must dash, have work to do.' He swished out the door with a wave.

Terry sat for a while after Michael left. This case was proving to be a mystery. Rubbing her forehead, she looked down at the Higgins notebook. At the moment it was all just random thoughts. That was the purpose of the notebook, jotting down ideas as they sprang to mind. She had one for every murder she had dealt with. Slowly, over the course of an investigation, the hope was that random pieces would become organised, and the answers would be staring her in the face. She wrote: *Body moved v. shot at scene.* Then she snapped the book closed and picked up her dictation machine.

'Post-mortem report on the body of Martin Higgins performed on the instructions of the Dublin coroner. Stop. Fill in the details from the C71 form as usual, Mrs Carey. New heading, scene. New line. I attended the scene at Delaney Gardens at 12.30 p.m. on Friday ...'

She dropped the paperwork and her dictation machine on Mrs Carey's desk on the way out.

Terry's flat was cold and dark when she arrived home, and for a brief second, she wished she had someone waiting for her with a homemade dinner. She couldn't be bothered cooking and stood looking in the kitchen cupboard, swithering between tomato soup and noodles. She spotted the bottle of fish sauce – noodles won.

Minutes later, she balanced the steaming bowl on the arm of the couch and went to retrieve her bag from the hall table while the noodles cooled. She still had to do Wordle. She checked her WhatsApp messages first. Her dad always did it first thing and let her know how many attempts it had taken him. He won last week, so she needed to up her game. The screen flashed with a message – 4 – straight to the point. Respectable score. He had started with the word 'chain'. That was the only rule: they both had to start with the same word.

'Guile! Who thinks up these words?' Terry exclaimed to her dad three minutes later. 'I nearly did it in four too, Dad.'

'Nearly doesn't count, Terry.'

'Well, I got the U, the I and the E, but I went for guide.'

'Rookie mistake.' Her dad chuckled down the phone, delighted to retain his title as champion. 'How did your weekend go? Anything interesting? There was a huge barney over at Ibrox after the game on Saturday. Nobody died, but.'

'That's a good thing, Dad,' she reminded him.

'Any roads, never mind here, have they got the animal that shot the guard?' he asked, always keen to hear the latest police news.

'It's early days – you know how it goes,' she said, knowing her dad would embark on a one-sided conversation about how things were done in his day. She could finish her noodles and then have a cup of tea, chipping in the occasional 'really!' or 'no!' or laugh at the right moment. It was as good as one of those mindfulness apps for clearing her head.

He eventually ran out of steam. 'Now, you mind yourself, Terry. You've a chance here to make a difference.'

She knew he was thinking about her sister, Jenny, who had been murdered just over twenty years ago. Jenny had been only fourteen when her body was found in the woods beside their house after she'd taken a shortcut home. She had been strangled, and her killer had never been found. Her dad never let on how gutted he was that the police, his colleagues, had failed him. Them. But Terry knew it ate him up that the bastard roamed free. 'Just doing my job, Dad. Just doing my job.'

7

The next morning, Terry woke with a determination to get her new office in the OSP organised. An ordered space was an ordered mind, she reminded herself. She rummaged through the cardboard boxes piled in the corner of her flat's spare bedroom, trying to locate her office essentials. Instead, she found two new jigsaws. Her dad had bought her a Christmas jigsaw for as long as she could remember. They had grown in size and complexity and these were going to be challenging: one was 3D and the other had no image of the final picture, just a short story depicting the scene.

Eventually she located the three boxes that contained the books, notebooks and assorted stationery destined for her office. She left the jigsaw boxes on the glass dining table in the kitchen on her way out. They would be a welcome distraction from work and her increasing intrusive thoughts about Fraser in the evenings.

It took three trips in the lift to get the boxes into the boot of her car. When she arrived at the OSP, her luck was in and she was greeted cheerily by Tomas, who was only too happy to help her carry the boxes inside. He dropped them on the floor beside her desk with a thud.

'What have you got in there? A body?'

'Ha bloody ha.' Terry sighed. 'The old ones are the best. Just books.'

'You're definitely staying then?' he asked hopefully.

'Well, until I piss someone off again.'

Tomas laughed, before closing the door behind him as he left.

She couldn't put the meeting off any longer. It was time to speak to Professor Charlie Boyd.

Mrs Carey looked up from her desk as she heard Terry's footsteps coming up the stairs.

'Hi, Mrs C, is the bossman in?'

'Professor Boyd is on a call,' she said, her fingers tapping furiously on her keyboard, not missing a beat. 'He won't be long.'

Terry dropped onto one of the sofas in the waiting area of the open-plan admin space. Thinking she might as well take advantage of the opportunity to grab a few minutes' rest, she leaned back and closed her eyes. After a few minutes she became aware of a voice and realised Mrs Carey was calling her. Blurry-eyed, she scrambled up from her seat and walked over to Boyd's door.

'Dr O'Brien, Terry, it's good to see you looking so well,' said a tanned Professor Boyd, greeting her with a warmth that was distinctly unfamiliar.

'You too, Prof. The weather must have been good in Madeira.'

'Good enough for a few games of golf.' He motioned for her to sit on the chair opposite his desk. 'This garda murder is a terrible situation.' Charlie was not one for unnecessary small talk. 'Sorry you got landed with it on your first week back. Do you need any assistance?'

Terry bristled. This was exactly what she didn't want. She was fully recovered – physically, at any rate. Then again, she'd always felt that Boyd wasn't quite sure about her and how to handle her. But she didn't need her hand held.

'All under control, Prof. It's early days. The gardaí have a lot to do.' She smiled, indicating that was the end of that particular conversation.

Boyd sat back in his chair and folded his arms. 'I hear congratulations are also in order,' he said with a brief smile. 'I hope the minister realises that what we do here is much more important than rummaging around in dusty corners. The deaths we deal with need one hundred per cent commitment.'

Terry fought hard not to roll her eyes. 'Of course. But, as I know only too well, we shouldn't rest until justice is served. Even if it is a long time coming. And on that note ...' She pushed the chair back and stood up. Boyd looked at her stony-faced. In turn, she gave him a dazzling smile. 'I won't keep you any longer, Prof. I guess we've both got a lot to do.'

As she turned towards the door, she saw him shaking his head in bemusement. Her smile turned genuine.

Relieved at having her first chat with Professor Boyd over

and done with, she walked down the stairs to the mortuary floor and slipped into her office. The Higgins file was back on her desk, Mrs C efficient as ever.

Terry sat looking at the typed report for a few seconds before reaching for her phone.

Her finger hovered over John Fraser's number. She scrolled through her contacts and selected DI Alan Ahern instead.

He answered on the second ring. 'Terry, I was just about to give you a call.'

'I was wondering if you had any update on the Higgins death?'

'There's a case conference tomorrow afternoon – just the investigating officers and the forensic team. Fraser wants the assistant commissioner to know that we're taking this seriously. Can you make 1 p.m. at WSH? I'll check if Michael and Monica are free too.'

Terry let herself into her flat just after 6 p.m., weary after an exhausting afternoon and struggling under the weight of two bags filled with M&S ready meals that she hoped would do her for the week. She decanted the food into the fridge, packing it in in no particular order: it made menu selection interesting – food Russian roulette. The last pack out of the bag would do tonight, she thought, pulling out a packet of prawns its depths. Leaning against the kitchen counter, she squeezed some mayonnaise into the corner of the plastic tray, speared a couple of spicy prawns with a fork and dunked them in.

Also among her purchases was some wine, a white and a red. She lifted the tumbler on the draining board and reached for the white. Unscrewing the cap, she inhaled the fumes. Then she screwed the cap back on and filled the glass with cold water instead. A quiet night in was what she needed.

She glanced at her phone for what seemed like the hundredth time that day. Fraser still hadn't tried to contact her. Seeing him on Friday had reignited old feelings. She had to admit, he had looked good. Some guards at his level had that clean-cut executive look, but he had a hint of scruffy rebel that appealed to her. There was a barrier between them, though, and she feared it was of her own making. And now he was keeping her at arm's length, professional rather than personal. Was he waiting for her to make the first move? Well, that wasn't going to happen. *Stop thinking about him*, she chastised herself and stuck on some *Real Housewives of New York City*. No doubt some melodramatic socialites screaming at one another would take her mind off Fraser.

Terry woke with a start. She was still on the sofa. Her new fur throw had obviously kept her warm and cosy all night. An ad for a mobility scooter had now replaced the sound of screeching housewives. Glancing at the time – 7 a.m. – she dragged herself up from the sofa and into the bathroom. After a shower and a quick cup of coffee, she set off, anxious to get started on her work at the OCRU. The traffic on the quays crawled along, and her frustrations were compounded by the lack of parking at Walter Scott House. Three rounds of the car park later, she gave up and abandoned her car in front of the bins.

Mary and Bob were already sitting at their desks in the OCRU office, with boxes of historic files covering every available space. It looked like they had been busy since she was there last.

'How did you get on with the list of garda murders, Bob?' Terry said to the back of his head a few minutes later. She was perched on her desk beside Mary, a packet of chocolate digestives already open between them, mugs of coffee in hand.

He replied without turning. 'Nothing out of the ordinary. I went back twenty years. A handful of shootings and a fair number of road deaths – a couple of hit and runs and one feckin' eejit who was run over by his own car.'

Spluttering, Mary spat a mouthful of soggy crumbs into her mug.

Bob spun his chair around. 'Gross! So I also checked out the gangland killings, like you asked. I went back as far as that scumbag Cahill. Most of the hits were shootings, nothing fancy. Bang, bang, you're dead!' He pointed a finger at Mary, who scowled in return. 'Most of them couldn't hit a cow on the arse with a shovel, mind you. Then they just scarper. Some bodies turned up in torched cars and there were a couple of bad beatings. Pure animals, they are! But at least they mainly stick to their own. Although there was that young lass in Coolock a couple of years ago. Collateral damage.'

Terry gave a non-committal hmm and then realised what he had said. 'Jesus, that's awful.'

He shrugged. 'Ah well.'

He didn't look the least bit upset that an innocent woman had been shot and killed. Terry took a deep breath. She waited for Bob to continue. After a few seconds of silence, she asked, 'Anything strange or startling in any of them?'

'No.' He wouldn't meet her eye. She waited. *Why the hesitancy?* He was probably just being deliberately obtuse to wind her up. Finally, he spoke. 'Nothing like Martin, if that's what you mean. That's what I don't get – why did they hack out Martin's tongue? What's that all about?' He spun back around and hunched over his screen, signalling an end to this conversation with her.

Terry stared at his back for a moment, then got off the desk and wiped her hands on her jeans. 'Good work, Bob.' Her voice was flat. She had no intention of letting this little fucker ruin everything – she had to make the OCRU a success. He was an irritant, but she had a job to do.

What is *it all about?* she thought, as she tapped a Sharpie on the blank page of the flip chart at the side of her desk. She transcribed the information about garda and gangland killings onto the page, drew a line and wrote 'NO MUTILATIONS'.

'So Higgins is different.' Terry tapped the Sharpie against her front teeth. 'Why?' She wrote 'Martin Higgins???'

'Any information we should know about him to add to the chart?' she asked over her shoulder. 'Mary? Bob?' Mary shook her head, Bob grunted.

Maybe she would have more to add following this afternoon's conference. 'Bob, there's a case conference for the Higgins murder at 1p.m.' Suddenly he was interested. He twisted around to grab his leather jacket, which was draped over the back of his chair. Terry paused for a tantalising second, then said, 'Only those central to the investigation have been invited.' Was it wrong that she liked winding him up a little? She had to get her kicks somehow. His expression darkened and he spun back around to face his screen.

'I'll pass on any information relevant to this team's part of the investigation asap,' she continued. 'Meanwhile, that's not the only case we're dealing with. We're here specifically to deal with cold cases and missing persons. We need to focus on unsolved murders and other cases that have been put on the back-burner due to lack of progress or evidence. Got it?' No response from Bob. Even the way his hair curled greasily over his collar annoyed her.

'Sure, boss!' Mary gave her a mock salute. Terry smiled despite herself and turned back. She replaced the Higgins chart with a fresh one and flipped back the cover page. 'Right. Mary, how did you get on with the coroners? Any joy? Do any of them have a mysterious death lurking in the dark recesses of an old filing cabinet that they might want us to cast an eye over? Maybe they were unhappy with the garda investigation at the time? Anything, really.'

She saw Mary cast an anxious glance at Bob prompting Terry put up her hands. 'We're not here to judge anyone, gardaí or coroners. We're just here to ...' She struggled to find the right word. 'Assist. If anyone wants us to. You need to make that clear to them.'

Mary nodded. 'Not much at the moment. I've contacted a good few of them, and I'm waiting for them to send me files. I got the impression that some of them weren't too happy. Thought this was the Department of Justice, or the gardaí, interfering with their decisions.' Mary shot Terry a look. 'Especially the country coroners.'

Terry rolled her eyes. She could probably guess which ones.

Mary opened her notebook. 'Some were delighted, though. They thought the gardaí didn't take them seriously when they asked them to keep cases open or enquire further.'

'I guess you didn't mention you were a detective sergeant?'

'I might not have. I just said I was working in your new unit.

They might have thought I was your secretary.' Mary looked pleased with her subterfuge. 'At any rate, I've got a few names to get started on.'

'Great. Well done, Mary. Give me the names of the coroners who have a gripe about the garda investigations or are a bit suspicious of our motives and I'll get Mrs Carey on to them. She has a way of dealing with difficult folk. You concentrate on the cases of the coroners already on board.'

Bob muttered something, but Terry didn't catch what he said. Mary obviously did, as she kicked the back of his seat. 'Stop sulking,' she warned him. 'Get a fucking grip.'

'Fuck off,' he muttered. That earned his chair another kick.

Annoyed, Terry thumped her mug on her desk. 'Like it or lump it, Bob, you're part of the team. You can play nicely or I'll ask for you to be moved elsewhere. And that would mean you won't get a sniff of your pal's investigation. Your choice!' She grimaced. It was like dealing with a petulant teenager.

'Right. I'm going to grab some lunch before this meeting.

Sort yourselves out,' Terry said, shrugging on her coat and grabbing her bag. 'See you there,' she mouthed at Mary.

Bob breathed out a long sigh of relief as Mary slammed the office door behind her. Unlucky for him that he had to spend his days shoved in this shitty office with two bitches lording it over him. Just who did they think they were? He couldn't believe that Fraser had booted him from one of the most high-profile investigations in recent years to do – what? Look at dusty old files from twenty years ago? But it wasn't all for nothing. He had uncovered something interesting when he was looking into old gangland shootings.

He rose heavily from his chair and went over to the office door. Quietly tugging it open, he peered out into the corridor. It was deserted. Closing the door again, he pulled out his mobile. After two rings, a female voice answered. 'This better be good, Bob. You've fucked up big time. How d'ya think you're going to fix this? Swear to God, yer on thin ice.'

'Listen, I've got some info, but it'll cost you,' said Bob, ignoring the threat. He wasn't going to kowtow to this woman either. He had the intel. He held the power in this dynamic.

Putting his feet up on the desk, he leaned back in his chair. 'It's to do with your brother. I have a connection you might like to know more about.'

8

Fraser, Ahern and the team from the Technical Bureau were standing in a loose group by the conference table, watching the technical guys set up a couple of screens. The atmosphere was sombre. Fraser had been watching for Terry. Out of the corner of his eye, he saw her come in and go straight to the coffee station before sitting down beside Michael Flynn and Monica MacKenzie from FSI. She didn't look at him.

Suddenly Martin Higgins's face filled the screens and the room quietened.

Fraser moved in front of the table to face the group as everyone took their seats. 'Afternoon. Thank you for coming. It is important we keep up the momentum and we keep the investigation tight. This is where we are.' He stepped back and stood beside one of the screens. Martin's face morphed into the details of the investigation.

'Higgins was last seen alive in the flesh, so to speak, in the CCJ on Thursday afternoon, in Court 17 at the Boyle trial.

It's not clear what he was doing there. He wasn't part of the investigation.'

'Probably popped in for a chat or a nosey. We all do it, boss.'

'Fair enough, Mick,' replied Fraser. 'But normally that's because you're attending a case in another court. As far as we know he wasn't involved in any trial.'

'Might have been on a call out in the area?'

'No record of that either. He didn't speak to the other guards at the Robbo Boyle trial, just stood at the back, nodded at the lads he knew and left. He was then caught on the CCTV camera outside Court 18 at 3.32 p.m. talking to a male – possibly mid-forties, white, about six foot. Other than that, he doesn't seem to have interacted with anyone.' Fraser nodded at the tech guy and suddenly the CCTV footage appeared on the screen behind him.

'Maybe he was up in front of Henderson for beating the crap out of his wife?' piped up a voice from the back of the room.

'Owen!' Fraser glowered at the ruddy- faced detective garda.

'Just banter, boss,' he mumbled by way of apology.

'That type of talk is totally unacceptable. I'll deal with you later.'

The young guard went beetroot and his colleagues moved their chairs a fraction away from his.

Fraser glanced behind him and spotted that the footage had been paused while Owen was being berated. 'As far as we can ascertain, he had no reason to be in or near Henderson's court.' Fraser signalled to restart the video. Martin Higgins walked up to a man standing outside Court 18 whose face was partly hidden from view. There were so many bodies crammed together outside the court door it was difficult to get a clear view of either male. The only thing that stood out to Terry was an expensive-looking bag the other man held in his right hand. The logo was vaguely familiar, definitely designer. Then the door opened and the man turned as if to enter and Martin walked off towards the stairs.

'The man he was talking to hasn't been identified yet. We need to look into what connection Higgins had with Henderson's court.' Fraser looked pointedly at Owen, daring him to make some other remark.

The tech guy rewound and zoomed in on the man. Fraser heard Terry gasp. He whipped around and looked at the image filling the screen, trying to figure out what had prompted her reaction. The mystery man had his back to the camera but he appeared to be dressed head to toe in black. Fraser realised that from that angle there was some similarity to her assailant Hunt. Of course, Hunt was in prison – but fear was not always logical.

Fraser noticed Michael grasp Terry's hand and squeeze. As Michael handed her a bottle of water he pulled out of his backpack, Fraser signalled to the tech guy to cut the footage, and Higgins's face was back on the screen. When Terry looked up, Fraser nodded at her. She mouthed 'okay' and took a sip of water.

Clearing his throat, Fraser continued: 'We've been able to track Higgins through the public areas. The last sighting is of him leaving the courts building alone. His car was found in the car park here at WSH. It seems he walked to court. And therefore, he may have walked up to Delaney Gardens from the CCJ, if he was killed there or thereabouts. Our outside cameras are trained on the courts complex and so only capture the exterior perimeter. We're checking local CCTV from shops and Ring cameras right now. House-to-house hasn't confirmed any sighting so far.'

He signalled to Michael. 'Dr Flynn, I believe you've had an opportunity to visit the scene and discuss the forensic evidence harvested from the body?'

Michael pushed his chair back and stood. 'DI Ahern and Dr O'Brien were good enough to share their findings and thoughts. I've discussed the case with Dr MacKenzie.' He nodded at his boss sitting beside him and Monica smiled back. 'We agree with their interpretation of the findings. When I visited the spot where Martin Higgins was found, the pattern of bloodstaining appears consistent with him being killed there, or pretty close by. There were no visible blood trails to suggest his body had been moved or dragged to that location. But even if they're very careful or try to clean up, there's always a speck missed, so if it's there we'll find it.' Michael nodded at Terry, who made a face back. He ignored her and went on. 'We haven't finished with the flats in the complex, so can't completely rule out the possibility of him being shot inside yet.'

'Thank you, Doctor. Do you think, on balance, that is the primary scene?' Fraser turned back to the screen as a new image appeared: Higgins on the ground in the area behind the flat complex. 'So far, we have no one admitting to hearing a shot.'

'Well, as I said, so far there is nothing at the scene to suggest to me that he had been shot elsewhere, but I suppose we need to keep an open mind. It'll be another few days. We haven't found a bullet either, but they'll keep searching. It wasn't in the ground under the head. If he was upright, it could be anywhere. It would still have been going at a pace when it left the head.' Michael looked at Monica, who nodded in agreement.

Beside Michael, Fraser saw Terry make as if to stand. 'Dr O'Brien, have you something to add?'

Terry cleared her throat. 'Could you rerun the CCTV footage of Higgins?'

Fraser nodded at the tech guy. He watched as Terry walked up to position herself between him and the screen. As the footage replayed, he kept his eyes on her until she shouted, 'Stop!'

Fraser looked at the screen and back to Terry. The still was of Higgins after his encounter with the man outside Court 18. It showed him midstride on his way to the stairs.

'Can you zoom in on that?' She was pointing at the screen, specifically to Higgins's right hand.

The room was silent as the image enlarged.

'He's carrying a grey woollen scarf. That wasn't with his body. Was it found anywhere at the scene?'

Fraser turned to Ahern, who shook his head.

'I thought it looked as if some textured material had been pressed into the blood on his face – that scarf could have made the patterned mark.' Terry looked directly at Fraser. 'Something could have been wrapped around his face and head to soak up the blood from the injury, stop him leaking and leaving a bloody trail behind. Of course, that supposes he was shot elsewhere and his body moved. But if he was shot where he was found, could the scarf have been used for another purpose?'

The room remained quiet.

'Could it have been used to muffle the sound of a shot?' she asked. 'Like a makeshift silencer?'

Fraser looked at Alan Ahern. 'You're the ballistics expert – do you think that would work?'

Ahern looked thoughtful. 'Maybe. I'll do some controlled experiments in the bunker at our shooting range. It might dampen the sound of a shot, but I wouldn't have thought completely. Though it might explain why those residents we've spoken to said they didn't hear a gun going off.'

'The oul' ones probably had their tellies up full blast anyway.'

Ahern gave the guard beside him a wry smile. 'You're probably right, Mick.'

'Great, you get on that, Alan,' said Fraser. 'Meantime, get the forensics team to look for the scarf. Good spot, Terry.'

He turned his attention back to the others in the room. 'Suspects.' The chatter quietened again. This was what the team wanted to know. 'Higgins was part of the surveillance team on the brothel we suspected the Hayes gang were running from that building. They could have been involved in his death in some way.' Fraser nodded back towards the building shown on the screen. 'Higgins wasn't on duty on Thursday, but maybe he dropped by as he was in the general area and ran into someone he shouldn't have. Still, it would be a bit sloppy leaving the body in their own backyard. These gangs are usually a bit savvier. That just doesn't sit right.'

'It is a bit of a coincidence, boss.' Alan Ahern didn't look convinced. 'Higgins's body found on the doorstep of a flat we're keeping an eye on? Maybe someone trying to set up the Hayes gang?'

'So it could be some other gang trying to take them out. Most likely the Carrolls.' Fraser gave a quick run-through of what they knew of the Hayeses' and Carrolls' activities. Intel suggested that the Hayeses were muscling into the Carrolls' territory. 'Problem is, the flat under surveillance was cleared out before we got there. None of it adds up at the moment.' He turned to Monica MacKenzie. 'Monica, I need your team to pull it apart. Find me something, anything, that puts Higgins in there and links back to the Hayeses.'

Monica MacKenzie's face was a picture. You'd think he'd asked her to send a forensics team in to take prints from a number 16 bus to confirm the taoiseach had taken a trip to the airport a week before.

He moved on before Monica could protest. 'Alan, can you deal with Mrs Higgins?'

'Sure, boss. We've all but ruled her out as a suspect. She came in and made a statement.' Ahern referred to his notes. 'She's an English teacher at Loreto on the Green. She runs an am-dram after-school club on Thursdays – they're doing *The King and I*. After she left the rehearsals, she went straight to Terenure to her book club. That checks out, so she seems to be in the clear, but I haven't had a chance to speak directly to the other women who were there yet. We'll be doing that this afternoon. They take it in turns to host it.' He tapped his pen on his notebook. 'We should check this out: Mrs Higgins said the group met through marriage counselling? I got the impression they all had a problem with the men in their lives. It might be best if Mary takes the lead with that.'

'That's a bit sexist,' Mary piped up from the back of the room.

Fraser suppressed a smile – he recognised the combative expression on Mary's face. He looked back at Ahern, who had turned red.

Out of the corner of his eye, Fraser saw Terry signal to him. 'Dr O'Brien?'

'Sorry to interrupt. This might be relevant given what Alan just said. Mrs Higgins came to the mortuary to do the formal identification of her husband. As she was leaving, she said, "May he rot in hell".'

'No love lost there so,' Mary muttered.

Fraser cut in. 'Alan, call Mrs Higgins back in. Take a closer look at their relationship.' Ahern nodded. Fraser went on. 'Higgins was no angel, and like most of us, he'll have made a few enemies along the way. That will take a bit of digging around.'

He spent the next fifteen minutes allocating tasks. He could feel the resentment from some of the team. Higgins was one of them. Fraser knew he needed to be careful how he handled this investigation. The pressure was on.

9

Terry flipped up the hood of her puffer coat as she walked out towards Military Road. She needed to clear her head, so had slipped out before anyone tried to talk to her. She was annoyed at herself for her reaction when she saw the black-clad figure on the screen. *I can't let that bastard Hunt affect me like this.* Maybe she should contact Dr Price, that psychiatrist who saw her while she was being treated in hospital? She had her card somewhere. Dr Price had warned her that she might suffer flashbacks and that she should continue seeing someone. Terry would call her and arrange an appointment. She knew she normally wouldn't be triggered so easily and she didn't want it to become a regular occurrence.

She picked up her pace. The investigation didn't seem to be much further on, and there were plenty of suspects. Let the guards worry about that though. Terry was more concerned with why the killer had cut out the tongue. It was bizarre. This new king of the dung heap, Hayes, was a worry. Originally from Dublin, according to Mary, Hayes had been operating out of Liverpool, and more recently Spain, for the past couple of years. Fraser was liaising with the team in the Garda National Drugs and Organised Crime Bureau, trying to suss out his operation. What if hacking out tongues was Hayes's thing? She could contact Tim Scott, the forensic pathologist in Liverpool, and ask if he had seen anything like this. It might be this Hayes guy's calling card. It was worth a shot.

She passed the train station and crossed the bridge, turning left onto Parkgate Street with the intention of grabbing a good coffee from one of the cafés there. As she passed Londis, a figure caught her eye, huddled in a stained sleeping bag outside the shop. Terry dug into her pocket and produced a couple of two-euro coins and some small change. As she bent to drop the coins in the paper cup, a head emerged. 'Thanks, missus.'

Terry stared at the woman. She was thinner than when she had last seen her. 'Mags? Is it you, Mags, Tina's friend?' Tina McCabe was a drug addict who had been another victim of Hunt's. 'Do you remember me? Dr O'Brien. Terry. I met you in the Phoenix Park after Tina died. I got you a new sleeping bag,' she added, hoping to jog her memory.

The dishevelled woman looked up. Terry noticed that she had trouble focusing. 'You were with that guard? The one that got a doing?'

Terry winced at the memory of the vicious attack on her and Fraser in the Phoenix Park during their investigation into the Tina McCabe and Rachel Reece murders. 'Not our finest hour, I admit, but yes, that was me.' Terry's mind was buzzing with all of the things she knew she needed to do at the office but …'You look frozen. Can I get you a hot drink and something to eat? Get you out of the cold for a while?'

'I'd rather have the money,' Mags grumbled, burying her head back into the relative warmth of her sleeping bag.

'Well, you've got all the cash I've got on me,' said Terry. Mags peeped out over the top of the bag. She was obviously considering her options.

'They won't serve me in any of these places.' Mags nodded towards the shops and cafés along that stretch of road.

'Well, I'm heading back towards Kilmainham. How about Heuston Station? They can't stop you going in, and you'll be with me.'

And so Terry retraced her route, hoping that Mags would take her up on her suggestion. After crossing the road again, she looked over her shoulder and saw Mags, sleeping bag under her arm, shuffling behind her.

Terry took Mags's arm as they approached the entrance to the train station. As well as a good meal, Mags probably also could have used a hot shower and a set of fresh clothes. Unfortunately, a quick bite to eat would have to do for now.

Terry ignored the stares of the commuters and looked around for a seat in the station concourse. Finding two near the ticket machines, she settled Mags and her sleeping bag beside a young couple, who looked very uncomfortable. The woman wrapped her coat tighter around her and shuffled as far away as she could without sitting on her boyfriend's knee. Both were wrinkling their noses. Terry thought they could have been a bit more discreet.

'Right. What do you fancy?'

'Nothing too chewy,' Mags replied. 'Me tooth's givin' me bother. And I don't like cheese. I'll have a Diet Coke and one of them chocolate chip cookies.'

Terry smiled at the preciseness of the order. 'I'll see what I can do. Keep that seat for me.' She knew that was a moot point – she'd put good money on her seat buddies moving off once her back was turned.

Five minutes later, Terry watched as Mags nibbled around the edges of the burger she'd brought her – it seemed to take her forever to eat it. The bag of cookies and the Coke had disappeared into the folds of the sleeping bag, presumably for later. She waited until Mags gave a contented sigh before she started questioning her.

With a bit of prompting, Terry gleaned that Mags was still living in the little hidey hole in the Phoenix Park that she had shared with Tina. She had a new boyfriend, but Bernice didn't like him. Terry had met Bernice during the investigation into Tina McCabe's death – she played 'mother' to the women working and living rough in the area. Men treated the Castleknock end of the park like a McDonald's drive-through for prostitutes. She had to admit that Bernice had tried her best to keep Tina and Mags off the game. Looked like it was a losing battle with Mags, unfortunately. If Bernice didn't approve of Mags's boyfriend, he was probably well dodgy.

'How did you meet him?'

'I was looking to score and he'd just taken over Puggie's pitch. He was the one I told you Tina used?'

'What happened to … Puggie?'

Mags shrugged. 'Dunno. A new bloke took over. Real class, Canada Goose jacket. None of yer knock-offs. Ye can tell. I was a bit short one night and he helped me out.'

Terry knew drug dealers didn't do favours. Maybe it had been a simple transaction, sex for drugs. But she sussed it wasn't that straightforward, as Mags wouldn't meet her eyes.

'What's his name?' Terry asked, trying to sound as nonchalant as possible.

Mags looked wary. 'Jake.'

'Is he from around here?'

'He doesn't sound like no one from round here.'

'Is he living with you in Phoenix Park?'

'Sometimes.' Mags picked at a sore-looking scab at the side of her mouth. Despite her lifestyle there was a certain innocence about her. Terry could have wept at her lack of guile. Mags trusted this guy. 'He has a place up the road. One of them new flats. He was trying to get me in.'

'Up around Delaney Gardens?' 'Yeah.'

Fuck, Terry thought. *He must be one of the Hayes gang.* No wonder Bernice wasn't happy – Mags was being groomed for the brothel.

Terry barely slept that night. She had felt bad watching Mags trudging back towards the park with her head down, avoiding the scrutiny of passers-by. She had been so close to taking Mags home with her, but she told herself she wasn't equipped to deal with Mags's situation. What she could do is pass on the information she had gleaned from Mags (which would hopefully help her in the long run): that it was definite that someone from out of town, possibly a member of the Hayes gang, was trading in both drugs and women. No doubt Fraser was across that, but there was no harm in letting him know the reality of Mags's situation. She wouldn't be the only victim, that's for sure.

Terry certainly wasn't using this as an excuse to contact Fraser.

She was hanging up her coat in her office at the OSP the following morning when Jimmy arrived at her door. 'It's the good stuff,' he said gruffly, as he handed her the steaming mug. And there it was, that little crack in his stony veneer again. As he turned to leave, he inclined his head towards the ceiling. 'The boss upstairs is looking for you.' She knew he was referring to Mrs Carey, not the professor.

Terry found Mrs Carey seated at her desk with a face like thunder. 'I've been working through the list you emailed over for your OCRU work. That little pup in the Galway coroner's office has sent up all the cases from the past ten years.' It was only then that Terry noticed the pile of cardboard boxes, five in total, stacked beside the office manager's desk. 'Every death reported to the office over that time.'

Terry suppressed a giggle. She bent down and grabbed one of the boxes, stumbling under its weight. 'Jesus, I'll need to get the boys downstairs to give me a hand.'

Tomas was only too happy to help, as always, and he was soon moving the boxes into the lift.

'Watch yourself, Doc,' he said, pushing the final box into the far corner beside Terry.

'Will do, Tomas.' The doors slid closed after them. 'No thanks to Jimmy. What's up with him anyway? He brought me a coffee this morning. Very out of character.'

'Hope it was drinkable.'

'He used the posh stuff and he didn't make any snide remarks. Is he all right? He seemed a bit down.'

'It's Bella, his dog,' said Tomas. 'She's got a slipped disc. Can't race anymore.'

'Oh! Poor dog. What do you do with a greyhound you can't race? Does he have to put her down?'

'No!' Tomas looked shocked at her question. 'I think they just become a pet.'

'That's okay, surely? You just move them into the house.'

'That's the problem. I think he loves that dog more than his wife, and she won't allow her inside. He's looking for a home for her. The dog, not the wife,' Tomas clarified, lest Terry thought otherwise.

Terry laughed as the lift doors pinged open and Jimmy appeared at the door of his office. He did not approve of merriment in the workplace. 'What's going on out here?'

Terry and Tomas looked at one another and started laughing again. Jimmy went back into his room, slamming the door behind him.

'Oh dear.' Terry tried to sober up. 'I don't think he's in the mood for a bit of fun. I'll go and have a word.'

Jimmy was sitting hunched over on the tatty old sofa in his office, an unlit cigarette dangling from his lips, a sure-fire indication that he was having a tough time. He had quit smoking about ten years previously but kept a cigarette in the top pocket of his lab coat for emergencies. At least he hadn't lit it.

She looked around – sitting beside him didn't feel right. She dragged one of the high-backed chairs over. 'Tomas told me about Bella. What's going to happen to her?'

Jimmy looked broken-hearted. He spoke, trying not to drop the cigarette. Watching it bob up and down on his bottom lip was strangely mesmerising. 'She can't stay with me.'

Terry thought his eyes looked a little watery. She was uncomfortable – she wasn't used to an emotional Jimmy. 'Can you find her a home?'

'Suppose so.'

'Can you keep her your place until then?'

He gulped and shook his head sadly.

'So where is she?'

'She's in the back of my jeep.'

'You can't keep a dog in your jeep.' Terry snapped into business mode. 'Why don't you bring her in here temporarily?'

'Ah, well ...' Jimmy plucked the cigarette from his mouth and wiped his nose on his sleeve. 'I had her in here.' He patted the smelly sofa and a flurry of dog hair floated upwards. 'Prof Boyd came in about something and she jumped up on him to greet him. She's a friendly soul. Problem is that I'd just taken her for a walk and she had big muddy paws.'

Terry grimaced. She couldn't imagine Charlie being too enamoured by a mucky dog messing up his expensive clothes.

Jimmy looked so dejected that she made a rash decision. 'Bella can stay in my office for the time being,' she told him. 'No one else need know.'

Terry spent the rest of the day going through the case boxes. Bella snored softly in the corner. She really was a handsome dog. And the fact that Charlie wasn't too fond of Bella was a bonus – doggy subterfuge. He might be reluctant to stop by her office. *Maybe this could be a permanent arrangement*, she thought to herself. And she had to admit that she found Bella's presence calming. She'd always fancied having a dog but could never commit.

Crouching down by the sleeping dog, she rubbed her silky ears. 'How would you feel about staying with me sometimes?' She would have a word with Jimmy.

First, she had to update Fraser.

10

John Fraser was surprised to get a call from Terry that afternoon. She had been avoiding him since the day he had driven her from the hospital to Dublin airport to catch her flight to Glasgow. DS Mary Healy had since pointed out to him that he had come across as controlling when he had advised Terry to take a break from her career, but he'd genuinely thought he was just looking out for her welfare. He had grown to like her a lot and had thought that their blossoming relationship could grow into something more. Now he knew he had probably blown his chances.

He couldn't help but feel responsible for Terry being kidnapped and nearly killed by Hunt – he should have figured him out earlier. And he should have kept a closer eye on her. He knew she was a bit of a maverick, and he'd got caught up in her enthusiasm. He admired that in her. He had tried to apologise for his badly phrased advice, but she refused to take his calls when she was in Glasgow. Don, her dad, had at least kept him updated on her progress. He said to give her time. So Fraser had taken the hint and backed off completely, but he had been more upset by her rebuff than he let on. He had kept a respectful distance so far during the Higgins investigation – it had all been very professional. He hadn't wanted to scare her off, but now he couldn't help but feel worried that she thought he didn't care about her at all. That couldn't have been further from the truth.

When Terry said she wanted to meet up to give him some information it would have been wiser to suggest WSH the following day. But he was going to be in the city centre anyway and thought maybe over a couple of drinks she might thaw a little. Also, Croke's on Nassau Street could be regarded as neutral ground. She wasn't as likely to kick off in a pub. Well, he hoped not.

Terry was already sitting at a table, fiddling with a beer mat, when Fraser came in through the side door. He knew that she would expect him to come through the front entrance. He was used to the cat-and-mouse game of surveillance and he could tell by her body language that she was not as relaxed as she would look to a casual observer. There was a definite edge to her.

She looked good, but then again, he thought she always looked good. She'd cut her hair up above her shoulders while in Glasgow and it suited her. The drastic change had been a bit of a shock when he first saw her at the scene at Delaney Gardens, nearly a week ago now. This evening, she was dressed in jeans and a cream jumper – subtle and casual, definitely not giving any vibes that she was dressing for a date. She looked like she had lost weight too. He hoped she was looking after herself but he doubted it, going by the already empty glass on the table. She was probably on her second gin and tonic. He turned to the bar and ordered two more. Holding a glass in each hand would mean he didn't have to go in for a hug and risk her turning away.

She looked up warily as he set the glasses down on the table. He smiled and thought, *What the heck*, and bent over and kissed her quickly on the cheek. No reaction. But at least she didn't flinch.

'Sorry I'm a bit late,' said Fraser, sitting down opposite her. 'Thanks for meeting me here.' He took a sip from his glass but kept his eyes on hers. 'You're looking good.' She made no response. 'May I start with an apology?'

Terry remained silent, so he took that as his cue to continue. 'I realise I was out of order suggesting you give up your work. I just …' He reached across and put his hand over hers. 'I didn't handle the situation very well. You frightened the shit out of me. I'd prefer it if you stayed alive.'

She glanced down at his hand and back up at him, but didn't pull her hand away. 'You were probably delighted when Paul came back. I'd have no job to return to, and you could forget about me.'

He heard the challenge in her voice, but he couldn't read her face. He didn't want to say the wrong thing. Again. 'That's not fair, Terry,' he said, frowning slightly. She had him on the back foot already.

'Isn't it?'

'Look, he's a good-looking bloke, but he's not my type.' The frosty look on her face told him this wasn't the time to introduce some levity to the situation. 'Anyway, it's a moot point. You're back. And I'm really glad you are.'

'Uh-huh.' She wasn't going to make this easy.

'And back in the thick of it too,' Fraser said, looking into her eyes. He sat back. 'To tell you the truth, it was a bit dull without you about the place.' Finally, a smile from her. He felt himself relax.

She mirrored his movement and sat back too. 'I guess you know about the new unit I've been tasked with?'

And there she was, Dr O'Brien – the professional mask was firmly back in place. He saluted her. 'Just promise me you'll be careful?'

Terry gave a non-committal shrug, and a little smirk flashed across her face. *Always the rebel.*

'So, Dr O'Brien. What is it you want to tell me?'

Terry told him about meeting Mags and her concern that she had gotten herself embroiled with a dodgy dealer, potentially part of the Hayes network he was investigating. She thought this Jake guy had been intent on getting Mags into the Delaney Gardens brothel.

Fraser was concerned that Terry was perhaps getting too personally involved again, but let it slide. 'I'll ramp up surveillance in the Phoenix Park to see if we can catch this Jake in action. We'll look out for Mags too. The Hayes gang are dangerous and they've got plenty of European connections. We're worried about conflicts with established gangs.'

Terry frowned, taking in all the information. 'We've got the new unit looking into previous gangland and garda murders to see if there are any patterns. Hopefully we'll land on something that might help with the Higgins investigation.'

'I thought Mary would be a good fit for you in the OCRU,' said Fraser, glad that the awkwardness of earlier had lifted now they were talking shop. 'She's a good investigator. But I think you should keep a close eye on Bob.'

'Ha!' exclaimed Terry, almost spitting out her drink. 'You don't need to tell me that. He's proving himself to be a complete pain in the arse.'

Fraser laughed, happy that Terry seemed to be relaxing a little in his presence, enough to complain about Bob at least. He'd take that. It was his fault they had been estranged. He would take it slow. She was worth it.

11

'Michael! A word in my office.'

Michael watched as Monica MacKenzie turned and strode out of the main lab. He was immediately on edge. Much as he respected his boss, he was also a wee bit frightened of her. He trailed along the corridor a few seconds behind her. It didn't pay to keep her waiting.

'Have a seat.'

Michael sat obediently. Monica was busy riffling through a file, her glasses perched at a perilous angle at the end of her nose. He was growing more and more nervous. For some reason, he wasn't sure what to do with his hands – he clasped then unclasped them, then settled on sitting on them, which tipped him forward.

Finally, she pulled out a document. 'Michael,' she said, adjusting her glasses and looking intently at him. Her tone was soft so he relaxed a little. 'This is rather delicate.'

She obviously expected him to make some response. He nodded for her to continue. *Where is she going with this?*

'I just had a call from Professor Alastair Wilkes, the head of the Scottish Forensic Science Department.'

Michael was immediately on the alert.

'It seems they are seeking our co-operation.' Monica sat forward in her chair, her mouth pursed and her brow furrowed. This was something serious. He could feel his heart rate rising.

'It would appear there were irregularities in a historical high-profile murder in Scotland and the senior investigating officer's actions are under the microscope. All his previous cases are being questioned and will be subject to investigation. The bottom line is that Dr O'Brien's sister's murder is one of said cases.

'What? Jenny?' It was the best he could muster, he was completely flummoxed. 'What's it got to do with us?'

'It seems that it's something to do with the fingerprint evidence. The reason we have been asked to get involved is because there's a potential Irish angle to Jenny's case – and Scottish forensics want us to rule it in or out. They're already under scrutiny, so they can't leave any stone unturned.'

'Right, okay. But I'm still not following,' said Michael hesitantly, afraid that Monica would think he was a complete moron. 'Jenny lived in Scotland, was murdered in Scotland. Where's the Irish angle?'

'I know, and I do realise this is tenuous, but we have to get involved,' said Monica reassuringly. 'Don O'Brien, Terry's dad, was re-interviewed by the police a couple of days ago.

He told them that he had been a serving member of An Garda Síochána before moving to Scotland in the nineties and joining the Glasgow police. They're looking at the possibility that someone from his past had tracked him down. Maybe he had been the target, and Jenny just happened to be in the wrong place at the wrong time? Or maybe it was retribution of sorts? Who knows?'

Michael was dumbfounded. This seemed like a total stretch.

Monica continued, ignoring hiss open-mouthed reaction. 'Professor Wilkes thinks this is a futile exercise but, given Don's garda background, his Irish links and the fact that he was well known by the paramilitary groups, it's another avenue they have to explore.'

After a moment he realised that his boss was staring at him, waiting for some response.

'You don't look convinced yourself, Michael.'

'It's just … I'm not sure I should be involved in this. You know I'm one of Terry's closest friends. Would it not be a conflict of interest?' What he really meant was that he knew Terry would be on his back constantly. 'I don't want to let her down. She would be devastated if it all came to nothing. Again.'

'Well, let's make sure we do everything to prevent that happening,' said Monica sternly. She was not going to take no for an answer.

'Fine,' said Michael grudgingly. 'Maybe I should look at what they've got first.'

'Marvellous. I'll forward the information Alastair emailed to me. Call him if you need anything else.' She gave him a dismissive wave. The meeting was over.

Michael sighed as he closed the door behind him. He had just been handed a bomb, and now he had to make sure it didn't explode.

Back in his office he speed-read the email then reached for his desk phone.

'Hi, George!' Michael had no intention of contacting Professor Wilkes, head of the Scottish lab. He had his own contact, George McLaughlin, a forensic scientist in the biology section. They'd met at a forensic conference a couple of years earlier. He was a decent enough chap and they could talk on equal terms.

'Hullo, Michael. I thought I might hear from you. Let me guess: Jennifer O'Brien. She's a very popular girl it seems. Yours is the second call today. Alistair's like a bear with a sore head. He takes criticism of the service personally. He's not happy with the boys upstairs rooting around in his dirty laundry.'

George gave Michael a quick summary of the investigation into Jenny O'Brien's murder. 'In fact, the only forensic evidence they recovered was a partial fingerprint lifted from a necklace she had been wearing at the time. No match was made from the Scottish or UK databases at the time.'

'Nothing? Not even an inkling?' Michael was incredulous.

'Well …'

Michael heard the hesitation in the other man's voice. 'Come on, George,' he demanded. 'Spill!'

'I hate criticising my colleagues but … Remember it was in 2005, before fingerprints were part of the remit of forensic scientists. Before that, fingerprinters were the polis. And let's say that things were a bit fraught in the fingerprint section around that time.'

Michael listened intently as George launched into the details. 'In 1997, a woman was stabbed to death in her home in Kilmarnock. After a full-scale murder inquiry, a chap who had been doing some building work in the house was charged with her murder, based on fingerprint evidence. So far, so good. But the case took an unprecedented twist. The police fingerprinter had also lifted a print from the house that allegedly matched with a policewoman.'

Michael's first thought was that she must have been sloppy, attending a crime scene without wearing gloves.

'Anyway,' George went on, 'the policewoman strongly denied having ever been near the scene. She couldn't explain how her print got there. Of course, the fingerprinters stood over the match. It was incidental to the murder trial, which was otherwise pretty straightforward, and the builder chappie was convicted. Job done.'

'Okay, but what happened to the policewoman?' Michael had a feeling this story was not going to have a happy ending.

'She was charged with perjury, lying to the court. The fingerprint evidence proved beyond doubt she had been there – she could deny it all she liked.'

'Surely that fingerprint evidence was questioned? Why would she say she wasn't there if she was – it doesn't make sense.'

'Yes, well, the fingerprinters were adamant they were right. You know what the police are like. They dig their heels in. No way they got it wrong.'

'But, George, we know fingerprint evidence is not foolproof. Not like DNA.'

'Ah! Scientists versus fingerprinters.'

'I'm not saying we're better. It's just different – a different standard of proof. To be crass, it's just wallpaper matching. A looks like B, so they match. It's not very scientific.'

'Try telling that to the polis back then,' sighed George.

'What did happen?'

'At the policewoman's trial, a fingerprint expert from the States gave evidence in her defence. He annihilated the fingerprinters' evidence, pointing out that not only had they erroneously identified that print, but the methods of verification they used were outdated and prone to human error. It was a masterclass in decimating an expert's evidence. First, he confirmed the similarities that led them to conclude that the print from the scene matched her fingerprint. He even went so far as to point them out one by one, matching whorls, loops and ridge shapes, twelve in total. The police were all smiles. But then he delivered the killer blow. He pointed out the dissimilarities, where the print didn't match. They had only done half the job. It seems obvious to us scientists that straightforward wallpaper matching isn't scientific. We routinely test evidence, make sure it's robust. But pig-headed police experts, huh!' Michael could hear the contempt in George's voice. 'They were wrong, on all counts. Well, all hell broke loose. The police, the fingerprinters and the courts were in uproar. The perjury case against the policewoman disintegrated, and she was exonerated. Thank God.'

'Poor woman.' Michael tutted. 'That ordeal must have been awful for her.'

'It was. After that, all should have been well with the world. But then, didn't the builder chap convicted of the murder appeal on the basis that the fingerprint evidence on which he was convicted was unreliable? What did they expect? Any defence lawyer worth his salt would have gone for the jugular. He walked free. Egg on the faces of the police.'

'Well, they had no one to blame but themselves.'

'There's the rub, though. The Scottish fingerprinters refused to accept their failings and continued with their archaic system for several more years until they were forced to relinquish fingerprint evidence to us in forensic science in 2006.'

Michael was aghast. 'Fuck's sake. How many people could have been wrongly accused of a crime based on fingerprint evidence alone? And what about unsolved murders – shouldn't the fingerprint evidence be reviewed? Maybe they could have been solved.' It dawned on him that Jenny's murder could have fallen foul of this monumental cock-up.

'Well, it isn't such an issue now that we have access to DNA evidence, which gives a level of certainty that wasn't attainable before. But you're right, Jenny O'Brien's murder investigation might have been hampered by not just a dodgy police officer, but also dodgy interpretation of fingerprint evidence. This investigation has opened up a real can of worms. God help us.'

Michael ended the call and sat with his head in his hands. He felt the weight of this. Monica wanted him to examine the fingerprint evidence to see if he could trace a match on the Irish database. That was easy enough. But the dodgy stuff was at the Scottish end, and by the sound of things George was up to his neck with it.

Just when he thought things couldn't get any worse, Terry's dad rang him as he was about to leave the lab for the day.

'Hi, Don.'

'Ah, Mikey, good to hear your voice!' Michael rolled his eyes as Don went through the pleasantries. They both knew what this call was about.

'Now, Michael, we know Terry has been through the mill with all this Hunt business. I need to look after her and make sure she focuses on her new job. I was interviewed by the police a couple of days ago and they told me that FSI would be reviewing the trace evidence, so I guessed you might be involved. I don't want her upsetting herself with this review into Jenny's death,' said Don.

Michael could hear the quiver in the gruff man's voice. What could he do? It was a catch-22. He couldn't win. He assured Don he wouldn't breathe a word. All he knew was that Terry was going to be raging with him when she found out what he had been up to behind her back.

He would do anything for Terry. She blamed herself for Jenny's death – they'd had this discussion many times over the years, usually after too much Sauv Blanc. She believed if she had taken the shortcut through the woods with Jenny that day, she would have been there and she could have prevented the attack.

In Terry's mind, she deserved all the bad things that happened to her. Michael sometimes wondered if she went looking for them, by deliberately placing herself in danger. Like with Hunt. She had actively involved him in Rachel Reece's murder investigation, had sought him out, so she thought it was only right she was punished for that. As if getting half killed would solve anything. Michael shook his head as if to banish his intrusive thoughts. *No, Terry would never do anything like that. Get a grip,* he chided himself.

12

Terry agreed a co-parenting arrangement with Jimmy: she would provide Bella with bed and board and he would dog-sit while she was working. Dog maintenance was not discussed, but she thought it was a small price to pay for Bella's company and the peace of mind Terry felt when she was around. Jimmy had insisted on bringing Bella to her flat on Sunday morning. Terry suspected that he actually wanted one last night curled up with Bella on the smelly sofa in his office. Quite sweet, really.

After a long goodbye with Jimmy, she decked Bella out in her coat and they set off for a walk along the quays. It was cold but dry, the perfect day for a stroll. But after only twenty minutes Bella decided enough was enough and pulled at the lead, almost tripping Terry up as she did a U-turn. Secretly, Terry was relieved. She had been under the assumption that a greyhound would need hours of walking but it seemed the dog was going to fit in with her sedentary lifestyle. The two spent the rest of Sunday sprawled on the couch together.

The other benefit was that Terry didn't feel the need to constantly check and recheck the locks. Whenever any of her neighbours opened or closed their doors, Bella's ears twitched and she rallied to her feet, a self-appointed guard dog.

The next morning, after the soundest sleep Terry had had in ages, she dropped Bella in to the mortuary to be looked after by Jimmy before driving to Walter Scott House. She was writing up her case notes in the OCRU office when Mary and Bob arrived.

Mary noticed Terry warily eyeing the teetering stack of files on her desk. 'This is only half of those coroners' cases.'

'This is all a waste of time,' moaned Bob. 'These deaths are from years ago.' He shuffled past and deliberately elbowed the pile, files scattering to the floor.

Terry counted to five. She would need the patience of a saint to deal with Bob. 'And your point is, Bob? That's the way cold case reviews work. The clue is in cold.'

Despite his attitude, Mary had assured Terry that Bob Paterson was actually a very good detective. He just had this knack of rubbing his seniors up the wrong way. Terry hoped Mary was right about the good detective part, because his anti-authoritarian sentiment was really beginning to annoy her. It wasn't just his attitude. She was well used to men underestimating her, but she could use that to her advantage – they never saw her coming. She had heard Bob referred to as a man's man, and to her this was shorthand for a hardened misogynist. This was something else. She didn't think she could trust him. In fact, she was sure she couldn't trust him. She would have to be careful with him, not give the impression she felt threatened. But she did.

He ignored her, letting Mary gather up what had fallen on the floor, and sat heavily into his chair. Terry picked a bundle of the remaining files from Mary's desk and dropped them in front of Bob. 'You can concentrate on these. Check out your esteemed colleagues' investigatory techniques.'

She picked up her jacket and her bag. 'Mary, I've an appointment this afternoon. I'll leave you in charge.'

Terry was glad to be out of the oppressive atmosphere of the OCRU. She needed to find a way to navigate this new role. It would be a disaster if she failed because she couldn't manage that prick. For now, she was off to her first therapy session with her psychiatrist, Dr Maeve Price. She was dreading this appointment. Talking about her feelings was not her thing. Maybe she could vent about Bob, if nothing else.

She parked in the grounds of the Rockroad Clinic, squeezing in between a couple of huge Range Rovers, neither of which looked like they had seen much off-road activity. The building was similarly oversized and intimidating. It was at times like this she wondered about her choice of profession. There was little money in forensic pathology, at least in comparison to some other branches of medicine, where you could make extra income with nixers or private cases. Still, money wasn't everything.

The main reception area was tastefully decorated and quiet, designed to have a calming effect. Not far up the road, she knew that the same could not be said for St Vincent's. No wonder the HSE was haemorrhaging doctors and nurses to the private sector.

She was directed to the first floor. The psychiatry unit was at the end of the corridor behind glass double doors. Inside, in the waiting area, were pairs of large comfy-looking sofas sufficiently distanced to afford the occupants some degree of privacy. Adorning the walls were framed photographs of the current psychiatrists and psychologists. She thought they must be heavily airbrushed – surely they couldn't all be that good-looking?

Terry was glad she was seeing a bona fide psychiatrist rather than a psychologist or psychoanalyst. She still wasn't entirely sure what the differences were, but she trusted medical doctors, and Maeve Price was a medical doctor, not a PhD doctor. Terry was uncomfortable to be in this position, but as her dad had said to her on the phone the night before, 'You're not doolally, you've been traumatised,' and Dr Price was a specialist in post-traumatic stress disorder.

Terry walked over to the receptionist, who appeared not to have noticed her coming in. She was cocooned in an oversized fuchsia-pink cardigan, which looked like she'd knitted it herself, and appeared to be engrossed in a book. Terry cleared her throat to announce her presence. Startled, the receptionist quickly dropped her book and straightened herself up, cheeks flushing with embarrassment at being caught skiving from her job. Terry couldn't help but notice that the book she had pushed to the corner of her desk was one of those modern romances, a favourite of her dad's partner, Aileen.

'Sorry. I'm a bit early. I didn't mean to interrupt your break. I'm here for an appointment with Dr Price.'

The woman quickly regained her composure and turned her attention to the computer screen in front of her. 'Dr O'Brien?' she asked.

She seemed unsure and Terry realised she probably didn't look anything like the woman's medical colleagues. Normally she thought that was an advantage, but here, in this rarefied atmosphere, she felt a tad out of place. The doctors in this building would no doubt shop in Brown Thomas for muted designer clothes suitable for treating their well-heeled Dublin clientele in. It was more likely that they were coiffed, perfumed and manicured, not dressed as if at any moment they could be trudging through a field to a gruesome murder scene or wrestling with a decomposing body. Forensic pathologists didn't do dry-cleaning. If it couldn't be bunged in a washing machine, it wasn't worth having. Although, having said that, she wasn't averse to a nice pair of shoes. Everyone has a weakness.

She nodded in reply to the receptionist's query.

'Dr Price is still in a consultation. She'll be with you presently. Meanwhile, please take a seat. Can I offer you a coffee?'

'That would be great' – Terry looked at the name tag pinned to the cardigan – 'Aoife.'

Dr Price appeared at exactly 2.30 p.m. and led Terry through more double doors into the office area and then into a beautifully furnished room, decorated in soothing tones of greens and creams. Lamps were dotted around, creating a relaxing glow. *This is nicer than my flat*, she thought ruefully. Dr Price gently guided Terry over to one of the plush armchairs, and the psychiatrist sat down opposite her. Terry wondered how much the Department of Justice was being billed for this session.

She had little recollection of exactly what she had told Dr Price when she had visited her in ICU. She had been on an opiate high most of the time. She did have a feeling, though, that the psychiatrist knew more about her than Terry would ever divulge, even to Michael, and he was her best friend and confidante.

Thankfully, once more she found Dr Price, who'd told her she could call her Maeve, easy to talk to. Terry liked her and immediately relaxed in her company.

'So, Terry. Tell me how you've been since I last saw you in hospital.'

'Oh, you know. Fine,' Terry said non-committally, shrugging her shoulders.

Maeve folded her hands in her lap and cocked her head to the side. That didn't feel like a good sign – she obviously had given the wrong answer. 'Well, not really fine.' She looked expectantly at the woman opposite, but her face was expressionless, her expertly made-up eyes staring back, waiting for Terry to continue. She didn't even seem to blink.

Terry could feel herself tensing. Silence made her uncomfortable. She rubbed her hands together, then noticed her bitten nails and tucked her hands under her thighs.

'Why don't you tell me how you feel about Rupert Hunt,' suggested Maeve.

Hearing his name caused Terry's body to recoil. She felt like she had been slapped in the face. 'I hate him,' she spat, surprising herself. 'He made a fool of me. I still can't believe I was taken in by him. I'm not the type of person that would be so easily manipulated by anyone.'

'So you're angry because you feel he made a fool of you, as you say, rather than because he tried to kill you?'

'But he didn't kill me,' retorted Terry.

'You do realise that you are not to blame for Rupert Hunt's actions? From what you told me before' – Terry felt the heat rising in her face and she held her breath, wondering what she had said – 'you were groomed by this man. This was a long game he had been playing, waiting for a worthy opponent, someone who would recognise his genius.'

'Yes. And that patsy was me.' Terry sank back in the chair, deflated, and pulled her feet up under her.

'You are not responsible for what happened, Terry. Hunt is,' said Maeve, trying to reassure her.

Terry squeezed her eyes shut. 'I still see him, you know. When I close my eyes, I see him lunging towards me and I feel that flint in my hand.' She blinked her eyes open again. 'And sometimes I even wish I had killed him.' She stared defiantly at Maeve.

'That's perfectly understandable. But you must remember, he cannot harm you now. He's safely behind bars where he's not a risk to you or any other women.'

'I know. I know.' Terry lowered her feet back to the floor. 'The breathing techniques help.' She desperately did not want the psychiatrist to think badly of her or that she was mentally unstable.

'Have you thought about medication?' asked Maeve as she scribbled on her notepad.

Terry gave a wry smile. 'Does alcohol count?'

Maeve returned the smile. 'No.'

Terry talked about how she had been since she came back to work and the trigger points that she had encountered, making sure to keep on safer ground – less like a woman with a murderous vendetta. She even threw in a bit about work relationships, making light of her problem with Bob. It was something they could come back to. She was starting to feel wrung out, exhausted by talking so much.

Towards the end of the session, Terry told the psychiatrist, tongue in cheek, that she had adopted Bella as her therapy dog. 'What an excellent idea!' exclaimed Maeve. She herself was a dog lover. She spent the remaining few minutes showing Terry photographs of her bearded collie and her lurcher. Terry assured her she would take a photo of Bella, and show it to her at their next appointment.

On the way back into town, Terry tried to blank out the therapy session by focusing on what she needed to get done in the next few days. An ambulance whizzed past her, sirens blaring. There were people a lot worse off than her. Mags popped into her mind.

Jimmy had Bella ready for handover by the time she pulled

up outside the mortuary. She decided that she would detour to the park to see if she could spot Mags, so she didn't hang about, although Jimmy wasn't much for small talk anyway.

Terry parked as close to the Castleknock gates as she could. Bella got out of the car reluctantly. The light was fading but there were still a good few people about. She reckoned that nefarious activities would soon replace the wholesome dog walkers and joggers. She shuddered at a momentary flashback to the time she was attacked in the park, and Bella looked up at her with her gentle hazel eyes as if she could sense Terry's fear. She patted the dog's head, seeking reassurance, and walked on, pulling up the hood of her coat to give her a bit of protection from the chilly breeze.

Bella trotted by her side, ears pricked, as Terry walked to the spot where she had last spoken to Bernice, the Phoenix Park's self-appointed mother to homeless girls. Terry hoped that she was still presiding over this end of the park, keeping an eye on her girls.

After a few minutes dawdling by some trees that Bella deemed worthy of extensive sniffing, a figure emerged from the shadows.

'The good lady doctor has returned.' Terry recognised the distinctive thick Dublin-accented voice. 'Glad to see you're keeping better company.'

Terry smiled at the tall redhead. 'Hi, Bernice. Good to see you again.'

'Who's your friend?'

'Bella.' Terry kept a tight hold of the dog's collar, as she was pulling against the lead trying to meet the stranger properly. To

Terry's amazement, Bernice walked over and knelt down beside the dog. Bella's tail whacked against Terry's leg as she licked Bernice's face in friendly greeting.

'I prefer animals to men,' Bernice said drily. She stood up then, towering over Terry. 'So, what are you hanging around these parts for?'

'I was hoping to bump into Mags. I'm worried about her. You heard about the detective who got shot?'

Bernice pulled a face. 'No loss.'

Terry tried to remain nonchalant. 'You knew him?'

'You could say that. And I'll say it again: no loss. But what has that to do with Mags?' Bernice looked wary.

'I met her and she told me about her new friend. Some dealer – Jake? I hear talk of a new gang muscling in and I'm just concerned that Mags might be out of her depth. She seemed to think this guy was trying to help her.' Terry pulled Bella closer. Bernice pulled a vape from her jacket pocket and inhaled deeply. She blew a cloud of sweet-smelling smoke into Terry's face.

'Any idea where she could be?' asked Terry hopefully.

Bernice finally spoke. 'That scumbag Jake has got his hooks in her. She's only seventeen, you know? She's gone through some shit in her life. When she was fourteen, her ma moved her loser boyfriend into their house. He abused Mags, and do you think her ma wanted to believe her when she finally told her what he was up to?' Terry shook her head. 'Nope, she chucked her out on her arse, with nowhere to go and no money. Her own daughter. Sometimes it's the women you have to be wary of.'

Terry looked intently at Bernice and wondered about her

own back story. *How did she end up here?* There was something compelling about her. Terry liked her, and evidently so did Bella.

Bernice took another drag. 'You didn't hear this from me, but word is the Hayeses, well, they're a bad crowd. They're lying low since Higgins was done. I hear they moved their operation to Drogheda. Stupid little bitch'll be chained to a bed by now.'

Terry felt deflated at this bit of news. 'I guess you can't keep them all safe.'

'No, but you have to try. You best get yourself out of here, Dr O'Brien. That lapdog'll not keep you safe around here either,' she said, giving Bella's ears a scratch.

Terry and Bella watched until Bernice disappeared into the shadows. Terry realised it was nearly dark. She shivered. She suddenly felt exposed and vulnerable. The dog looked up at her. 'Good girl. Like Bernice said, let's get the hell out of here.'

13

Detective Superintendent John Fraser sifted through the pile of statements on his desk. It was always like this a week or so into the investigation of any murder – information overload, but little hard evidence. But this was not where he wanted to be in this particular investigation. A murdered detective was big news and the press were constantly looking for quotes and updates. That he could cope with – it was the assistant commissioner who was the issue. The 'I have full confidence in your abilities, John' pep talk earlier that morning was intended to leave him on edge.

The most obvious answer was that it was an organised hit by the Hayes gang, and an enlightening conversation the previous evening with C.I. Perez of the Policía Nacional in Girona, his Spanish contact in the Drugs and Organised Crime Unit, seemed to suggest that his suspicions might be correct.

Donal Hayes was a career criminal, going way back to his teens when he was involved in petty crime: breaking and entering, car theft, dealing with stolen goods – nothing major. Later he had moved up a gear into drugs. but the rot had really set in when Donal married Lou Ward in 1985.

Lou had aspirations and she wanted Donal to be top dog in Dublin. The Hayeses soon became notorious – they were violent and money-obsessed, which essentially led to their downfall. It was alleged that Donal was responsible for an armed robbery at a Bank of Ireland branch on St Stephen's Green in the nineties, during which Lou's brother, Seamus, was shot and killed and her dad was arrested. Ward Senior later died in Mountjoy while serving a life sentence.

At any rate, the family disappeared shortly thereafter, then popped up in Liverpool, where they thrived once more. Ireland's loss, et cetera. With his Irish connections, Donal infiltrated the local inner city drug scene, and they also opened a couple of sex shops – a front for their foray into the sex trade and a handy means to launder money. They now had a few legitimate businesses in the UK, including an aesthetic cosmetic clinic in the trendy Liverpool Docks, run by their daughter, Caoimhe. She had since reinvented herself as Cherry Hayes, a more anglicised and glamorous moniker befitting her new enterprise. Fraser had seen photographs of Lou taken at a footballer's wedding in 2022 and it looked like she was a loyal customer of her daughter's clinic. It was around then that Donal and Lou upped sticks and moved to Spain.

Perez told Fraser that the Spanish authorities had been monitoring the Hayes family since their move, and he was more than happy to trade information. Problem was there wasn't much of it. Fraser had been taken aback when Perez explained that Donal Hayes was out of the game. He was said to be suffering from dementia and was holed up in the secluded family villa in a little coastal village just outside of Girona, with carers attending to him around the clock.

Perez suspected that the family were making a move out of Spain, as they hadn't been very active for the past year. He suggested that a combination of Donal's dementia and the dominance of powerful Russian, Eastern European and North African gangs meant that they couldn't get a strong foothold in the Spanish market, and several high-profile drug seizures at Southampton Port had detrimentally affected their UK importation business. Ireland seemed the obvious choice if Donal's wife, Lou, had taken over the role of head of the family. Going back to her roots. It was worrying if she had full control. She could be ruthless and unpredictable. As for the rest of them, Cherry was her mother's daughter. Her younger brothers, Donal Jr and Liam, were vicious, but not the brightest – a volatile combination.

If Lou was coming home, she might have scores to settle. Was Higgins one of those scores?

There was no record of any of the Hayeses travelling to Ireland, but that didn't mean Lou wasn't orchestrating the expansion operation from her luxury villa or that any of them couldn't slip in through Belfast undetected. Fraser had been looking into the possibility that the Hayeses had had a foothold in Ireland for quite a while, biding their time, rebuilding contacts. Higgins had heard this from his contacts, and he saw no reason to doubt the information. Fraser suspected that they may have been concentrating on the sex-trade side, and not drugs, which allowed them to operate covertly.

But now, if the Hayeses were moving drugs into the Irish market, they would be upsetting the tenuous status quo amongst the existing drug families. That would be dangerous to all concerned. He didn't need another all-out turf war.

Fraser had had his eye on Higgins prior to his murder – he'd suspected he was up to something dodgy. It was no coincidence that many of his team's raids had been thwarted. Someone on the inside had to be passing on information to the Hayeses, and Higgins's name had come to the fore. He had been clever, there was no doubt about that, but his financial situation had been under secret investigation. A guard and a teacher recently buying an expensive house in leafy Foxrock didn't stack up.

Picking up Bob Paterson's statement, Fraser reviewed the details again. Bob had disclosed that he thought Higgins was a little too interested in the flat they had had under surveillance, but he thought it was just a case of sampling the goods. He suspected that Martin was slipping in and out of the flat under the radar. Fraser had read the riot act to the officers who were supposed to be keeping an eye on the place, but they were all stretched, and he accepted it wasn't possible to watch the flat all the time. Higgins had plenty of opportunity to go in unnoticed – he knew the rota.

Fraser had asked Bob directly if Higgins was in the Hayeses' pocket. He had vehemently denied it, but Fraser wasn't sure whether Bob was being loyal to Higgins or covering something up. The next few weeks would be critical in assessing whether their information leak had dried up. If so, Higgins would be the obvious source. If not … well, they were in serious trouble.

Even so, it didn't sit right that whoever was running the show would order Higgins to be taken out and then leave the body in plain sight. Rule number one: never shit on your own doorstep. Fraser had been building a human-trafficking case, watching and waiting. His colleagues in the National Drugs and Organised Crime Bureau were closing in on where the increased influx of drugs in the Irish market was coming from and who was distributing them. They had been planning a coordinated raid on the operation and the players. But now the Hayeses were on alert. They had cleared out the flat pretty thoroughly – Monica MacKenzie was still giving him grief over it. They had doused the place in bleach, but it was still awash with prints and DNA. If there was something useful in there, he knew her team would find it.

He put his head in his hands. Sometimes the obvious answer wasn't necessarily the right one. He agreed with Terry about the mutilation of Higgins's body. He hadn't come across it before in this type of hit. Maybe the Hayes gang had other ideas. Did they think Higgins had double-crossed them? Had his murder been an intimidation ploy to others who might be stupid enough to threaten to rat them out? Or could it have been the established Carroll gang sending a warning to the Hayes family? There were so many permutations and not enough evidence at the moment.

Fraser massaged his temples – he could feel the dull throb of an imminent headache. He had other pressing concerns too, and closer to home. He picked up his mobile – he couldn't put this off any longer.

'Hi, Terry,' he said as she answered the call. 'There's no easy way to say this: I've some news on Hunt.' He suddenly wished he had driven over to make sure she was okay when she heard what he had to tell her. 'He's in court tomorrow. The DPP has agreed to charge him with his sisters' murders and your attempted murder.' He was trying to be matter of fact about it.

'What about the others?' said Terry, outraged. 'Don't drug addicts and prostitutes count?'

Prickly as ever, thought Fraser, relieved, before he continued. 'We're still working on them at the moment. Thanks to Michael we've also got some leads on the skeletal remains excavated from Hunt's storage unit.'

'Have I to go to court?'

Fraser heard the waver in her voice. 'No. It's just a formality,' he reassured her. 'Probably best for your own sake if you don't go. And don't worry, there's no chance he'll get bail.'

There was a pause at the other end. 'Has he admitted to anything?'

'No. Nothing. And it doesn't look like he will.'

After Fraser's phone call, Terry couldn't relax all evening and didn't sleep a wink. Eventually, at 4 a.m., she gave up and stuck on the television, comfort watching *Selling Sunset* and fantasising about living in a luxury multi-million-dollar house with an infinity pool in the Hollywood Hills. As she sat nursing her second cup of coffee, she decided she had to go to court.

Dr Price had said she had to confront her demons. And Rupert Hunt was one big fucking demon.

Tomas was a bit taken aback when she rocked up to the mortuary just before 7.30 with Bella in tow, but he kept his counsel. He made her tea and toast and gave Bella a dog biscuit and left her to it. For an hour, Terry sat looking out the window, psyching herself up for seeing Hunt. Then she ordered a taxi, wanting to be at the CCJ in plenty of time to clock who would show up for the court appearance of a serial killer.

The media were out in full force. She recognised a few of the reporters so hung back outside, waiting until the rush died down. The other courts were also in session, and there was much pushing and shoving and arguments at security, the queue snaking out onto the steps outside the building. Smug lawyers and officious gardaí bypassed the scrum. Terry stood beside a group of smokers having a last drag before they likely had to go in and face their fates.

She waited until the security area had quietened before she approached the glass doors of the Criminal Courts of Justice, with her head kept down. She was dressed like most of the regulars, in a hoodie, jeans and runners, so no one took any notice of her.

The third floor was crammed with gardaí, lawyers and their clients, and anxious relatives, all milling about in front of the courts' doors. The doors of Court 20, where Hunt was due to appear, were still closed to the general public, but gardaí and court personnel were drifting in and out. Terry didn't want to risk being spotted. She didn't want anyone, particularly Fraser, to know she was there. When the door to Court 18 opened and people filed in, she sidled over and slipped in with them, taking a seat at the back, a safe place to wait until she could sneak into the other court unseen.

There were huddles of lawyers at the front of the room, and a couple of men hovering at the periphery. A few seats in front of her sat a well-dressed middle-aged woman accompanied by a man in an expensive suit. Terry watched as he patted the woman's hand. She wondered who he was – he was too dapper for your regular court volunteer or FLO.

She was startled by a loud bang. A door behind the bench opened and a stocky man with jet-black hair to match his black robe appeared, holding a long staff. His face was pug-like, and his beady eyes darted around the courtroom as if he could quieten it by his mere presence. He suddenly raised the staff, banged it three times on the floor and roared, 'All rise for Judge Henderson.'

Terry jumped up from her seat. After a couple of seconds Judge Henderson strutted in, his thick hair, just visible beneath his wig, curling around his ears, his robe flaring out behind him. He examined the courtroom with his flinty grey eyes, seemingly displeased by what he saw in front of him, and eventually settled himself. The shorter man bowed and backed out.

So that's Hanging Henderson, she thought. He certainly looked the part. She had heard the stories of the goings-on in his court. She had never appeared before him – he didn't do murder trials, the near-death experiences of domestic abuse were his area of expertise. He demanded respect from all parties, and to be fair, by all accounts, it was deserved. He had a reputation for being pretty astute and his determinations were usually on the money. He took no prisoners and, according to DS Mary Healy, he had no problem dishing out hefty sentences if he thought them appropriate.

The first case was called. She noticed that the lawyers were almost reverential in their discourses with the judge. They knew that one wrong word could have dire consequences for their client. Terry glanced at her watch – 10.15. She quietly got up and left.

Court 20 was standing room only. Word had got out that Ireland's most prolific serial killer was appearing. Everyone wanted a look at the monster. The gardaí involved in the case had set up at the back of the court to the left of the door. Terry kept her head down and slunk over to the opposite side. Spotting a tiny gap on a bench, she wedged herself in between a guy dressed much like herself and a reporter tapping away on her laptop, oblivious to the people around her. Armed detectives were positioned around the room, covering all entry and exit doors as well as either side of the dock – the bench where Hunt would sit.

She was shaking and felt sick. She closed her eyes, but that was worse – she could see Hunt's mocking face, smell his rancid breath as he straddled her. She could feel the cold sharp flint in her hand and how her arm had juddered as the makeshift knife struck his spine, and then, the relief when it slid to the side and plunged into the spinal canal. She had hoped he would never walk again. It was what had kept her going.

The reporter leaned over. 'Are you okay?' she whispered,

a concerned look on her face. Terry froze, sure she had been recognised, then nodded and pulled a bottle of water from her bag, took a swig and leaned back, thankful that chopping off her hair had at least afforded her some anonymity.

The court fell silent and she realised the judge had entered, his entrance less dramatic than Henderson's. There was a Mexican wave of people rising to their feet and immediately flopping down again. Terry sank back into her seat and concentrated on her breathing: four in, four out. The atmosphere was charged, the anticipation palpable. The door behind the dock opened and what looked like a frail old man was wheeled into court. There was a collective exhale.

Terry heard a man along the row from her ask incredulously, 'Is that him?' She hadn't thought he was dangerous either, at the time. She looked at Hunt critically now, sitting with his head bowed, his pale skin sagging around his neck. His scrawny body was swamped by his cheap polyester suit, and his hair was now grey and wispy. She had been taken in by the suave professor but his look, even his hair colour, had been a façade, hiding the ugliness deep within. This pathetic specimen was the man responsible for her sleepless nights? She felt angry, but she wasn't afraid of him now. She had gotten the better of him.

Despite that, she wasn't buying his damaged victim persona and meek demeanour. As the charges were read out she watched as every so often his eyes flicked around the court. Looking for someone. Looking for her.

The guard accompanying Hunt grabbed the handles of the wheelchair, and the sudden movement caused Terry to shrink back in alarm, her right hand instinctively reaching for the scar on her shoulder. The courtroom was suddenly a buzz of excitement. She realised it was over. He had been charged with two counts of murder and one of attempted murder and she hadn't heard one word of it.

She waited until only the court staff remained before leaving the room. Relief flooded through her system. Hunt being formally charged was one step closer to him being locked up for his remaining years. A miserable existence, and one that he thoroughly deserved.

A short time later, Terry slipped in through the back door of the mortuary, avoiding Tomas and Jimmy who were busy helping an undertaker load a coffin into the back of a hearse. Bella raised her head when she opened her office door, but remained in her bed. Terry was desperately trying to process her feelings. She'd thought she would feel more upset, but she was just relieved that Hunt would be soon put away for good. Maybe it was a good thing that she'd gone to court, maybe she could start to move on.

She rolled her shoulders and rubbed her neck. Now it was time to get back to the day job, and she had work to do. She had to put this morning's events out of her mind and she could think of no better way to do it than by performing a post-mortem. By the time she had changed into scrubs, Tomas had pulled a body bag onto the post-mortem table and was in the process of unzipping it to reveal the body of a male, possibly in his early twenties. Concentrating on the task at hand, Terry got down to work. Performing a post-mortem was her version of mindfulness – the intricacies of dissection focused her thoughts.

The gardaí attending the post-mortem knew the deceased of old. He was a seasoned addict, a fixture on the Liffey Boardwalk, who would know to the microgram what he could take and survive. This led the gardaí to speculate that there could be a dodgy batch of drugs on the streets. These addicts dodged death on a daily basis, so why not today? The post-mortem couldn't answer that question, but she knew someone who could – the new toxicologist.

Terry called up the state laboratory and explained who she was and was put through to Dr Fionnuala Brady. Dr Brady she hadn't noticed anything odd in recent drug screens on potential overdose victims, dead or alive, she told Terry, but she promised to check the samples from this case herself. There wasn't much else Terry could do but wait and hope that the toxicological analyses identified what she too suspected – that the addict had taken a potentially lethal drug.

14

In the early hours of Saturday morning, Fraser sat in his car outside a run-down semi-detached house in a bleak Drogheda estate, watching closely as the Emergency Response Unit surrounded the house they suspected was being used as a brothel by the Hayeses. The local lads had done a great job identifying where the Dublin business had relocated to since the Higgins murder.

It went like clockwork. Fraser was in a benevolent mood, so he had the ERU wait until the punters had dried up – it could become very messy if they inadvertently lifted one of the local worthies. More bother than it was worth. As it was, the clientele consisted of two average Joes, who probably had wives and kids tucked up at home.

Six women and two men were found when the guards stormed the premises. The men were less than co-operative, but the element of surprise prevented anything more than a bit of bravado and a few harsh words. He wasn't sure, but their body language suggested something stronger than 'get off'. These guys had the air of seasoned criminals to him.

Fraser got out of his car as soon as the men were safely contained. He watched as four scantily clad women filed out under armed guard. If he expected high fives and cheering at their being liberated, he would have been sadly disappointed. These women looked as if they were about to face a firing squad, their heads bowed and their arms wrapped tightly around themselves. He sighed as he watched a couple of female guards lead them away.

Suddenly there were shouts from inside the house and he was immediately on alert. The remaining two women were being dragged out kicking and screaming, an armed officer on either side of them. Fraser stifled a laugh as one of the officers got a kick in the groin before the women were cuffed and put in the back of a patrol car. They were to be taken to Drogheda garda station, where Fraser was now headed, and the men to Dublin, where his team would interview them.

Arriving at the station a short time later, he spotted the women huddled together in the reception area. A specialist team was waiting to speak to them but it wouldn't be easy – one of the guards told him that only two spoke fluent English – they would need to bring in interpreters for the rest. The feisty ones had now calmed down but were still cuffed. Then Fraser realised he recognised one of them. It was Mags.

Normally he would leave the interviews to the local gardaí, but he decided that Mags might respond better to a familiar face.

Fifteen minutes later, Mags sat at the table in the interview room, concentrating on her constantly fidgeting hands. Fraser placed a paper cup of water on the table in front of her and sat down. 'Mags, isn't it?' Her eyes remained transfixed on her hands. She looked quite different to when he'd last seen her – when she had tried to thump him on the back of the head in her den in the park. Her greasy hair was pulled up into a bun so tight the skin on her face was drawn up and back – council-house Botox. And her new living and working arrangements meant she had been cleaned up.

She eventually looked up, but stayed silent.

'Do you remember me from the Phoenix Park? After Tina McCabe died? I was with Dr O'Brien.'

At the mention of Terry's name, Mags glanced hopefully towards the door.

'Dr O'Brien's not here.'

The young woman was shaking, jumpy. He guessed she was coming down from whatever cocktail of drugs she had been fed.

'You're not under arrest or anything,' Fraser said reassuringly. 'I just wanted a chat. We want to help you.'

Mags's face contorted into a grimace. 'Yeah, right! I don't need your help.' She folded her arms defiantly across her chest and looked away from him.

'What can you tell me about your friends? Who are they? Do you know who brought them to the flat?' Mags remained silent. He decided on a different tack. 'Dr O'Brien told me you had a new boyfriend?' He looked down at his notes. 'Jake, is it?'

'Don't know who you're talking about.' Mags sat up and stared defiantly at Fraser. He sighed. This was futile. Her defensive behaviour was the norm. And he didn't have the time to try and talk her round – he needed to get back to Dublin. He could only hope that someone at Ruhama would be able to get through to her. If anyone could make her see sense it would be them. The organisation bore the brunt of supporting prostitutes in Ireland, whether they continued working or whether they wanted help to get out. It was sad to think that the state depended on a charity to provide help to these women.

Terry scrolled aimlessly on her phone as she waited for Michael in the bar on the ground floor of the Bord Gáis Energy Theatre for a matinee performance. Rule number one of any visit to the theatre was to pre-order interval drinks, and Michael had woefully neglected his assigned duty. At this rate they would be lucky to get a sip before they had to be back in their seats. She scanned the crowd. Her attention was caught by a striking young woman wearing a cap a dead ringer for Eponine's. Terry always wondered what Marius saw in Cosette, but then he was a bit of a drip too. Eponine would be a bit of a challenge for him.

She watched the woman squeeze through the crowd to join her friends and was taken aback to see that one of them was Martin Higgins's wife, Pat. Terry hadn't seen her since that day in the mortuary last week. She swithered over going over to ask her how she was, but Michael suddenly appeared clutching four glasses of wine.

'Quick, get one down you,' he said, plonking the glasses on the table then shoving one into her hand. Terry cast a disparaging look at the deep yellow liquid masquerading as Chardonnay, but took a large gulp regardless.

Wincing as the acrid wine hit her tastebuds, she checked the time on her phone. 'We've only got ten minutes. We'll never neck all this.' She took another sip and leaned in closer to Michael. 'Don't look round, but Martin Higgins's wife is over there.'

Typically, her friend immediately turned around. 'Where?'

She grabbed his arm. 'Jesus, Michael!' Before she could remonstrate about his lack of subtlety further, she saw a tall well-dressed man walk over and hug Higgins's wife. 'He looks familiar. I'm sure I recognise him from somewhere. Have you seen him before?'

The screen of her phone lit up. They both stared at the name of the caller. John Fraser.

'Are you not going to answer it?'

Terry stared at the screen until it went black. She began texting. 'Just letting him know I can't answer because we're at the theatre.'

Michael raised his eyebrows and drained his glass. Her phone screen flashed again.

'He wants to meet up after?'

From his vantage point at the bar, Fraser watched Terry and Michael walk into the Marker Hotel and scan the room, looking for a table. He smiled as he saw them hustle a couple of women who had made the mistake of reaching for their coats. Michael appeared to offer to assist one of the women as she struggled getting her arm in the sleeve, while Terry hovered behind the other, ready to pounce as soon as she rose and pushed her seat back.

Fraser swirled his pint around in the glass and checked his phone. Still no word on Mags, who, along with the other girls, had done a runner at the first opportunity. It wasn't anyone's fault they had gone to ground – they hadn't done anything illegal. They were victims and the gardaí only wanted to protect them. Mags and the other Irish girl hadn't seen it that way though. There was no reasoning with them. Fraser suspected that Mags had somehow got a message to someone, likely one of her keepers. Or there was always the possibility that one of the gang had clocked the gardaí and avoided the raid but followed them on to the garda station, waiting for a chance to reclaim the women: their chattels. He wondered if the Jake guy was somehow involved, but he wasn't either of the men currently being questioned at Walter Scott House. They weren't local lads – they had Scouse accents, although they were refusing to say much. But it was enough to confirm that the Hayeses had indeed moved their business to Ireland.

Fraser had sent a team to the Phoenix Park to see if they could spot Mags there. He was sure she would scurry back to where she felt safe, and hopefully back into the arms of Jake. The team had only come across a group of scumbags, low-level criminals – drug addicts with a penchant for shoplifting. But they did have some useful information: Bernice and her girls hadn't been around since the day after Terry said she had spoken to her. Fraser hoped to God that she was just lying low – he didn't need another body turning up. But someone must be putting pressure on her.

He drained his glass and headed over to Terry and Michael. A group of people caught his eye. Centre stage was Pat Higgins, Martin Higgins's widow. He recognised the other two women as Cait and Saoirse Paterson, Bob Paterson's ex-wife and their daughter. He also unfortunately knew the man who was with them, Ronan Reagan, a sanctimonious, poisonous creep. Fraser couldn't stand him and suspected the feeling was mutual.

Reagan was a psychologist and lauded as a champion of, and spokesperson for, abused women. He popped up on daytime television on a regular basis, fake sincerity oozing out of him. Fraser shivered. He couldn't understand why people didn't see through his sleazy demeanour. He would love to wipe that smirk off his face.

Fraser skirted around the tables, making sure he wasn't seen by Pat, Cait or Ronan, as he made his way to where Terry and Michael were sitting. He gave Michael a pat on the back and leaned over to kiss Terry on the cheek. She smiled. But that might just be the effect of the drink.

'Saved you a seat.' Terry grabbed her jacket and bag from the stool next to her.

'Thanks. How was the show?'

'Brilliant!'

'What do you want, John? We're on white wine.' Michael waved a waiter over.

'Guinness Zero, please.' The waiter nodded and headed back to the bar. 'Driving,' Fraser said, rattling his car keys.

'So I guess this isn't pleasure.' Terry turned to face him. 'Why the urgency?'

'We followed up on that information you gave us about Mags and the alleged boyfriend.'

'You've found her? Them?' Terry said hopefully.

'Yes. And no.' Her face fell. 'We raided an address in Drogheda that was operating as a brothel. Mags was there, with five other women.'

'Oh no. So that means Jake managed to get her into sex work. Is she all right?'

'Physically speaking, yes. But mentally … you know, it's hard to tell. Not great, I'm sure. She wouldn't talk to me, and as soon as she could, she legged it along with the other girls. I had hoped she'd stay and talk to Mairead Dunne from Ruhama. Guess you can take the horse to water but you can't …' He shrugged.

'She's not a bloody mare,' said Terry, banging her glass on the table. 'What about the Jake guy?'

'No sign of him. He wasn't one of the lads we picked up. They're both Scousers, which I guess Jake is too. It's possible he followed us to the station and waited until Mags came out and picked her up.'

'Or maybe she just headed back to the park. It was her home. God forbid.' She stood and grabbed her jacket and bag. 'We need to get over there.'

Fraser put his hand on her arm, halting her in her tracks.

'Not so fast, Miss Marple. We've got lads out looking for her. She hasn't turned up in the park.'

'Yet! We need to let Bernice know. She'll look out for her. She—'

He cut her off. 'That's going to be a problem. Bernice has gone to ground. She hasn't been seen for a few days.'

'Shit!' Terry collapsed back into her seat.

Michael and Fraser exchanged looks. Then, Fraser took a deep breath. 'Hopefully she's just lying low. She's not stupid.'

At that moment the waiter returned with the drinks.

Michael tapped the card machine.

'Cheers!' Fraser raised his glass to Michael. 'We'll keep an eye out for Bernice. She's the least of my worries. Four of the women we found in Drogheda are non-nationals. No papers. No English. No idea who they are or how they got here, but most likely they're victims of sex trafficking. We've a problem getting interpreters, but we managed a game of charades and they've agreed to be swabbed.' He looked over the rim of his glass at Michael. 'DNA might be a shortcut to identifying them – seeing if they're on a database somewhere. They might have been reported missing in their countries of origin.'

'Are you sure miming is valid consent?' Michael looked uncertain.

'I take full responsibility.'

'Does Monica know? She's a real stickler.'

'Well, she wasn't thrilled, but she authorised technicians from FSI to take the samples and have a look at the scene. We need to know more about these women ASAP.'

'Just another wee DNA job then. Thanks! I'll add it to the list,' he said, a note of sarcasm creeping into his voice.

'It's your job, Michael. Suck it up.' Terry glared at him then turned to face Fraser. 'Anyway, on a related subject, we saw Martin Higgins's wife in the theatre. Didn't we?' She knocked her glass against Michael's and made a face.

Michael made to say something, but Fraser interjected. 'Yes. I saw her in here too. She's back there near the door with her sister – Cait, Bob Paterson's ex-wife.'

Terry started choking and sprayed wine out of her mouth and across the table. Michael slapped her back. She took another swig of wine, swallowed and took a deep breath. 'You're saying Pat Higgins is Bob's sister-in-law? When was someone going to tell me?'

'I thought you knew,' said Fraser, perplexed. 'Sure, he came with her to the mortuary to do the ID.'

'I just thought it was because Bob was pally with Higgins. I didn't know they were related through their wives.' Terry slapped her forehead. 'Shit! He must think I'm a right cold bitch. I just thought he was being a prick. As usual!'

'I wouldn't lose sleep over upsetting him,' Fraser reassured her. 'Sorry, I was sure Mary or Bob would have told you.'

'No wonder you didn't want him in the middle of the investigation. I thought you'd deliberately sent him to me to wind me up.'

Fraser smiled. 'That was just a bonus. No, I knew he would have to toe the line with you. He was loyal to Martin, but Martin could be a real shit. It always surprised me that Archie Sinnott had him on his team – I just inherited him. Seems behind closed doors he gave Pat a hell of a time. Problem was she would never make a complaint. I think she was embarrassed – she's big in the church and a teacher in Loreto. She wasn't going anywhere. Bob's wife, well … that's a different matter.'

'But they split up?' asked Terry, keen for all the scandal. 'That was a few years ago.'

'Who's the young woman with them? Martin's daughter?'

'Saoirse? No. Pat and Martin didn't have any children. She's Bob's daughter. A really nice girl, despite her dad. He dotes on her, but Cait does her best to keep them apart.'

'She probably has her reasons,' said Terry with a glimmer of a smile.

'That's a bit harsh!' Up until now Michael had been happy to listen. 'I never get it when parents make children take sides.'

'Well, John Boy Walton, not everyone is lucky enough to have a mum and dad like yours.' Terry shot him a look. She turned back to Fraser. 'There was a man with them. I'm convinced I've seen him somewhere recently. I just can't remember where.' She lifted her glass and sat back, looking in the man's direction.

Fraser glanced over to where Pat and the others were sitting. 'He's a psychologist, Ronan Reagan,' he said. 'You might have seen him on one of those afternoon chat shows.'

Terry suddenly sat up. 'No, that's not it. I know where it was. He was in the CCJ in Henderson's court when I …'

'What were you doing in Court 18? Why would you …?' Fraser's voice tailed off. He shook his head and looked at her askance. 'Court 18 doesn't deal with murders. When was this?'

Terry's face reddened. He could practically feel the heat.

'You were in court for Hunt's appearance?' Fraser couldn't believe it. She must have hidden herself near the back of the courtroom so he wouldn't spot her. 'Why would you put yourself through that ordeal? You weren't required to be there.'

He shook his head again and took a deep breath, trying to keep his emotions in check. He quickly composed himself. He wasn't Terry's keeper. If Terry felt strong enough in herself to go to court to see Hunt charged, that was her prerogative. No, he told himself, he was going to approach things differently this time.

15

Terry was reeling from the family connection between Bob and Martin. She couldn't believe it. She chatted companionably with Fraser and Michael for another hour, before Fraser drained his glass and made his excuses. He was heading to Walter Scott House to see if there were any further updates on the two men arrested in Drogheda. Paul called Michael to see if they both fancied dinner and a box set, but Terry wasn't in the mood. Her social battery was rapidly depleting, and anyway, she had left Bella in the flat, fully intending to come back early.

Tonight would be a good night to start her jigsaw. It would help calm her whirring brain.

Her phone rang at 11 p.m. She had only just crawled into bed. Pushing Bella off her legs, she grabbed the phone from the bedside table. Her heart sank when she saw Prof Charlie flash on the screen.

'Evening, Prof. Is there a problem?'

'I'm sorry to bother you so late.' She knew he wasn't sorry. He expected her to be available around the clock, so she stayed silent. 'I've been informed of the death of someone I know.'

'Oh. Sorry for your loss. What can I do to help?'

'Thank you, but we weren't close. He was in my year at college. Actually, I didn't particularly like him and I haven't seen him since our thirty-year reunion. He was a gynaecologist so our paths didn't cross. But that's by the by. His death is being treated as suspicious. At the moment, the guards' theory is that it was suicide, but I think there may have been' – he paused and coughed – 'an auto-erotic element to his death. Also, I've heard that several allegations of sexual assault have been made against him by some former patients. I've explained my predicament to the DI investigating the death. We don't want any hint of a conflict of interest, so I've told him to expect you at the scene tomorrow morning. They're holding it overnight.'

'Okay.' She couldn't think what to say.

'Is that a problem, Terry?'

She wanted to reply, 'I've got a fucking life and it's not my weekend on call.' But instead, she said, 'Of course not. Give me the details.' She took down the address from Charlie and hung up. She was wide awake – it would take her ages to get to sleep now. 'All part of the job, I guess,' she said wearily to Bella, who was snoring away, stretched over the length of the bed.

It was a sunny Sunday morning and the roads were relatively quiet, which was a blessing as Terry didn't know Dún Laoghaire very well. The house she was looking for was on the road overlooking the coast. As she drove towards Sandycove she ignored the glittering sea view – she was more fascinated by the spectacular houses. The prof's classmate must have had a healthy private practice.

The traffic slowed and she realised that the Technical Bureau had abandoned their Transit van on the road, causing a gridlock. It was easy to spot the house, as there were garda cars, marked and unmarked, spilling out of the drive. When traffic finally started moving again, she was able to tuck her car behind a small van with RTÉ emblazoned on the side.

Luckily the press was expecting Charlie so no one took any notice of her and she was able to slip into the drive unchallenged. She was almost at the front door before a guard finally noticed her and hurried over to stop her from entering. Just then, Vinnie appeared at Terry's side. 'This is Dr O'Brien, she's the state pathologist,' he informed the fresh-faced guard. Vinnie grabbed her arm and pulled her into the porch. 'Bunch of amateurs! Any Tom, Dick or Harry could walk in here.'

She followed him through the front door. 'I wasn't expecting you,' said Vinnie. 'I thought it was Professor Boyd's weekend on call?'

'He asked me to take it,' she said, looking around the beautiful hall, with its high ceilings and ornate cornicing.

'Fair enough. Give me another ten minutes to check where the SOCOs are at and then you can get into the room. It's up there.' Vinnie pointed to the top of the staircase, then started to make his way upstairs.

'Dr O'Brien?'

Terry turned. A guard in his late thirties, dressed in a white shirt and dark jeans, strode across the hall towards her. 'Cian Nolan, DI.' He held out his right hand. She took a quick head-to-toe glance.

'Dress-down Sunday?' she asked. Nolan smiled and let his hand drop. He had dimples. He was not technically her type – blond hair, clean-cut, piercing blue eyes – but she guessed she could make an exception.

'Thanks for coming out. Professor Boyd explained it might be a conflict of interest if he got involved.' DI Nolan shrugged.

'The prof filled me in that some patients had made complaints against the deceased. Charlie probably doesn't want his name dragged into any of that.' She gave the DI her best winning smile. 'And he's a bit of a prude. He told me that there might be an element of auto-erotic activity. If he saw his friend wearing a pair of women's frilly knickers, he would never unsee it.'

Nolan laughed. 'Sorry to disappoint, but no frilly knickers involved.'

She felt herself redden. And there was that little smile of his again. She was a sucker for dimples.

Terry followed him up the stairs. They had to squeeze past a group of SOCOs and a couple of detectives sorting exhibits. The doors of the rooms were lying open.

DI Nolan looked back over his shoulder. 'Some gaff, eh?' He stopped at the third door. 'Master bedroom by the look of it.'

Terry peered in. Master was the right word. This room had masculine vibes, decorated in a deep forest green and replete with dark mahogany furniture. It was in direct contrast to what she had seen of the house so far. The hall was light and airy and appeared to have been recently decorated by someone with expensive taste.

Nolan had moved on to the next door along. 'This is the wife's bedroom, according to the cleaning lady who found the body.'

Her room was like something out of an interiors magazine. 'Nice.' It was at least double the size of Terry's bedroom and lavishly furnished in various shades of creams and golds. Money *can* buy you happiness, it seemed. The lucky woman got all the trappings of wealth and didn't even have to sleep in the same room as her husband.

The next two rooms were more modest, but still bigger than most average bedrooms. There was no bathroom off the landing area so she assumed the bedrooms were all en suite.

'He's in here.' The DI knocked on the final door on the landing, the doctor's office. It was opened by Vinnie. He held up his right index finger. 'One minute.'

Terry picked up a white suit from a pile beside the door and pulled it on. 'So he was found yesterday afternoon?'

'Yes, the cleaner came in about 3 p.m. she said. It was about 5 p.m. when she finished up and she came up here to let Dr Maguire know she was leaving. Poor woman got a bit of a shock.'

'So she saw him at 3 p.m.?'

'No. She has her own key and she didn't want to bother him. He gets a bit tetchy about being disturbed if he's working in his office. She only went in to let him know she had left his dinner in the fridge.'

'What about Mrs Maguire?' asked Terry.

'She's away for the weekend.'

'She didn't come back last night?'

'No. But then again, she was told she couldn't get in the house until we finished with it.'

'Still. You'd think she'd want to be close by when her husband had just been found dead.'

The DI nodded in the direction of the his-and-her bedrooms. 'Maybe she had her reasons. This last month can't have been easy. Living with someone accused of sex offences.'

'Is there anything in the allegations?'

'Two women came forward, both former patients. It's still early days. But there was a letter on his desk about a meeting with the hospital board in the Rockroad Clinic next Monday.'

Vinnie appeared in the doorway. 'Ready for you now, Doc.'

Dr Maguire's office was the smallest of the rooms, but still larger than most double bedrooms. Voluminous burgundy velvet drapes had been pulled closed and the room was illuminated by bright lights set up by the SOCOs.

Directly opposite the door was an oversized marble fireplace, and above it was an ornate over-mantel mirror that seemed to be fixed at a precarious angle, the top leaning away from the wall. To the right, at the window end and overlooking Dublin Bay, was a large mahogany desk, with a dark leather recliner behind it. He obviously preferred working without the distraction of the view.

She stepped into the room and Dr Maguire came into view. The disgraced gynaecologist was reclining on a velvet chaise longue. The opulence of the room somewhat softened the disturbing scene.

The SOCOs had set out a path of metal plates, the obligatory stepping stones, snaking left to the body, ensuring no one stood on the carpet on the way. Vinnie took the lead. He slung the strap of his camera around his neck and bent to pick up an armful of plates. As he moved from station to station, he placed a parallel line of plates for Terry so they could walk side by side.

Dr Maguire was naked, his clothes neatly folded on the floor. He looked middle-aged, maybe early fifties, but must be older if he was at college with Boyd. His hair was dark brown and, she suspected from the slight mahogany hue, was dyed. He looked like he had slumped back onto the seat – his right foot was on the floor, his left draped over the side. His arms lay limp at his sides. He appeared to have kept himself fit and looked in good shape for his age.

Terry moved closer to get a better look. Vinnie directed the lights at the doctor's head. The face was swollen and purple. There was a ligature wound around the neck. One free end, about ten centimetres long, lay over his collarbone, the other end disappeared over the back of the chaise. She moved back two plates to get a wider view. She took in the area around the chaise: there was no evidence of any disturbance – all was neat and tidy. She looked up. Directly above was a large ornate chandelier.

'Vinnie, do you have a torch?' He reached inside his suit and produced one. She pointed towards the ceiling and Vinnie swung the beam upwards.

'Suspension point?' he queried. 'Mmm.'

'Hanging?' Another voice came unexpectedly from behind, causing her to wobble on the plate she was perched on. She hadn't realised the DI was standing there.

It was Vinnie who replied. 'Looks like it.'

Terry motioned for Vinnie to move back so she could stand closer to the doctor's head. She stuck her hand behind her and Vinnie put the torch in it. She leaned in, illuminated each eye and followed the course of the thick gold-coloured cord around his neck.

'Classic asphyxial signs. Cyanosis, that's the purple colour, and petechiae in and around the eyes. Actually, they're over the whole of his face.' She turned to the DI. She knew Vinnie had seen these before. 'See the tiny red blood spots?'

DI Nolan nodded, but kept his distance. She guessed he wasn't that familiar with dead bodies – he seemed like the ambitious type who had probably been fast-tracked through the garda ranks.

'Thing is, these signs are more common in strangulation and partial suspension.'

'What do you mean, Dr O'Brien?'

'If you look up, there's a piece of cord dangling from one of the arms of the chandelier. If he was fully suspended, his feet clear of the ground or the seat, death would be pretty quick and there wouldn't be time for these haemorrhages to develop, and the face would usually be pale.' She shone the torch on the doctor's face. 'It wouldn't be purple.'

'So he was standing on the couch?'

'Hmm …' Terry motioned for the men to move back towards the door and she carefully stepped towards the middle of the room. She slowly turned around, shining the torchlight around the space.

'A-ha!' She pointed the light beam towards the curtains. 'That's where the ligature came from. The match to that.' She pointed to the curtain tie-back hanging at the left side of the window. 'Minus the tassel.'

'So it's likely just a suicide?' Terry could hear the hope in Nolan's voice. Open and shut case, no need for a prolonged investigation.

'The manner of death is not for me to decide. I'll tell you the cause of death, which is asphyxia, and the mechanism. What the possibilities are. But if this is suicide, it's not typical for a number of reasons. He's naked, which is odd. And then there's all that stuff.' Terry pointed the torch at the end of the chaise where there was a pile of photographs showing images of women's genitals.

Walking back over to where Maguire lay, she shone the torchlight at the feet and slowly scanned the body. She stopped at the groin. There was a smear of blood at the tip of the penis, but she couldn't see any injury. Terry didn't say anything to the DI – she needed to have a closer look when she got the body back to the mortuary. No point in jumping to conclusions.

Tomas was setting up in the post-mortem room when she arrived at the OSP with Bella just after lunchtime. The dog had been as good as gold waiting in the car until she finished at the scene. As a reward they had walked along the pier in Dún Laoghaire before going to the mortuary.

Terry popped her head around the door of the post-mortem room. 'Two this afternoon okay for you, Tomas?'

'Sure, Doc. The body's on its way in. There was no mention of anyone doing an ID.'

'Their regular cleaning lady found the body so the DI seems happy enough. Seems she's known him for years.'

The team arrived in dribs and drabs, Vinnie and DI Nolan leading the pack. The local SOCOs were new to her. As long as they didn't interfere in the mortuary, all would be fine. Including them in the discussion about the forensic strategy was lip service. It would be done her way. She was responsible for collecting the forensic trace evidence at the post-mortem. It was rare that she had to consult with a forensic scientist at this stage. She didn't want any SOCOs touching the body. While the body was in her mortuary, she was in charge.

'All the usual swabs, but remember we'll need penile, scrotal and nipple swabs as well as tape lifts from the neck.'

They all nodded and set about gathering the equipment needed.

'I'm going to cut the ligature to get it off his neck. We need to keep the knot intact. It will have to be checked for DNA transfer, but we also need to check it's a bog-standard knot, not anything fancy.'

'Like what?'

Terry looked at the SOCO who'd asked the question – he looked fresh out of the box. 'Dun Laoghaire is a sailing spot so it could be something a sailor would do. Was he into sailing?'

The SOCO shrugged and went back to filling out forms. Terry set about taking forensic samples, leaving the ligature to last. She changed her gloves and asked Tomas for fresh sterile scissors. The knot was on the left side of his neck, below and behind the ear. The cord was tight around the neck but she managed to slip two fingers under it, directly opposite the knot. Tomas handed her a length of tape, which she wound around the cord, and then divided the cord by cutting through the taped area so Michael could identify her cut.

She looked back over her shoulder to Tomas. 'Exhibit bag, please.' She dropped the cord inside.

Vinnie photographed every step of the process. Terry re-swabbed the neck and had Tomas pull the body onto its side so she could get a look at the back. The cord had left a ring of abrasion encircling the neck. It was more or less horizontal. She looped the tape measure around the neck to get an idea of the circumference.

The tongue was clamped between the teeth. The jaw muscles had stiffened and it took a bit of effort to prise the mouth open. She would have to check with the GP called out to pronounce death to determine what examination she had made at the scene. It might help to narrow down when he had died. All they knew at the moment was that he was last seen by his wife at lunchtime on Friday and he was found dead at 5 p.m. on Saturday.

The dissection was fairly straightforward, until it came to the pelvic organs and the genitalia. Tomas handed her a needle and syringe to siphon off a sample of urine from the bladder. The urine was bloodstained. The kidneys and the ureters looked fine, so she guessed there might be a bladder problem. She decided to do a complete resection of the bladder, penis and testes. It was a tricky dissection that rarely needed to be carried out, and only in unusual cases. Potential auto-erotic deaths fell squarely into that category.

When Terry grasped the bladder, she could feel something inside, so she carefully sliced into the bladder wall. Inside she could see a piece of metal protruding into the base of the bladder that looked like a needle. It seemed to be lodged in the urethra. She felt the base of the penis and there was something inside too. She had Vinnie photograph it and then deftly freed the bladder and the shaft of the penis, turning it inside out, leaving only the skin.

She turned to take a large glass specimen jar from Tomas just as one of the SOCOs raced out of the room, tugging his mask away from his face and retching. His colleague looked to be coping better. Terry stood upright and rolled her shoulders back. These dissections took a lot of concentration, and she wasn't about to be distracted by amateurs.

By the time she had finished, DI Cian Nolan was sitting in her office, speaking to someone on his mobile. Bella's head was resting on his knees and he was idly stroking her head with his free hand.

'Gotta go,' he said quickly when he saw Terry come into

the room. 'Dr O'Brien has just finished the PM. I'll update you later.' He smiled and pointed to the phone. 'The super. Wanted to know where we were with everything.'

Terry kicked off her clogs and collapsed onto her chair, rubbing her neck. 'Curiouser and curiouser!'

The DI sat poised, pen in hand. 'Fire away.'

'Bottom line, death was due to ligature strangulation.' The DI interrupted. 'Not hanging?'

'I'm not saying that. If – and it's a big if – this was a hanging, he couldn't have been fully suspended.'

'So it could be a hanging?' he asked.

Terry was not in the mood for a game of semantics. 'As I said earlier, there are unusual features. The scene suggests auto-erotic asphyxia and I found a foreign body, a needle possibly, inserted into the penis.'

'That's definitely not normal.' DI Nolan winced.

'To you, maybe. But guys who get their kicks this way do other strange things as well. All part of the fun. Or so I'm told.'

'Doesn't sound much like fun to me.'

'Well, reducing their oxygen levels is said to heighten the sexual experience. Each to his own. And I mean his – women don't go in for it much. But ...'

The DI looked up sharply. 'I don't like buts. Is it a good but or a bad but?'

Terry smiled as a sudden image of DI Nolan's butt flashed across her mind. 'Is there ever a good but? The thing is, the whole point of this practice is to not kill yourself. In fact, they often use padding around their necks because they don't want marks left. And there is usually a fail-safe mechanism that releases the pressure on the neck should they go too far and collapse unconscious. Neither of which was found.'

'So have I got this right? It's not a typical suicidal hanging and it's not a typical sex hanging, or whatever it's called. But it could still be a suicide or an accident.'

'What we haven't excluded is third-party involvement.'

'You think it's a murder?' said DI Nolan, putting his head in his hands.

'I can't rule anything out at the moment. I think you should get FSI in.'

Terry had barely finished the sentence when Nolan whipped out his phone. He pressed a single number, someone on speed dial.

'Hi, Monica. Yes, I'm sorry I missed your lunch, but I'm in the mortuary.' He listened to what was being said. 'Yes, Dr O'Brien. It's an odd case, and she thinks it best if someone from your team checks it out. We're still holding onto the scene. The local SOCOs have done preliminaries. We were waiting for the results of the PM. Okay.'

He moved the phone away from his ear. 'Monica MacKenzie. She had a lunch do on. I was supposed to be there, hence the outfit. I was at college with her son. Anyway, she's gone to have a chat with one of her staff from FSI, see if she can set up something for tomorrow.'

He put the phone back to his ear. 'That's great. I'll let her know. Sorry to have disturbed you. Say hi to Conor for me.'

He slipped the phone back into his pocket. 'She's sending out a Dr Flynn tomorrow morning.'

'Perfect. I can meet him there,' said Terry, getting up from her chair. She was tired. It had been an exhausting Sunday.

The DI looked at his watch. 'We're a bit late for lunch – what about a drink?'

Terry was taken off-guard. 'Thanks. But I've got Bella,' she said, nodding to the dog who was now attempting to straddle Nolan.

'Mulholland's is dog friendly,' said Nolan, giving Bella an affectionate scratch under her chin.

Terry guessed if Bella was a fan of Nolan's, he must be okay.

She grabbed her bag and Bella's harness. 'Well then, let's go!'

16

Terry woke with a start. The room was still dark. She reached her left hand out from under the covers and scrabbled for her phone. It was already 8 a.m. Her head was throbbing. She should have left the pub earlier. As she frantically tried to piece together the evening, a wave of nausea rushed over her. Had she said or done anything she shouldn't? Cian Nolan had been easy company. One drink led to another, and another, and she had been more than a little tipsy when they left Mulholland's. She remembered swaying into Cian and at that moment, when their faces were so close, it was easier than not to kiss him. But as soon as their lips touched, she'd known she was making a mistake. A delicious mistake, she'd thought, and strutted off into the cold night with Bella leading the way.

She sank back onto the pillows now and closed her eyes as relief ran through her – thank God she hadn't taken it any further than a brief kiss. Swinging her legs out of the warmth of her bed, she made for the shower. She stood under the scalding water, trying to wash away any feelings of mortification at letting her guard down so easily.

At 9.30 a.m., she picked Michael up outside his flat, as arranged, and drove them both over to Sandycove. She filled him in on the details of the post-mortem on the way. There was less activity at the doctor's house this morning, and she was able to squeeze her car in the drive behind Vinnie's white van. Vinnie had the back door open and was perched on the edge of its storage area, his legs dangling, engrossed in his phone. He jumped down when he saw them and pulled up the hood of his white suit, falling into step beside Terry and Michael as they made their way up to the front door.

'The DI told the SOCOs to hang back until you got here, so it's pretty much how it was yesterday. Minus the body. Here!' Vinnie handed them each a suit and headed to the house. 'See you inside.'

'I don't really see what the issue is,' said Michael. 'Sleazy doc gets caught out interfering with his patients, can't take the embarrassment of being exposed. Pardon the pun. Then hangs himself.'

'That's one narrative,' agreed Terry. 'And it's highly plausible, but that's not how I read the scene. The scene says sleazy doc jerks off while he's oxygen deprived. And we've seen what happens when auto-erotic practice goes horribly wrong. But …'

'I hate your buts.'

'I said that too.' Michael and Terry hadn't noticed anyone come up behind them. She recognised the voice and froze. She had been naive to think that DI Nolan wouldn't turn up. She kept her back to him, feigning difficulty zipping up her white protective suit. Michael was completely unaware of the awkwardness and turned around to see who it was.

'Hi. Dr Flynn?' said Nolan warmly. 'I'm DI Cian Nolan, the senior investigating officer, and I think you already know my colleague,' he gestured to the man standing next to him, 'Superintendent John Fraser.'

Oh God, thought Terry. *Could my day get any worse?*

Luckily, Fraser only seemed interested in Michael.

'Hi, Michael,' said Fraser. 'I just wanted to get a handle on the problem with this case. I was the duty super for the weekend. Dr MacKenzie told me you were coming out this morning.'

Terry fiddled with her zip for as long as possible, trying to compose herself. Then she had a sudden realisation. *Superintendent!* Shit, she had been so wrapped up in herself she hadn't picked up on his promotion. *When did that happen?* How many times had she met him and not realised the change of title? It must have washed over her at the Martin Higgins conference. *He must think me a right self- obsessed cow.*

'Morning, Superintendent!' Terry did her best to sound relaxed and breezy. 'We're just about to go in.' She turned and pushed Michael up the doorstep.

'Give us a minute,' Michael managed as he stumbled into the hall. Under his breath he hissed at Terry. 'What's going on?' She ignored him and, in an unnaturally loud voice, said, 'Here, let me help you with your bag.' She picked his kit bag up, whispering, 'Move it.'

Michael looked back over his shoulder at her, and then at Nolan and Fraser, who were now engaged in deep conversation. A grin broke out on his face. 'You didn't?' he whispered back.

'Shush! No, I didn't!'

'But you thought about it. Which one? Or was it both? You little minx, you!' said Michael with a lascivious wink.

Terry thumped him on the back. 'Vinnie's waiting,' she said in a raised voice, pushing him up the stairs.

Up in Dr Maguire's study, Vinnie explained to Michael what forensic samples had been taken, and Terry scanned the room, refreshing her memory.

'Vinnie.' She interrupted their conversation. 'Did you bring the ligature?'

Vinnie produced a brown paper bag with a clear plastic window to allow the contents to be seen without having it and handed it to Michael.

'I removed this from the body,' said Terry.

'Good job, Dr O'Brien. You're getting good at this forensic malarkey.'

Terry shot Michael a sharp glance, she didn't need sarcasm on top of a hangover. She pointed at the evidence bag. 'This is why I want you here. I want you to test if this cord would break under his weight.' She looked up at the ceiling and pointed. 'And if the light fitting would hold his weight. It's the free end of the ligature that I'm interested in, just in case someone handled it.'

She squeezed past him and stepped from plate to plate to the chaise longue. 'Head was here and feet were here.' Her hand swept across the seat. 'He was naked. Ligature around the neck.' She stepped back to allow Michael a clear view. The curtains had been opened and now natural light flooded the room, revealing its true grandeur.

'Vinnie, can you get a sterile sheet to cover the couch? Tez, is it all right if I take this down?' Terry looked over. Michael was pointing up at the cord dangling from the chandelier.

'Fire away.' Terry carefully, stepping plate by stepping plate, went over to the desk. The sea view from the window was mesmerising. She watched as the sun danced across the waves. She could now fully appreciate the reason the doctor kept his back to it while he was working. Less distracting.

Speaking of distraction, she heard Fraser and Nolan appear in the doorway then, but Vinnie and Michael's ongoing chatter meant she couldn't quite hear what they were discussing. Terry did her best to keep her mind on further analysis of the crime scene.

There were two framed photographs on Dr Maguire's desk: one of him with the president at some posh do, the other of a gangly young man in a graduation gown and cap flanked by Dr Maguire and an elegant, well-preserved brunette, most likely Mrs Maguire.

'Give us a hand here, Tez,' Michael said, interrupting her thoughts. 'Can you take some notes?'

Terry looked over to see Michael clambering onto the chaise, hand on Vinnie's shoulder. 'I need to take a few measurements. We'll want to know the length of the cord and the height of the suspension point above the ground and this seat.'

Automatically, she replied, 'It's a chaise. Yeah, I need to know if he could have been fully suspended and dangling or if his feet were on the floor or the chaise.'

Fraser and Nolan left after taking a cursory look at the room, realising they were surplus to requirements. Terry had successfully and steadfastly ignored them both. Once they had gone, she could relax and concentrate fully on the task in hand.

After about an hour, Terry realised there was nothing further she could do at the scene and suggested to Michael that he take a break so they could go for a walk. 'I need some fresh air after all this.' They released a delighted Bella from the car and walked down to get a coffee in Sandycove village. They settled on a bench near the Yacht Club. Terry was just beginning to feel human again.

'Well, what do you think?' she asked, blowing on her cappuccino before taking a sip.

Michael looked at her, all wide-eyed innocence. 'What?

Fraser and Nolan? Well, I never thought you had it in you!' She gave him a sharp elbow in the ribs, knocking his arm.

He clutched his cup in both hands. 'You need to stop doing that,' Michael admonished her. 'I nearly scalded myself. There's no need to be so touchy. It's a valid question: the blond blue-eyed young blood versus the ... brooding Mr Rochester.'

Terry glared at him. 'Dr Maguire. Accident, suicide or murder?'

'Meanie!' said Michael. 'Oh, okay. Dr Maguire. Accidental suicide? Is that an option?' He took the lid off his coffee and drained the cup. 'When I stood on that couch, I could see myself reflected in the mirror, so if he suspended himself from the light fitting, he'd have got a grand view of his bits. And Vinnie said there was porn found beside him. That all fits with an auto-erotic doodah. But ...'

'So you have a but, too?' Terry turned round to look directly at him.

'Cool your jets, Tez. Leave me to deal with the equations. It's what you've asked me to do. There's just a couple of things – The cord ...' His voice tailed off.

Terry knew better than to push him. Michael stood up. 'Lots still to do.'

Later that day, Vinnie sourced weights from a boxing club in Dún Laoghaire and helped Michael rig up a pulley system to test whether the chandelier could support Dr Maguire's full weight – around 83 kilos, according to Tomas.

The chandelier held firm up to 90 kilos. Michael didn't test it to breaking point, which, as a scientist, he would prefer to do, but that would be at the expense of wrecking the room. Monica MacKenzie would not be happy if she had to cover the cost of repairing the ceiling. But he had to be satisfied that the chandelier could withstand the doctor's weight, fully suspended. As it was, they had to unscrew the fitting from the ceiling so he could check the type of knot used to secure the cord to it. It was all a bit of a kerfuffle.

Back at FSI, his next task was to test the material properties of the ligature, the gold cord. On face value from the findings at the scene, the doctor had been suspended from the light fitting and, while the light fitting had held strong, the cord had snapped under his weight, depositing him on the fancy sofa.

This was basic science: forces, stresses, strains, stretching to breaking point, determining the strength of the material. But that didn't matter a jot if the cord had been cut.

First things first. He had to check for DNA transferred onto the cord Terry had removed from the doctor's neck from anyone handling it. Anyone other than the doctor himself. Michael shook the cord out of its bag onto the bench in the preparation room and swabbed its entire length, taking special care with the knot, which looked like a typical noose knot, quite different from the knot used to secure the cord to the light. He would get to that later, when Vinnie transported the chandelier to the lab. After labelling the samples, Michael left them in the in-tray for the technician to process, then washed down and decontaminated the bench and changed his protective clothing. It was now a waiting game.

Terry drove straight from Sandycove to Rockroad Clinic, and so was early for her weekly appointment with Dr Maeve Price. She settled on a couch on the first-floor concourse outside the psychiatric clinic, looking down onto the main reception area. It was an excellent spot to watch rich folk come and go. One other person was seated on a matching couch further along, at the other side of the glass double doors into the unit – a stylish dark-haired woman, perched on the edge of her seat, gripping a handbag, her legs crossed at the ankles, staring blankly ahead. She reeked of money. Terry was conscious of her own slouched position, sunk deep in the cushions, and her casual jeans, sweatshirt and runners. No point dressing up for a morning at a crime scene. She was sure the woman was oblivious to her presence. Still, Terry didn't want to stare but there was something vaguely familiar about her. Maybe she was just a stereotypical D4 lady who lunches. They tended to scare the shit out of her.

The woman stood up abruptly. Terry looked around and saw a tall, well-dressed man striding across the concourse towards her. He clasped her hands in his. Terry shrank back into the cushions – it was the man from the court, the man who had been with Pat Higgins in the Marker. What had Fraser said his name was again?

'I thought I'd wait out here, Ronan. I just wanted a quiet moment.' The woman's voice was husky and low. Terry had to strain to hear her.

'It's over now,' Terry heard the man, Ronan, say quietly. He took the woman by the elbow and guided her through the glass doors into the psychiatric clinic's reception. As Terry watched, they went into one of the consultation rooms opposite Dr Price's. She checked her watch – she had only a couple of minutes before her appointment. Maybe she could get some information about them from the receptionist?

Aoife was at her desk, head bent. She must have heard Terry approaching because she looked up and plastered a smile across her face. Terry smiled in return. 'Hi, Aoife. What are you up to there?'

Aoife looked down. 'Knitting. Sorry. Very unprofessional of me.'

'I'm a wee bit early again,' said Terry apologetically. 'So it's me who's disturbing you. What are you knitting? I could never get the hang of it at school.'

'Just a little something for a knit and natter session I run.'

'That sounds ... fun! But unless they serve wine, it's not something I could get on board with.'

Aoife tittered. 'You can't drink and knit. You'd end up with a lot of wonky stitches. Although we do serve wine at my book club.'

'That's much more my cup of tea. Or should I say glass of wine.'

'Dr Price is a member,' said Aoife, as if imparting a great secret. Maybe now she was a co-conspirator, Terry could ask her some questions.

'Aoife, that man who just came in with a dark-haired lady, who is he? I'm sure I know him from somewhere.'

Aoife's smile disappeared. 'That's Dr Ronan Reagan,' she said, pointing at the picture of him on the wall behind Terry, with Dr Ronan Reagan, Clinical Psychologist, written below on a polished nameplate. 'He's one of our top psychologists here. He's always on TV.'

'Ah, of course. I should have seen the picture.' Terry was kicking herself. How had she failed to notice it? She was off her game. But the hair was darker, probably the result of L'Oréal. *Because middle-aged men are worth it too.* 'And the woman he was with – I feel like I might know her from around. Is she a doctor as well?'

Aoife picked up her needles and resumed her knitting. 'I'm not at liberty to give out personal information about clients,' she said tersely.

Terry was starting to regret asking the question in the first place. 'I'll just take a seat until Dr Price is ready?'

The receptionist nodded.

Returning to her seat, Terry flicked through the stack of magazines, obviously aimed at a horsey crowd, all country sports and manor houses. 'Dr O'Brien! Terry.' Maeve Price was standing at the open door of her office. 'Come on in.'

Terry dropped the magazine and turned to pick up her bag. As she straightened up, she pointed to Dr Reagan's photo on the wall. 'A handsome man, your colleague,' she said.

'Ronan?' Maeve frowned. 'Yes, you could say so.'

The clipped response surprised Terry. Maeve Price was not going to be drawn on his attributes. She decided to change tack as she walked into the room, Maeve closing the door softly behind them. 'Aoife seems very nice. She was telling me about her hobbies.'

The warmth returned to Maeve's expression. 'She's a great one for trying to bring people together, a real people-pleaser. She organises all these clubs.' Maeve dropped her voice. 'Bless her, I guess she just likes to keep herself busy. Now, where did we leave off last week?'

Terry could barely concentrate during the session, which meant that she over-shared, something she had been deliberately avoiding. She had even mentioned Fraser in passing, though she didn't go into any great detail about their relationship. There was no point including her other issues – Hunt was more than enough to deal with. Maeve was delighted to hear that he had been formally charged and hoped this would help Terry to achieve some sort of closure.

When Terry eventually escaped the psychiatrist's room, she noticed Aoife had swapped her knitting for a book. Obviously it wasn't too taxing working as a receptionist in a private practice.

'That looks a bit … worthy?' said Terry, gesturing at the book. 'It's certainly thick enough.'

Aoife slapped the book shut. 'It's this month's choice for the book club. *The Island at the Centre of the World*. Mrs Maguire picked it. You saw her earlier – she's in bits,' Aoife said in hushed tones. 'Her husband died at the weekend so I'm not sure if we'll hold the book club this week out of respect.'

As Terry had suspected, Aoife wasn't the sharpest tool in the box and had forgotten about her commitment to patient confidentiality. So Dr Maguire's wife was a client of Ronan Reagan's.

'Well, enjoy the book, and see you next week,' said Terry, her instincts telling her it was best not to pry about Dr Reagan or his patients any further.

17

Terry was relishing the challenge of this hybrid job. She was mindful that having two office locations wasn't ideal, but it did help her separate her roles: the hot from the cold cases. She just hoped that it wasn't an issue for her colleagues.

Today was a day for the OCRU and she hoped that Mary and Bob had been making some inroads in the investigations while she had been busy at the OSP. When she arrived, she checked if anything had been added to the flip charts. Nothing. Clearly there had been little progress. She sighed in frustration and decided to make a coffee before she got stuck in.

Bob and Mary arrived together, already bickering. Terry kept her back to them and added milk to her mug. Then she picked up her coffee and plastered on a smile to greet her colleagues. 'Morning, Mary. Bob. Kettle's just boiled.'

She sat down at her desk for a few minutes, drinking her coffee and surreptitiously watching Bob as he got himself organised. It was painful viewing, as he shuffled a few files around his desk. Then Terry's mobile rang. It was a garda number she didn't recognise.

'Dr O'Brien, Cian Nolan here. Just a quick call to check whether you had any more thoughts on the Maguire death?'

'No,' Terry told him. 'I'm waiting for Michael to finish his side of things.'

'Vinnie told me they did some experiment with the chandelier,' he continued. 'He said it took the equivalent of Maguire's weight and a bit more.'

'I'd suspected as much. These old houses are fairly robust. The light fitting in my flat can barely take a lampshade. But I don't think that was the issue.'

'So you think it could be a suicidal hanging, or even a sex act without a happy ending?'

She ignored the innuendo. 'No, I don't think it's that straightforward. The scene smacks of being staged.'

'Staged?'

Nolan was beginning to aggravate her. Without the benefits of a pretty face and dimples, he was just another annoying guard wanting the easy solution. 'He's a gynaecologist. Patients have made an allegation of sexual assault. He isn't the first doctor, and certainly won't be the last, to find themselves in that position. One thing's for sure, I doubt he was the type to roll over and admit to anything. Nor does he strike me as the suicidal type – although, to be fair, I didn't know the man, and I'm a pathologist not a psychologist. And if he was into auto-erotic practices, would he be stupid enough to do it on the day the cleaner was coming in?'

'Maybe that was part of the thrill,' suggested Nolan unhelpfully.

'Maybe.' She wanted to close this conversation. 'It just doesn't ring true to me. It's like a textbook scene. Life, and death, aren't usually so prescriptive. It's the way he was lying there for a start. Reclining … Displayed more like. Too neat. I just need to figure it out.'

'Okay. I'll continue running it as a suspicious death. For now!'

Terry cast her eyes up to the ceiling. Thank God she hadn't been stupid enough to sleep with him. 'I'll let you know as soon as I have something more concrete.'

'Great. By the way, I enjoyed the other night. We could maybe grab a drink later in the week?'

She gave a non-committal 'Mmm' and hung up. Nolan was just like the rest: he only had one thing on his mind and it wasn't his job.

Fraser flung his phone onto his desk and rubbed his eyes. Another hopeful lead had ended in a dead end. Higgins's death was a conundrum – nothing was adding up. He kept coming back to Martin's potential links with a criminal organisation.

Fraser got up and stretched, looking out the window at the busy street below. It was entirely possible that Higgins's death was totally unrelated to gang activity. He did have a knack for irritating people and he might just have upset the wrong guy. On a whim, Fraser decided to give his old boss, Archie Sinnott, a call. If anyone could give him some greater insight into Higgins's character, it was him. Fraser hadn't spoken to Sinnott since his retirement dinner. They had parted on fairly amicable terms, despite clashing during the investigation into the murder of Rachel Reece.

Sinnott answered after a couple of rings. 'Fraser, good to hear from you,' he said warmly. 'I assume this a work-related call? It'll have to be quick – I'm due on the golf course in half an hour.'

'Well, Archie, retirement must be suiting you. I'll only take a minute of your time. The reason I'm calling is Martin Higgins.'

Fraser could hear Sinnott exhaling slowly at the end of the line. 'How's the investigation going?'

'Not as quickly as I'd like. I want to know more about who Higgins was and what could have got him killed. I never thought he was your kind of man.'

'And who is my kind of man, John? You?' Sinnott retorted coldly. Fraser sighed – his old boss was as prickly as ever. Sinnott continued, obviously not expecting a response. 'Higgins. What can I tell you? He was cut from a very different cloth. There was talk of some dodgy dealings when he was working undercover a few years back in Galway, but that's the trouble with undercover work – sometimes the lines get blurred, and there's nothing in it. Chief Superintendent Maura Murphy organised his transfer to Dublin, and she advised me to keep an eye on him. If he was dodgy, it was only a matter of time before he shot himself in the foot.' Sinnott sighed. 'I didn't think someone would kill him.'

'Have you any idea who would target him, boss?' asked Fraser.

'Maura had the Carrolls on her radar. They were running

the show in Galway at that time. If Higgins was mixed up with anyone it would be them. It was around when the Carroll boys were looking at taking over the dad's pitch up in Dublin. Maybe he ran into them there.'

'I don't think it's them. Recent intel is that the Carrolls aren't doing that well in Dublin. It looks like someone else is muscling in. Did the chief super mention the Hayeses sniffing around?'

'Donal Hayes. Well, I'll be damned. What's that headcase doing back here? Last I heard he was lording it over in Liverpool and expanding his empire into Spain. It's bad news for Dublin. It's bad news for you, John.'

'It was possibly bad news for Higgins.'

Fraser ended the call with his old boss, frustrated at the lack of hard evidence either way on Higgins's past. He pulled open the left-hand drawer of his desk and lifted out a can of Red Bull – he needed a bit of a pick-me-up. And now this Maguire case was proving to be complicated too. Terry had doubts that it was a suicide, and she had called him yesterday evening to tell him that Mrs Maguire had been a client of that slimeball Ronan Reagan. He flicked over Mrs Maguire's statement again, taking a gulp of the sickly medicinal-tasting liquid. He screwed up his face as he swallowed. *Why would anyone drink this for pleasure?*

It was clear that Mrs Maguire had been keeping her distance from Dr Maguire in the months leading up to his death. Fraser understood all too well the pain of a failed marriage and the desire to leave it behind. His own divorce still smarted. Not because he still loved Sandra, he just hated failing. His ex-wife had only been partly right that the job was to blame – the woman had no insight. Her affair with Robert Hill, a weaselly defence barrister, had been the last straw, but she even turned that on its head, saying Fraser had driven her to it. It was no surprise that Robert hadn't hung around for long. Sandra was a complete nightmare, disguised as an angel. She promised heaven, but the reality had been hell. Work had been his succour, not her rival.

He had agreed to couples counselling as a last resort, and that was when he had come across Dr Reagan. Fraser had been naive enough back then to believe it might make a difference. But his last meeting with Ronan Reagan had not ended well. He had lost his temper with the psychologist, who had fully accepted Sandra's account of their marriage. He could have smashed his fist into Reagan's smug face, but instead walked out of that final session with his hands firmly in his pockets, vowing never to see either party again. And Fraser hadn't seen his ex-wife in a long time.

But now Reagan was back on his radar. Terry had a bee in her bonnet about him, and he did seem to keep popping up, first in relation to Higgins's death, schmoozing with his widow at the theatre, and now to Dr Maguire's.

Maybe Fraser should have checked the psychologist out back then, when he was dubious about his counselling skills. He certainly would now. But first he would have another chat with Mrs Maguire.

18

The past few days had been unsettling for Terry, and there was only one person she could talk to who she knew would ground her and make her feel better.

'Hi, Dad,' she said brightly, smiling when she heard that familiar gruff voice. 'How are you doing?'

'Great, hen. What's the latest with you? How's the new job going?'

'Fine. Busy. Got a lot on the go,' she said wearily. 'I've a suicide, but it looks a bit suspicious.'

'Sounds right up your street. Just don't be getting yourself into any bother,' he chided.

Terry thought her dad sounded a bit subdued. 'As if! No, this is all very pedestrian. I can't get myself in trouble. Are you sure everything is okay with you? You don't seem like yourself.' She crossed her fingers. Memories of his stroke weighed heavily on her mind. She couldn't help being anxious that he might have another one at any moment.

'Don't be so daft,' he reassured her. 'Have you spoken to John recently?'

Terry raised her eyes to the ceiling. 'Not really. He's been promoted to superintendent.'

'Aye, I know. He's a good lad. You could do worse.'

'I didn't come to Ireland for a man, Dad!' said Terry indignantly. 'Anyway, I think I blew that one. But how come you know about his promotion? Have you been speaking to him?'

'No, no,' he protested.

'You've not been talking to him behind my back, keeping an eye on me?'

'No. He must have mentioned it when he called to see how you were when you were home. You were the one who said you didn't want to speak to him or hear what he had to say. And he's been very helpful with—' Her dad started coughing and spluttering. 'Sorry, Terry, got a frog …'

There was a long pause, silence on the line. 'Dad! Dad? Are you still there? Are you all right?'

'Hi, Terry.' It was Aileen. 'Your dad's gone to get a drink of water. Just threw the phone at me. What did you say to him to bring on a coughing fit?'

'Nothing!' said Terry. But maybe she could glean some information from Aileen. She had a feeling her dad was hiding something from her. 'He was just talking about how helpful Fraser has been recently.'

'Oh! He decided to tell you then,' said Aileen, a note of relief coming into her voice. 'I'm glad. I really thought you should know. But I can tell you, it was a bit of a shock at first.'

I knew it. I knew he was acting cagey. Well, Terry was quite happy to play along. 'I bet it was,' she agreed.

'Well, Don was a bit taken aback. He thought the police had exhausted all avenues at the time, but this new development has really thrown him.'

Terry was thankful she was sitting – she felt dizzy. This must be about Jenny's death. Her chest felt tight and she couldn't speak.

Aileen didn't seem to notice her silence. 'I mean, Terry, he was devastated. He knows that iffy detective. It was a slap in the face. You know your dad, he's straight as a die, and this wee bastard has been mucking up all these investigations. I thought he'd have another stroke.'

Terry swallowed hard. 'So they're reopening all this detective's old cases?'

'Aye, hen. Not just your sister's. God help all those families. Of course, Don couldn't refuse to co-operate. I think it's hit him hard, the thought that they might have been able to catch Jenny's killer back then, and now all this time has passed.'

'Is he all right, though, Aileen?'

'He's … he's putting on a brave face. He was more worried about how it would affect you. That's why he told Fraser and Michael not to let on to you what was going on. Wee Michael wasn't happy about it at all. Jesus, he's phoned umpteen times trying to get your dad to change his mind. He's awful fond of you, that one.'

So everyone but her knew. Fantastic. She had to keep her cool, although she was simmering with rage. 'Dad won't be happy at them raking up Jenny's death again. It's taken him years to come to terms with the fact he won't ever get answers.'

'Don't you think he just pretends that he's okay with things as they stand for your sake?'

'What?' Terry had never dug down into why her dad hadn't kept the pressure on the police. Maybe he did want to know but wanted to shield her. How self-centred had she been?

'He knows there's nothing he can do to stop it,' Aileen carried on. 'His old polis pals have rallied around. Big Jim's been great. He's doing what he can to take the pressure off your dad. It's a blessing. He's dealing with the polis for us. It's been great having him about, especially as him and your dad go way back in the guards. He's been chatting to your John about the Irish side of the investigation.'

'He's not my John,' Terry reminded her. 'So it's a joint investigation. Is Michael reviewing the forensic evidence?'

'Oh, hen. You know I don't understand all that. But you can ask him yourself now.'

Terry had a sudden thought. 'Aileen, could you do me a wee favour? If you look upstairs in my old room, there should be a jewellery box on the shelf in the wardrobe. If it's there, can you check if there's a wad of tissue paper under the top tray? But don't open it up.' She felt sick – her head was spinning. She needed to end this conversation. 'Sorry, Aileen. There's a call I need to make. Look after Dad. I'll ring you tomorrow.'

Terry flung her mobile onto the kitchen worktop and pulled open the fridge door. Lifting the bottle of wine, she looked at it for a long moment, but decided against it. She turned as she heard the clipping of Bella's nails across the tiles. She hunkered down beside her.

'Hello, gorgeous girl.' She gave the dog a hug. 'I'll let you into a secret. Sometimes only gin will do.'

Terry woke in the early hours of the morning, disoriented. She was on the sofa and Bella was snuggled into her. After wiping some semi-dried drool from her face, hoping it was her own and not the dog's, she gently moved Bella and struggled to sit up. The television was showing a shopping channel. She grabbed the remote and killed it. Spotting the gin bottle on the coffee table, she gingerly picked it up, heaving a sigh of relief at the level. She must have fallen asleep after one, albeit hefty, glass.

She dragged her phone across the table to check the time: 4.50 a.m. There were multiple notifications, missed calls from her dad and Michael. Surprise, surprise. Guilty consciences, no doubt. *Fuck them.*

'Come on, girl. Bedtime. As Michael is wont to say, "tomorrow is another day".' She chose to ignore the fact that it was technically already tomorrow. Terry sighed. Even Scarlett O'Hara had better luck with the men in her life, though, which was saying something. She could swear Bella nodded.

Michael knew they should have been upfront about the reopening of the investigation into Jenny's murder. Terry was old and wise enough to be trusted to take it in her stride. What she would not appreciate was having been kept in the dark.

But Don had been trying to protect his daughter, and there was nothing Michael could have done to convince him otherwise.

When he'd got the panicked phone call from Don last night letting him know that Aileen had inadvertently spilled the beans, Michael knew he would be the one taking the flak for the whole thing.

He had tried to call Terry several times afterwards but had given up at midnight. As soon as he got in this morning, he tried again. Still radio silence. She could keep a huff going for weeks.

'John. Michael here.' He decided it was wise to let Fraser know the situation. 'We've got a huge problem. Terry has found out about the reopening of Jenny's investigation.'

'Shit! Shit! Shit! I knew it would come out.' Fraser sighed heavily. 'I should have got Don to listen to reason, for as sure as fate, Terry won't. We're going to be the bad guys in this. How did she find out?'

Michael heard the accusation in his voice. 'Hang on, don't blame me. It was Aileen. She let slip. But I need to fix it.'

'*We* need to fix it. This is not good. The old gang are having drinks tonight – do you think she could be persuaded to go? We could try and speak to her there?' said Fraser hopefully.

'Oh, I don't know.' Michael was sceptical. 'Maybe get Mary to ask her?'

Mulholland's was neutral territory. Michael hoped Terry would turn up, despite Fraser telling him that Mary wasn't hopeful, but she'd tried her best. Terry still hadn't returned his calls. He thought this ambush might be a mistake – he usually left her alone, gave her space. But he agreed with Fraser: she was pivotal to the current murder investigations, investigations where they would all need to work closely together, so there wasn't time to wait.

He fortified himself with a quick shot. He was leaning on the bar beside Fraser, who was on his phone, when he heard Terry's voice behind them. 'Hi, guys!' She greeted Vinnie, Alan and Mary who were all clustered around a high table. 'It's been a while since we were all here.' She sounded normal, but that meant nothing with Terry. Michael signalled to the barman and ordered a round of G&Ts.

'Sure has, Doc. Take my seat.' Vinnie got up to grab some extra chairs, pulling them over to the table.

Once the drinks had been made, Michael and Fraser sauntered over from the bar. Only Mary had any inkling that there was a bit of friction between them and Terry, but she hadn't asked any questions. She didn't want to get involved, but had nonetheless agreed to broker peace.

Fraser sat a G&T in front of Terry. 'Peace be with you!'

'Thanks.' She lifted the glass and raised it. 'Cheers, all!'

Michael knew her smile was forced.

After a while, when Michael couldn't bear the tension any longer, he asked Terry to help him at the bar, to which she grudgingly acquiesced. Fraser followed them over. Michael wiped away a bead of sweat from his forehead. He didn't know what to expect – Terry was as unpredictable as they come – but surely the fact she hadn't run off as soon as he and Fraser had appeared was a good sign. He just hoped she was willing to talk.

As soon as they moved away from the others, her smile vanished. Fraser led the way to a table in the corner. Michael sat, but Terry and Fraser remained standing.

'Okay, what's the score?' She looked from Michael to Fraser, her eyes narrowed.

Michael patted the stool beside him. 'Here, sit beside me?'

'No thank you.' Her arms were folded and she was glaring at them both.

Oh God, he was really in for it. There was nothing he hated more than upsetting Terry. Underneath that hard exterior, she was just as vulnerable as anyone else. Michael looked up at her and then lowered his eyes when he saw the anger in her face. 'I'm so sorry, Tez.' There was a catch in his voice. He couldn't look at her as he could feel tears welling. He waited for Fraser to jump in, but he said nothing.

Terry slammed her glass on the table in front of him. 'Is that it?'

He grabbed her arm. She looked down pointedly at his hand and he released his grip. 'Your dad swore me to secrecy. I kept telling him I didn't think it was right but ...' He saw her expression change from anger to derision and then to disappointment.

'I thought I could always rely on you to have my back, Michael. How could you not tell me? You know how important this is to me.'

Michael croaked, 'I know.' He looked at Fraser, a silent plea to help him out.

Fraser took a seat and met Terry's eye. 'Terry, please sit down and talk to us. I totally understand why you're angry with us – you have every right to be. But we had to respect your father's wishes. And don't blame him – he was just worried about how opening up Jenny's murder investigation would affect you. Things have been difficult for you over the last couple of months. He thought he was acting in your best interests.'

Michael could see Terry was struggling to contain her emotions. Finally, she relented and sat down. He took her hand in his and leaned in towards her. 'I'm really, really, really sorry.'

She folded her arms in front of her chest again. 'Tell me everything you know about the investigation or I walk.' When no one said anything for a few seconds, she made to stand up, but Fraser motioned for her to stay put.

Michael was aware that Mary was watching them. He raised his glass towards her and mouthed 'thanks'. He knew they were on the path to forgiveness.

19

Terry had only intended to stay for one drink in Mulholland's the night before – she hadn't expected to be ambushed by Michael and Fraser. She was still a little annoyed with them, and her dad, but at least she now knew what was happening. It was lucky her dad had been so adamant that they look into the possibility of an Irish connection to Jenny's death when the Scottish police had spoken to him because it gave her the opportunity to get access to all the evidence. Fraser and Michael wouldn't want to upset her any more than they already had. She could use that to her advantage – they weren't off the hook yet. This was her chance to get justice for her sister and she wasn't going to blow it.

The next few days passed in a blur of post-mortem procedures and flitting between the two offices. Motivating Bob was a tougher job than dissecting a dead body. Michael called into the tea room in the OSP on Friday afternoon with a box of Krispy

Kreme doughnuts. He was still grovelling, and doing a good job of it. Everyone was benefitting from his misdemeanour. It didn't take long for the box to be emptied and the others to drift back to work.

'How are things your end?' Terry swiped her finger through the puddle of chocolate hazelnut filling on her plate and licked it off.

'Really good,' murmured Michael, his mouth crammed with a Boston Kreme. 'Got the results back on the Drogheda prostitutes. The DNA shows one is of Nigerian origin, and the others are Romanian and Albanian.'

'It's sickening. Those poor women, coming to Ireland and hoping for a better life. Instead, they're taken advantage of, drugged up to their eyeballs to sell their bodies to make money for a gang. It's just not fair.' Terry had lost her appetite. 'Were any of the women on the DNA database?'

'Nope. I let Fraser know. The rest is up to him.'

'Good work, Michael.' Terry smiled, glad that they were on good terms again.

Terry was hyped up when she got home that night. Everything was adding up, but nothing was adding up. They were going around in a big circle in every case she was involved in. And none of them made any sense to her. She thought a glass of wine might help her drift off, but settled for hot milk. While she was looking for some honey to sweeten it, she came across a miniature of brandy and added a dash.

Wrapping a throw around her shoulders, she settled down at

the table. Maybe focusing on the jigsaw would calm her nerves and settle her mind. She was going through the pieces for the third time, looking for the Highland cow's nose, when her phone suddenly rang, causing her to jump and drop the piece she had just found. She noticed the time on the oven's digital clock: 1.30 a.m. She groaned. It could only be about her dad or a call from Command and Control.

She didn't understand the knee-jerk reaction of calling her at silly o'clock to tell her they needed her at a scene some time the next day, the actual time to be determined by the team from the Technical Bureau, who weren't known for their early starts.

It turned out that all Sergeant Willis knew at that point was there had been a fatal shooting at Blanchardstown Shopping Centre, at around 10 p.m. A couple having a smoke outside Eddie Rocket's were gunned down by a guy on a motorbike. She had thought that kind of very public drive-by shooting only happened in America. Television and films had a lot to answer for.

Both victims had been taken to Connolly Hospital, but the female had been dead on arrival. However, that wasn't the reason Terry wasn't required at the scene straightaway. The situation was too dangerous. Sergeant Willis did not elaborate, but Terry suspected that was because he didn't know exactly what was going on himself. The fact that the victims had been removed by paramedics meant there was no need for her to attend anyway. She could sort it out in the morning.

Terry waited until nine the following morning to call the coroner – there was no point in heading out until she knew what had been arranged. Tomas had phoned earlier to inform her that the post-mortem was scheduled for 2 p.m. in the City Mortuary. She would have been happy enough to do the post-mortem in Connolly, but apparently the families of the two victims were kicking off, and the hospital had requested the woman's body be taken to the City Mortuary. They had enough on their plate dealing with the injured man. That would mean a detour to the Mater radiology department for X-rays of the dead victim's body.

She sat on the sofa with Bella, waiting for the news to come on the TV. She had listened to the radio bulletins but was none the wiser: names withheld, ongoing enquiries – the usual garda speak for 'mind your own business'.

When the story came up, she watched as the camera panned past the Technical Bureau's white transit, picking out the white-suited gardaí, totally anonymous to the general public. She could make out the shape of Alan Ahern, very obviously in charge, this being a ballistics case, and Vincent Green, with his camera slung around his neck.

A tent had been erected, blocking the entrance to Eddie Rocket's, the garda tape roping off access to the shopping centre. The camera panned to the crime reporter standing as close as he could to the tent. Terry ignored him and his spiel – he wasn't going to have anything more than she already knew, which was sweet FA. She was more interested in what was going on behind the tape.

Suddenly the reporter's voice was drowned out by shouting and screaming. The camera moved away to the right and zoomed out. A crowd had gathered. They certainly didn't sound happy and their faces were covered by hoods, scarves and masks, even a couple of balaclavas. Two uniformed gardaí were trying to control them.

Terry sat forward, tense, her heart racing, recognising the potential danger. A strip of flimsy garda tape would be no deterrent to a raging mob.

The camera swung past the rabble to two jeeps that had just pulled up. She watched intently as gardaí from the Armed Support Unit came spilling out.

And suddenly they were back in the television studio and Terry relaxed. She hadn't realised she was on edge.

'The woman was pronounced dead and a post-mortem will be carried out this afternoon by Assistant State Pathologist Dr Terry O'Brien. The gardaí will not release the names of the two victims until their families have been informed.' The studio presenter shifted her position, presumably towards a different camera, and her solemn expression morphed into a wide smile. It was almost seamless – you had to admire her professionalism. 'Now. This morning in studio we have members of the cast of *Sister Act*, performing a number from the upcoming show in the Bord Gáis Energy Theatre.'

A fatal shooting dismissed in favour of light entertainment, even if it was a bloody good musical.

After a quick walk, Terry settled Bella into her bed and ordered a taxi. There was no use even trying to get parking at the Mater.

Several uniformed gardaí were stationed about the radiology department when she arrived. One of them recognised her and nodded her through. She had a chat with the radiographer as she filled out the request form for the examination.

As it was a Saturday morning, there was no queue of patients waiting for the CT scanner, so the body could be fitted in between live emergencies. It only took a few minutes for it to pass through the scanner. The radiographer assured Terry that the images would be examined, interpreted and reported by the forensic radiologist and she would be able to access them when she got back to the mortuary.

One of the guards gave her a lift back to her flat, probably hoping she would tell him some unreleased details that he could share with his cronies. He was sorely disappointed. Bella was ready and waiting for her, and Terry drove straight over to the mortuary with the dog in the passenger seat, her nose twitching at the smells wafting in through the half-opened window.

'Morning, Doc.' Jimmy bent and ruffled Bella's head. The dog followed him into the kitchen and Terry went into her office and logged onto her laptop. The scans were in a file labelled 'Ms X'. She preferred to check them out herself before she read the radiologist's report.

She had been lucky enough to do a course in forensic radiology while she was in Boston. The forensic radiologists were of the opinion that the virtopsy – scanning the body, no knives, no cuts, no direct look inside – was the future of death investigation. There was some truth in that, and Terry embraced the technology, but forensic pathologists weren't going anywhere. Someone still needed to dig out the bullets.

It was obvious from the images that Ms X didn't stand a chance. There was a bullet-shaped piece of metal inside the skull, as well as a trail of tiny metal fragments across the neck and another diagonally through the trunk from the right shoulder to the left lower back. Three separate bullet tracks. Any one of them could have been responsible for her death.

Fraser and Ahern arrived together for the autopsy.

'So, what's the story?' Terry asked, motioning for both men to take a seat in her office.

Fraser took the lead. 'The deceased is Orla Kielty – the local gardaí know her. She was having a smoke with her boyfriend, Feargal Hannigan, outside Eddie Rocket's when a motorbike drove up and the rider opened fire. Luckily no one else was injured. He was the target – she was collateral damage. Hannigan is one of Sean Carroll's boys. Carroll was one of the big players on the northside but he's gone into semi-retirement in Galway, leaving his sons to run the Dublin branch of the operation. They're nowhere near as savvy as their father. No one would have considered making a move on them if Carroll senior was still in charge. It could have emboldened the Hayeses to move in if they suspected any hint of weakness in the control of the Carroll operation. If so, this could just be a warning.' Fraser did not sound happy about this.

'It was a Friday night,' Terry said. 'Isn't there a cinema there? It could have been a lot worse.'

'It could *get* a lot worse.'

Fraser nodded at Ahern, who took up the story. 'According to witness statements six shots were fired. Seems the first shot was wide of the target, but then the gunman fired off two in quick succession. Feargal had his back to the road and one caught the side of his head and split the scalp open, and one got him in the back of the left shoulder. He had surgery last night. He'll live.'

'What about her?' asked Terry. 'Where was she during the shooting?'

Ahern went on. 'She was behind him but he ducked down and that's probably when she was hit.'

'From what I've seen so far from the X-rays, she got hit in the head, neck and chest, but there's only a bullet in her head – two went straight through her.' Terry turned to Ahern. 'Did you recover any bullets at the scene?'

'Dug four out of the walls. But they're worse than useless, completely flattened. No chance of being able to match them to any gun.'

'That means there's still one bullet unaccounted for if there were six shots. It might have ricocheted off a wall and is lying somewhere,' Terry said. 'You never know your luck. Anyway, this won't get the post-mortem done. Vinnie is already setting up in the PM room. I'll just go and get changed. You know your way to the observation room.'

Terry gowned up and made her way into the post-mortem room. She lifted her knife and did a quick check of the body, in case there was something that the X-rays hadn't shown. As post-mortems went, this was a textbook case. One bullet had penetrated her head, just above her right eyebrow. The bullet entry wound was what Terry would describe as atypical: instead of a small round hole caused as the bullet struck nose on, there was an oval wound caused by the bullet having been knocked off course before it reached her. The bullet could have ricocheted off a wall, but she suspected the bullet lurking inside the woman's skull had passed through her boyfriend first, so by the time it reached her it was tumbling, having lost speed and power.

Terry leaned over and rapped on the glass separating the investigating officers from the post-mortem room. 'She's tiny. About 150 centimetres. How tall is the boyfriend?'

Fraser looked at the guards standing behind him. 'Anyone here know Hannigan?'

A uniformed guard at the back of the viewing room nodded. 'Yes, sir. I know the two of them. He was a good head taller than her.'

It was Terry's turn to nod. It was very likely that the bullet that hit Hannigan on the back of the shoulder had exited and hit his girlfriend's head.

She had been struck on her neck and chest by two further bullets. Both entry wounds were small and round, smaller than the tip of Terry's little finger. She could tell from the tell-tale bullet wipe, the rim of grease around the hole, on the right side of the woman's neck that the bullet had gone through from right to left.

The same grease wipe was around a tear in the right sleeve of her denim jacket. Tomas pulled the body up to let her get a look at the back. There was no hole in the back of the right sleeve or around the upper back. She pulled up the jacket to expose the T-shirt the woman had on underneath. On the left side of the back of the garment, just above the waistband of her jeans, was a tiny tear. There wasn't much blood around it but tiny globules of fat were clinging to the inside of the material from the bullet exploding out through her back, dragging subcutaneous fat with it.

This was an odd trajectory, the bullet passing down and through the chest from right to left, but Terry needed to see inside the body to know what damage had been done. Shootings were dynamic events and it was up to her to envisage who was where and who did what after the first bullet was fired.

Terry, Vinnie and Tomas assumed their usual positions and snapped into action. As soon as she signalled, they could get started: describing, photographing and stripping the body, as well as taking relevant forensic evidence.

Terry turned to Tomas. 'Okay, you take the head from here.' She walked over to where she had set up her laptop. She pointed at the CT image on the screen. 'Tomas, there's the bullet we need to retrieve. It looks like it barely burst through the skull into the brain. It seems to have run out of gas pretty quickly, which fits with it going through an intermediary target first, most likely the boyfriend. Just make sure you keep the saw away from it. I'll start on the chest and I'll leave the neck until last. Let me know when you're ready to take off the skullcap.' She turned to Vinnie, who was busy changing his camera lens. 'That suit you?'

'Ready when you are, Doc,' he said, giving her the thumbs-up.

She sliced open the chest and followed the track of the bullet that had struck the woman's right arm, just below the shoulder. The bullet had gone across the armpit and on in through the ribcage. Terry removed the front of the ribcage. There wasn't much blood inside the chest cavity, which made it easy to see the injuries to the lungs and the heart caused by the bullet ripping through the tissues as it passed down and across the chest cavity, fracturing the left ninth rib before exiting the back of the chest. The lack of bleeding suggested she had been near death when that bullet hit her.

Tomas called her over then and she stood at his side as he carefully opened the skull. There was a flash as Vinnie snapped the interior. Tomas had done a brilliant job keeping the thick dura covering the brain intact, and there was a hole in it over the frontal lobe. Tomas handed her a scissors and she snipped the thick layer of tissue encasing the brain open. There was blood coating the brain and a large bruise on the front surface of the right half, surrounding a hole in the tissue. Terry could see the glint from the light striking the metal bullet. She carefully eased the bullet out of the brain with her thumb and index finger and placed it on her left palm.

When she held it up so that it could be seen more clearly from the viewing room, Ahern came right up to the glass have a closer look and pressed the intercom button. 'That's looking good, Terry. It's in much better shape than the ones I retrieved. If you put it in a bag, I can get it under the stereomicroscope.'

'Vinnie will take some pics and then I want to swab it. I think this is the bullet that went through the boyfriend first. It should have sliced through the brain like butter. It wasn't firing on all cylinders when it struck her. We might pick up his DNA on it.'

'Sure.' Ahern already had his hand on the handle of the door at the back of the room.

Terry turned her attention to the gunshot injury to the neck. The bullet had ripped the right carotid artery apart and torn the jugular vein before penetrating the voice box and exiting the left side of the neck. It was probably one of the bullets Ahern had removed from Eddie Rocket's wall.

'Vinnie, have you got photos of the scene?' asked Terry.

He held up the camera screen and she flicked through the pictures, stopping at one taken near the door of the restaurant. On the wall was a wave pattern in blood, caused when the carotid artery was punctured, the blood pulsing out with every heartbeat. There was also a large pool of blood on the ground below that. That alone would have been sufficient to kill her.

Terry motioned to Fraser to meet her outside.

She pulled off her protective clothing, kicked off her wellies and went out into the corridor where Fraser was leaning against the wall.

'No surprises. Three gunshot injuries. Probably head first, the bullet having gone through the boyfriend. He goes down and she's an open target. She gets one in the neck and then tips over, collapsing towards the ground, when she gets a third one in the shoulder. She was a goner by the time the third bullet ripped through her chest.'

'Christ! What's to come?' Fraser shook his head and walked off.

20

Tomas ordered in pizzas for the team after they finished up the post-mortem. Once everyone else had eaten, packed up and left, Terry stayed on to dictate her notes. It was close to midnight when she and Bella eventually got back to the flat. She decided she would take advantage and have a lie-in the next morning, but she woke early and tossed and turned before eventually cutting her losses and getting out of bed. When she was on call she could never fully relax. She couldn't predict when the gardaí would phone looking for her. Her day would be spent constantly on alert, checking her phone in case it had accidentally been put on silent, and listening to every news bulletin on RTÉ. For this reason, she never made arrangements to meet up with friends, even for a coffee. Even settling down and watch a film was a bad idea in case someone died somewhere in Ireland and she never got to find out what happened in the end – did they live happily ever after, which obviously was a load of bollocks, or did the main character die? That ending was truer to life – in her world anyway.

She spent the morning cleaning, a task she wouldn't have minded being interrupted. When there was nothing imminent on the one o'clock news, she decided to bundle Bella into the car and go for a walk in the Phoenix Park. If by any chance someone did die in unusual circumstances, at least she would be handy for Walter Scott House. She parked near the zoo. It was a miserable day – the sky was an ominous dark grey, with rain likely on the way– so the sole users of the park were mainly joggers and dog walkers, the hardy ones at any rate. She was walking towards the café when she noticed a vaguely familiar figure seated on a bench watching her approach.

'Hi, Doc.'

The person on the bench tipped back her hood. Red hair cascaded out. 'Bernice!' Terry was both pleased and a little disconcerted at seeing her here. 'I thought you'd moved out of the park after that business with Mags and that Jake character?'

Bernice was stony-faced. 'I thought it best to lie low for a while.'

Terry sat down beside her. 'Have you seen anything of Mags? It's days now since she disappeared in Drogheda.'

'No. I was just in the area and came to check on things,' Bernice said, her eyes constantly darting around.

Terry stared at Bernice. 'Are you … em … living somewhere else now?'

Bernice tapped the side of her nose. 'Keep that out.' She leaned in closer to Terry and dropped her voice. 'I've heard some rumblings. Your name came up.'

Rather than be scared by this, Terry was indignant. 'What are you talking about? Who brought my name up?'

'It was something to do with Lou's brother, Seamus.'

'Who the fuck is Lou? And Seamus?' asked Terry, looking confused.

'Lou Hayes. Donal Hayes's wife.'

'The drug dealer? What's her brother got to do with me? Did he die or something? Did I do his post-mortem?'

'Nah! Seamus died about thirty years ago. Maybe even longer.'

'I don't understand then. Who exactly is talking about me and what are they saying?' Terry's voice was rising. She was starting to panic now. 'Is it something to do with the Blanch shooting?'

Bernice shook her head as she pulled her hood back up. 'I'm just giving you a friendly warning. These are bad people – you don't want to be on their radar.' She stood up, her body hunched over, arms folded across her chest. As Bernice walked off, Terry realised she must be trying to conceal her height, protect her identity. After a few steps, she looked back over her shoulder. 'Just keep your head down and watch your back. You and that little pal of yours.'

Instinctively, Terry grabbed Bella's collar. She was stunned. She sat for a moment thinking about what Bernice had said. She had been warned off, but nothing made sense. None of this had anything to do with her. She was no threat to anyone. The bench shuddered as a man sat down beside her. She got up and tugged on Bella's lead, pulling her out from under the bench, and set off at a sprint back to her car.

She locked the door and looked back towards the bench. It was empty. She checked her mirrors. No one to be seen.

Birthday drinks in Mulholland's at 7 p.m. for Mary.

Terry read Vinnie's WhatsApp message for the third time. Her phone had pinged on the way back from the park, but she had to wait until she was safe in her flat before she could even think to look.

Fortunately, the security guard had been hovering about the entrance to the underground car park when she got back to the flat complex. She'd parked as close to the entrance as she could and walked out onto the street rather than take the lift to her floor, checking over her shoulder as she had climbed the internal stairs.

She was still shaken. Once inside the flat, she had locked, unlocked and relocked the front door, and then checked the door again. She knew it was stupid, but what Bernice had told her had unsettled her.

She sat looking at the phone in her hand. She thought about calling Fraser but wasn't sure if she was overreacting. Bernice was warning Terry off, but she couldn't understand why. It hadn't been a direct threat. What had she said? *Her name came up.* Came up with who? Who had Bernice been speaking to?

And what had Terry got to do with Lou Hayes and her long-dead brother? It was truly bizarre.

She pressed Michael's number, desperate to talk this through with him. It went straight to voicemail. He was away with Paul for a make-or-break weekend, and she wasn't entirely sure which way he wanted it to go.

She put on the kettle and dropped a teabag in a mug. When she opened the fridge to get some milk, the bottle of white wine stared back at her. She looked at it longingly, but couldn't risk a glass knowing a call might come in. This was the longest a bottle had ever lasted in her fridge.

She flicked through the channels until she found an old Bette Davis film she had watched with her dad so often she could repeat the lines. Just as the credits started to roll, the sound of her phone ringing made her jump. She grabbed it from the coffee table. The screen showed it was Charlie. She sank back into the cushions – better respond to the boss.

'Ah, Terry! Saw the fatal shooting on the news. Any problems with it?'

Even if she had any, she knew it was unlikely that Professor Charlie Boyd would care. 'No, Prof. It was pretty straight-forward. No surprises.'

'Good, good! Well, just to let you know that I'll take over the on-call as you've had a lot to deal with already this weekend. I'll let Command and Control know.'

She sighed gratefully. 'If you're sure?'

'Is everything all right? You sound a bit ... subdued?'

'I'm fine, Prof,' she said reassuringly. 'It was just a bit of a long one.'

'Good. You can tell us all about it at the case review meeting on Wednesday.'

'Will do. Hope you have a quiet night.'

'Terry!' Mary stood, swaying a little, waving both hands in the air. 'I didn't think you were going to make it.' She gave her a lopsided hug. 'Fraser cried off. Too busy.' She pouted. 'Party pooper!'

Terry had swithered about coming, but she didn't relish sitting on her own with Bella all night, jumping at every sound. And she thought Fraser might pop in to the party. She couldn't lie: that was the real reason she'd made the effort. She had decided in the taxi over that she would use her meeting with Bernice as an excuse to have a cosy chat with him. She wasn't going to roll over easily though. He needed to do a bit of grovelling first. But there was no point cutting off her nose.

Trying to shrug off her disappointment, she looked around the table and her heart sank when she saw Bob Paterson. He was holding a bottle of Budweiser and seemed to be having difficulty directing it to his mouth. She squeezed through the group gathered and chose a seat as far from him as possible, hoping he wouldn't see her. 'G&T, thanks.' She turned to Mary, seated next to her, handing her a hastily bought card and bottle of wine. 'Happy birthday. Is it a special one?'

'Sure, aren't they all special?' Vinnie passed her a G&T with no ice, seemingly having ordered for her as soon as he saw her arrive.

'Service is quick here tonight!' she quipped and clasped it in both hands – it was warm.

At that moment, Vinnie plopped two ice cubes into the glass, causing the drink to spill over. 'Thought it might need this.'

Terry tried not to show alarm, realising that he had a handful of ice cubes he was randomly dropping into people's drinks. She really hoped his hands were clean. She smiled her thanks as she wiped the drips from the base of the glass on her sleeve, and then took a large gulp. She could tell by the noise level, and the stack of empties on the table, that she was some way behind the others. She took another swig and listened to the chatter around her.

Ahern, who was opposite her, leaned over. 'I've got some news on the bullet you retrieved from the girl's head. I got a match on it. Same gun's been used in a couple of instances recently. Nothing this serious. Nothing requiring your expertise, anyway. One was a potshot at a guy on a bike and another involved a car's tyres being taken out. I guess it was only a matter of time before the gun was used to kill someone—'

A sudden thud caused her to look to her right. Bob Paterson was being hauled to his feet. He struggled with the two men trying to keep him upright, trying to wrest himself free. Looking up just as he tipped forward, he caught sight of Terry. Bob pulled his right arm free and stabbed a finger towards her. 'That's the bitch!' he roared, swaying away from the guards holding him up.

One of the men grabbed the back of his jacket to keep him on his feet. 'Get off!' He elbowed the man in his stomach, and Vinnie moved around the table and came up behind Bob, wrapping his arms around him, pinning his arms to his sides. 'Enough!' He took hold of the bottle Bob was still clutching and put it on the table out of his reach.

Meanwhile Bob continued struggling. 'I'll wipe that smile off her smug face. Sanctimonious bitch. She's got me filing when I should be out there finding out who killed Martin.' He looked back at Vinnie. 'He was my best mate, man.'

Vinnie nodded. 'I know. I think it's home time.'

Bob allowed Vinnie to manoeuvre him through the chairs. When they got to the door, Bob grabbed hold of the doorjamb and shouted over his shoulder at Vinnie, loud enough for them all to hear. 'She'll get what's coming to her. Don't think I don't know about you and your fucking family. You'd better watch yourself, you bitch!' Vinnie huckled him out.

Mary looked pissed off at her party being disrupted. She reached over and patted Terry's arm. 'He's wasted.'

Terry shrugged, trying to look like she didn't care, but really she was close to tears. Wasted or not, he had threatened her and, bizarrely, her family. She couldn't make sense of what he'd said. Bob was obnoxious, but she didn't expect this level of vitriol from him. And in a room full of guards too.

'It's Martin's funeral tomorrow ...' Mary's voice tailed off. 'I guess he's a bit emotional.'

Terry gave her a hug. 'It's okay, Mary. I get it. No harm done.'

She stood up, suddenly desperate to get back to the safety of her flat and Bella. Bob was the second person that day who had told her to watch her back.

21

Terry pressed snooze, even though there was no chance of dropping back to sleep. She lay staring at the ceiling. She still felt on edge after Bob's outburst last night. Martin Higgins's funeral was starting at ten o'clock. She could imagine the troops gathering. Despite what they thought about him, he was getting the full garda send-off. Normally the coroner would have released the body for burial after two weeks maximum, but between the guards wanting to wait a bit longer and then the minister for justice going off for a two-week break in the Caribbean, it had taken until now to get the full razzamatazz organised. She was surprised that Mrs Higgins wasn't more incensed at the long delay.

She had tried to call Fraser when she got back from Mulholland's but her calls had gone to voicemail, not that she had left a message. He was obviously up to his eyes in it, between the investigations and the funeral.

She pulled on jeans and a jumper and went into the kitchen

to get Bella's lead. The empty wine bottle on the draining board explained her thick head. She ran the cold tap, filled the discarded wine glass and glugged the water down. She had been too keyed up to sleep and the wine was a means to the end – she didn't stir all night.

As she walked along the quays, she decided she was glad she hadn't reached Fraser. In the cold light of day, she was more rational. He didn't need to know about Bernice's warning. She had overreacted. As for Bob, he was just being himself: a total arsehole with too much drink on board and emotionally labile. Excuses would be made for his behaviour – no one would take his threats seriously. Neither should she, although she dreaded having to work with him. This might be something she could talk through with Dr Price at her session this afternoon. For the moment, it was good to savour a chance to de-stress. Working from home had its perks and she didn't have to answer to anyone.

When it was time to leave for her appointment, she showered and changed, intending to drive straight to the Rockroad Clinic. The car park was now half empty. As she walked towards her car, she realised that something didn't look right. Her car was sitting lower than normal.

Terry groaned. A flat tyre was not what she needed today. Putting her hand on the bonnet, she bent to have a look, and discovered both front tyres were flat as pancakes. She sighed and walked towards the back of the car. All four tyres were flat. Trying to remain calm, she squatted down beside the rear wheel on the driver's side to inspect it. She rocked back and had to grab the wheel to steady herself – the tyre had been slashed.

As she stood up, Terry saw the message sprayed in vivid blood- red paint on the rear window. WATCH OUT BITCH.

She glanced around, but the place was deserted. Her heart was pounding as she ran to the lift and repeatedly thumped the Ascend button until the lift doors opened. Inside, she dug her flat key out of her bag and held it in her right fist, blade protruding. As soon as the lift doors opened, she ran to her door, fumbled to get it open and, once inside, slammed it behind her.

Panting, she rested her back against it for a few moments, then flung her bag across the floor and went into her bedroom. She dragged the chest of drawers out, scraping it along the floor, and rammed it against the door.

Then, she pressed 9 on her phone keypad. She expected the call to go to voicemail yet again, so she was surprised when Fraser answered after just a couple of rings. She was so relieved to hear his voice that she surprised herself by bursting into tears as she haltingly explained what was going on.

She sat on the floor, propped up against the chest of drawers, Bella looking pensive beside her, until Fraser pounded at the door fifteen minutes later. Moving the drawers to get the door open was a struggle. When she did, he took one look at her blotchy red face and guided her into the kitchen, sitting her down in a chair. He busied himself putting on the kettle, making encouraging noises as she talked non-stop.

She grimaced as she took a sip from the mug that he handed her.

'Sorry. Garda training – tea with two sugars for shock, and just about any natural or unnatural disaster.'

Terry gave a half-hearted smile at his attempt at humour.

They sat quietly sipping tea after she had finished her account of the last couple of days. Fraser asked a few general questions, clarifying the timeline and who said what and when. She felt she was under interrogation, though a gentle one.

'Lou Hayes? You're sure Bernice said Lou? The information from Perez must be correct – Lou is in charge. And Seamus?'

'Bernice said Lou mentioned something about her brother's death,' Terry replied. 'It was definitely Lou. It doesn't mean she had anything to do with slashing my tyres. That doesn't make any sense to me. I have no idea why she would be in any way interested in me. My money's on Bob. It's the kind of mean, juvenile thing I could imagine him doing.'

'Paterson's a dickhead, I agree, but he's not entirely stupid. Something like this would end his career.'

'Yes, but he was pissed out of his head last night and not entirely rational.'

'Still doubtful,' said Fraser, but a note of uncertainty had crept into his voice. 'But that was way out of order and needs to be dealt with anyway.'

'Well, Bernice said to watch my back, and Bob told me to watch my back too. And lo and behold, the same message is scrawled across my car.'

Fraser put his mug down and dragged his hand across the rough stubble on his jaw. 'What's going on? Nothing is making sense.'

His phone buzzed and he checked the screen. 'I need to go. Are you going to be all right on your own?'

'I'm not alone.' They both looked over at Bella, sleeping soundly under the table. 'We'll be fine.'

'If you're sure? I'll get the boys to pick up your car and get it to forensics. Will you be okay for transport?'

'Oh! I hadn't thought about that. I'll give Michael a ring – he can give me a lift back and forth to the mortuary. FSI is only next door.'

Fraser left to speak to the SOCOs in the car park and meet the local gardaí who would investigate the car damage. Terry had told him she wanted the investigation to be low-key. She didn't want any panic. She phoned the Rockroad Clinic and rearranged her appointment with Aoife. Maeve Price must think she attracted trouble. Maybe she was right. The only person she wanted to speak to was Michael, who insisted on coming straight over from the lab. He just had to check with his boss first.

'Thanks for calling in, Michael, but I'm fine. Really,' Terry said, flopping down on the couch. 'You don't have to fuss. I'm a big girl, I can look after myself.'

'Come on, Tez. Don't be so daft. You can't stay here. The place is hoaching with guards. You can stay with me, at least until this dies down. You know how I love a bit of drama.'

'I don't want to put you out,' said Terry, but she was warming to the idea. It would be nice to have a bit of human company.

'Hardly. I'm your best friend. And anyway, I owe you for the Jenny thing.'

She had forgotten about that with all that had happened. 'You sure do. This is only a down payment. You're not fully forgiven,' she said, with a glimmer of a smile. 'But thanks.'

'Go and pack a few essentials, but don't be getting any big ideas. There's no room service and you'll have to wash your own knickers.'

Terry didn't need any further convincing. She disappeared into her bedroom and started throwing her clothes into a suitcase.

'It was just as well I walked over,' he called in to her. He was peering out her window. 'With the guards all over the place, I'd never have got parked. I'll order a taxi once you're sorted.' He did a double take as she trundled a massive suitcase into the room.

'Christ almighty. Are you moving in permanently?'

Terry laughed when she saw the horrified look on Michael's face. 'Just the bare essentials, like you said.'

Michael whined about the size of the case all the way down in the lift.

'Would you rather take Bella?' Terry asked, holding out the dog's lead and resisting the urge to roll her eyes at his mini-tantrum.

'Just get out' he snapped, barking instructions as they manoeuvred their way out of the building and into the waiting taxi. Terry thought this wasn't a great start to her moving in with him.

The taxi driver sat staring ahead, having no intention of helping them to get both case and dog into the car. When they got to Michael's, Terry got a fit of the giggles as they tried to manhandle the case out of the taxi, which started Michael off, infuriating the driver.

Once they were safely ensconced in Michael's flat, he sighed dramatically and went over to the kitchen, peering into the fridge as if looking for divine inspiration. 'Drink? Tea? Coffee?'

'Is wine an option?' asked Terry. 'I need a glass – it's been a bitch of a day.'

Michael grabbed a bottle from the fridge and busied himself getting glasses out of the cupboard. 'What about Bella?' he shouted over his shoulder.

'She'll have a Pinot Grigio. What do you think? Just fill an old bowl with water.'

'I'm gay. I don't do old bowls,' he said, sweeping a hand across his forehead in feigned shock. 'Only artisan tableware sourced from Positano in this flat.'

'How's Paul?' Terry looked around then as if he might pop out of a cupboard.

'More to the point, Tez, what's this all about? Someone wrecking your car? I would have thought Fraser would have gone into full macho mode. Come to the rescue of the fair maiden.'

'He thinks this is something and nothing. Anyway, I'm not overly worried. You haven't answered my question about Paul.'

Again, Michael deflected. 'So Fraser doesn't think you're in any danger?' he asked as he screwed off the wine lid.

Terry pulled herself up onto the counter top while Michael poured two sizeable glasses of Chardonnay. 'No, but I was shitting myself after Bernice cornered me in the park. And then that bollocks Bob Paterson turned on me at Mary's night out.'

'What's he mad at you for? I get his mate's dead, but why take it out on you?'

'Fuck knows what his problem is. Women! Life! Who knows?' 'What does Fraser think?' Michael handed her a glass. 'About Paterson possibly slashing my tyres?' She jumped down and went over to the sofa. 'He doesn't think it was him. Bob's one of them, isn't he? They've already uncovered one bad apple in the form of Martin Higgins. He probably doesn't want the hassle or the bad press of another.'

'Maybe there's an orchard of them.' Terry laughed at his quip. Michael sat down beside her. 'Do you think he slashed your tyres?'

'Maybe.'

Michael walked over to the window and looked out onto the bustling quays. 'Well, you'll be safe here with me.'

'No offence, but I think Paul would be more use.' She expected Michael to make some smart retort but he kept his back to her. She got up and went over to him and put her arms around his waist, resting her head on his back. 'Oh, Michael! You've split up. He's not moving back in, is he?'

Michael leaned back against her. 'No.'

'I'm so sorry,' said Terry.

He turned around and hugged her. 'I knew it was coming. But I thought we should give it a last shot. Paul's right, we're better off as friends.'

'It does mean we can stay up eating pizza and watching *Real Housewives* without heavy sighs. I mean, I do like him, but he can be a bit serious. He needs to lighten up.'

'Worst of all is that I'll have to tell my mum. She loved him.

Oh well.' He walked over and picked up his glass. 'Here's to being single. But seriously, back to you. Do you think you're going to feel safe here?' He flexed his non-existent biceps. 'As you said, I'm not much of a bodyguard.'

Terry laughed. 'Luckily we have Bella.' They looked over at the dog, who was lying on her back, legs splayed in the air, out for the count.

22

When he had checked in that evening, Fraser had been surprised when Terry told him she was staying at Michael's for a few days, but he seemed to buy her explanation of her being a shoulder to cry on after Michael and Paul's break-up. And it wasn't a complete lie.

He had offered her a lift to Walter Scott House in the morning. The thought of being in that small office with Bob Paterson made her flesh crawl, but she wasn't going to let him think she was scared of him. Even if she was.

The next morning, she made sure she was standing at the kerb a few minutes before 8.30 a.m.

'Morning, Terry,' shouted Fraser, leaning over and pushing open the passenger door. 'How's the new digs?'

'Fine.' She snapped the seatbelt buckle and turned and grinned. 'You know Michael – he's going to milk this break-up for what it's worth. Poor lamb. Copious amounts of alcohol and crisps and he'll get over it.'

'You're all heart, Dr O'Brien.'

'I know. Forensic pathologists are known for their empathy. If it didn't kill you, what are you greeting about?' She noticed Fraser's look of puzzlement. 'Greeting. Crying. It's a Scottish saying. Anyway, never mind him, what about my poor car?'

'Uniforms have spoken to the security guards. There've been no other recent acts of vandalism, and none of them had noticed any dodgy characters hanging about. I asked them to check the CCTV footage for the last few days but coverage of the area where you parked is patchy – most cameras are trained on the areas further from the entrance. Whoever slashed your tyres slipped in and out unseen. Sorry.'

Terry nodded. 'Security isn't there 24/7. After midnight there's only one security guard, who does regular patrols of the entire complex. Anyone could have sneaked in to the car park while he was on his rounds.'

'Well, so far we've drawn a blank.' Fraser indicated and pulled into the bus lane.

'Superintendent, that's a bit cheeky,' chided Terry.

'I'm on official garda business,' he said, giving her a wink.

Terry laughed then sat back. 'I've been thinking, John.' She had a quick squint at him to see how he was reacting. He kept his eyes on the road ahead. 'I agree with you.' She sensed him flinch. 'I don't think it was Paterson. It was probably a random attack.'

'Well, I've news for you on that front. Paterson has been put on sick leave. Alan had an informal chat about his conduct in Mulholland's and asked him if he had anything to do with your car damage. Bob did not take it well, and he denied any wrongdoing. Alan was concerned about his state of mind and Dr Maher, the garda doctor, got involved. She's signed him off, citing mental health issues.'

Terry felt herself relax. At least that was one threat she didn't need to worry about now.

Fraser dropped her off outside Walter Scott House and went to find a parking space. She walked up the stairs to the fourth floor feeling very relieved and looking forward to the day. When she arrived outside the door of the OCRU office however, she was surprised to hear Bob Paterson's voice coming from inside. Terry stood at the door but couldn't make out what was being said. She hadn't expected to have to confront him and she realised she was trembling. She couldn't believe the gall of the man – this was intimidation.

Giving herself a shake, she took a deep breath and boldly opened the door. She looked around the small office. He was nowhere to be seen. Mary was seated at her desk with her back to the door, scooping sugar into the mug in front of her. Terry noticed the mobile propped up against the bag of sugar.

Mary turned and smiled and pressed her finger to her lips.

'Right, Bob, I hope your ma is fine. We'll manage here. I'll let the doc know. There's no rush to get back. Family first. Look after yourself. Yep, see ya, bye.' She spun round in her seat to face Terry. 'That was Bob. Seems his ma isn't too well so he's going down to Wexford to look after her for a few days. Probably better off after the way he behaved on Sunday night. And he could barely keep it together at the funeral.'

'A few days with his mother might sober him up,' said Terry. Mary seemed oblivious to the sarcasm. Terry decided it was best if Mary believed the lie Bob told her about his absence from work. She would allow him to save face. 'We'll manage without him.'

Terry sat at her own desk, pulled her current notebooks from the bookcase and read through the recent cases for the umpteenth time, trying to make sense of them all. She picked up the Higgins flip chart and on a fresh page wrote 'Martin Higgins'. To the right she wrote 'Hayes?', then she added 'Dr Maguire' at the bottom of the page.

Mary came up behind her and looked at the chart. 'Does Fraser think Hayes killed Martin?'

'Uh-huh.' Terry drew an arrow between the two names. 'What about the shooting on Friday night? Was that down to the Hayeses as well?'

'Fraser thinks they might be involved, yes.'

'So we have a gang war kicking off?'

'Maybe ... I don't know. Let's assume that both shooting deaths were carried out on Hayes's instructions. What doesn't feel right is ... why cut out Higgins's tongue? I keep coming back to that.'

Mary looked nonplussed. 'He's a guard! A warning to others not to snitch?'

'A warning?' Terry was sceptical. 'Would they be bothered? Killing him would be enough to scare the shit out of any other guards they had on their books.' She tapped her Sharpie against the paper. 'Why? Why? Why?'

'He was found outside a known brothel,' Mary reminded her. 'Maybe he had been sampling the goods? Taking liberties? Overstepped the mark?'

'Maybe.' Terry flipped back a few sheets. 'What if it was someone else who had a gripe with Higgins? Maybe the message was not cutting out his tongue. Maybe it was the location his body was found – outside a brothel that looks like it's part of the Hayes portfolio. Why would the Hayes gang shit in their own backyard? Finding Higgins there only brought attention to their business. It just doesn't make sense to me.'

Mary shrugged.

Terry took the lid off the Sharpie. 'Let's go back to our original plan: looking for murder victims whose bodies were mutilated.' She went back to the last page and drew a star beside Dr Maguire's name. 'Just like Dr Maguire, our gynaecologist.'

The coroner had asked Fraser to have a word with Mrs Maguire. She had been hassling the office to get her husband's body released, much to their annoyance, so he was surprised that she seemed totally indifferent to her husband's death when he called in to her at a friend's house for an informal chat later that day. 'I just want rid. The sooner he's buried the better. This whole sorry business has been difficult. I don't expect you to understand, but we move in certain circles, and while a blind eye is turned at certain behaviours, Cillian overstepped the mark completely.'

Fraser raised his eyebrows. Sexual assault pole-vaulted over any mark. He suspected she didn't know about the photographs they had found at the scene.

Mrs Maguire waved a hand at Fraser. 'Believe me, Superintendent, I am only doing this for the sake of our son. My son, Senan. Otherwise, he would be caught up in this fiasco. At least Cillian had the good grace to fall on his sword and spare us all the ghastly details of his proclivities being aired in court. Ireland's a small place. I wanted Senan to graduate from Trinity unsullied by his father's reputation.'

'How was your relationship with your husband, Mrs Maguire?' 'No better or worse than most I know. We had an arrangement that suited us both,' she said sniffily.

'Was the marriage abusive?' Fraser decided this was a straight-talking woman and so he could get straight to the point.

'Abusive?' She gave a harsh laugh. 'You could say that. But I don't want to dwell on it. It's in the past.'

'But you never thought of divorcing?'

'No,' she snapped back. Fraser had touched a nerve. 'I was his wife for over twenty years. I was a nurse when we met. I supported us while he studied. I invested in that man.' She shook her head and seemed to slump. 'You may think I'm shallow, but I put up with so much, I wasn't going to let one of his bimbos come along and take what was rightfully mine and Senan's. It was the only control I had.' She looked away. 'It took its toll. We tried counselling, and even Dr Reagan said that divorce was the best solution, a clean break. But I couldn't take the chance that he would renege on his alimony payments. And of course, Father Murphy wouldn't have condoned divorce.'

There he was again, the psychologist, Ronan Reagan. Fraser put a question mark beside Reagan's name. He was due a little chat with his old friend.

'Did your husband agree to counselling?' asked Fraser gently. 'Unfortunately, he didn't take to Dr Reagan,' she said, plucking at a loose thread on the sleeve of her jumper. 'Ronan was very supportive. I continued seeing him even after Cillian refused to join our sessions.'

'Mmm. You were away over the weekend when your husband's body was found?' he said, looking down at her original statement.

'Yes, a spa break with friends. Cillian even managed to ruin that. He always was a selfish man.'

The hard veneer was back. Fraser looked at his notebook. 'Did your husband have any enemies?'

'I think it would be more appropriate to ask whether he had any friends, Superintendent.'

'The house is just a short distance from the Yacht Club – was he a member?'

She laughed. 'He couldn't even swim. The closest he got to sailing was a Mediterranean cruise we took in 2018. He would have loved to be involved in the club. Not as a sailor, no, that wasn't his style – he wanted to be propping up the bar with his cronies. It was all about the power and the glory. He had been on the waiting list for years, but Judge Henderson saw to it that he didn't get a foot in the door.'

'So, he wasn't a sailing man.' Fraser looked quizzically at the woman in front of him. He wasn't entirely sure what to make of her. She turned a blind eye to her husband's activities, but it must have hurt. Enough to do something about it? He snapped his notebook closed. 'Our investigations into your husband's death are not yet complete. The coroner's office will notify you when your husband's body is ready to be released. I'll be in touch if I have any more questions for you.' He stood, signalling an end to their chat.

23

After work, Terry jumped on the Luas to Michael's flat on the quays. Bella bowled her over as she came through the door. She could hear Michael singing in the shower, so she grabbed Bella's leash and went straight back out. There was a green behind the building, which would have to do for Bella's walk.

She sat on a bench with her plastic poo bag in hand, alert for any attempt by Bella to squat while she mooched around the flower beds. Suddenly, Terry became aware of someone with a small dog approaching. She felt a sudden increase in tension on the lead – Bella had also spotted the newcomer. Terry gave the lead a sharp tug and warned, 'Bella!'

As the person got nearer, she immediately felt vulnerable. She looked around – they were the only people there. It was probably a legitimate dogwalker, but she couldn't make out if they were male or female. The uniform of dark hoodie and joggers disguised identity and intent. She called Bella over to the bench. She was big, but not likely much of a deterrent. She pulled off Bella's muzzle and held her collar in a tight grip. She took out her phone and hovered her finger over 9 on the keypad, ready to contact Fraser if need be.

The person was only a few strides away when she realised it was a man. She gripped the lead tighter. He looked at Terry and then at Bella and stopped, turned and scooped up his dog and tucked it under his arm. He glared at Terry as he walked past. Bella was a big softy, but greyhounds got a bad rap. Terry felt the tension leave her body. She slipped Bella's muzzle back on. She pressed 1 and put her phone to her ear.

'Hi, Dad.'

'Hang on a minute, hen, until I put my tea down.' She heard the scraping of a chair being pulled out and she could imagine her dad in his kitchen, sitting down at the table. 'That's better. Everything okay?'

'Yes. Just called for a wee chat,' she said cheerfully. 'How was your weekend?' he asked.

She was immediately on the defensive – surely Fraser hadn't spoken to him? 'What do you mean?'

'Weren't you on call?'

'Oh! Yes. It was busy. I had a gangland shooting.'

'There were two stabbings here after the old firm match on Saturday. One of each.'

Terry rolled her eyes. Her dad was referring to the great Protestant–Catholic divide in Glasgow that reared its ugly head when Rangers faced Celtic on the football field. The friendly rivalry often spilled out onto the streets. She remembered that when she had been working in Glasgow the forensic pathologists on call were on high alert on those occasions.

'Aye, even-stevens. Thank God the wee toerags don't have guns here.'

Terry laughed. 'Makes me feel nostalgic for my home town.'

'There's bampots everywhere. You're never going to be out of a job. I was going to give you a ring anyway. Big Jim's going over to Dublin to an Eddi Reader concert this week. He was wondering if you could put him up in your spare room?'

Big Jim was her dad's best friend. Back in the day, they had been in An Garda Síochána together, and when her dad decided to bring the family to Scotland, Jim followed him over and into Strathclyde Police. They were very close-mouthed about their time as gardaí. Her dad had implied it was something to do with the IRA and that he felt Ireland wasn't a safe place for them. He thought that it was best left in the past.

Uncle Jim, as she had called him when she was little, was a fixture in her life, and normally she would be fine with him staying with her for a couple of days. But that wasn't possible in the circumstances. She scrambled for an excuse. 'Well, I'd love to, but ... there's a problem with the plumbing in the flat – some sort of leak or something – and I've had to move in with Michael until it gets sorted. I could check out some places for Jim?'

'Oh, don't worry about him. He can doss in with some of his own family. He's only being a lazy bugger because he knows you're in town and his family is out in Balbriggan. What's up with the flat? I hope you're not having to shell out for any work that needs to be done. Those landlords are a shower of chancers.'

She realised that she had now started a lie that her dad wouldn't let go. 'No, Dad. Don't get worked up. It's fine. It's all in hand. It's just going to take a week or so to get it fixed.'

'Well, if they try any shenanigans, Big Jim could have a word,' he grumbled.

'Dad! I'm not ten.' She hadn't the heart to be annoyed – he had always looked out for her. 'Tell Uncle Jim to give me a call and I can meet him for a coffee.'

She heard spluttering from her dad's end and realised he was laughing. 'Near choked myself!'

She couldn't help but smile. 'A pint of the black stuff, then. Away and sort yourself out and let me have a word with Aileen.'

'What were you two talking about? He near wet himself.'

Terry could hear the smile in Aileen's voice as her dad passed the phone over.

'I'm sure he'll fill you in,' said Terry. 'I didn't like to ask him, I know it's a sensitive topic, but has there been any update on Jenny's death? I get he's trying to keep me out of it, but the genie's out of the bottle now.'

'No,' Aileen replied, her voice dropping to a whisper. 'He doesn't like to talk about it, and I don't like upsetting him. Best ask Big Jim, he's been dealing with it for your dad. I think he's feart your dad'll have another stroke. His blood pressure is awfie bad.'

'Make sure Dad keeps on top of that. I'm sure I'll hear about the investigation in due course. Aileen, while I've got you, remember I asked you to check out the jewellery box in my old room?'

'Aye, hen. There was a wee wad of tissue paper with something inside.'

'That's it. Could you put it in an envelope or something and give it to Big Jim to bring over?'

'Of course I will. Anything else you want?'

'No, that's it. How's your lot getting on?'

'Great. They're all doing just fine.'

'I'd better go, my bum's numb sitting on this bench. I'm out with the dog.' Terry stood. 'Say bye to Dad. And Aileen, don't say anything to him about the package, and just let Big Jim think it's a wee something from you.'

Terry knew that if her dad or Big Jim got wind that she still had Jenny's necklace and that she intended to get Michael to examine it they wouldn't be best pleased. She knew it was a long shot. They had got a partial fingerprint from it before, but as far as she knew they hadn't looked for traces of DNA – they wouldn't have had the technology in those days. If there was any chance of recovering something, Michael was her best bet. Now she would just have to persuade FSI to run the tests.

'Aoife, thanks for fitting me in this morning.'

With all that was going on, Terry had had to cancel her appointment on Monday afternoon. She had promised her dad that she would continue to see someone about her issues, as he called them, and she realised she did need to speak to Maeve Price, but not because she was in dire need of counselling – she had believed she could handle any perceived danger, but maybe she couldn't. Hunt had damaged her mentally more than she had realised.

She needed a neutral party to bounce her thoughts off. The psychiatrist rarely said much, but Terry could tell by the expression on her face exactly what she thought of Terry's ideas. She couldn't risk talking to Michael or Mary as they might feed it back to Fraser or, worse, her dad.

'Dr Price always leaves an hour in the day in case of emergency referrals. It was a system I introduced when I started here. I know how crucial it is to see someone when you really need help,' Aoife said, with a note of pride in her voice.

Terry wondered what trials Aoife herself had faced. 'Well, it's much appreciated. How long have you worked here?'

Aoife seemed not to notice her question, but when the door behind Terry thumped closed, she realised that someone had entered the clinic and the receptionist's attention was diverted to the newcomer. Terry noticed her demeanour change as a couple approached the reception desk, ignoring Terry's presence.

Terry moved away and sidled over to the seating area, intending to remain in the background. She was fascinated by this couple. The man was taking the lead. He had the woman, presumably his wife or partner, gripped by the elbow. Terry strained to hear what was being said. She thought she heard Dr Reagan mentioned but didn't catch the couple's name – it sounded like Watts? She was surprised by how sharp Aoife was with the man and how she turned her back to him as she spoke to someone on the desk phone.

The door of the office opposite Maeve's opened and Dr Reagan appeared. He walked over to the woman, skirting around the reception desk, and took her hand, smiling warmly. He gave a cursory nod to the man in lieu of a welcome. Terry thought the look on Reagan's face was one of simpering benevolence, like an insincere undertaker. He reminded her of a character in a Dickens novel: Uriah Heep, the humble man. She gave an involuntary shiver.

'Terry. Come on in.' She hadn't noticed Maeve Price standing in her doorway. Maeve smiled politely at the couple and Reagan as they passed her, then turned to Aoife.

'Aoife, my next appointment just messaged me, he's running late.'

'He should have contacted me,' the receptionist huffed. Maeve ignored her petulance.

Terry flashed Aoife a sympathetic smile as she followed the psychiatrist into her room.

After about thirty minutes Terry had run out of steam. She had ruminated over her frustrations with her recent investigations, but avoided mentioning her run-in with Bernice or Bob Paterson.

Maeve, as usual, said very little until Terry made to get up. 'You seem on edge, Terry. Has something happened? Something it might be useful to talk about?'

The other woman's poker face hid a perceptive eye – she could see behind Terry's façade. Meanwhile, Terry sat quietly, staring beyond the psychiatrist's head. She wasn't ready to deal with the recent threats. She needed to process them herself first, but not now, not today.

'Just a tad tired. Problems with my car and flat so I'm staying with a friend. It's difficult to sleep in a strange bed. That's all.'

Maeve held her gaze, waiting. Terry shifted uncomfortably and looked away, before standing and scuttling out the door before any more information could be weaselled out of her.

The reception area was deserted – Aoife was nowhere to be seen. Terry could hear voices from Reagan's room. She recognised Aoife's voice, but couldn't make out what was being said. Aoife started giggling then. *Oh God*, Terry thought, *Aoife has the hots for Reagan*. She didn't want to imagine what was going on behind that door.

The traffic was dreadful on the way back into town. The taxi dropped her off outside Michael's flat minutes before Fraser was due to pick her up and bring her to the OSP for her case review meeting. This was not sustainable: she needed her own transport – she hated being reliant on others. She just had time to nip in and get Bella.

Conversation was stilted on the drive to the OSP. Not only did she have that afternoon's case review meeting on her mind, but Terry was still mulling over Reagan's latest clients. Reagan gave her the willies, as they say in Glasgow. But something else was bugging her.

'John, what if Paterson or the Hayes crew had nothing to do with the damage to my car? When am I getting it back?'

He ignored the first question. 'You're not enjoying having your own private chauffeur?' He turned and mimed tipping an imaginary hat.

Terry suppressed a smile. 'It's just that I've been thinking.'

'I'm not going to like this, am I?'

She swivelled around to face him. 'Just hear me out.'

Fraser kept his eyes on the road. 'Do I have a choice?'

'If it wasn't Paterson, could it have anything to do with Hunt's court case?'

She waited for him to respond. When seconds passed and he remained silent, she looked around in case he was concentrating on the traffic or something else that had caught his attention outside the car.

He took a deep shaking breath then. 'Terry,

Hunt is behind bars.' He sounded worried. 'How the hell could he have arranged for someone to trash your car? That's what you're thinking, isn't it?'

'It's not like he doesn't have form for terrorising women,' she argued. But the last thing she needed was for Fraser to think she was losing it.

Fraser glanced at her and then said firmly, 'Hunt is no longer a danger to you. He's not your bogeyman.'

They sat in silence for the rest of the journey. She knew she wasn't being rational, but there was so much going on she didn't know what to think anymore.

24

At two o'clock sharp, Professor Charlie Boyd stood in front of the screen that was set up at the end of the conference table. 'Welcome. Thank you all for coming,' he said to the assembled group of pathologists. His eyes alighted on a woman in the group, and he smiled warmly in her direction. 'It's good to see you, Dr Farrell. Thank you for making the journey down.'

Rose Farrell was the state pathologist for Northern Ireland and had helped Terry on a missing-person case previously. Unfortunately, the woman in question had been another of the infamous Dr Hunt's murder victims. 'Thanks, Professor Boyd. It's great to get down to Dublin for the afternoon. I don't get much chance to get out and about, unlike yourselves. They keep me chained to the mortuary and bring the business to me.'

'Well, I'm glad you managed to get away.'

Charlie Boyd nodded at Rose and then looked around the room. 'It's a pleasant surprise that so many of you made time to attend our case review meeting.' He grimaced at the hospital pathologists huddled at the opposite end of the table.

It was mandatory for doctors to partake in continuing medical education to ensure they remained on top of their game. These case review meetings constituted part of this and sometimes attracted hospital pathologists with an interest in post-mortems, but they were a dying breed. Forensic pathologists were still treated as second class by some histopathologists, who much preferred dealing with the bits and pieces surgeons removed rather than be faced with an entire body. Today four hospital pathologists were in attendance.

The coroner system in Ireland gave the individual coroners – and there was at least one in each county – the autonomy to instruct any pathologist to carry out a post-mortem examination, unless the death was regarded as suspicious or was being treated as a murder. In those instances, only a very foolhardy coroner would elect not to use one of the state pathologists.

This meant, however, that hospital pathologists were called upon to perform post-mortems in suicides, road traffic accidents, work accidents and sudden deaths. Not trained in forensic pathology, they could sometimes come unstuck. Thankfully, some realised they were out of their depth and sought assistance or reassurance at the OSP. These case review meetings were the perfect venues for those with difficult or unusual cases and any case requiring a second or third opinion. These insightful pathologists were always welcome – well, mostly. Professor Boyd sometimes took exception to these 'blundering fools', as he was wont to call them. Today's visiting pathologists all had cases they wanted to discuss, and they probably hoped the state pathologists would be able to reassure them that they had come to the correct conclusions regarding the causes of death and there was nothing more they could, or should, do.

Terry noticed Charlie bristle when Dr McDonald from the Mater stood to present the death of a thirteen-year-old boy who died after inhaling aerosol deodorant fumes. He had been found dead in his bedroom, likely after suffering a cardiac arrhythmia.

Dr McDonald described the post-mortem findings, which amounted to brain swelling and signs of cardiac failure, all very non-specific. It was the toxicology that made the diagnosis: butane was identified in the sample of blood sent to the state laboratory for analysis. The pathologist concluded that death was as a result of inhaling the gas.

He looked around his audience as if expecting a round of applause. Terry caught Paul's eye and they smiled at one another. Terry did a countdown on her fingers. She knew Professor Boyd wouldn't be able to help himself. When only the fingers of her right hand remained raised, there was a clearing of a throat. Out of the corner of her eye she saw Boyd stand.

'Well, Fionn. You might not be aware that I published a research paper on deaths due to volatile substance abuse in the 1990s after a spate of teenage deaths in Ireland. Just a few pointers for the future, if you or your colleagues are faced with such a death again.' The professor was now centre stage and making the most of it. 'Speed is of the essence. Volatile substances are rapidly cleared from the body, and' – he looked around the table checking that everyone was listening intently – 'after death they simply evaporate from bodily fluids, unlike other drugs and toxins. So levels drop quickly. Blood is fine for analysis purposes, but it must be collected in a gas-tight vial, none of those plastic containers you keep in hospital mortuaries.'

Terry was watching Fionn McDonald's reaction to this dressing down, but he seemed oblivious that this lecture was being directed at him specifically.

But Boyd wasn't finished yet. 'And, as I'm sure you know, volatile hydrocarbons are lipophilic so tend to be found in the fatty tissues, so I suggest also sending samples of liver and brain tissue. Of course, in the nineties I would also tie off a lung and send it to toxicology. But perhaps that is excessive. But well done.' He couldn't sound more patronising if he tried.

There was an uncomfortable silence for a few seconds.

Terry got to her feet. 'Thanks, Dr McDonald. Mercifully those deaths are now relatively rare. Unfortunately, our young people have more sophisticated tastes and we are seeing an increase in ecstasy and cocaine abuse.'

'I agree, Dr O'Brien, and that's exactly what I would like to discuss,' said Dr Rose Farrell, standing up to address the table. She nodded to Niamh, who was manning the equipment. A graph showing the drug-related deaths, DRDs, in Northern Ireland appeared on the screen. 'As you can see, the number of DRDs had doubled in the ten years from 2010 to 2020, and it seems to be getting worse. We have now entered the big league. Although, per 100,000 of the population we are still less than half of Scotland.' She smiled at Terry. 'No offence.'

'None taken, Rose. What can I say? My fellow Scots tend to be a tad overenthusiastic when it comes to pumping their bodies full of toxins, from sugar to alcohol to heroin. We're just party people.'

Rose smiled and gave Niamh a nod for the next slide. 'But we're still double England and Wales. The drugs are much the same, with heroin, methadone, cocaine and benzos being the front-runners. What I'm seeing is an increased appetite for drug cocktails, which increases the risk of serious overdose.'

'That's always been the issue in Scotland,' Terry interjected.

Rose nodded and looked around the room. 'The big problem in the North is a newcomer, fentanyl,' she said. 'I don't want to teach my colleagues to suck eggs, so to speak, but fentanyl is a synthetic opioid, twenty – no, forty – times more potent than heroin. At the moment it is contained. It's coming into the country as transdermal patches.'

Niamh moved to the next photo, which showed the patches and the packaging.

Terry nodded. 'Ah! It's not an adulterant – it's not being mixed into the other drugs. It's an added extra. As they would say in Glasgow, "a wee something to sook on" while you're waiting for the hit to kick in. Enterprising.'

'Exactly. They're not slapping these on their arms – they're sucking on these patches.'

'So where are they coming from?' Paul Hannah pointed at the screen. 'They look like commercial packets. I've seen them back home in the States. Fentanyl is a huge problem there. It was supposed to be some sort of wonder drug for chronic pain. Marketed as a super-strength, non-addictive painkiller. And it turned out to be anything but.'

Rose carried on. 'And now it's our problem. The PSNI have

some inkling regarding the source. Put it this way, it's not some dodgy GP writing prescriptions for the local drug addicts. The good news for you down here is that, as far as they are aware, there is no cross-border activity. It's a local team supplying the patches, and a local problem, but it's good for those of you practising south of the border to know about it, just in case it tips over.'

'If there's a market ...' Terry looked over at the group of hospital pathologists. 'Your common or garden drug death doesn't always come the way of the OSP unless there's something suspicious about it, perhaps an indication that another party injected them with the drugs. Most drug overdoses and deaths end up in A&E and your local mortuaries. The coroners look to their local hospital pathologist to investigate these deaths. So you're now forewarned. I suggest adding fentanyl to your list of drugs to be analysed for in any suspected drug-related death. The state lab will be well aware of this problem through their links with the PSNI, but your hospital lab might not be. You don't want to be caught out.'

Charlie Boyd stood up. 'Thank you for your insightful presentation, Dr Farrell.' Rose took the hint and walked back to her seat. 'I'm sure you have all found that most informative. I realise that some of you will have to get back to your laboratories, but there is tea and coffee over there.' He pointed to Mrs Carey's generous spread on the side table. 'Please help yourselves.'

Terry hung back to have a word with Rose. She liked and respected the Northern Irish state pathologist and she wanted another woman's perspective – not only on the deaths she was dealing with, but also on recent events. Charlie Boyd was a good pathologist, but he was old school, and he tended to be a bit judgemental. And, much as she liked Paul, his split with Michael was making things a little awkward. She valued Charlie's and Paul's opinions on pathology matters, but not so much on any other aspect of her life.

Terry and Rose moved away from the others to the far end of the conference table. In a low voice, Terry began recounting the recent damage to her car. She knew that the state pathologists up north had worked under siege conditions during the Troubles. It had been routine for them to check under their cars for incendiary devices and they were largely confined to the mortuary in Belfast, such was the danger to them. They were only doing their jobs, but any situation which brought them into close proximity to the police made them a target. Terry wondered if this could be the case for her too.

Just as Rose opened her mouth to reply, her expression sympathetic, they were interrupted.

'Terry.' She turned as Dr Fionn McDonald put his cup and saucer onto the table and pulled out a chair and sat beside her. She gave him a wry smile, annoyed that her private conversation with Rose was being interrupted. 'What can you tell me about Cillian Maguire's death?' He leaned in towards her and patted her arm in a paternal fashion, a gesture she did not appreciate. She immediately pulled her arm away.

Terry was taken aback by the directness of his question, but before she could respond, Professor Charlie Boyd came up behind them. 'Precisely nothing, Fionn. Now, if you don't mind finishing your tea, Terry and I have a forensic pathology meeting due to commence.' He stood his ground while the hospital pathologist got to his feet.

Charlie watched him saunter away then turned to Terry. 'I should have guessed that was why he turned up today. He never usually attends our case review meetings. He always was a duplicitous character. The gall of the man to try and compromise you.' He shook his head and patted her shoulder before walking back to the tea and coffee table.

Terry was pleasantly surprised. It was good to know the prof had her back.

Then Rose grabbed her bag, shooting Terry an apologetic look, and called over to Professor Boyd. 'Sorry, Charlie, but I need to get off. I've an evening meeting in Stormont.'

Charlie raised his eyes ceilingward. 'My condolences. Politicians. Hah! Bureaucrats and jobsworths, the lot of them. You stick to your guns, Rose.'

Rose smiled at Terry. 'He never changes, does he? Give me a call anytime. Meantime just be careful.'

This was the first time in the last few weeks Terry had had a chance to discuss Martin Higgins, Dr Maguire and her recent gangland shooting with Professor Boyd and Paul. They covered the whole of the country, so one of them was always on the road and the others at inquests, in court or lecturing to students. It was a luxury for the three state pathologists to sit together over a cup of coffee.

Terry had decided it was best to present the bald post-mortem findings and let them make up their own minds about the whys and wherefores without showing her hand.

'I've seen body parts excised as an indication of torture before death, particularly when I was working close to the Mexican border. The Mexican drug cartels were brutal. Really nasty. But I've not come across anything like that since I moved to Ireland. Have you seen anything like this, Charlie?' Paul sat back in his chair, staring at the image of Martin Higgins on the screen.

The professor merely shook his head.

'Maybe it was because he was a cop?' Paul sighed.

'But it wasn't as if he was undercover at the time. It's possible he was working with some criminal organisation.' Terry flicked through the next few pictures. Niamh had been excluded – they all agreed she might let something slip to someone she shouldn't. She meant well but was a bit of a loose cannon. Terry was quite sure she'd looked at the photographs anyway, but it was best not to give her any extra information.

'All the previous gangland killings have been pretty straightforward. I don't like this new departure. The gardaí must be uneasy as well.' Boyd looked from Terry to the screen and back. He sat for a moment staring at her and she began to feel uncomfortable under his scrutiny. 'You don't agree that this is a gangland killing, do you, Terry?' It was a question, not an accusation.

Terry raised her eyebrows. 'No. Well, not no, but it just … doesn't add up. Tim Scott emailed me yesterday. You know, the forensic pathologist in Liverpool? I had asked him if he had seen any mutilations in drug-related murders or attempted murders allegedly carried out by the Hayes gang over there. I thought it might be a calling card of theirs. But no luck. No mutilations have been recorded. This one doesn't seem to stack up,' she ended glumly.

'On this occasion, I might just agree with you. It doesn't

fit the usual patterns, so that always rings alarm bells.' Terry was gobsmacked and looked at Boyd in amazement. Not that long ago he would have been dismissive of her opinions. 'Mrs Carey might be able to dig out some unusual cases for you. She can recall every death the office has dealt with since she started here. She really is a quite remarkable woman. She has her own system of cataloguing and cross-referencing our cases. I've always suspected she is a member of some secret service.'

With her body at an angle so the prof couldn't see her face, Terry looked at Paul and mouthed 'what the fuck?' Charlie had a sense of humour – who knew! Then she turned to face Boyd again. 'I'll certainly ask her.' She swung back to the keyboard and opened the next file. 'Speaking of unusual cases, let's move on to your old friend Dr Cillian Maguire.'

Dr Maguire's study loomed large on the screen, the naked doctor splayed on the chaise in the centre of the image.

'Well, I would never classify the man as a friend. An acquaintance at most. He was in my year at medical school, but it was probably a blessing our names were some distance apart in the alphabet so we tended to be in different classes.'

Boyd sounded very defensive to Terry, and he was avoiding looking directly at the screen. She reckoned a lot of old friends probably distanced themselves from Dr Maguire once there were whispers of sexual impropriety with patients. She looked over her shoulder at Paul. 'Do you know the background of this case?'

'You mean have I heard he's a sleazy git? In Niamh's parlance.'

'That's about right.' She turned and looked up at the picture on the screen. 'He was found in his study just as you see him.'

She got up and walked over and pointed. 'This is a curtain cord, a tie-back, around his neck and this is a length of the same cord dangling from the chandelier. First impressions are that his body was suspended from the chandelier, the cord snapped and he collapsed onto the chaise, into this position.'

'Why were we called in for a suicide?' Paul got up and moved over to stand at the other side of the screen. 'Because the gardaí were investigating allegations against him?'

'To be fair, the gardaí weren't so sure it was a suicidal hanging because of some findings at the scene. From what you've alluded to about his character, Prof, he doesn't sound as if he would contemplate suicide, but if we believe the claims made against him and the selection of sexually explicit material found beside him, auto-erotic asphyxia might have been right up his street. Which is what the gardaí thought was the case.'

Paul cut in. 'Who found him?'

'His cleaning lady. She called the gardaí.'

'The door wasn't locked?'

'Nup.'

'Odd! If you're going to be wanking off while you're choking yourself, you'd think you'd want a bit of privacy. He did know she was coming to clean that day?'

'She came every day, pardon the pun.'

'That's both distasteful and disrespectful, Dr O'Brien.' Professor Boyd was back to his normal self.

'Sorry, Prof. A wee bit of black humour eases the tension.' Terry attempted a conciliatory look. 'She was there that particular day because his wife asked her to drop in, do a tidy-up, but also fix him dinner, as she was away for the weekend.

She would normally be in and out and never see him, only dealing with Mrs Maguire otherwise.'

Paul pointed at the screen. 'Do you have close-up shots of the knots?' He pointed to Maguire's neck and then at the chandelier.

Terry was relieved to move on. 'Here we go.' She managed to pull up the two images and project them side by side on the screen.

'Interesting! Look, the ligature around his neck is secured by a bog-standard running noose knot. But' – his finger hovered over the chandelier – 'that's an anchor hitch knot.' He turned to Terry. 'Is he into sailing? I'm assuming Michael's got the knots for forensics.'

'Of course he has. He came out to the scene and to see the PM findings. I don't know if the doctor was into sailing. It's possible. I wondered the same thing myself. His house is about a kilometre away from the National Yacht Club in Dún Laoghaire, if that's any help.'

She turned her attention back to the keyboard and after a few clicks another image appeared. 'There's something else odd about this case.' Both men were staring at the penis emblazoned across the screen. 'The metal part of a disposable needle, like the ones for using with a syringe, was found in the urethra.' She smirked as she watched both men wince.

Paul recovered first. 'It's not unheard of as part of the ritual in auto-erotic practices. If you've spent any time in A&E, you'll have come across many an unusual foreign object stuck in the most unlikely orifices.'

'Yeah, folk do the strangest things. I'll do multiple sections of the urethra and check for scarring to see if he's stuck anything up his penis before. It might be his thing, though it's a bit extreme.'

At that moment the screen of Terry's phone began flashing, indicating an incoming call. 'It's the state lab. I'd better take it. I won't be a moment.' She pressed the green icon as she shouldered open the door into the corridor. 'Hello? Dr O'Brien here.'

'Hi! It's Dr Brady from toxicology. We – well, you – have a problem.'

'Oh?'

'It concerns Martin Higgins and the recent drug-overdose death, one of the drug addicts who hang about the boardwalk. I've double-checked but there is no doubt: both samples contain fentanyl.'

'Huh. We just heard from the Northern Irish state pathologist that they've got a big problem with fentanyl. I guess it was only a matter of time until it tipped over the border.'

'Yes, we've been keeping a watch on that. Our tox colleagues in Belfast have warned us of the influx of fentanyl patches. But that's not what you're dealing with.' Terry heard papers being rustled. 'Higgins had taken cocaine and the addict had taken heroin, but both drugs had been cut with fentanyl. It's there in tiny amounts along with the usual adulterants. The actual levels we've found are only a fraction of the fentanyl levels the NI lab is seeing with the patches. This is a completely different problem.'

Terry cut in. 'So fentanyl is just mixed in with the usual rubbish the dealers use to bulk out the principal drug?'

'That's what we think. There wasn't enough fentanyl in Higgins to cause a problem.'

'I think a bullet in the head was more of an issue for him.'

'The genuine overdose is a different kettle of fish,' Dr Brady said. 'While the level of fentanyl we found in the blood sample would not have been lethal, because it's way more powerful than heroin it was enough to potentiate the effects of heroin, even in such a small quantity. It ensured that the heroin proved fatal. This could mean that the cocaine and the heroin came from the same supplier. It's hard to tell if they realise how lethal fentanyl is. I mean, it's easy to make, and it's cheaper than heroin, which is in short supply given what's going on in the world. Supplies from Afghanistan have dried up. I suspect the supplier knows that adding fentanyl to heroin, or even cocaine, increases the power and effects of both drugs. It's a game of Russian roulette. Totally unpredictable.'

'That doesn't sound good. This could just be the tip of the iceberg. The gardaí need to know about this. We could be looking at a huge spike in drug overdoses and deaths if we don't act fast. I guess you can't say if the drugs were already contaminated when they reached the Irish dealers, or if this is a local phenomenon, the dealers cutting the good drugs with the potentially dangerous mix before they sell it on?'

'I'm going to check with the UK mainland labs. If they're not seeing fentanyl, it's an Irish problem.'

25

Fraser found Terry, Prof Boyd and Paul Hannah in the conference room of the OSP. They were discussing an image on the screen of Orla Kielty, the woman shot in Blanchardstown. He sat down at the table, nodding for them to continue, and waited until Terry had finished describing the injuries.

'Superintendent Fraser. Good to see you,' Charlie Boyd greeted him warmly. 'Congratulations on your promotion. My old friend Archie Sinnott must be missed?'

'Thanks, Prof. I don't know who's going to get the chief super's post yet.'

'Big shoes to fill! Are you here for something in particular?'

Terry butted in. 'I asked him to swing by. There's a potentially massive problem. I thought it best to wait until Fraser got here so I could update everyone together.' She pressed the remote control and the screen went blank. She sat down and looked from Paul to Boyd. 'That was Dr Brady in toxicology on the phone earlier. She's identified fentanyl in two deaths.'

Paul groaned. 'It didn't take long for the patches to cross the border.'

'No. Our problem is way worse. When you buy a patch, you know what you're getting: a prescribed dose of fentanyl. However, in our instances, fentanyl is being added to heroin and cocaine.' Fraser was taken aback – this was all he needed. 'So now we have definitive proof that fentanyl is being mixed into the parent drug and used to bulk it out. A bit like adding an extra tin of beans to a chilli to make it go further. But they're not using a measure – it's a game of chance.'

Charlie was shaking his head. Paul interjected. 'This is a disaster.'

'And that's not the worst of it. Martin Higgins was one of the two we know about who got a bum deal on his cocaine.' She directed this to Fraser.

This was catastrophic. Higgins had taken cocaine that had been laced with fentanyl, and that was just part of the issue. He was a prime example of the hidden drug users. Professionals, moneyed individuals, the party animals looking for a high – they saw themselves as superior to the street junkies. The truth was, they just had a bit more money. They could go to a better class of dealer, but the drugs all came from the same source.

Fraser groaned. 'Could this investigation get any more complicated? I've got the assistant commissioner breathing down my neck and now there are lethal drugs on the street. And to make matters worse, one of our own was actively using.' He pushed back his chair and picked up his keys. 'I'll have to get the information out to my team and the press office so they can alert the public.'

Terry nodded. 'I spoke with Dr Brady. She plans to get in touch with you today. She's going to source detection kits that can be used by addicts and dealers to check if the drugs are free from traces of fentanyl,' she told Fraser with a resigned note in her voice. 'After all, it's not in the dealers' interests to kill off their return customers.'

'Thanks, Terry,' he said. 'It just feels so hopeless sometimes, trying to battle against drugs and drug addiction. We simply don't have the ammunition to solve this problem. We need full government engagement. A radical overhaul of the whole system: drug treatment centres, proper programmes, housing, support – the list goes on.'

Professor Boyd nodded his head vigorously in agreement. 'How can the guards be expected to convince addicts to give up the one thing that gives them respite from a hellish existence?' Fraser sighed. 'Right, I'm going to shoot on. I need to get my team following leads to identify the source and I need to speak to the PSNI, the unit at the National Drugs and Organised Crime Bureau, and Edward Farrelly.' He glanced quickly at

Terry. 'Can you stay out of trouble, please?'

She gave a quick grin in return. 'No promises!'

When Terry arrived home that evening, she found a note from Michael on the kitchen table saying he was going out but to call if she needed him. She smiled when she read *Might not make it home. A little something to keep you from pining for me. Kiss, kiss.* She opened the Eason bag beside it and pulled out the jigsaw box inside. 'The cheeky beggar!' She held the box in front of Bella. '101 Iconic Women. And look what's he's scribbled across the picture: "Where's Wally?"'

The dog looked up at her and down at her empty food bowl. 'Okay, girl. I guess it's not that funny. Come on, then, dinner and a quick walk. Deal?' Bella nosed the bowl across the floor in reply.

While Bella mooched about on the little green behind the flat, Terry sat on the bench, mulling over this latest turn of events. This new development meant that the gardaí were going to be clamping down hard on the drug dealers. She just hoped there wouldn't be many more deaths, but the fentanyl had obviously been on the streets for a few weeks now. It was going to be a case of damage limitation. They had just been lucky so far.

Her phone rang. A garda number. 'Hello. Dr O'Brien.'

'Evening, Doc, Detective Inspector Brogan from the press office. I was trying to get John Fraser but he's not answering.'

'Why are you phoning me?' asked Terry.

'I've had one of the papers on – they're running a feature on those dodgy drugs. They want to speak to someone involved and who would know the details. I thought someone from the state lab might be good, but you know what it's like at this time of night – no chance. I know it's a bit of a liberty, Doc, but you did the overdose post-mortem, so I thought you might be best placed to speak to them.'

'Suppose so. It can't do any harm. Who's the journalist?'

'Julie Barry. *Irish Independent*. She just wants a quick quote.'

'Okay then, give her my number and I'll see what I can do.' She was still sitting on the bench when her phone rang again. A different garda number. She swithered whether or not to answer – she wasn't on call, but it might be important. 'Hi, Terry.'

She was surprised to hear the caller's voice. 'Oh! Detective Inspector Nolan. What can I do for you?'

Terry looked around Mulholland's. It was midweek, so she didn't expect to see any of the usual crowd. It wasn't that she was trying to avoid them, but they might read more into her meeting up with Cian Nolan than just a casual drink.

'I'm glad you agreed to come.' Cian pulled out a chair for her. There was already a flirty vibe and she wasn't sure that was the direction she wanted the evening to go in.

'Just for the one. I've left Bella alone, and I've work tomorrow.' Best to keep things at least semi-professional.

But soon one became two, then three – he was a charming companion. Who would have known he was such a good mimic? He had her in stitches with his take on his colleagues, including Fraser. Before she knew it, it was 10.30 p.m. Terry was pleased when he insisted on seeing her home. Still, she made it clear she was staying in Michael's flat and that she expected him to be waiting up for her.

She opened the door of the taxi and turned to Cian to say goodnight. She was surprised when he leaned in and kissed her. She pulled back, mumbled goodbye and clambered out of the car.

She kept her head down and didn't look back. She still wasn't sure if she wanted him to kiss her? He was fun, but she wasn't sure she could trust him. Fraser was solid, reliable, bordering on sensible. And Cian probably wasn't interested in a long-term relationship. He didn't seem the settling-down type. Was the bird in the hand a better bet?

26

Terry had gone straight to bed, although she hadn't slept particularly well. She wasn't sure what to make of Cian Nolan. Maybe she should have just gone with the flow, had a bit of fun, but she just wasn't the type of person to have a one- night stand. Those times with Fraser didn't really count. He was definitely something more. She'd heard Michael come in a couple of hours after her. Normally she would have sprung out of bed and pinned him to the wall until he coughed up all the gory details of his date, but she wasn't in the mood.

Michael was still in bed when she got up the next day. She guessed he would be taking the opportunity to work from home this morning. She wrote on the back of his note from the night before, lunch OSP, and propped it up against his posh and ludicrously complicated coffee machine. First, she had to go to Walter Scott House.

Mary arrived at their office in OCRU shortly after Terry,

bearing two americanos and two almond croissants, much to Terry's delight. The perfect remedy for a slight hangover.

'How's your research on unusual deaths and mutilations going, Mary?' Terry wiped her left hand across her mouth and shook loose flakes from her pastry into the bin at the side of her desk.

Mary tipped her head back and shook her crumbs into her mouth. 'There's nothing screaming out at me.' She leaned over and grabbed a pad of Post-it notes and pulled off the top sheet. 'The Wicklow coroner got back to me. He's asked us to look at one of his deaths from three years back.'

Terry peeled the pink square from Mary's outstretched fingers.

'It was a drowning. He was found in the bath. He'd been drinking.' Mary shrugged. 'It just sounds like the usual. You know, the family not happy with the garda investigation. Blah blah blah. We're always the bad guys.'

Terry looked at the name written on the paper, Owen O'Neill.

She looked up at Mary. 'So what's the family's gripe?'

'Well, to be fair to them, the coroner wasn't happy either. The gardaí treated the death as accidental from the get-go. And when the tox came back positive, that was it as far as they were concerned. He'd had a drink, took some drugs, went for a bath and drowned. Job done.' She rubbed her hands together.

'An accident or suicide?' asked Terry. 'Was he depressed?'

'Well, him and the wife were separated.'

'He took it badly?'

'Nobody said that. But the family don't think it adds up.

243

They say he wasn't much of a drinker and he wasn't on any medication.'

'But even I say I don't drink much.'

'Fair point,' said Mary, her eyes scanning the coroner's report.

'Do we know what drugs were found?'

'It says temazepam here in the report. The coroner returned an open verdict.'

'Interesting. That's a bit like the Scottish not proven verdict in murder trials – the evidence doesn't quite add up so we'll give you the benefit of the doubt. Neither of these outcomes is particularly satisfactory for families. Right, pull up the garda file and drop the PM and tox reports on my desk. Let's see if we can do anything better for the O'Neills. Meantime I've a hot date at the OSP. You couldn't give me a lift over in that cute little white van of yours?' Terry wheedled. 'Please.'

Niamh, Mrs Carey and Michael were already in the OSP tea room when Mary dropped Terry off.

'Hi, folks. All good?' she asked as she flicked the kettle on.

Michael pushed a brown paper bag across the table. 'Cream cheese and smoked salmon bagel with pickled cucumber.'

Terry gratefully grabbed the food and dropped into the seat beside Niamh, who gave her a sly smile. 'Hangover cure?'

Terry turned sharply to the pathology technician. 'What do you mean?'

'You were seen in Mulholland's with a dishy DI.' Niamh bit into her sandwich and smirked at Michael. 'Bit of a boy, I hear.'

'You know what I think about gossiping. No one wants to hear.' Mrs Carey frowned at Niamh. 'It's none of your business whom Terry cavorts with.'

Niamh gave a snort. 'Cavorts! Is that what you call it?'

Michael clattered his mug onto the table. 'Not DI Cian Nolan? You're fu—'

'Michael!' Mrs Carey slapped the table in front of him. 'And mop up that mess.' She pointed at the coffee he had spilled.

Terry got up and wrung out a cloth in the sink. She was aware of Niamh and Michael sniggering together like schoolkids. She sat back down and wiped the table, then threw the cloth back over her shoulder into the sink. 'It was just a drink. Definitely no cavorting.' She looked defiantly at them and took a large bite of her bagel. All three watched silently as she chewed, waiting for her to expand. She knew she was defeated. 'He's just a colleague. All right? I'm not interested in his reputation.'

'Keep your hair on, Tez. We're just joking.' Michael gave her a cheeky grin. But she knew her face very obviously showed that she didn't think it was funny.

An awkward silence ensued, broken only by Niamh rustling a packet of crisps, peeved because she had been admonished.

Mrs Carey cleared her throat. 'Professor Boyd asked me to check my database for unusual murder cases on your behalf.' She addressed this to Terry. 'I've double-checked my Uncommon, Atypical and Bizarre files.' Terry stared open-mouthed at this middle-aged, middle-class apparent superwoman. 'Mercifully, it is a short list. I've asked for the court transcripts but one has still to come to court. Apparently, the alleged perpetrator in that particular case, the deceased's son, is incarcerated in the Central Mental Hospital, unfit to stand trial.'

Niamh had sat nodding along as the office manager spoke and now she pitched in. 'That's the one where he cut off his dad's dick and stuck it—'

'Niamh!'

'What?' she asked innocently. 'You left the files on your desk. I just had a peek.'

Mrs Carey turned back to Terry. 'It was a most unsavoury case. But it is alleged that the father had sexually abused his daughters.'

Terry wondered what the category this had been filed under – uncommon, atypical or bizarre. Unsavoury? *Justifiable*, she thought.

Niamh obviously agreed. 'He deserved all he got.'

Mrs Carey ignored Niamh's comment. 'They are all rather nasty killings' – she wrinkled her nose in disgust – 'but all of the deaths themselves were straightforward.'

'Thanks, Mrs C. It was really helpful of you to trawl through your database. I doubt I would have been able to navigate your system so efficiently.'

Michael turned towards her, his mouth open in feigned shock. 'You think? We all know about your technological prowess.'

Mrs Carey stood and took her cup and saucer over to the dishwasher, signalling that this little chat was over. 'Niamh. It's two o'clock,' she said as she left the room.

Niamh made a face behind her back but got up and followed her out. Terry called after her, 'I'm still waiting on Martin Higgins's histology slides. Today, please.'

As soon as the door closed behind them, Michael got up. 'Refill?'

Terry nodded.

'So,' he continued, 'DI Nolan.'

She chose to ignore the remark. 'Where were you last night?'

Michael reddened. 'Out.' He was on the defensive.

'Don't be smart. Who were you out with? Paul?' 'With whom were you out?' he corrected her.

'Now you're just pissing me off.' She stared at him unblinking, which she knew from the past would force him to cave in.

'Ahern,' he mumbled.

'No!' Terry sat back, a smile spreading over her face. 'Alan Ahern. Who would have thunk it.'

Michael had a ton of work to do before Fraser and Terry came over to FSI for an update on the ongoing investigations later that afternoon. He wanted to double-check a few of his results on Maguire, Higgins and Drogheda. DNA was a double-edged sword: it didn't always supply the answer you were looking for, sometimes it answered a question you hadn't thought needed asking.

The DNA results on the knots in the ligature used in Maguire's death had thrown up some surprises, but he needed to be sure before sharing any information. Terry had a tendency to go off half-cocked, and that nearly got her killed previously. If Dr Maguire's death was either an accident or a suicide, Michael would have expected to find Dr Maguire's DNA on the ligature, confirming he had tied the knots. But there wasn't a trace of his DNA on the knot used to tie the cord to the chandelier.

Paul had called earlier to tell him his thoughts on the Maguire case. The knot securing the cord to the chandelier was an anchor hitch knot used by sailors. And Paul should know, he sailed most weekends, which, Michael had to admit, was always a bone of contention between them. Michael couldn't see the point. He'd tried valiantly to muster up the enthusiasm when they started going out, and spent many a Sunday waiting for Paul on a blustery dock while he competed in a race. Not to mention the other sporting events he'd had to attend with his sports-mad ex-boyfriend: standing on the side-lines of a mucky rugby pitch or sitting through interminable cricket matches. They say opposites attract, but eventually they repel – well, in their case anyway.

At any rate this information only added to the confusion.

And then there was the Higgins murder. He would also have to brief Fraser on that. There was definitely an overlap between the Drogheda brothel workers and Higgins.

Fair play to Terry – she had noticed the marks on Martin Higgins's wrists caused by handcuffs, and his were missing. The search team had scoured Delaney Gardens and turned up all sorts of shit, but there had been no sign of Higgins's handcuffs. Until now.

He had been so wrapped up in prioritising the DNA analyses to help identify the women taken from the brothel in Drogheda that he had initially ignored the evidence the SOCOs had taken from the house. It hadn't been a priority for him, the women weren't going to be prosecuted. But Monica had said all evidence must be logged and, at the very least, looked at, which was why he had pulled the lot.

About twenty bags of evidence had been taken from the house in Drogheda – some SOCOs were more discriminating than others, particularly the Technical Bureau, which is why he preferred working with them. The local SOCO teams seemed to just bag and tag anything that wasn't nailed down, just in case they missed something. This house had obviously been searched by overzealous amateurs. He wondered what they taught them in Templemore.

He had sifted through the mound. Some items had been easily dealt with without opening the clear plastic bags they were in. Other objects he hadn't been quite so sure about but took a photograph, just in case. Midway through, there had been a bag labelled 'handcuffs'. The hairs on the back of his neck had stood up. He had taken the bag over to the DNA lab, where he separated the more Ann Summers-esque fur and leather handcuffs from the sturdy pairs. He had looked for fingerprints and taken swabs for DNA. Only one pair wasn't covered in smudged prints, so he concentrated on those. And he wasn't disappointed when he got the results.

'Thanks for coming in, John,' said Michael, as he showed Fraser into the general lab area. Terry was already there, peering at the evidence bags laid out on a bench.

Fraser merely nodded at Michael and Terry. 'I don't have much time. Can we keep this snappy?' he directed at Michael. Terry and Michael exchanged a look.

'There's something I need to show you first.' Michael led Fraser over to the bench where Terry was standing. He turned to them and held up a clear plastic evidence bag. 'Are these official garda handcuffs?' Michael knew they were, but he wanted confirmation from the horse's mouth, so to speak.

Fraser turned the plastic specimen bag over and back. 'They certainly look like standard garda handcuffs. Where are they from?'

'The house in Drogheda – and wait until you hear this.' Michael was in his element, he looked like he was going to burst from excitement. 'I found Higgins's DNA on them.'

Fraser and Terry looked dumbstruck.

Michael nodded, more than a little enthusiastically. 'Uh-huh. And we know there was no way he could have been in the Drogheda house. Him being dead.'

'No need to state the blooming obvious,' Terry quipped.

He ignored her interruption. 'There were some smudged fingerprints, but none useful. But that's not the best of it.' He stopped for effect. Terry was looking exasperated, so he quickly went on. 'There was a second DNA profile.' He looked from one to the other. 'Chisom Hassan, the Nigerian prostitute working in the brothel.' He took a bow. 'You're very welcome.'

'One of the prostitutes? You're sure?'

Michael nodded at Terry.

'So let me get this right. This Chisom Hassan handled Higgins's handcuffs?' Terry looked puzzled. 'Did she take them with her from Dublin to Drogheda?'

'I didn't get any other useful profiles, so it's possible. But then they might just have been lying around the flat in Delaney

Gardens and got scooped into a bag when the gang cleared it out and did a runner.'

This was the frustrating thing about DNA – it never told the whole story. The problem was that people tried to fill in the blanks. And Michael knew Terry never failed to have a go.

She didn't disappoint now.

'So Higgins was involved in some way with a prostitute. Business or pleasure? This Chisom could have killed him or at least been involved in his death. That could be why she's done a runner? Maybe she killed him while he was chained to the bed with his own cuffs?' Terry directed this to Michael.

He stared back open-mouthed. 'You didn't just say that! That's a bit of a leap.' He looked over at Fraser, but he seemed lost in thought.

Terry ignored him. She got up and walked around the room. 'From the photos I've seen of the women found in Drogheda, Chisom is tiny, and Higgins was a bruiser. So she would have needed someone to help drag him outside after she shot him.'

Michael found himself being pulled into Terry's version of events. 'But I didn't find any blood in the flat in Dublin. There was no forensic evidence to support him being shot in that flat.'

'Fun as this speculation has been' – Fraser spoke directly to Terry, and Michael could tell he did not appreciate her thoughts regarding Higgins's death – 'I need to find Chisom Hassan. Meantime, let's just stick to the facts.' He gave Terry a warning look. He turned his attention to Michael. 'Thanks, Michael. If there isn't anything else urgent that I need to know, I'd better get back to WSH and release an all-points bulletin to the gardaí on the ground, let them know she's a priority. We need to find Chisom before someone else does.'

'I've got an update on Dr Maguire as well,' Michael stated, but Fraser was already at the door.

'Send it over.'

Michael and Terry watched as he strode off along the corridor.

As soon as Fraser was gone, they settled themselves in Michael's office and Michael turned on his friend. 'You made a right hames of that!'

Terry sat, staring into space.

'You've got to admit, Michael, that it's all very odd. All these random connections that just don't add up.'

'I'll get us a couple of coffees.' While he waited for the kettle to boil, he watched Terry. He was worried about her. She wasn't her usual self, he thought she was putting on a brave face. There was so much going on – Higgins, Maguire and Jenny – it would test anyone. He felt bad because he had been busy trying to sort out his own life and hadn't been much of a friend.

He put the mug on the table in front of her. 'Well, we can't do anything about the Hassan stuff, but I've something else for you.' He took a folder from his Out tray and sat down. 'Dr Maguire!' He waved the folder in her face. 'I processed the swabs from the knots and I got a DNA profile.'

'What?' She moved the mug out of the way.

'It's not his! Maguire didn't tie the knots. Someone else did.' She slapped the table with both hands and coffee spilled onto its surface. 'I knew it! I knew it wasn't an accident or a suicide. I just needed the proof. So whose DNA is it?'

'Well, I don't know.' He grabbed her hand in case she knocked the mug over. 'There was a match on the database. It came from the scene of a death a few years back. It wasn't identified at the time. But I haven't had a chance to pull the case and review the evidence yet. I want to be a hundred per cent sure – you just saw how Fraser is. It wasn't a Dublin case, and as far as I can see the gardaí were treating the death as a suicide. Leave it with me for now.'

'Well, don't take forever. Potentially we're looking at a murder.'

27

Terry went back over to the mortuary to wait until Michael was ready to leave and found Niamh had left a stack of trays of glass microscopy slides on her desk. She wasn't really in the mood for a session at the microscope, but she noticed that the top tray was the Higgins tissues, including the slivers of skin she had taken from his wrists, and decided to have a quick look.

Picking a slide at random, she placed it on the microscope stage and focused on the image as she flicked through the lenses, increasing the magnification by four times, by ten times and by forty times. She homed in on the reddened areas of grazing she had seen on Higgins's wrists, which she had thought were caused by rigid handcuffs rubbing against the skin. She had been right: something had scraped off the surface layers of the skin. The epidermis was missing in those areas, exposing the layer below, the dermis. Had Higgins survived, this would have scabbed over and eventually healed as good as new.

But that wasn't what caught her attention. As she zoomed in on the cellular detail, it became apparent that the skin tissue was more cellular than it should be. If Higgins had been cuffed just before he was killed, the tissues wouldn't have had time to react to the surface injury. But the small blood vessels in the dermis were lined by eosinophils, meaning the inflammatory response had kicked in, the body attempting to begin the healing process. A few of these cells had even spilled out into the tissues. Bottom line was that Higgins had been cuffed way before he was shot.

The handcuffs were found with the brothel paraphernalia because, apparently, that was his thing. The clincher was finding macrophage cells, the Pac-Man cells of the body, stuffed with a dark-brown pigment, haemosiderin, between the normal cells of the dermis: a marker of previous injury to his wrist. It seemed Higgins liked being strung up and restrained during sex. Guess this time he had simply left his cuffs behind. Chisom Hassan had a tale to tell. Fraser definitely needed to speak to her.

Back at Michael's flat, Terry had no appetite and declined his offer of a Domino's pizza. She couldn't settle, and when Michael's phone rang and he slunk off to his bedroom, she decided to take Bella out for a walk.

It was only when the cold air hit that she snapped out of her self-pity. Her thoughts returned to the important things that had happened this afternoon: DNA results for the Higgins murder with the discovery of his handcuffs, the histology giving a perfectly simple explanation for said cuffs, and the big surprise, Dr Maguire. It was all getting very complicated.

Terry pulled her beanie as low as she could. It was freezing and there was a slight drizzle of rain. She looked at the faces of the passers-by – most ignored her, the occasional female gave a slight smile and quickened their step. It was not a night to linger. She wondered about those living on the streets. Where were Mags and the others? Would Mags know where Chisom was? They were vulnerable, in all senses of the word. She just hoped they were safe and had shelter. She wondered what she would do in these circumstances, where would she go?

Not the Phoenix Park, that would be reckless. She suspected that Mags and the others were keeping under the radar, but they would need money to survive, which might drive them back to prostitution. She just hoped that they would get help where they could. There was a soup kitchen on Thursday nights outside the Bank of Ireland building on College Green. She had seen it when she was late-night shopping on Grafton Street, and it had made her feel guilty. She kept meaning to do some voluntary work. Wasn't that what good people did? Maybe when this was over.

Terry wasn't hopeful that she would see any of the women at the soup kitchen, but it was worth a chance. Better than doing nothing. She would need to contact Ruhama at some point. They had offered to assist the girls before they'd disappeared. Someone in the organisation might give her some insight into the underworld of prostitution.

When she arrived, there was already a queue waiting for the food to be distributed. She scanned the faces, hoping to see someone familiar, but the vast majority were men. She slowly walked past, trying not to look too conspicuous. Bella proved a distraction – people trusted animals and, by extension, the person on the end of the lead. She listened out for foreign accents, but she didn't want to get too close and raise any suspicion.

Terry and Bella hovered near the taxi rank, watching the comings and goings. An hour later the queue was dwindling, her feet were freezing, and the dog was restless. She decided to give it another five minutes.

Out of the corner of her eye she saw someone skulk up behind the volunteers. She could only make out a slim figure in tracksuit bottoms and a hoodie. Like most of the others, the hood was up, concealing their face. They seemed a bit skittish. She watched them closely as they seemed to decide to approach the volunteer handing out sandwiches.

They knocked the hood back a little to speak to him. 'Mags!' She recognised her immediately. Terry pulled Bella to her feet just as Mags spotted her and took to her heels, sprinting across the road and heedless of the traffic. The Luas thundered past and Bella refused to budge, startled by the noise. By the time it had passed, Mags had disappeared through the gates of Trinity.

Terry stood at the entrance. 'Fuck! Fuck! Fuck!' She knew there was no chance of catching up with Mags. She checked her phone: three missed calls from Michael. She patted Bella. 'Come on, girl, time to go home. At least I know she's alive.'

Her phone chirped, indicating a text message. Where the hell are you? Your uncle Jim is here. Why did you give him my address? Get your arse back here now!

On my way, she texted back quickly, before breaking into a

trot. She knew Michael felt uncomfortable around Big Jim. She had to rescue him. Big Jim might be her dad's best friend but he was a bit … old-fashioned macho, her dad called it. She would say homophobic.

'Hi there!' Terry pushed the door closed behind her and let Bella off the lead. The dog made straight for her water bowl.

'And how's little Anne Therese?' Jim got up and pulled her into a bear hug. Bella gave a throaty growl and he took a step back. 'Jesus, that's a queer guard dog.'

'She's Bella and I'm Terry,' she admonished him. He had an infuriating tendency to treat her as if she was still a little girl. She patted the dog's head. 'It's okay, the big scary man won't hurt us. Sit down.' She smiled at her uncle. 'I mean you, Jim, not Bella.'

She pulled off her coat and her beanie hat. Jim suddenly stiffened. 'You're the image of your mother with your hair like that.'

She touched her hair. She had always worn it long, more often than not in a ponytail. This was the first time she had cut it short. She went over to the mirror, ran her fingers through it and stared briefly at her reflection. Did she look like her mother? She had left them so long ago, Terry hardly remembered what she looked like. Her dad had got rid of all the photographs. It was almost as if she had never existed. As far as Terry was concerned, she and her father had been abandoned, just when they should all have been pulling together. She lost a sister and a mother. How many times since she had become a forensic pathologist had she witnessed the fracturing of families after a death? Her position wasn't special.

'You think so?' She spun around to face him. He just sat staring at her. 'Did Michael offer you a drink? Jim!' She snapped her fingers to get his attention.

He seemed to rally. 'What, love?'

'Do you want a beer, or a wine, or a … Michael, do you have anything other than gin?'

'I gave him a beer.' Michael sounded surly.

She mouthed sorry, and turned back to her uncle, who was still unusually quiet. He was normally loud, brash and bordering on the offensive. 'Dad said you were over to see Eddi Reader. Sorry I couldn't put you up.'

Jim lifted the bottle of beer he had at his feet and took a gulp. 'No worries, it's only for a couple of nights. The concert is tomorrow and I'm back home early next week. Your dad gave me Michael's address. He told me you had a problem with your flat?'

'Oh, that's something and nothing. It's getting sorted. This is just for a week or so.' Michael handed her a glass of white wine, which she accepted gratefully. 'Cheers. It's nice to see you anyway. Did you get anything to eat?'

'Now, don't you bother about me. I'm fine, I had something in the airport. Your dad said you've been busy.' He patted the seat beside him, and she settled back on the couch.

'Nothing I can't handle.' She didn't like her dad telling Jim about her work. Even though Jim, like her dad, was police.

Jim suddenly sat forward and felt inside his jacket pocket. 'Aileen said to make sure you got this.' He opened his right hand, revealing a small package wrapped in shiny Christmas paper with cartoon reindeers with luminous red noses, securely fastened with Sellotape. He set it down on the coffee table. 'I'd have thought Aileen would have given you your presents at Christmas. She's fierce organised.'

'It's probably just something she forgot at the time.' Terry attempted a conciliatory smile.

'Well, let her know or she'll be at me.'

The conversation flagged after a while. Terry was tired and wanted to go to bed so was deliberately monosyllabic, hoping Jim would take the hint. He didn't.

'Another beer wouldn't go amiss, young man.' Big Jim shook his empty bottle towards Michael, who gave a tight-lipped smile before storming into the kitchen.

'So, what are you working on anyway? Anything interesting?' said Jim, ignoring the tension in the room.

'Oh, just the usual.' Terry kept it vague, not wanting to be drawn into this conversation.

'What about that scumbag that nearly killed you? What's the story with him?'

Terry felt her chest contract. She took a sip of wine to mask her consternation. She hadn't expected him to bring up Hunt. 'He's been charged with murder and attempted murder.'

Jim didn't seem to notice her discomfiture. 'Fucking hanging is too good for the likes of him. Don't you worry, love, he'll get his comeuppance. You just concentrate on doing your job. You're lucky. Things are pretty tame here now. Back in the day, me and your dad were dodging bombs and bullets. Lads these days have it easy. They should have been around when the IRA were on the go.'

'I think the bad guys do enough damage without having the IRA as role models,' said Terry ruefully.

'Fair dos.' He swirled the beer in the bottle Michael ungraciously handed him. 'Your dad mentioned to you that they're having another look at your Jennifer's death. Have you heard if they came up with something new?'

Terry looked down at the parcel on the table, but before she could respond Michael jumped in. 'Oh, it's probably just routine. A box-ticking exercise. Little usually comes from them. Waste of time from what I hear from my Scottish counterparts.'

Jim looked from Michael to Terry. 'Ah! Now, don't you get your hopes up, Anne Therese.' He squeezed her arm. 'Remember what happened last time.' He nodded at the glass she was holding.

Terry bristled. 'Don't worry about me, Jim.'

'Maybe that boyfriend of yours could find out where they are with it, if it would make you feel better.'

'I think he's got enough on his plate without getting involved in Scottish police business. Why don't you ask your pals in Police Scotland? Aileen said you were dealing with things for Dad.'

'Well, I don't think your dad trusts them. Maybe a fresh pair of Irish eyes might have picked up on something they missed.' He looked over to Michael and then continued, 'I just heard from some old pals in the gardaí ...'

Terry jumped up off the sofa, stopping Jim in his tracks.

She'd officially had enough. 'Sorry, Jim, to cut you off, but I'm exhausted and we've an early start tomorrow. Do you mind?'

Big Jim struggled to get up. Terry forgot sometimes that he and her dad were getting older. She felt a pang of affection for him. He pulled on his coat. 'You do look done in, love. You need to mind yourself. Stay away from the bad guys. Watch your back.'

She walked him to the door. 'Don't worry about me, Jim. It's just been a long day at work. I hope you enjoy your concert.' As the door clicked closed behind him, Terry leaned back against the wall, closed her eyes and exhaled heavily. *Thank God he's gone*, she thought to herself.

'So! What was that all about?' Michael topped up her glass.

'It was just Jim being Jim.'

'I really don't like him. He gives me the creeps.'

'I know. I'm sorry. I wasn't in the mood for him either. He's hard going when my dad's not there.'

'Banter is what they call it.' Terry could see Michael was angry. 'How's the gay boy?' He picked up the empty beer bottle and walked over to the kitchen area. 'I shouldn't be surprised – I've heard much the same from some gardaí.' Terry heard the thud of the bottle as it hit the bottom of the bin.

'I'm sorry,' she said. 'I'll speak to him about it.'

'Don't waste your breath. I was just a bit taken aback at him turning up out of the blue like that.'

'He thought he was doing me a favour, I suppose, bringing this over.' She pointed to the shiny parcel on the coffee table.

'Forget him. This is a present from me to you.' Terry gave him a sly smile.

He made to grab the small parcel. She leaned over and knocked his hand away. 'Uh-uh, not so fast.'

'What's going on?'

'Sorry. I just didn't want you messing with it. Gloves!'

Michael pulled back. 'What?'

'Evidence, Watson.'

'You've lost the plot,' Michael said, shaking his head. 'A Chrissie pressie is evidence of what?'

'Jenny's murder.' She couldn't read his face. 'It's Jenny's necklace.' She waited. She relaxed a little when she saw he looked more quizzical than angry. Subconsciously, she reached for the chain bearing her name that she wore around her neck. 'We both got a necklace with our name on it one Christmas, like this one.' She held up the necklace around her neck so he could see it. 'Anne Therese for me and Jennifer for her.'

'But that says "Terry".'

'It's new. I'm Terry now.' She shrugged.

'Where did you get it? Hers?' Michael pointed at the parcel.

'She was wearing it when she was murdered. We got it back along with her clothes and bag once the police were finished with them. Mum and Dad couldn't bear to look at her things so the bag was put in her room. I used to sleep with her jumper. It smelled of her – well, the Britney Spears perfume she wore. The perfume was in this really nice blue bottle. I kept that for years until it all evaporated. But it was part of her.'

Michael came over and sat beside her. He put his right arm around her shoulders and pulled her close. 'I'm sorry, Tez.'

They sat quietly for a few minutes. Michael pulled his arm away and sat forward, staring at the small package. 'So that's where they got the partial fingerprint from.' He turned and looked at Terry. 'So why didn't you give the police this when they did that last review?'

'No one asked for it. Anyway, it was maybe about ten years ago. They were dealing with Dad and I don't think he even remembered she had it. As soon as I left home, he cleared out her room. All the evidence that had been returned was dumped. This' – she pointed at the package – 'and a moth-eaten jumper stuffed in the back of my wardrobe, that's all I've left of my sister.'

'So no one knows about this?'

'No. I told Aileen I had something I wanted sent over but I didn't say what it was. She probably suspects it has something to do with Jenny because I said not to mention it to Dad. But, to be fair, it was just a memento to me initially. It was only when I did that course in Boston, when they mentioned the success they had had with touch DNA, that I thought maybe one day ...' Her voice tailed off.

'And you pushed and pushed to get the case reviewed, and in the process royally pissed off the Scottish police and the Scottish forensic science services to the extent you ended up here.'

'That's a bit harsh. I just pointed out that they needed to be a bit more thorough. And guess what? It looks like I was right all along. Now I don't trust any of them.'

'From what I heard, the word you used to describe their investigation was incompetent. Jesus, Terry, you were lucky for the sake of your career that Charlie Boyd took you.'

'Hmmphh! I was doing him a favour. Your Paul left him in the lurch.' When she saw Michael's face fall at the reminder of his failed relationship, she felt bad. 'That was below the belt. I'm sorry.' She was saying sorry too much these days. 'It was just frustrating that they didn't want to try.' She sat back, defeated. 'And even Dad told me to back off.' Terry ran her fingers through her hair and wiped her hands across her face. She looked at Michael and saw him sag.

'Okay, okay.'

She perked up. 'So you'll do it? You'll check Jenny's necklace for traces of her murderer's DNA?'

Michael nodded. 'Well, I'll need to run it past Monica and the lads in the Scottish forensic science lab. No promises.'

She leaned over and kissed his cheek. 'Thank you. You're the best. And don't you worry about Jim. He still sees me as some stupid kid. He's just being protective. I guess it's because he doesn't have kids of his own. But how he talks to you is not ok – and I will talk to him, I promise.'

Interesting. Maybe freezing his ass off tailing that bitch all night had been worth it. She'd had a visitor – one he knew a certain someone would be very interested in. Maybe he'd even see some cash for his trouble. God knows he needed it now. His career was in tatters thanks to that stuck-up cow. She'd had him shunted into a desk job and booted off the force indefinitely. No, if anyone who deserved what was coming to them, it was her.

28

Mary had already downloaded the garda files Mrs C had sent on the three cases of interest – the drowning in Bettystown, the pervert bludgeoned by his son and the Carlow fire death – and was busy making notes in the OCRU office when Terry arrived at 8.30 a.m. The post-mortem reports were sitting on Terry's desk, thanks to Mrs Carey. She knew this was a fishing exercise, but if you didn't try, you never caught the big fish.

The least promising was the guy who had been 'bobbitted', for want of a better expression than Niamh's frank appraisal of the circumstances. His penis had been chopped off after he was brutally pummelled to death with a chair leg by his son. The story had obviously caught the imagination of the press at the time. There was a thick wad of newspaper cuttings in the post- mortem file, the majority referring to him as the Irish Bobbitt, comparing him to John Bobbitt who had been assaulted by his wife who alleged that he had been abusing her.

Terry checked the date –2014, eleven years ago. Professor Boyd had performed the post- mortem, but his report had remained under cover, waiting for the day the son was deemed mentally fit to stand trial. At this stage it didn't look likely. She threw the PM file onto her desk. 'We can discount this one, Mary. Unless you've found anything in the garda notes.'

'The gardaí seem to have been fairly sympathetic towards the son because of the history of sexual abuse. Open and shut case. He's in the Central Mental Hospital and likely to remain.' Terry slumped back, staring into space. She suddenly sat up. 'It got a lot of press at the time.' She rifled through the newspaper cuttings. 'I mean, look at this headline.' She brandished a photocopy of the front page of a red-top. '"An eye for an eye, a tooth for a tooth, and a dick for a dick."'

'Nice work by the journalist.' Mary smirked.

'Maybe not a literary genius, but they're fairly accurate in the summation. I'm not critiquing the content, but the sentiment.' Mary looked puzzled. Terry explained. 'What if it gave someone ideas on retribution for crimes? Like a copy-cat thing.'

'I think we would have noticed a spate of knob-related killings.'

'Nice. Have you thought of going into journalism – you have such a lovely turn of phrase? I mean, not just hacking off a penis, but making the punishment fit the crime.'

'You mean like the Saudis chopping off the hands of thieves?'

'Yes, something like that.'

'So Martin Higgins was a nark. He got shot and his tongue hacked out by someone like the Hayeses? That's what we thought anyway.'

'I don't know. That's too easy. Why would they bother? Remember, you checked. There were no other gangland killings with such specific mutilations and nothing similar reported in the UK.'

'You keep saying that. But maybe their go-to guy for the odd execution is a fucked-up bastard who thought it would be fun.'

'I don't know,' said Terry, her brow furrowed. 'I still think we're missing something.'

Mary was going to a hen night in Temple Bar, so they called it a day at about four o'clock.

Terry got a taxi to the OSP. She knew Jimmy would be on call, as Tomas and his girlfriend were going to Edinburgh for the weekend for the rugby. It was Friday night so she hoped he was true to form and intending to spend the night on the sofa in his office. The on-call suite he called it if anyone asked.

The OSP was quiet as she went into the conference room, where she dumped her files on the table, before going downstairs to leave Bella with Jimmy while she worked in her office.

When she looked back, Jimmy and Bella were already snuggled up together on the moth-eaten sofa Jimmy used as a bed when he was in the doghouse, which strangely seemed to be at weekends. Those in the know avoided sitting on it and he reserved it for eejits and arseholes – his words – of whom he thought there were many in the gardaí.

She decided to finish going through the files Mrs C had identified. The first one she looked at was from November 2015: the body of an Eastern European chap found on the beach at Bettystown. Apparently, this was enough for the gardaí to treat the death as suspicious. The gist of it was that he and his mate, same nationality, had gone late-night fishing. It wasn't clear how it happened, but the boat capsized and only one of them made it back to shore alive. The body was brought in by the tide and found late the next day by a dogwalker. To cut a long story short, there was no evidence of any animosity between the friends and it appeared to be an accident. She speed-read the PM report. And there it was, towards the end of the section External Examination – the reason Mrs C had filed this under Bizarre: the eyes had been gouged out. Obviously, Dr Tomlinson, the pathologist at the time, was unaware that biggish birds can peck at the eyes of carrion. Ask any farmer: dead lambs are fair game.

Dr Tomlinson brought this to the attention of the SIO, as he was adamant this was an example of post-mortem mutilation. Well, it was, but not in the way the doctor meant. It was obvious that the gardaí took no notice of the doctor's concerns. But it wasn't clear how the report had found its way into the archives of the OSP.

At the back of the file were the notes from a case review meeting. Dr Tomlinson had come along to one, presumably hoping that Professor Charlie Boyd would agree with his opinion. Of course, he hadn't. She was sure Charlie had taken great pleasure in educating the city pathologist on the vagaries of nature. She'd bet it was a lesson Dr Tomlinson never forgot. But that explained why Mrs C had a copy of the report on file. The next was a fire death from 2021. They were always tricky cases anyway. Mrs C had categorised it as *Unusual*. Terry fully expected it to have been misclassified as *Spontaneous human combustion*, a favourite diagnosis of the press. But that wasn't the cause of death. It was one of Charlie's cases. He had given the cause of death as *Death in a fire*.

On the face of it, Mr Emmett Tormey had died in a fire in his garden shed. What was unusual about that? The fact that Charlie had not been the first port of call. The coroner had asked a hospital pathologist to carry out the post-mortem, and the death had only been referred to the OSP when the gardaí had worries about the examination of the shed. Unfortunately, by the time that was complete, within a mere forty-eight hours, Mr Tormey was already six feet under.

Charlie only had the notes that the hospital pathologist had taken during the post-mortem. He had summarised the salient findings: there had been soot and smoke in the trachea and way down into the depths of the lungs. This man had been fighting for breath. Confirming that he had been suffocated by the noxious fire fumes, toxicology showed a high level of carbon monoxide, 63 per cent, as well as other toxic substances, including hydrogen cyanide, but no alcohol or drugs.

She skimmed the conclusions: *Previously healthy male. Severe burns and charring. Post-mortem?* Not a pleasant way to go.

She sifted through the paperwork looking for the Technical Bureau report. It was standard practice in fire fatalities that the ballistics expert took the lead. She checked the signatory: DI Alan Ahern. Perfect.

As she would have expected from him, the examination of the scene had been meticulous. There had been precious little left of the original structure by the time the fire brigade brought the fire under control. Alan had raised a couple of concerns: there were remnants of paint tins and a petrol can, which would act as accelerants, fuelling the fire. Mrs Tormey couldn't identify them. She said she had no idea what was in the shed. It was her husband's domain and he kept it locked.

And that fed into Alan's other concern. There was practically only the hardware left of the shed door, and the lock was in the locked position and there was no sign of the key.

On the basis of these anomalies the SIO flagged the death as suspicious, but it was too late. Reading between the lines, it was with reluctance that the coroner referred it to Professor Boyd. Terry had had dealings with the Carlow coroner before. She was a rather terse individual.

With the body buried, Charlie Boyd had done what he could with the limited information available. Terry knew he would have been furious. He was never done telling the gardaí and the coroners that if there was any doubt at all about any death, they were to call his office, day or night. Terry and Paul agreed with this sentiment, even if they were the ones who usually had to deal with the night-time queries.

She looked at the front cover of the file. It showed the name of deceased, date of death and post-mortem, and the coroner and pathologist details. But there was also a column to be completed by the state pathologist, or Mrs C, to indicate further actions. The list included toxicology, forensic evidence, neuropathology, inquest and court attendance.

Beside Inquest was a date, around eight weeks after the death and a week after the date on the toxicology report.

One might admire the coroner's efficiency, whoever the hell one was. Below that, written in Mrs C's neat and precise handwriting, was Verdict – accidental death (Professor Boyd not required to attend). He would have been livid, he loved a day in court.

In the pocket at the back of the file were the press clippings. It would appear that Mr Tormey had been a local solicitor. One release showed a photograph of him holding a trophy aloft – from his attire, she reckoned it was for golf. Others showed views of the garden and house, a pretty impressive pile. Only one showed the burnt-out shed.

This shed did not in any shape or form resemble her dad's garden hut. This had been one of those posh affairs you see advertised in the country-house magazines she had flicked through while waiting to see Maeve Price. Still, a burnt-out shed is a burnt-out shed – useless, no matter what it cost.

Terry stretched and checked her watch – 6.15 p.m. Time to head home, but first she had a call to make.

It was after hours on a Friday night, but she rang the station of the guard who had compiled the C71 form informing the coroner of the circumstances of the death of Emmett Tormey. Luck was with her. It was obviously a slow night in Rathoe, County Carlow, and Garda Dunphy, who answered the phone, knew exactly who she was. Apparently, he had met her at another scene. She feigned recognition, although she had no memory of the encounter.

She explained what she was looking for and he seemed more than happy to look out Tormey's inquest file. He had been at the coroner's court that day in another case. It wasn't a death he had dealt with but he knew about it. He had a melodic voice and she imagined him as nearing the end of his thirty years on the force, a little rotund and not that fit. Overlooked for promotion, but a cheery chappy nonetheless.

'Now, the coroner is very good. She doesn't like distressing the families with too many unpleasant details. So she has us read summaries of all the reports into evidence. The pathologists prefer that too.'

I bet they do, she thought, *that way they don't have to answer any difficult questions.* Not the style of the OSP pathologists, who relish being challenged by barristers and coroners. Problem was that also meant that the families got a sanitised version of the events leading to a death. They should get all the information, warts and all. They had a right to it. 'That's very … thoughtful of her, but sometimes the families want the details. And they want to ask questions.'

'Ms Harkins, the coroner, doesn't encourage that.'

There was no point in taking out her frustration on this man. 'Did the family instruct a solicitor?' She heard him rustling the papers in his file.

'No. The only person who gave evidence was Mrs Tormey. She identified her husband.'

'How on earth did she do that? He was burnt beyond recognition by all accounts.'

'Well, there was only one person who had access to the shed – it had to be him.'

Duh! 'I'm sure you're right, Garda Dunphy. Surely DNA was done?'

'Of course, Doctor.' Bless, he sounded so proud. Thank the

Lord nothing much happened in that neck of the woods. 'It proved it was him.'

'Did the wife have any concerns? You know, about her husband's death, or even about the fire?'

'No. Well, not about the death anyway. It was about the wedding ring.'

She waited. It was like pulling teeth.

'It wasn't on him. And it wasn't found at the scene. But then the fire brigade was a bit overenthusiastic with their hoses, so they could have blasted it anywhere. It might turn up in the garden someday.'

Terry shook her head. She revised her image of an affable guard – the man at the other end of the phone was now akin to Homer Simpson. 'Well, unless there's anything else relevant in the file, I'll let you get back to work. You've been very helpful. Thanks.'

'It was lovely talking to you, Doctor. The thing I do remember at the time was that the coroner was really hacked off at the hospital. They billed her for cleaning the X-ray department. She sent the sergeant to deal with it. She had to cough up in the end.'

Terry stifled a laugh. You couldn't make this stuff up. But death could be a very messy business. She managed to persuade her new friend to ask the hospital for copies of the X-rays and email them to her. She hoped he knew how to do that.

It would be Monday before she would get anything. She had another look at the file. Charlie did not seem to have been informed that X-rays of the body were available. On the front of the file, she wrote X-rays and today's date with an asterisk beside to remind her to tell the prof, or maybe just let Mrs C know and she could tell him. He would take it better from her. Terry also made a note to check on the missing ring – it might have been overlooked in the debris in the body bag. It happened. It might even show up on the X-rays.

29

Terry left a note on Mrs Carey's desk asking her to get on to the Wicklow coroner for the inquest file on Owen O'Neill, the man who had drowned in his bath. She had the garda file Mary had downloaded but she couldn't face it tonight. It had been a hell of a week: Higgins, the prostitutes, the DNA results, Fraser ... especially Fraser. Monday would be soon enough.

As she stacked the files on the shelf in her office her phone rang. Fraser. She swithered but thought, *What the hell.* 'Hi, John. Can I just apologise to you?' she said quickly, eager to get in what she wanted to say first and avoid his wrath. 'I was a complete arse yesterday. I just got carried away. I didn't mean to upset you.'

'And yet you have.'

She wasn't sure what to say. Why had he called? 'I know you must be mad at me for my—'

'Theatrics?' Fraser asked. There was a distinct lack of warmth in his voice.

'I was going to say *speculations*. But, yes.'

'But that's not the reason,' he went on. 'Do you realise how absolutely frustrating you are?'

Terry's heart was in her mouth. She couldn't think what else she had done. She decided it was best to stay quiet.

'Does this ring any bells, Terry? *Ruthless drug gang pushes deadly drug on Dublin streets*. An interesting headline.'

'Oh!' Realisation dawned. *Julie fucking whoever.* That sweet-talking reporter. She had forgotten all about that. 'I can explain.'

'Go right ahead. I'm all ears,' he said patronisingly.

She immediately went on the defensive. 'I didn't mention Hayes.' She knew that was the issue.

'Here,' he said. She could hear a newspaper rustling. 'Let me refresh your memory of what you did say.' Fraser cleared his throat theatrically. '"A deadly new drug gang has infiltrated the Irish market, warns Assistant State Pathologist Dr Terry O'Brien. The once notorious Hayes gang, run out of town back in the mid-1990s after a failed bank raid, are now back on the Dublin drug scene and are proving to be more dangerous than ever. They are said to be responsible for supplying a lethal mix of heroin and cocaine cut with fentanyl, which has already caused several overdoses and at least one fatality. Described by Dr O'Brien as 'a group of murdering scumbags', this gang are 'targeting highly vulnerable individuals who do not realise the potency of this highly addictive drug'." I could go on. Any of that sounding familiar?'

'Well, it's all true.' Her bravado was faltering.

'For fuck's sake, Terry. You're a state pathologist. What you say matters. You need to be more careful.'

'It's not my fault. I just gave that Julie one a quote like the press office asked me to because they couldn't get hold of you or Dr Brady. I was only chatting with her. I didn't think she would print it all.'

'And this was after Bernice warned you that you were in Lou Hayes's sights. It doesn't make sense to poke the bear.'

'I just said that these fentanyl-laced drugs were dangerous and people needed to be aware.' She was trying to justify her words but it sounded lame even to her.

Fraser was not going to be easily appeased. And he wasn't done yet. 'You don't remember calling the Hayeses a group of murdering scumbags? Have you a death wish?'

'I'm really sorry, John. I know I've messed up,' said Terry, now feeling contrite. Yet another apology she was having to make.

Fraser suddenly sounded serious. 'I'm annoyed with the press office for asking you to speak to that journalist. It's not your remit. I'm worried it might put a spotlight on you and draw unnecessary attention.'

'Do you think it's really that bad?'

'Let's hope not. It'll probably blow over. But no more quotes. Agreed?'

Terry couldn't think how to make it better. On impulse, she threw caution to the wind. 'I suppose a drink is out of the question?'

She was so relieved when he laughed, and so desperate to

make amends, that she found herself agreeing to not only a drink, but also a meal that same evening.

Terry left Jimmy and Bella lolling on the sofa in the mortuary office watching *Reeling in the Years*. Neither moved nor acknowledged her when she said goodnight.

She had been surprised when Fraser suggested a curry – she didn't think Dublin was renowned for its Indian cuisine. The place on Dame Street looked fine, but it was no Shish, the famous Glaswegian Indian restaurant, a staple of Glasgow Uni students. They didn't have long to wait for a table. The place was buzzing, the noise level loud enough that they could have a modicum of privacy.

They slugged beers from the bottle as they waited for their order to arrive. It was always a case of Russian roulette where Indian food was concerned. Fraser, despite his conservative nature, chose one of the hotter curries on the menu. She was impressed. In her student days, the level of heat was used as a measure of the suitability of someone as boyfriend material. She would probably have passed on a second date with him if he'd ordered a korma. Terry, on the other hand, had no such yardstick for herself and stuck to her favourite Glaswegian invention, chicken tikka masala.

When the food arrived, she scooped up the lurid orange sauce with a piece of chapati. 'So, what are your plans for the weekend? Cinema? Theatre?' They had agreed no work talk, which was difficult. She knew it was best to avoid her new theory on Higgins and the handcuffs.

Fraser busied himself chasing a chunk of lamb around his plate. 'I'm actually going to Waterford to see my mum. I wondered if you might like to come along? If you've nothing else planned, that is.'

Terry was stunned into silence. Was he really suggesting going straight to the meet-the-parents stage?

Eventually he looked up. They sat quietly for a couple of seconds, eyes locked.

Fraser dropped his napkin on the table. 'Well? You're very quiet all of a sudden. I'll take that as a no then.'

'No. I mean, yes. I would like to come, thanks.' She became wary when a thought struck her. 'Did you know Alan and Michael were going away for the weekend? Do you just feel sorry for me?'

Fraser pushed his plate to the side and leaned his elbows on the table. 'I heard Alan making plans, but that wasn't why I asked you. I'd really like you to come along. I want to spend some time with you.'

She had to admit she hadn't been relishing a weekend alone, especially now Bella was staying with Jimmy to keep him company while he was on call.

'Right, then. I suppose I could.' She didn't want to seem too keen. Desperate, even. But when his attention had returned to his food, she smiled to herself.

The woman flung the newspaper onto the marble island. 'Have you seen this bullshit?' she seethed.

On the sunken leather sofa, her son barely glanced up from

his phone. 'Yeah, so what, Mam? Makes no difference to us. All publicity is good publicity, amirite?' he said, smirking at his younger brother, who rolled his eyes at him and slid his headphones back on.

Their mother stabbed a finger at the newspaper and then at him. 'That one there needs a lesson in manners – and respect.' She snatched up the paper and hurled it into the bin. 'Sort it – mess with her head some more. Maybe give our pal a call.'

Almost as an afterthought, she added, 'Don't do anything stupid.'

30

Alan arrived at the flat at 9.30 the following morning, looking positively giddy. Terry liked this softer side of him. In the work arena he tended to give off macho vibes. She felt a pang of jealousy, which she quickly tried to suppress. It just stung to see a happy couple when she wasn't sure what was going on between her and Fraser. All she'd got at the end of the night was a peck on the cheek, although curry breath was a bit of a passion killer.

'Michael's still packing. Do you want a coffee?' she asked Alan.

'Yes, please – thanks, Terry.' He followed her down the hall. 'We're taking my Range Rover just in case the roads are a bit ...'

'Shitty? Full of potholes? Blocked by tractors and sheep? Where are you off to anyway? Michael didn't say.'

Alan merely smiled and tapped his nose.

'Oh! That doesn't bode well. Michael doesn't like surprises.

I hope there's at least a flushing loo. You know how particular he is.'

'Don't be such a Debbie Downer, Tez. I love surprises.' Michael brushed past her and gave Alan a kiss on the cheek and took the cake box he was holding. He turned back to her. 'Say thank you to Alan for the croissants.'

Terry filled three mugs with coffee. 'Thank you, Alan, for the croissants.' She opened the box and pulled out an almond one and took a bite. 'Oh! They're very good. Thanks.' She raised her pastry in a salute.

'I'll just finish packing.' Michael waved towards his room.

Alan smiled and sat down beside Terry. He shouted at Michael's retreating back, 'Pack your Speedos.'

Terry looked askance. 'That's not something I want to think about. It could nearly put me off my croissant.' She took a bite, then brushed some flakes of pastry off her jumper. 'Any update on my car? Did you find anything?'

'Sorry, Terry, I should have said. I got sweet FA. Whoever slashed your tyres didn't so much as breathe on them.'

'So I can collect it then?'

'Sure. Anytime, now that Fraser has arranged for new tyres for it. But it will have to be after the weekend when I'm there to sign it out.'

'Great. Thanks, Alan,' she said, happy now she knew she was getting her car back.

Then Michael appeared with his weekend bag. 'Shouldn't you two get on the road?' she asked, glancing at the text she'd just received.

'Will you be okay on your own?' Michael put his bag down

and looked around the room. 'Did you not bring Bella home last night?'

Terry busied herself putting mugs in the dishwasher. 'I'm going to Waterford with John.' She slammed the door shut and stood up defiantly. 'I need to get ready.'

Michael and Alan exchanged pointed looks but said nothing.

'It's not what you think. We're just friends. Now bugger off.' She walked down the hall and opened the front door. Alan picked up Michael's bag and, grinning, they both kissed her goodbye. She could hear them laughing all the way to the lift.

After she closed the door behind them, she reached for her coat and slung her backpack over her shoulder. But she waited until she heard the lift doors close before she left.

Terry felt very self-conscious as she climbed into the passenger seat. In the cold light of day this now seemed a bad idea. Fraser, however, appeared to be enjoying her discomfiture.

'Worried about Bella?' he asked, raising an eyebrow.

She gave him a side eye, not sure if he was serious. 'No. She's fine. Jimmy's taking her to a meet tonight. She can get reacquainted with her old running mates.'

'Good. Right. Before we set off, I'm just going to lay some ground rules.' He looked like he was enjoying this. 'I've told my mother I'm bringing a friend. But before you get any ideas, I've told her to make up the spare room. No funny business.' He waggled a finger at her.

She was totally confused. He took her out, arranged for new tyres for her car, invited her away for a weekend to meet his mother and then acted as if they're two buddies on a road trip. Were they just friends or did he want something more? She couldn't cope with all these mixed signals.

He started the car and music filled the interior. She looked out the window, watching the city streets go by.

Fraser didn't seem to mind that she wasn't in a chatty mood. He regaled her with anecdotes of growing up in Waterford with his sister, Mo, who was married with two children and now lived in France. She realised he must be nervous, bringing her down to meet the mother. Terry wondered what John's mother would be like and if he looked anything like her.

They stopped for coffee and the caffeine helped her relax. By the time they were driving along the quays in Waterford, she had a picture in her head of a small plump woman in an apron, pruning roses in the garden of her terraced cottage.

They drove to the end of the quays and then headed uphill, as if they were going to Waterford Hospital. She had been in the mortuary there on a few occasions. But when they got to the top of the hill, he turned right instead of left. The street was flanked by grey sandstone houses. Halfway along he turned in to the drive of a grand-looking period house. She assumed it was divided into flats.

Fraser parked beside a startlingly vivid blue 8 series convertible BMW, a bit gaudy for her taste. He grabbed both bags from the boot and started up the stone steps to the main entrance. The stained glass of the inner doors was as impressive as the building, and they opened out into an equally grand hall. In the centre was an expensive-looking antique table decked out with a fussy floral arrangement.

Terry looked around, expecting to see doors leading off to separate private apartments, but the doors on either side looked more like internal doors, no locks or nameplates. She followed Fraser around the table. It dawned on her that this was a house: one house. Her childhood home had been a three-bedroom semi. It could fit into the downstairs hall of this place. She could see through to French doors in the room beyond, leading right out to the garden.

Fraser's family had money.

He dropped the bags. He turned and smiled. 'Time to meet the mammy.'

'Mammy' preferred to be called Jacinta. She was the CEO of an IT company founded by Fraser's dad, who'd died of a heart attack seven years earlier. She looked the epitome of Irish money. Terry could imagine her at ladies' day at the races. The woman was gardening in a dress that Terry knew cost a small fortune.

Mrs Fraser, Jacinta, noticed her gawping. 'This old thing? Last season. Only fit for housework and gardening.' But there was a mischievous glint in her eye.

'Don't listen to her, Terry. Jacinta has a housekeeper and a gardener. And thank God. Mo and I would have starved otherwise.' He smiled fondly at his mother. 'She might be a business whizz but she can't boil an egg.' They all laughed as Jacinta took Terry by the arm and led them into a light-filled, cosy kitchen where a bottle of chilled white wine was waiting to be opened. Not a bad way to spend a weekend afternoon, Terry thought happily to herself.

'Your mum's lovely.' Terry waved goodbye to Jacinta as they drove off after lunch on Sunday.

'Of course she is,' Fraser agreed. 'She can be a bit of a nightmare, but she likes a laugh. And good wine.'

'Thanks, John.' She squeezed his arm. Jacinta had been a great hostess, and she felt refreshed after being looked after the whole weekend.

They had spent Saturday afternoon chatting over a few glasses of wine. Dinner had been a splendid affair, whoever cooked it. She had felt comfortable and relaxed, and she hadn't laughed so much in a long time. The only disappointment was that, true to his word, Fraser had kept to his own bed. A little part of her had hoped for a knock on the bedroom door.

She phoned Jimmy to say they were on their way back. He insisted that he was happy keeping Bella another night, which suited her. With a bit of luck, Fraser would suggest drinks tonight. *And who knows what could happen?*

The silence on the drive this time was companionable. Terry was starting to wonder if she should suggest drinks, when that silence was suddenly broken by Fraser's phone ringing. He pressed a button on the steering wheel. 'Superintendent John Fraser.'

DI Cian Nolan's voice came over the speaker. 'Hi, John.'

Terry tensed, assuming this must be about Dr Maguire's death. 'I've a bit of good news.' She sat upright, waiting.

Nolan continued: 'Sal had a boy early this morning. I'm a dad.'

'Oh! Delighted for you, mate. That's the best news.'

Terry sat back, stunned. Fraser was grinning.

'Just wanted to let you know. I've another hundred calls to make. I'll probably be in Mulholland's tonight. If you can't make it, no worries – we'll wet the baby's head soon.'

'Give my love to Sal.'

Terry felt as if she had been slapped in the face. The cheating scumbag. She felt sick. She had very nearly … No, she didn't want to think about what she nearly did. What would Fraser think of her? The weekend had soured. Now she just wanted to go home.

Fraser thought Terry had really thawed out over the weekend. He hadn't wanted to push his luck, but he would have liked to get closer to her. Jacinta hadn't helped, dropping heavy hints. She liked Terry, and Terry had fallen under his mother's spell. The two most important women in his life got along – it should all be good.

And it had been – until halfway home, when she seemed to shut down. He was sure she was pretending to be asleep. When he pulled off the motorway for coffee, she didn't stir. He got her an Americano anyway, but it sat untouched.

Her phone rang just as they hit the M50. He guessed it was Michael by her reaction. She suddenly perked up and became animated. He couldn't hear Michael's side of the conversation but he heard Terry saying, 'Plan A: a Chinese takeaway and a bottle of wine, Plan B: just the wine, but that could be dangerous.' There didn't appear to be any plan that included him. She agreed to Thai and ended the call.

And she had her seat belt unbuckled before he slowed down outside Michael's apartment block. He got out and retrieved her bag from the boot while Terry stood dejectedly at the kerb. He couldn't fathom her. He wondered if he should have been more upfront about his feelings for her rather than play it cool. Was she annoyed with him for not making a move?

She wouldn't even look him in the eye. She just took her bag, and turned and walked to the main entrance of the building. At the door, she stopped and looked back over her shoulder. 'Thanks, John. I did have a good weekend. 'Night.' She didn't wait for an answer, just disappeared into the foyer.

He stood for a few seconds before getting back into his car. She was infuriating. All these mixed messages. He thought they'd had a good time. She had seemed relaxed and hadn't pulled away when he'd kissed her goodnight. For a moment, he'd thought she was going to invite him into her room. He had stood at the closed door wondering whether he should just knock. But he had said there were no strings. He was a man of his word.

And now it seemed they were back in the friend zone.

31

Terry felt a little fragile on Monday morning. She could put it down to the inferiority of the wine of the previous night, compared to Jacinta's finest. You get what you pay for, and they rarely paid more than a tenner and always went for what was on special offer. But no, it was the quantity that was the issue.

Michael always knew when something was up with her. They had been one bottle down when she'd told him about Cian Nolan's call to Fraser. By bottle three she had been in agreement – nothing had happened between her and Cian, other than a kiss or two, and thoughts weren't actions. She wasn't to know he had a heavily pregnant partner at home – that was on him – and she wasn't going to let two stupid nights out with Cian jeopardise a potential relationship with John Fraser. Realistically, the thing with Cian had just been after-work drinks, not real dates. But she didn't want Fraser to find out about them either.

She was drying her hair when Fraser called. She couldn't help but smile with relief. During her heart-to-heart with Michael last night, she had vowed to stop sabotaging what could be a good relationship. This was a second, or was it more like third, or fourth, chance? At any rate she would take it.

The reason he had called was because he was going to Rockroad Clinic that afternoon to have a word with Dr Reagan. Seemed he had spoken to Mrs Maguire, and she had told him her and the husband had gone for counselling. No surprise to Terry it hadn't worked out.

Fraser knew she had her weekly appointment there and did she want a lift? She jumped at the chance and hopped straight into his car when he pulled up outside her building that afternoon. This time she was the one trying to defuse the situation and make amends for her coolness the day before. It was a one-sided conversation, and she felt exhausted by the time they arrived at the hospital. She decided to cut him some slack – he was obviously geeing himself up for his interview with Dr Reagan. She told herself it wasn't anything to do with losing interest in her – she hoped.

Fraser had to take a call as they got out of the lift, so Terry went on ahead. Aoife looked up, phone receiver in hand, and smiled at her as she walked towards the reception desk. 'Dr O'Brien. Can you wait for a moment, please? I've just put an urgent call through to Dr Price.'

Terry nodded and stood to the side as Aoife replaced the handset. Then, she heard the swoosh of the door opening and it clicking closed again behind her. Fraser had arrived.

Terry noticed that Aoife's eyes had narrowed, and the welcoming smile had faded from her face. 'Detective Inspector,

I'm sorry, but if you want an appointment with Dr Reagan, his diary is full. Perhaps I can arrange something for another day? Would that be with your wife?'

Terry had no idea what was going on. She was definitely getting passive-aggressive vibes from Aoife, who stood, pen poised over the page of a diary, a hard look on her face. Fraser gave Aoife a charming smile and pulled out his garda ID. 'Superintendent now. And I'm here to see him on official business. Mrs Foster, isn't it?'

The receptionist stared back coldly. Terry was dumbstruck by her unfriendly demeanour. What had Fraser done to her? 'Is Dr Reagan expecting you?' asked Aoife curtly.

Fraser stood his ground. 'Would you please let him know I'm here? Thank you.'

He walked away, hands in pockets, before taking a seat. Terry watched as Aoife bustled over to Dr Reagan's office, knocked on the door and walked into the room. *There must be a school for office managers*, Terry thought. Aoife was not as scary as Mrs C, but they both appeared to be devoted to their bosses, although she sincerely doubted Reagan was as terrified of Aoife as Prof Boyd was of Mrs Carey. She daren't look at Fraser, as she might laugh.

A few minutes later, Aoife came out of Reagan's office and closed the door quietly behind her. She walked slowly back behind her desk before she spoke. 'Dr Reagan will see you now.' She scrutinised Fraser with a sour look on her face until the door closed behind him.

Terry was intrigued by the dynamic between Fraser and the receptionist. They obviously knew one another.

She walked over and, leaning against the reception counter, she nodded towards Dr Reagan's door. 'He's quite dishy for a guard, isn't he? He came up in the lift with me. He wasn't very chatty, but I quite like that – silent and broody is my thing.'

But Aoife was not entertaining her at all, and continued to look through her diary.

Terry persisted. 'Did I detect a little frisson between the two of you?' She winked, aiming for girlie confidential, but she suspected she was failing miserably given Aoife's lack of response. She tried a warm smile.

Aoife either didn't notice or didn't think her remarks were worth acknowledging. She gave Terry a long look. 'Please excuse me. I'm going to the bathroom. Dr Price will be with you presently. Do take a seat.'

As soon as the door into the toilets closed, Terry peered over the edge of the counter, hoping to have a look at the diary Aoife had been writing in when she came in. When she leaned over to reach for it, she accidentally knocked a magazine off Aoife's desk onto the floor. Panicking, she scooted around to pick it up. She put it back on the edge of the desk, smiling as she saw it was *Real Crime*, a true-crime magazine. Not what she'd expected. Some women appeared to lap up this type of gutter journalism – 'true' was a gross overstatement.

As she straightened up, she saw the line of diaries packed together on the shelf under the countertop. She was impressed. Aoife liked to keep hard copies of the workings of the office, just like Terry kept her notebooks. Maybe they had more in common than she had thought.

She turned back to the day of her last appointment. There

was the name of the couple who'd come in to see Reagan – Watson. So she had almost heard it correctly – it wasn't too far from Watts. There was an exclamation mark beside it.

Out of the corner of her eye she saw a rather snazzy overnight-style bag with bright-blue handles tucked behind Aoife's desk. The design was vaguely familiar. It was the unusual blue colour of the handles – she was convinced she had seen that bag somewhere before. She pulled out her mobile and took a few photographs of it and some pages in the diary.

Then, Terry heard the door opening and barely made it back to the patient, or rather *client*, side of the reception desk before Aoife reappeared, straightening the front of her skirt.

'True crime fan?' Terry pointed at the magazine on the edge of the desk.

After taking her seat once more, Aoife looked down. 'What? Oh, that! Someone left it behind. It's not really my thing. I was going to add it to the stack of magazines, but maybe I shouldn't.'

'You're right. It's a bit grisly. I prefer a bit of fiction myself. What's the latest at the book club?'

'This month it's the memoirs of Paulo Coia. It was supposed to be *Strange Sally Diamond*, but Dr Price vetoed it in light of recent events.'

'That's a great book – I love Liz Nugent. Who's this bloke Coia? I've never heard of him.'

'He's an Italian chef.'

'None the wiser. But I do love Italy. The food, the fashion ...' Terry said wistfully. 'I couldn't help but notice that gorgeous bag you've got,' she continued, pointing to where it sat on the floor behind Aoife. 'I would absolutely love one like that. It's so unique-looking. I'm sure my friend Becs has one similar, but in a different colour. She's a label fiend. What brand is it?'

Aoife glanced around to see what Terry was referring to. 'Oh, that's not mine. I could never afford that bag on my salary. It's Dr Reagan's. He leaves it out here so I can remind him to take it home. He always used to go without it. He keeps his case files in it.'

At that moment, Maeve Price called Terry into her room. Terry gave a little wiggle of her fingers by way of goodbye to Aoife. Was it her imagination or did a look of relief flash across the woman's face?

Terry followed Maeve into her office. 'Have you had a break-in or something?' she asked, feigning innocence. 'A detective has come in to see Dr Reagan.'

'No. There's nothing I know about. It's probably about one of his patients.' The psychiatrist settled in her chair across from Terry.

'Has something happened to one of them?'

'I've really no idea.' Dr Price was not going to be drawn. 'Now, how have you been?'

'Much the same.' Terry watched as Maeve typed something. She decided to have another try. 'I see Aoife prefers pen and paper. I haven't seen a desk diary in years.'

'What?' she looked at Terry, puzzled. 'Aoife's diary?'

Terry smiled. 'She was scribbling away in it when I came in.'

Maeve sat back. 'Oh, that. Well, that's more for Dr Reagan's sake. We had gone electronic before Aoife started, but Dr Reagan is a bit paranoid about hackers getting into his patient notes. He still keeps paper files. Aoife has been a godsend since he took her on after her husband's death. She's reorganised the office and more besides. As long as they don't expect *me* to go back to all that writing, I don't really care. It would be a nightmare.'

Then Maeve rested her hands on the keyboard and looked at her intently. 'Actually, a diary might not be a bad idea, Terry. Maybe you should try keeping one. Record your feelings. That kind of thing.'

Terry was horrified at the thought. Her notebooks were for her cases, not her feelings. And she wasn't going to give up pumping Maeve for information.

Time to try a different tack. 'I've been having anxiety attacks.' Maeve looked interested and waited for Terry to expand. 'I think it's to do with these recent cases I'm working on. I think it's because they both had difficult relationships and I find that …' She looked vague.

'Traumatic?' Maeve asked.

'Challenging. Weirdly, they were both patients, or clients or whatever, of Dr Reagan's.'

Maeve closed down at that. 'You know I cannot discuss other patients with you.'

'Oh, sorry. It's not about them, per se, but about trying to understand what compels people to do what they do. The unpredictability of people – and, well, life – can make me anxious.' Terry tried to look and sound contrite. She knew she could not press anything further without alerting Dr Price. She would hear everything from Fraser later.

Terry gave Aoife a quick wave as she headed for the lift. The doors opened and she was almost bowled over by a short stocky man with dark hair exiting.

She steadied herself. 'Wanker!' she muttered under her breath as she saw him disappear through the glass doors into the reception area she had just left. There was something vaguely familiar about him. Then she felt bad. If he was here for therapy, he might have good reason to be rude.

Taking her phone out of her bag, she turned it back on. On a whim she googled Aoife Foster. She scrolled down a few entries and then found an *Evening Herald* article. *Dublin businessman Francis Foster killed in freak accident.* She opened the link just as the lift reached the ground floor. Francis had fallen over the edge of a balcony while on a golfing trip to Spain. Poor Aoife, that must have been a terrible shock. But the fact that Maeve Price mentioned Reagan taking Aoife on was interesting. Had he felt sorry for her? Terry decided it might be no harm to have a look at Aoife's husband's death.

Fraser was waiting downstairs, hands in pockets, pacing back and forth on the marble concourse. She could tell by his demeanour that his interview with Reagan hadn't gone particularly well.

'You don't look too happy. Was Dr Reagan not very forthcoming?'

'I'd forgotten how infuriating that man could be.'

He cast a quick glance at her and she realised he had let slip something he hadn't wanted her to know about. Her guess was that he and his ex-wife had been another of those hopeful, or rather hopeless, couples seeking help from Reagan. This wasn't the time to press it. She'd keep that for another time.

Terry deliberately kept her face impassive. 'So, what did he have to say?'

'He admitted to knowing Martin Higgins and Dr Maguire in a professional capacity, but said he hadn't seen either recently. He played the confidentiality card and he's refusing to release their files.'

'Does he have to?' she asked. 'Don't you need to make an application under some data act or something?' She was desperate to redeem herself after their depressing end to the weekend. 'What if I ask the coroner to get access to them because I think it's relevant as part of the post-mortem? It is, in a way. It might save you getting in the midst of a legal wrangle?'

Fraser didn't respond, he seemed to be deep in thought. They pushed through the doors out to the car park. Terry got in the car and fastened her seat belt. She turned to Fraser. 'Have you had dealings with Reagan in the past? You said—'

'I know what I said. Just leave it,' said Fraser, his teeth gritted.

Terry sat back thinking on the drive into town. She suddenly remembered the bag.

'John? I need to go to WSH.' She looked at Fraser's profile – there was not as much as a flicker. He was lost in thought. She ploughed on. 'Fraser. This could be important. I saw a bag behind Aoife's desk. She said it was Reagan's. I need to see that

CCTV footage from outside Court 18 when we were looking for sightings of Higgins.'

She saw his jaw tense. She wasn't sure whether it was because he didn't want her in the incident room or he didn't want her to look at the footage. Either way, she wasn't going to be fobbed off.

'There!' Terry stabbed a finger at Fraser's laptop screen an hour later. 'Look!' She held up her mobile in front of him to show him the photos she'd taken. 'There's the bag beside Aoife's desk. It was the blue handles that struck me instantly.' She held her phone up so they could look at the photo and the CCTV footage side by side. 'It's the exact same colour, a Gucci bag. They're identical.'

'They certainly look alike,' he agreed. She could tell he was trying not to seem too excited by this development.

Then, she tapped her phone to pull up the website she'd looked at earlier and showed it to him. 'Here, it's on the Gucci website: the Gucci Savoy large duffle bag. "Part of the Gucci Lido collection, beige and blue supreme canvas with bright-blue handles and blue leather trim",' she read aloud from the screen. 'It has a blue and red web trim – that's the stripe, there.' She pointed back to Fraser's laptop. 'See?'

Gucci bags don't usually have these bright-blue leather handles. This one was exclusive to the States until recently. Not that I know much about fancy labels. But it's a bit of a—'

'Don't say coincidence.' Fraser groaned. 'I'll get it checked out, but even if it turns out to be the same bag, it doesn't mean the man holding it is Reagan, or that he had anything to do with Higgins's murder.'

'Well, it's a potential new lead,' said Terry. 'He might have been the last person to be seen speaking with Higgins, who then turns up dead the next day. There might be something in it.'

'I guess so,' said Fraser, who had picked up his phone and was typing a message.

Terry replayed the full CCTV footage. She jumped up. 'John! Look!'

Fraser put down his mobile and gave her his full attention.

'This is Higgins leaving the CCJ. There are people exiting the main door after him. But look ...' Terry zoomed in to a darkly attired short man keeping a steady pace behind Higgins. 'See this man coming through the court doors, walking behind Higgins. Does it look like he's following him? He's definitely familiar. I'm sure I saw him today when we were leaving the psych clinic. He was going in. I knew I recognised his face. He was in Court 18 on the day of Hunt's appearance.'

Fraser squinted at the screen. 'He looks like Judge Henderson's cousin, his tipstaff.'

Terry was maddening, but Fraser had to admit she was astute. But what had a judge, his tipstaff and a psychologist got to do with Higgins, if anything? And where did the Hayes gang stand in all of this mess? He rubbed his forehead. This investigation was wearing him down, and the pressure from above was intense. He needed evidence. But he hoped he had persuaded

Terry to leave this to him. She hadn't complained when he said he needed all hands, and that included DS Mary Healy.

What he hadn't told her was that DG Bob Paterson, Higgins's best friend and thorn in Terry's side, had been in touch with both him and the garda doctor, begging to come back to work. That certainly wasn't a given. He knew Bob had been influenced by Higgins, but Bob was a good cop, despite his attitude. Could he trust Bob? He knew Terry wouldn't want him back on her team for sure.

He watched as Terry walked off to find Ahern. He would check in with her later.

32

Terry drove out of the car park at Walter Scott House, delighted to have her car back. She had to admit it looked better than before: it had been spruced up with a valet and brand new tyres. Now she was mobile again it was an opportunity to pop in to her flat to get some more clothes. She had packed in such a hurry that she hadn't brought a lot of her work clothes with her, and she was fed up of repeating the same outfits. She could be in and out in minutes.

As she drove along the quays towards Spencer Dock, she thought about what they had just learned. She had promised not to interfere and let Fraser take the investigation into Martin Higgins's death from here. But that didn't mean she was walking away from the Maguire investigation and the cold case reviews. She needed to see if she could find links between some of the cases. That was her strength.

The security guard at the entrance to the car park of her building flagged her down. 'Hi, Doc! Good to see you back.

You can park in your usual space. They've installed a few more cameras in the black spots, but I'll keep a close eye on your car.' He slapped her roof and took a step back, then seemed to reconsider and leaned back into her open window. 'There've been a couple of people asking about you. I told them you were away on holiday.'

'Thanks. Did they say who they were?'

'Nah. One was a big bloke, but he seemed okay. The other guy was a bit ... jittery. I threatened to call the guards and he scarpered.'

'Well, if anyone else turns up asking for me, just call the guards straightaway,' she said, trying to sound nonchalant. Who the hell was asking around about her? She wouldn't be letting Fraser know anyway. Next thing she'd know, she'd be under constant garda supervision.

'You're the boss.'

The flat was as she had left it, apart from a pungent smell that she traced to an open milk carton in the fridge. She swept the entire contents of the fridge, all looking quite wilted or suspect in some way, into a black plastic bag and dropped it in the bin in the car park on her way out, glancing warily about as she did so. The feeling of unease lingered until she had driven out of the car park and was safely on the quays.

She parked outside the mortuary and popped in to see Bella before sprinting upstairs to the OSP.

'Mrs C, could you check up on the Tormey death for me, please? It seems the prof wasn't informed that X-rays had been taken at the time.'

'Preposterous!' Mrs C looked horrified. 'How dare that

coroner conceal information from Professor Boyd. He will be furious. He gave an opinion in good faith. Something like that could have harmed his reputation.'

'It might not be a big deal,' said Terry calmly. 'I can check them out first. There might not be anything worth worrying about.'

'I'll still have to let him know. I've a good mind to get onto the coroner,' Mrs C said, bustling over to her desk. 'I know her type. She's only the coroner for Carlow.'

Terry rolled her eyes – she seemed to do that a lot when she was dealing with Mrs Carey. She guessed from that statement there was a pecking order among the coroners, the Dublin coroner being top dog. 'Well, maybe start with Garda Dunphy. I spoke to him on Friday night.' Terry felt bad setting an irate office manager on him, he had sounded like a gentle soul. 'He might already have persuaded the radiology department to send him copies.'

'Leave it with me.' Mrs Carey picked up a large brown envelope from her desk and held it out to Terry. 'The inquest file you asked for, a Mr O'Neill. The Wicklow coroner is a lovely man. He is very grateful to you for reviewing the death. He said if there is anything else you need, to get back to him.'

'Good. Just don't expect the Carlow coroner to be so obliging.' Despite that, Terry knew that Mrs Carey would have the Tormey X-rays by the end of the day. 'Is Niamh in her lab?'

It was Mrs Carey's turn to roll her eyes. 'She's in the tea room.'

Terry smiled. 'I'm guessing she's entertaining by the look on your face.'

'The guard who brought that up.' Mrs C pointed at the envelope in Terry's hand.

At that moment they heard Niamh's voice – it appeared to be a one-sided conversation. They watched as Niamh waved off the guard. She turned and grinned at them. 'Result!' She punched the air. 'He'll be in Mulholland's Thursday night.'

Mrs Carey shook her head and muttered, 'God help him.'

Terry coughed to cover up a laugh. 'Niamh, enough about your love life – can you get hold of the histology for these cases?' She handed the technician a Post-it note with the cases she was interested in, including Owen O'Neill and Emmett Tormey. 'Ask Mrs C if you need more details. I have to speak to Michael about another name to add – it's to do with the Maguire death. He was double-checking the details. You'll have to get onto your pals in the hospital histology labs for them as they weren't state cases, so the PMs were carried out by hospital pathologists. Tell the pathologists to speak to their coroner if they have an issue.'

She had more or less dismissed Mr Irish Bobbitt and the guy who'd drowned at sea as not of any real interest, but she had to be a hundred per cent sure there wasn't anything she was missing. The histology would be helpful.

Terry took the brown envelope into the conference room and emptied its contents onto the table. What was it about Owen O'Neill's death that perturbed the Wicklow coroner?

The gardaí had prepared a C71 form informing the coroner of the circumstances of Mr O'Neill's death in 2022. He had been fifty-two years old when he died, and living in the family home with his nearly adult children. He had recently separated from his wife and ran a kitchen-fitting business.

His daughter, Aisling O'Neill, had found him dead at home, submerged in the bath on a Sunday evening. She had stayed at her boyfriend's on the Saturday night. Terry made a note – *When last seen alive? By whom? Other children?*

His GP had said he was healthy and on no medication. Beside this she wrote – *Drinker?*

The local gardaí had attended. The death was not thought suspicious and was treated as an accident/suicide. She circled that.

That was the first red flag. She knew from experience that once some gardaí had a theory, it would take a juggernaut to dissuade them. She hated when she was called to a scene only to be talked at and told what the guard thought had happened. She knew it pissed them off when she stopped them mid-flow, telling them she preferred to make up her own mind, thank you very much. *Just give me the facts, not opinions*, was her mantra. Maybe she should heed her own advice and row in her theories on Higgins and his death.

The post-mortem report was fairly comprehensive, but succinct. There were no injuries described. The skin was white and wrinkled, indicating he had been submerged for some hours at least. The death wasn't treated as suspicious so no post-mortem photographs were taken. The only photograph in the file was one of O'Neill in his garden. He was a rather handsome chap, she thought, all floppy hair and cheeky smile. A bit like someone else she knew.

Internally, all was good except for froth in his airways and waterlogged lungs, part drowning, part heart failure, which is what she would expect in freshwater drowning, quite different from the lung changes in the guy who drowned in the sea at Bettystown. She would check the histology in both to confirm her interpretation.

The toxicology report showed that only a blood sample had been analysed – his bladder must have been empty. He might have had a seizure in the terminal stages of drowning or had taken a pee before he got in the bath. There was no doubt he had been drinking – not a shitload, but enough to make him a bit dopey – and he had taken temazepam. Not a good combination – both are depressants and would likely have knocked him out.

It would be easy for him to slip under the water and drown in that state. So it could have been an accident, not necessarily a suicide. But where did the temazepam come from if he hadn't been prescribed it by his GP? He didn't seem the type to have a dealer, but you never knew. Or he might have gone to another GP if he was having mental health issues after his wife left and didn't want people who knew him to find out he was struggling.

At the moment there were a few question marks, but nothing to get excited about. She would wait until Niamh got the histology slides from the lab in the hospital in Loughlinstown.

There wasn't any more Terry could do at the moment to help the family.

'Hi, roomie. Are you busy?' Terry put her phone on loudspeaker as she doodled on the brown envelope the O'Neill file had been in.

'What do you think, Tez?' Michael sounded frazzled. 'What do you want now?'

'You know the rogue DNA profile you found in the knot from Dr Maguire's ligature? Can you please give me the name of the case it matched with?'

'I might have known. Hold on. I need to go get the report.' A few seconds later she heard paper rustling. 'Still there?' 'Uh-huh.' She sat, pen poised. 'Shoot!'

'Right. The DNA profile from the knot was not a match with Dr Maguire. It matched with a profile obtained from a pill bottle found at the scene of a death a couple of years ago. The deceased was an Owen O'Neill.'

33

Fraser sat in the office at FSI with Terry and Michael. 'Let me get this straight. Randomly, two deaths you're involved with, a recent suspicious death and a cold case, are linked. Right?'

'Right!' Terry and Michael answered in unison.

'Dr Maguire and Owen O'Neill,' Terry continued. 'DNA in the knot of the ligature in Dr Maguire's death and a DNA profile from a pill bottle from Owen O'Neill's house match.'

'You're sure?'

Terry looked askance. 'Do you need to ask? It's Michael. He double-, no, triple-checked before he would even give me the deceased's name.'

'And the DNA profile hasn't been identified,' Michael butted in, giving Terry a side eye.

'So you don't know who this person is who's involved in the two deaths?'

Michael just shrugged.

'And there is no reasonable explanation for this?' Fraser looked from one to the other. This was an almighty headache. Upping the Maguire case to a murder enquiry had been on the cards since Terry had expressed her doubts, but this was a whole different ball game. Randomly linking with a death a few years earlier. And in a different county. Bugger DNA.

As if reading his mind, Michael responded, 'DNA doesn't lie!' He threw his hands up in the air. 'And I don't make mistakes.'

'But gardaí do.' Fraser knew he had touched a nerve. 'I wasn't implying cross-contamination here, but we've had problems with people tampering with evidence in the past.'

'There is no immediate other connection between these cases.'

'Why would anyone tamper with the evidence?' seethed Terry, her frustration with Fraser clearly increasing by the second.

'No need to be so sarky, Tez. Fraser has a point.' Michael looked directly at Fraser. 'It was the first thing I checked – the trail, who had handled the specimens. There was no crossover. In fact, the pill bottle in the O'Neill case was handed in by the O'Neill family. It wasn't found until a few days after the scene was examined.'

Fraser nodded, but he would ask Mary Healy to do a thorough check. You could never be certain that there wasn't a dodgy guard somewhere.

Terry cut in. 'We were already considering that Maguire's death wasn't suicide or an accident.'

Fraser shot her a look.

'Okay, I thought his death was suspicious. What else will it take to convince you? Right from the get-go I said there was something fishy about it – and that wasn't because Maguire's house was a stone's throw from the sea.' Fraser glared at her, Terry's attempt at humour falling flat. She ploughed on. 'Michael proved that the chandelier could take his weight. The ligature was at least part cut through and then made to look as if it was frayed.'

Michael chipped in. 'It was part cut with something sharp, and part rough cut to make it look as if it snapped. I stressed a length of the same cord and it could definitely have taken his weight.'

Terry nodded in agreement and continued counting off her points on her fingers. 'Then, point three' – she pointed at her left middle finger – 'one of the knots is a type used by fishermen.'

'Sailors, sailing people, yachties,' Michael explained.

'Thanks, Michael, we get it.' Terry rolled her eyes. 'And we know Maguire didn't know his port from his starboard. He was asphyxiated, there is no doubt about that, but not necessarily by hanging. The cord could have been looped around his neck and pulled tight. I don't think he was suspended.' Terry smirked, seemingly to realise that she now had Fraser's full attention. 'Then there's the way he was laid out – draped over that couch like one of those reclining nudes you see in the National Gallery. I'd have expected him to be lying in a heap if he'd strung himself up and the cord simply snapped.' She pointed at her left thumb. 'And then there's the needle in his penis.'

Fraser flinched and put up his hand. 'Okay, okay, I get the picture. Let's say I accept your hypothesis, Dr O'Brien, then whoever killed Maguire was somehow involved with this other man.'

'Owen O'Neill, a fifty-two-year-old chippie from Wicklow,'

clarified Terry. 'What I don't know is what he would have in common with a prick like Maguire.'

Michael sniggered. Fraser glared at him. 'I just thought that was funny. Prick. Penis.' Michael gave a shrug and continued. 'Maybe he fitted Maguire's kitchen. It was pretty spectacular. Although, I'd have put in bifold doors opening onto the garden.'

'Not helpful, Michael.' Terry scowled at him.

'I really don't need this. Another body in the mix.' Fraser was perplexed.

'Probably two.' Terry gave him an apologetic smile.

Fraser stood. 'Liaise with Mary about this O'Neill death. Anything else I should know?'

Terry and Michael exchanged a look and Terry shook her head.

'Right. I'll need to speak to Cian Nolan – Maguire is his case.' Fraser stretched and made to leave. 'Why didn't you contact him about all this?'

'I thought you were the senior investigating officer.' For some reason, Terry couldn't meet his eyes.

'And make sure you leave the investigating to us. An Garda Síochána.' Fraser made sure there was a warning in his tone.

'Right!' Terry and Michael said in unison.

He stifled a smile as they both nodded like recalcitrant schoolchildren. *And just as reckless*, he thought.

Fraser went straight to WSH. Mary had interviewed the women allegedly assaulted by Maguire. The impression she'd got was that they were decidedly unhappy that Maguire had escaped going to court. As far as they were concerned, the coward had committed suicide to avoid being convicted and punished for his crimes.

Meanwhile, Ahern was looking for links between Dr Reagan, Judge Henderson and Henderson's cousin, who worked as his personal aide or tipstaff, and rechecking the CCTV footage from the court complex.

Fraser still wasn't sure where Higgins's death fitted in. He was sure the Hayeses were involved somehow, given the prostitute's DNA being found on Higgins's handcuffs and Terry having evidence that the handcuffs weren't necessarily anything to do with his murder. He was kicking himself at losing the opportunity to ask the women they had found in the brothel about Higgins. If it wasn't the Hayeses who'd murdered Higgins, someone must have known he was going to be at Delaney Gardens that Thursday afternoon and set a trap for him.

More urgently, there had been a couple more drug-related deaths and God knows how many near misses. The information from the undercover guards all pointed to drugs cut with fentanyl being imported and distributed by gang members affiliated with the Hayeses. The other gangs weren't happy – the tenuously balanced status quo was being disrupted. It could all kick off at any time. This had to be nipped in the bud.

34

Terry sat at the conference table of the OSP staring at the pile of files in front of her. It was like juggling sand. Impossible. She needed to get a handle on what was going on with all these investigations. But she couldn't concentrate. Her mind was on Mags again. Where was she? And where were the rest of the missing prostitutes? Were they okay? Were they being hidden somewhere by the Hayeses because they knew they had something to do with Higgins? Had they been moved out of the country? Terry pushed back her chair, grabbed her coat, and her car keys and put Bella's harness on her. 'Come on, girl, let's get some air.'

She had a route mapped out in her head: after parking her car at the multi-storey car park near the Spire, she would walk down Gardiner Street, cross the Liffey, past Tara Street Station, back across O'Connell Bridge, along the boardwalk and up to Phoenix Park. She knew the main congregation points of the local addicts and dealers – she might just spot someone she knew or someone who knew Mags or Bernice. Maybe they would be more inclined to speak to her than the gardaí – it was worth a try.

Terry walked the length of the quays, all the way to the Phoenix Park entrance, but didn't come across anyone she recognised. Her last hope was the Luas, Dublin's bargain-basement equivalent to Hotel California, transporting cocaine-snorting professionals and heroin-addled addicts amongst the good people of Dublin just trying to get to the shops.

She turned back towards Heuston Station and crossed the road at the lights, keeping her eyes peeled for Mags. This was where she had seen her about three weeks ago. She started over the bridge and, sadly, as always, there was someone sitting begging. All the passers-by quickened their steps and tried to hurry past, pretending he wasn't there. And Terry planned to do the same, such was her determination to complete her mission and get home before dark.

But Bella had other ideas. She came to a halt right in front of him. Terry grimaced and tried to pull her on, but she stood her ground. Terry watched, appalled, as the dog nosed the paper cup at the man's feet and knocked it over. Terry knelt to pick up the few coins that had spilled onto the pavement, feeling terrible.

'Sorry about that. Look, can I get you a tea or something? Maybe a sandwich?'

The man raised his head, but had trouble focusing. Then Terry started. She recognised him, though he was in much worse shape than the last time she'd encountered him.

'I know you. You were Tina's dealer.' She couldn't for the life of her remember his name.

He looked at her blankly.

She tried again. 'Tina McCabe. She OD'd in the park end of last year. You had a patch up near the big house in there.'

A middle-aged woman shoved past her, nearly toppling her. 'Wasting your time on that scum.'

Terry's head whipped around. 'Sorry, were we in your way?' The woman ignored her and walked on. 'Stuck-up bitch,' Terry muttered. She turned back to the man, who was now almost stuporous. 'Have you seen Bernice or Mags?'

There was a flicker of recognition. 'Bernie?' he slurred. 'No, I'm not Bernie, but I need to find her.'

His head dropped onto his chest. She was reluctant to shake him. Instead, she unzipped her bag and rifled through until she dug out a pen and one of her notebooks. Ripping out a page, she wrote down her name and mobile number. 'Here's my number. Please get Bernie or Mags to phone me.'

His head jerked a few times, but she doubted it was in the affirmative – he was barely conscious. She folded up the piece of paper and put it at the bottom of his cup. Digging around in her bag again, she found a few euros and dropped them on top. Gingerly, she placed the cup between his thighs in the hope that any passing opportunist would think twice about grabbing it from his crotch.

She patted his arm then and walked away. It was the best she could do, but it never seemed to be enough.

That night, Terry wakened every hour, checking her phone. It was futile, she knew. The dealer had turned user and he was so out of it that it would be a miracle – if the note was even still there when he rallied – if he knew what it was about. Her number was probably fluttering in the breeze somewhere around Heuston Station.

Terry was in a ratty mood by the time she got to the mortuary the next day. Michael had chosen to ignore her – he wasn't much of a morning person and he preferred amicable silence first thing – and Bella kept her head down in the back seat. It's lucky she wasn't easily offended.

She went up the back stairs from the mortuary, straight into the conference room, and was sitting with her head in her hands when Mrs Carey came in and put a mug of coffee on the table in front of her.

'Thanks, Mrs C. I didn't sleep much last night.'

'I've downloaded Mr Tormey's X-rays onto the system. You'll find them in his file.'

Terry gave her a half-hearted smile in thanks – the woman's efficiency was unparalleled. Picking up her mug, she went over to the table where the desktop computer and the microscope sat. She doodled on the cover of Tormey's file while she waited for the X-ray images to appear.

The computer screen suddenly filled with a rather out-of-focus X-ray of a body. The reason for the poor quality was that the body was encased in a body bag, which meant the radiographer would have had to alter the penetration of the X-rays to get a clear image. It was like standing on the beach trying to take a photograph of fish swimming in the water.

The next image was much better. The body bag must have been opened. That explained the mess in the X-ray department the hospital had complained about. As soon as the bag was unzipped, all the detritus from the fire would have come spilling out. It was the same problem she had in the mortuary when dealing with fire deaths: smoke, ash and soot seemed to have the ability to adhere to any and all surfaces, and was difficult to remove. It was a bugbear of all mortuary technicians, so she was surprised the radiographer had made that decision.

They had probably tried to clear some of the debris off the body to get a clearer view on the X-ray, and maybe they even tried to move the body into a more suitable position by straightening out limbs. Their gloves would have been blackened and that would have transferred soot onto everything they touched and every surface, from floor to ceiling. Black dust and handprints everywhere. A nightmare to clean.

She clicked through all the images, then put them in order: unopened body bag, opened body bag, full body, close-ups head to toes. First, she scanned the debris on and around the body, looking for the missing ring. There were all sorts of metallic objects in the mix, not surprising as the fire had been in a shed. She could make out nails, screws and washers among the little bits and pieces in the bottom of the body bag. Nothing ring-shaped.

Next, she concentrated on the body, or what was left of it. The skull was part burnt through. If she remembered correctly, the pathologist had mentioned an extradural haemorrhage, a large blood clot inside the head, that he attributed to the fire, which might be correct, but he would have needed to send the clot for toxicology to be sure. If Tormey had been whacked over the head and knocked out before the shed was set on fire, the blood leaking into the skull wouldn't have had the same high levels of carbon monoxide as the blood in the body. She needed to check that out.

The left lower leg was detached and the right foot was up by the left shoulder. It must have been a pretty fierce fire – he was part cremated. The arms were in the typical pugilistic pose – elbow, wrist and finger joints flexed, as if sparring with an opponent – which was just due to the heat cooking and shrinking the muscles, a bit like the Sunday joint in the oven. The wrists had fractured under the strain, and she could see the jagged shards of the broken ends of the bone. Part of the lower ribcage was burnt through, and she imagined the internal organs would be similarly heat damaged – puppet organs, they were called, as they shrivelled and shrank in the heat.

So far, there was nothing that Terry wouldn't expect in a fire death. She would double-check what she could see on these images with what was described in the post-mortem report. But she needed to speak to someone who had attended the scene at the time the body was found. She wanted to know where he was in the shed and what position the body was in.

Terry went back to the hands. The family had asked about his wedding ring so that was one question she should be able to answer. She checked the right hand first. Despite the fingers being curled into a fist, she could make out the individual hand bones. Except for the right little finger – it was missing. She tried to magnify the image but it still wasn't a clear view.

She looked through a few images until she found the best X-ray of the left arm and hand. She enlarged the image. All four fingers were missing from just below the knuckles. Zooming in further affected the clarity so she fiddled with the focus until she was satisfied. This didn't make sense.

Terry went back to the right arm and hand. Something caught her eye on the shaft of the ulna, midway up the forearm: a V-shaped chip out of the bone.

'Hi, Alan. Sorry to disturb you.'

'No problem. What can I help you with?'

'I need your help. I'm looking into a fire death from about three years back. A chap died in a fire in his shed in Carlow. You're down as crime scene manager.'

'It rings a bell. Sort of.' He didn't sound so sure.

'His name was Tormey. It was treated as an accidental fire death at the time. The PM was done in the mortuary in Loughlinstown. Does that jog any memories? The OSP was only involved later because there had been some concerns after the initial examinations. The prof didn't get to see the body and he wasn't told about X-rays being taken.'

'Hang on a sec, I'm just retrieving the file.' Terry heard the sound of a mouse clicking. 'Yeah. I remember it now. I wasn't happy about a few things at the scene. I'd need to get out my original notes, but it was something about the lock on the door. Just give me a minute to pull it up on the screen. Ah! I remember. The SIO was a bollocks. Wouldn't listen. I'd forgotten about it. Is the inquest coming up?'

'Long done and dusted,' said Terry. The coroner didn't call anyone other than the wife. But that's not why I rang you. It just came on my radar because I asked the divine Mrs Carey to help me find any unusual cases as part of my investigations into Higgins and Maguire. This is one of them.'

'So what can I tell you?'

'For a start, how did you think the fire started?'

'It was hard to be certain, but he was a smoker and the shed was full of flammable materials. I didn't find anything that shouldn't have been there. But you know how these scenes are. Especially after high-pressure hoses have pulverised everything.'

'I'm amazed you can determine anything from them. I can usually barely see the body in the fire debris.' Terry thought a bit of flattery might help.

'Years of experience.'

'There is one other thing,' said Terry. O'Neill's wedding ring. It wasn't found in the shed?'

'Yeah, I remember the family asked me to retrieve it, but it wasn't on the body. I sifted through the debris in what remained of the shed. I've nothing like that recorded in my report. It didn't get chucked into the body bag when they scooped up the body?'

'No. I would have thought if it came adrift it would have been under the body. And there's something bothering me. Did you find a biggish knife or an axe in the shed?'

'Spade, hammer, wrench, spanners, all kinds of tools in a tool box. Just what I would expect. Good brands too,' Alan said. 'Nothing exciting I can see.'

'Was the search confined to the shed?'

'Excuse me, Dr O'Brien. I'm a professional. What are you insinuating?' She could tell he was teasing her. 'I had a search team do a fingertip search of the garden. I was looking for a key.'

'Yes, I saw that.'

'As far as I know the key wasn't found either. It was put down to the fire brigade's overzealous hosing. I couldn't really argue with that. There wasn't any reason to suspect anyone else was involved.'

'Yeah, the guard I spoke to said the same about the ring.'

'Right. I've got the full report here – hold on while I scroll down through it. Ah! Here we are.' She heard him mumbling. 'Football, garden fork.' She tapped her pen on the table, waiting. 'I should get that lot to clear my dad's garden. So here's something interesting.' Ahern read out: '"Flower bed to right of remains of burnt-out shed. Small axe part buried in soil beneath shrub. No fire damage." Is that the kind of sharp implement you're looking for?'

'It might be. Where was the axe taken?'

'Doesn't look like it was submitted to FSI, so it's probably still in a locker in the garda station.'

'Do you think you could check it out?'

'Okay. But if it's not urgent it might be in a week or so.'

'I think it is urgent,' said Terry. 'I think some of Mr Tormey's fingers could have been chopped off. The bone ends are very straight. I would expect splintering if the bone damage was due to the fire. And there's a definite chip out of the bone that runs from the elbow down towards the little finger.'

'Fuck!' Ahern gasped. 'Why would anyone do that? Are you sure?'

'Eighty per cent. I've only got pretty ropey X-rays to go on. I don't want to jump to conclusions.'

'Really?'

'There's no need to be so sarcastic,' she retorted.

'I believe you, Doc.' She heard him laugh. 'What do you want done with the axe if I find it?'

'Give it to your boyfriend in FSI.'

35

Mrs Carey spoke to the Wicklow coroner and got information on Owen O'Neill's family. His wife had since died and the children had dispersed. Only the younger daughter, Aisling, still lived locally. Aisling had been suspicious of Terry's motives when she called. She'd had negative experiences with the press and the gardaí, she explained. She only agreed to a meeting when Terry explained that it was the coroner who had asked her to look into her father's death.

The following day, Terry drove down to Wicklow, not sure how helpful this would be.

'Mam died six months ago. Breast cancer.' Aisling O'Neill stirred milk into her coffee. They had agreed to meet in a café on the main street, just along from the AIB where she worked.

'Sorry for your loss.' Terry mirrored Aisling's movements, hoping that would relax her. They both took a sip of coffee.

'Well. It was a blessing in the end. I'd had enough.' Terry was taken aback. The young woman didn't look or sound upset about her mother's death. 'My brother Tadhg took off on a gap year not long after she was diagnosed. He was always selfish. She spoiled him rotten – fat lot of good it did her. Donna's down in west Cork, so she was no use either. I was left looking after her.' She sounded bitter.

'That must have been hard on you,' Terry said sympathetically. 'Particularly so soon after losing your dad.'

Aisling's face softened. 'He was a great dad. I miss him.' Her teaspoon clattered onto the table.

'I hope you don't mind the coroner asking me to look into his death,' Terry said. 'I don't want to upset your family.'

'No. Me and Donna, we were never happy with the gardaí. They thought he'd committed suicide because she'd left him.'

'Your mum and dad were separated at the time of his death?'

'Yeah, but Dad thought she'd come back. She had before. Honestly, I think she was happy he died. I know that's a terrible thing to say, but she didn't care about him. She was the one who walked out, leaving Dad to look after us.' Aisling stared into her cup. 'She always acted the victim. Even got Dad to go and see the priest. Well not him exactly, some odd couples counsellor in the church. Tried to make out he abused her. Dad was so embarrassed he stopped going to mass. And then one of her snobby friends told her about this big-shot counsellor in Rockroad Clinic. It cost a fortune but Dad went along with it. He would have done anything for her. From Dad's accounts of their sessions, she twisted everything he said. It was easier for him to go along with her narrative.'

'He still loved her?'

'He doted on her. Wouldn't let us say anything against her. Even though she took up with a new fella when she and Dad were technically still together.'

'You've had a difficult few years. Are you sure you're up to talking to me?' Terry wasn't great in these situations when people were a tad emotional. She liked things matter-of-fact.

Aisling sat up straight and pushed her cup aside. 'Don't mind me, just feeling sorry for myself.' She reached over and grasped Terry's arm. 'Dad wasn't depressed. I know he would never have taken his own life.'

Terry pulled the file out of her bag and laid it on the table. She spun it around so they could look at it together. 'I've been through this. Your dad was found partly submerged in his bath and the post-mortem findings are consistent with him drowning.' She watched Aisling's expression carefully to gauge how she was handling this.

The other woman frowned. 'We already knew that the findings said he drowned. That's what you wanted to meet up to tell me? I thought there was new evidence or something.' There was a note of despair in Aisling's voice. She made to stand. 'Well. This was a waste of time.'

'Wait,' implored Terry. 'Just hear me out.' She picked up the bundle of papers and shuffled through it, putting the toxicology report on top of the pile. 'At the time of his death he had alcohol and a tranquilliser in his system.'

Aisling sat back and folded her arms. 'We've been through this before. Dad only took an occasional Guinness. Mam drank enough for both of them. The house was full of drink. He was always getting bottles as thank-you gifts from his customers.

I told the gardaí that, but Mam told them he had taken to the bottle when they split. She harped on about mental health issues, even said that was why she had to leave. Who was going to pay any heed to his children? To me?'

She looked so forlorn that Terry felt for her. She patted Aisling's arm. 'I will.'

Coughing to cover her embarrassment at her display of emotion, Terry snapped back into control. 'Have you heard of this drug?' She pointed at the report. 'Temazepam.'

'I've heard of it. But Dad wasn't on anything. I don't know where that came from.'

'Were there any drugs in the house?' Terry was startled when Aisling slammed her coffee cup onto the table so hard it seemed likely it would crack.

'No drugs! What kind of family do you think we are? I know that was what the gardaí were hinting at.'

'Sorry, I didn't mean to imply anyone taking illicit drugs,' Terry said, hoping her measured tone would re-establish calm. 'I just meant was he on any prescribed medication?'

'No. But when we were clearing up after the funeral, we found a little brown plastic pill bottle under Dad's bed. There was nothing in it and no label. I handed it into the garda station. Is it important?'

Terry guessed this was the bottle Michael had recovered a rogue DNA profile from. 'Did you ask your mother about it?'

'You kidding? I told you she didn't care.'

'Right.' Terry put a question mark on the tox report. 'What happened at the inquest?'

'It was a bit of a blur. I remember the coroner was very good trying to explain everything to us.'

'Did your solicitor not ask questions?'

'We didn't have one. I didn't know you could. Uncle Colin, Dad's brother, asked the gardaí about a few things, but they had made their minds up. He'd killed himself. They explained away everything. I didn't really understand what was going on, but I got the feeling the coroner wasn't convinced by the garda theories.'

'What about your mother?'

'Mam didn't want to be there. Didn't even sit with me and Donna. She sat across the aisle with Tadhg. And as soon as the coroner gave his verdict she got up and left. We didn't see her again until she got her diagnosis and the boyfriend did a runner.' She turned and looked directly at Terry, and Terry noticed the tears. 'I was left to deal with her.'

Aisling rummaged about in her bag and pulled out a little pack of tissues and blew her nose. She took out her purse and produced a photograph. 'That's Dad with us at Disney World in Florida.'

Terry saw a happy family snap. The man with his arms around the shoulders of two teenage girls was pretty handsome in a Hugh Grant kind of way, Terry observed again – all floppy strawberry-blond hair and a charming smile.

Aisling smoothed the picture out. 'I was always jealous of Donna – she got Dad's hair.'

Terry stared at the photo of Owen O'Neill. 'But you got his smile.'

'He had this habit of flicking his hair back out of his eyes.

He knew it annoyed the hell out of Mam. He thought it made him look sexy,' said Aisling with a small laugh.

Terry thought it very probably did.

Aisling's smile dropped then. 'I didn't even recognise him at first when I went to identify him at the mortuary. The guard thought I was just being awkward, that I didn't want to believe it was him.'

Terry patted her hand. 'It's not uncommon. You just don't want to accept he's dead.'

'No, it wasn't that. His head was shaved.'

Terry switched her phone on when she got back into her car. There were missed calls from Fraser, Mrs C, Michael and her dad. It was 1.30 p.m. – she would be back at the OSP before 3p.m. Whatever they wanted could wait. Mrs C had probably tracked something down for her, and Michael, well, Michael would be panicking. She had left Bella with him and he hated having to take her out for a walk, as he was afraid she might go for a poo. He even wore disposable gloves in case he had to use one of the poo bags, which always made him look suspect to other dog walkers. Fraser and her dad would no doubt be checking in. She switched the phone to silent.

A couple of things Aisling had said would need following up, most notably the mention of O'Neill's head being shaved. When Terry was stopped at the lights she scrolled through her contacts and dialled the mortuary at Loughlinstown.

'Hi, Stevie, it's Terry O'Brien. I'll not keep you. Do you keep records of the state of bodies when they're brought in?' She explained what she was looking for and he promised to call back. Stevie was the mortuary technician, an APT, and he was brilliant at his job. Terry loved working with him.

Her phone vibrated a couple of minutes later. She checked the caller ID before answering. 'Stevie. Thanks for getting back so quickly. Did you check the description of his hair?'

'Hair recently shaved, some skin nicks. Anything else?'

'No. So his head was shaved when he came in? It wasn't shaved during the post-mortem?'

'No way. You know what the doc's like. She'd get mad if I didn't send the bodies back to the family the way they came in. We've had families complain about us disfiguring their loved ones. So it's insurance. Sometimes she even has me take photographs.'

She thanked Stevie and rang off. Maybe Owen O'Neill had been having some sort of breakdown. Shaving his head might have been a cry for help. Despite what Aisling thought, maybe it *was* suicide.

At the next lights she noticed the sign for Rockroad Clinic and made up her mind. Couples counselling in Rockroad, Aisling had said. Who did Terry know was a *big-shot* counsellor? Dr Reagan. It was worth a punt.

She hoped Aoife would be out for lunch. No such luck. The receptionist was sitting at her desk as usual. Terry would have to brazen it out.

'Hi, Aoife,' she said cheerily.

'Dr O'Brien, do you have an appointment? Dr Price is

lecturing over at Maynooth.' Aoife's brow was furrowed, worried she had made a mistake, and Terry could see she was checking her appointment calendar on the screen.

Terry leaned over the reception desk. 'No. I don't have one.'

Aoife looked puzzled. 'Do you need an emergency appointment? I could squeeze you in tomorrow morning.'

'No, it's not that. It's …' Terry glanced at the reception desk, where a pen was lying next to an open page of her desk diary. *Aha!* 'I think my gold fountain pen might have fallen out of my bag when I was in with Dr Price on Monday. It's really special – my dad gave it to me when I graduated. It has my name engraved on it. Did Maeve find it? Or the cleaner, maybe?'

'She didn't mention anything, and the cleaners usually leave anything they find on my desk.' Aoife sounded a bit narked, as if Terry was accusing her of lying.

'It might have rolled under the couch. Would you mind taking a quick look? Dad's visiting this weekend and I'd feel really bad if I lost it. He'd be so upset if he knew.'

Aoife stood up slowly. 'I suppose, as it's quiet, I could check Dr Price's office.'

'Oh, thank you, Aoife.' Terry clasped her hands to her chest. 'You're so kind.'

As soon as the door closed behind Aoife, Terry leaned over the counter. It was difficult to scan the dates on the diaries at that angle so she hoisted herself up to get a better view. The furthest to her right was for 2001 and they ran consecutively up to 2016. The next was dated 2020, then up to 2024. And 2025 was lying open on Aoife's desk.

Owen O'Neill had died mid-2022, so Terry reckoned

he could have had counselling in the months beforehand. Plucking the 2022 diary from the shelf, she flicked through, looking for his name. She was sweating and kept checking over her shoulder in case someone came in Realising she couldn't read through quickly enough, and reckoning she could flick and click more pages than she could read, she fished out her phone and photographed the diary contents as best she could. It was random and she was probably looking for a needle in a haystack, but she might get lucky.

Then she heard a noise from Maeve's room that sounded like a piece of furniture being dragged across the floor. Terry shoved the 2022 diary back onto the shelf and grabbed the 2025 diary off Aoife's desk, laying it on the counter and taking photos of some of its pages. As soon as the noises lessened, she dropped the diary back onto the desk and walked away from the reception counter.

The door whipped open and a red-faced Aoife emerged, picking carpet fluff off her cardigan. 'Sorry, Dr O'Brien. It definitely isn't here.'

Terry gave a choked sob. She was impressing herself with her acting skills. 'Is there a lost property office for the hospital? Maybe I dropped it downstairs in the main reception area or even the lift.' She pulled a crumpled paper napkin bearing the Bewley's logo from the depths of her bag and dabbed at her eyes, surreptitiously gauging Aoife's reaction. She saw her check her watch.

Aoife sounded hesitant. 'Clara is the one who actually deals with lost items. She keeps the lost and found register.'

'Wow. You don't get that sort of service in the public

hospitals. It's every man for him, or her, self.' Terry realised that sounded more of a criticism and switched to contrite. 'You are so very lucky working in a place that really cares for people.'

'Clara's not working today, I'm afraid.'

Terry was disappointed – she wanted to get rid of Aoife so she could look at the other diaries. She would need to come back another day and try again.

Then Aoife picked up her hospital ID. 'It might take me a little while if you don't mind waiting?'

'It's not accessible online?' Terry was both incredulous and delighted.

'Clara prefers one copy she has full control over. She keeps it in her office on the ground floor.'

'I can't believe you would do that for me. Thank you, Aoife.'

As soon as the receptionist left, she hurried back behind the reception counter and grabbed the 2021 diary intending to try and get a few pages photographed. Her hands were shaking and she was breathing heavily as she worked her way through the pages.

When she heard the lift doors open a few minutes later, she slid the diary back and sprinted back to the seating area.

Aoife looked upset and immediately Terry was worried that she had seen what she was up to. 'Are you all right, Aoife? Has something happened?'

'I'm afraid I didn't have any luck, Dr O'Brien,' she said, her voice tinged with regret.

'You're so good for trying. I won't forget that.' She smiled at the receptionist, sharing a moment of gratitude. She counted to ten and then snapped back to normal and grabbed her bag.

'Thanks for looking anyway, Aoife. I guess I must have dropped it somewhere else.' She almost ran to the door.

'Maybe don't say anything to your father until you've checked everywhere,' Aoife shouted after her.

Terry was thrown briefly, then remembered her lie. 'Good advice.'

Terry sat in her car for a moment, waiting until her heart rate returned to normal before she would start towards the city. That had been equally terrifying and exciting. She felt bad about her deception and subterfuge. Aoife was one of those nice people, always ready to help out. She would bring her a little something at her next appointment.

Terry drove across the East Link but, desperate for the loo, she decided to divert for her flat, rather than head to the OSP. It was a good excuse to check on the place. And she could leave her car in the underground car park and walk back to Michael's.

Terry nodded at the security guard at the car park entrance – she didn't recognise him. They probably had employed a few more in the aftermath of an unknown intruder vandalising a car. Continuing up the ramp to the street, she walked around to the front entrance of her building. She was still wary about someone attacking her car. It felt safer getting the lift up from the lobby. As she pushed through the glass door, the lift doors began to open. She ran across and got in as the doors started closing. As Terry stepped out on her floor, she rifled through her bag for her keys. Suddenly, a door bang closed and she looked up to see a large man stepping away from her door.

'Jim!' she cried out in shock.

Her uncle Jim looked startled. 'Terry. Am I glad I got here before you.'

'What are you doing here? I thought you'd gone home?' She walked towards him then suddenly stopped. She remembered the missed calls. 'Dad! Has something happened? I missed a call from him earlier.'

'No, love. Your dad's fine. I decided to stay on for a few more days. I wasn't in any rush to get back home after the concert.'

'How did you know I'd be here?'

'I didn't. I was meeting an old pal close to here and thought I'd see if you'd moved back in. I took a chance you'd be working from home and it's just as well. Your door wasn't locked.'

'What?' Terry couldn't mask her fear. 'Have you called the guards?'

'No. There's no need to panic. I had a quick look around and there's no one in there. I was just about to call you.'

'I'd better have a look before I call Fraser.'

Despite her bravado, she was trembling as she pushed open the door to her flat. She was sure she had double locked it when she left after picking up those clothes. But then, maybe she just forgot. She had an armful of clothes and a black bin bag full of stinking food when she left. She must have assumed she'd locked the door behind her.

She stood in the hallway, her hand holding the door against the wall, and took a few deep breaths, letting Jim walk on into the living room. She stood behind him in the doorway and scanned the room – everything seemed in place. There was no sign of a disturbance. She turned and put her hand on her bedroom door and tentatively pushed it open. The bed was made but the wardrobe doors hung open and clothes were strewn on the floor.

Jim looked over her shoulder. 'What a mess. Does it look like anything's missing?'

Terry managed a smile. 'It's exactly like I left it.' She bent and gathered up the nearest clothes and dropped them in the wash basket.

Feeling a bit better, she opened the door to the spare room, stuck her head in and let out a screech. 'Jim!'

'What, love?' he said, rushing in behind her.

'I think someone's been in here. Does that bed look slept in?' She peered closely to see if she could find any actual evidence of uninvited visitors. The sheets definitely looked crumpled, and the pillows were askew.

He pushed the door fully open. 'Looks fine to me.'

'I never use this room. I know. I've just got a feeling.' Terry walked over and opened the wardrobe, then pulled out the drawers. Turning to face Jim, she said, 'Do you think someone could have been squatting here? I mean, the place has been empty. Anyone could have walked in.'

Jim took her arm and steered her back into the living room. 'I don't think so. You're panicking about nothing.' He went over to the kitchen area and opened and closed the cupboard doors. 'Nothing! It all looks good to me. I tell you what. You go back to Michael's and I'll get a locksmith in to change the locks. Get something a bit more robust. You should be more careful anyway. It wouldn't take much to get through that door, locked or not.'

Terry collapsed on the sofa. 'Fuck! I can't really handle any more grief. You're probably right, Jim. It was just a shock. Nobody else needs to know how stupid I was leaving my door unlocked.'

'We can sort this out without anyone else sticking their noses in.'

'You sure, though, that I don't need to worry?'

'Nah! Leave it to me, I'll sort you out with some new locks and keys,' he said reassuringly.

'Thanks, Jim. I'm glad you stuck around.' She gave him a quick hug and picked up her bag. 'And not a word to Dad. He already thinks I'm losing the plot. Come on, I'll treat you to a bite in the Harbourmaster.'

36

Feeling more relaxed after a couple of glasses of wine, Terry hugged Jim goodbye outside the restaurant and watched as he headed back in the direction of town, but a flicker of movement across the road made her feel suddenly unsettled. She could have sworn she had seen a man staring at her, but when she blinked again, there was nobody there, just the blur of passing traffic.

Terry shook her head, brushing off the uneasiness as wine-induced paranoia, and walked back towards Michael's flat, deciding to stop off at Fresh on Lower Mayor Street to pick up some dinner for them on the way. As she waited in the queue at the checkout, she glanced at her phone. She had forgotten to take it off silent. There were more missed calls from Michael and one from Fraser. There was also a text from Michael. She gasped as she opened it: At vet's with Bella. Phone ASAP. Dropping her basket, she rushed outside, waving frantically at passing taxis.

She felt sick all the way to the vet's surgery. She told the taxi driver to take the Tunnel and get a shift on. The car had barely stopped outside the vet's surgery when she flung open the door and threw a fifty-euro note at the driver. Barging through the door, she looked frantically from Michael to Alan, who were sitting side by side in the waiting area.

'Where is she?'

Michael was chalk white. 'Tez. I'm so sorry.' He looked down at the collar and lead on his lap.

'No!' Terry wailed. She looked around the waiting room and spotted the vet's receptionist behind the counter. She rushed over. 'Where's Bella? I need to see Bella!'

The receptionist seemed to be well used to emotional outbursts and was not perturbed by the distraught woman standing in front of her.

Michael walked over. 'This is Dr Terry O'Brien, Bella's owner.'

At that moment, the door opened and John Fraser strode into the clinic. He made a beeline for Terry and engulfed her in his arms. Michael watched as Terry sobbed into Fraser's chest. Fraser took charge. 'Superintendent Fraser. Can we speak to the vet?'

'He's with a patient at the moment. He'll be free soon.'

Fraser steered Terry over to the chairs and sat her down, keeping his arm around her. He looked over at Michael, whose face was stricken with grief. 'What happened?'

'I came back to the flat at lunchtime to check on Bella.' He sounded part defensive, part apologetic. 'I rang Terry to say I'd had a call-out and I couldn't take Bella with me. You weren't answering, but I knew I'd only be gone for a couple of hours and thought Bella would be fine.'

'I had my phone off and then it was on silent,' Terry whispered. 'I was working.' It sounded pathetic, even to her. Why hadn't she called him back as soon as she saw those first missed calls? She wiped her eyes with both hands. 'I wouldn't have left Bella if I thought something would happen to her. She seemed fine when I left her this morning. She ate her breakfast and everything. What happened?'

Alan said, 'Dr Copeland thinks someone's poisoned her.'

Terry let out a strangled sob.

Michael's tone softened. 'It was awful. When I came home, I found Bella lying in the hall, unconscious. She was barely breathing.' Alan came over and stood beside him, rubbing his shoulder. Michael looked up at him seeking reassurance. 'I phoned Alan – he's got a dog. I didn't know what you're supposed to do.'

Alan nodded at Fraser. 'I went straight round and brought them here to Barry's surgery. Dr Copeland's a brilliant vet.' He gave Terry a wan smile. 'But even he can't work miracles. Sorry, Terry. She was just too far gone.'

The door to the surgery opened and a huge brute of a man emerged. After introductions, Barry Copeland explained all that had happened since Bella was brought in. 'I did a quick dipstick test on her urine. It was positive for opiates and her pupils were pinpricks. Whatever she ate it was laced with something like heroin.'

'I fed her myself this morning. Just that dried stuff. She's got a sensitive stomach. I get her special food.' Terry's voice was barely audible.

Alan stepped in. 'There was some vomit on the floor, and I scooped it up into a plastic bag to give to Barry. It looked like minced meat, rather than dried food. Whatever it was she must have eaten quite a bit.'

Dr Barry addressed Fraser. 'I can arrange a sample to be sent for analysis.'

'Some bastard poisoned my dog.' Terry sat looking utterly dejected. Suddenly she jumped up. 'Fucking Hayes!' Terry had her voice back. 'It's a warning, I could be next.'

'Sorry, I don't understand.' The vet looked worried.

Fraser shot Terry a disapproving look, then addressed the vet. 'It's a gang we have under investigation. I doubt it's anything to do with a dog eating something it shouldn't.'

'It's all my fault.' Terry pulled away from Fraser. 'It's my fault she's dead. I left her and those bastards killed her.' She turned to the vet. 'Can you ask the lab to check for fentanyl?'

She turned to Fraser, her face stricken, as a sudden thought dawned on her. 'Oh my God, the newspaper article. Fraser! The bloody article! Do you think this is retaliation for what I said to that journalist?'

Fraser looked at her grimly, his mouth in a tight line. He shrugged. 'Dunno. Maybe?' He walked to the door, pulling out his mobile phone. 'Just need to make a call.'

Once the door closed behind him, Terry spoke to the vet. 'Would naloxone have reversed the effects?' Terry had seen drug addicts comatose and near to death making remarkable recoveries due to naloxone, or Narcan, reversing the effect of opiate drugs on the brain.

'Unfortunately, it was too late. I tried anyway but there wasn't a flicker of response. I'm sorry.'

Terry took a deep breath. 'Can I see her?'

Terry followed the vet into the surgery, leaving Michael and Alan alone in the waiting room. After about ten minutes with Bella, saying her goodbyes, she came out, wiping her nose on a blue paper towel.

In the meantime, Fraser had returned. He pocketed his phone now and pulled Terry towards him. 'I was just explaining to Michael that the flat is a crime scene so you can't stay there. He's going to Alan's. I've a spare room – I think you should come back with me. All right?'

She nodded, not fit to do much more.

Terry woke the following morning with a start. She'd had the strangest, most unsettling dream. She was walking Bella along the beach when a large wave washed her out to sea. The current was too strong and she got further and further from shore. Jimmy, Michael, Fraser and her dad surrounded her and began chanting, 'Killer! Killer!'

She became aware of someone in the bed beside her. Michael? It wasn't the first time they had shared a bed. They were so skint at uni that she, Michael and their friend Becs would often squeeze in together to keep warm. Glasgow mid-winter was freezing and they couldn't afford to heat their flat – it made perfect sense at the time. As her eyes accustomed to the dim light, she realised she wasn't in her or Michael's flat. So whose bed was she in? She shot up.

'Morning.' Fraser smiled and she pulled the duvet around her. Reality flooded back – the vet, Bella, a few glasses of wine. Unsolicited tears started.

'You all right?' Fraser leaned in close and tucked her hair behind her ear. She tensed up, realising how vulnerable she was.

'I'll make some coffee' Fraser swung his legs out of the bed and stretched as he got up. She relaxed when she saw he was wearing tracksuit bottoms and a T-shirt. As soon as he left, she checked under the covers and was relieved to find she was wearing a grey T-shirt, presumably one of his, and she had her pants and bra on beneath it.

Terry leaned back against the pillows and closed her eyes. Last night was the real nightmare. She had been more than happy for Fraser to take her back to his home. She hadn't wanted to be on her own. But she regretted those last drinks. She should know by now that alcohol wasn't a cure-all, and it certainly wouldn't change how she felt about losing Bella. It was all her fault. Fraser had had to listen to her self-flagellation and she must have looked a right mess. She wasn't a pretty crier.

A sudden wave of nausea engulfed her and she struggled out of the bed into the en suite, reaching the toilet a fraction of a second too late. Vomit splattered the floor and the toilet seat. She retched again, this time on target. Afterwards, she sat on the floor mopping up the mess with toilet paper.

'Better?' John Fraser stood behind her with a glass of water and a pack of paracetamol.

Groaning in reply she turned back to the toilet and rested her forehead on the seat. When she looked up, he was gone and the glass was on the floor beside her, seeming to know that she wanted space. Terry curled up and let the tears flow.

'Better?' Fraser looked up from his laptop as she hovered in the doorway to the living room ten minutes later.

She gave him a wan smile and flopped onto the sofa beside him. 'Isn't that the definition of madness, asking the same question and expecting a different answer? So, no, not really.' She folded her legs under her and pulled a throw from the back of the sofa and wrapped it around her. 'It's all my fault, isn't it?' Fraser kept quiet. 'Poor Bella. Who would poison a dog? Sick bastards! She was so innocent and trusting.'

'I doubt whoever did it will lose sleep over a dog,' said Fraser, shaking his head sadly.

'How did they get to her? She didn't pick up anything when I took her out for her walk. I need to call Michael. He might have some idea.'

'Look, Michael feels bad as it is,' said Fraser. 'I've spoken to him. When Mary and Vinnie were checking his flat, they found a chewed-up pouch of dog food in the hall.'

'But that doesn't make any sense. I only buy those big bags of dried food Jimmy told me to feed her. So what did Michael say? Did he buy it?'

'No. He said he took Bella out for a quick walk before he had to go to work. When he got back there was a package in reception addressed to you. He didn't think anything of it, just thought you'd ordered something online. He took it up to the flat and left it on the console in the hall so you'd see it when you came in. Bella obviously got into it in the meantime. Must have smelt the food inside.'

'Where did it come from?' asked Terry.

Fraser picked up his notebook from the coffee table to consult it. 'Zooplus, an online pet shop.'

'But I buy the food in a pet shop in town. I don't know anything about this Zoo company.'

'Zooplus. We've checked with them. They deny any knowledge of any delivery to you or to that address.'

'So where did it really come from then? What was in it?'

'Mary thought what was left looked like regular beef mince. Which matches what Alan said he found in the hall.'

'Poor Bella,' said Terry sadly. 'So they must have laced the mince with something – the opiates the vet found in her urine? At least she probably didn't suffer. I think they affect animals the same as humans. Poor wee soul would have lost consciousness and eventually stopped breathing. And I wasn't there.' Tears ran down her face. 'I would never have given her food that I wasn't sure of.'

'Whoever sent it was just chancing their arm that the poisoned meat would get to Bella. The state lab are on it,' said Fraser, pulling Terry in close to him for a hug. 'Mary brought the mince and the blood and urine samples the vet took up to the lab this morning, first thing. She dropped the packaging into FSI, and Monica is going to look for prints. But I doubt it will be helpful.'

Terry sniffed. 'But they don't do animals at the state lab, do they? Are you sure they'll do it?'

'It's all part of a bigger picture. I want to know if the opiate is heroin. But more importantly, I want to know if it's been cut with fentanyl. If so, I can prove it all leads back to whoever is infiltrating the market with these new drugs.'

'I wish they'd got to me and not Bella.' She settled into Fraser's embrace and closed her eyes. A moment later she shot up, his arms dropping in surprise. 'Jimmy! Oh God! He's going to blame me, and he's right – I got his dog killed.'

Fraser took her hand. 'I called him when we were at the vet's surgery. He knows.'

She headed for the shower where she mulled over her options. The first thing she needed to do was speak to Jimmy herself. She needed to apologise for not looking after his dog properly. Because Bella was his dog – Terry was just her foster mother. And she needed to know what to do next – do you bury the body or get it cremated? She had never asked her dad what he did with her fish and hamsters. She had been satisfied with 'they've gone to heaven'. It sucked being the adult.

If this was a warning, whoever thought it would make her back off could go and take a flying leap. Problem was, she didn't know what she was being warned about.

Terry asked Fraser to drop her at the front entrance of the OSP. She needed to mentally prepare herself before she saw Jimmy. Turning up at the mortuary door was too abrupt. She trudged up the stairs to the reception area, dreading seeing anyone. Sympathy would break her. Blame would shame her. Mrs Carey was on the phone so she put her head down and walked along the corridor to the tea room.

'Didn't think you'd be in today. Sorry about Bella. Tomas told us.'

'Thanks, Niamh. To be honest, it's only because John's got something to do up at WSH and I didn't fancy hanging around the house. I'm just plucking up the courage to go and see Jimmy. I don't think he'll ever forgive me for getting his dog killed.'

'Rather you than me. He's a real grumpy git. That's why I stay well out of his way. He only likes dogs.'

'Well, that makes me feel a whole lot better. Wish me luck.'

Terry knew it made her a coward but she was glad that Fraser had called Jimmy last night so he had had time to get his head around the death. She found Jimmy on his ratty old couch and shared an awkward hug with him and, if she hadn't known better, she would have been sure he was a wee bit teary. At least he wasn't angry with her, although that might have made her feel less shitty.

Jimmy had already been onto the vet's practice to make arrangements for Bella. He told her that Bella was being cremated. Terry was a bit taken aback when he asked if she wanted to help choose an urn. She tried to assure him that he was best placed to make the right decision, but he insisted she at least take a look at the brochure.

Eager to end the upsetting conversation, she promised Jimmy she'd look through the brochure and rushed back up the stairs to the OSP. Mrs C was still busy at her desk so Terry was going to sneak by her, but Mrs Carey looked up. 'How are you?'

Terry walked over to her. 'Hanging in there. Thanks.'

'You know I wasn't a fan, but I wouldn't have wished that dog any harm. Yesterday must have been very difficult for you.'

'Yes. It was.' Terry suddenly thought about her trip to the Rockroad Clinic and, more specifically, about the receptionist there. 'Mrs C, I've got a friend, well, an acquaintance, really, whose husband died on holiday in Spain. When bodies are repatriated to Ireland in those circumstances, do we routinely carry out a post-mortem?'

'No,' said Mrs C firmly.

Terry was taken aback by the abruptness of the answer. 'Oh! Never?'

'The coroners have no jurisdiction outside of Ireland, and if an Irish citizen dies abroad, even if they were murdered, there will be no investigation into the death in Ireland.'

Terry's shoulders slumped. 'I didn't realise that.'

'There are exceptions.' Terry perched on the edge of the desk and folded her arms and Mrs Carey smiled, knowing she had a captive audience. 'Families can approach the coroner if they are dissatisfied with the investigation in the country in which the death occurred. It is not a given, mind you.'

'And how would I find out if a post-mortem was done this end?'

'If the body was transported through Dublin airport, the Dublin coroner may have taken jurisdiction and this office would be involved.'

'Interesting. Would you mind checking this one, please? Francis Foster. He died in Spain in 2019.'

Terry's mobile rang and she jumped up off the desk. The number was withheld. She swithered then pressed the green Accept icon.

'Dr O'Brien?'

Terry recognised the raspy voice but couldn't immediately place it. 'Who is this?'

'I warned you to take care of your little friend.'

It dawned on Terry who was on the phone. 'Bernice? Was it Lou Hayes who poisoned Bella?'

Bernice was silent but Terry could hear her breathing – she was still there.

'Do you know where Mags is, Bernice?'

'I saw you at Heuston talking to that piece of shit Puggie. If I did, others did too. Mags and the other girls are safe. For now. Don't do anything to change that.' The line went dead.

37

Fraser threw his phone down in frustration. It bounced off the towering stack of files on his desk and onto the floor. The assistant commissioner had just given him the most almighty bollocking about the stalled Higgins investigation. It was all well and good throwing resources and manpower behind it, but Fraser's team had little evidence to go on. They were following all the leads they could, no matter how small. He scrabbled under the desk, feeling for his phone, when there was a rap on the door. Alan poked his head around.

'What the hell are you up to, Fraser? Things so bad you're hiding under the desk?' he quipped.

'Something like that,' he said, retrieving his phone and sitting back on his chair. 'The assistant commissioner is not happy. Anyway, that's my problem. How's Michael doing after yesterday?'

'Fine, boss.' Alan handed Fraser a Starbucks coffee. 'Double shot.' He took the seat opposite. 'I got Mary and Vinnie to pack up the essentials for Michael and Terry, to tide them over for a few days.'

Fraser took a swig of the coffee. 'We might have to make longer-term arrangements if the Hayeses have anything to do with this.'

'Terry won't be happy. Good luck telling her that.'

'I'd rather that than tell her Vinnie's been rifling through her knicker drawer,' said Fraser with a smile.

'Fair enough.' Alan laughed. 'I don't get it, though – surely they can't have a vendetta against a pathologist or even a scientist? They're just doing their jobs.'

'It does seem a bit far-fetched.' Fraser sighed. 'Lou's hot-headed but I can't see her taking umbrage at that. I just don't know anymore.'

'Maybe it's the sons. Flexing their muscles. Trying to impress the mammy. What if Terry backs off, lies low?' suggested Alan.

'Someone already told her to do that.'

'You?' Alan looked shocked at the thought. Fraser suspected that a little part of Ahern was frightened of Terry.

Fraser smiled. 'No! I value my own life. It was that woman Bernice. She looks after the prostitutes in the park.'

'I'll get one of the team to check her out. But even that seems odd. What's it got to do with her? Is she one of the Hayeses' girls? Sorry, women.'

'I don't know.' Fraser slammed his laptop shut and stood up.

Ahern tossed his paper cup in the bin and stood. 'Right, are you ready, boss?'

Fraser snatched his car keys off the desk. 'I'll drive. We'll go to the Rockroad Clinic to see Reagan first. I've tried calling him a few times but he's obviously avoiding my calls. This is the first chance I've had to follow it up. At any rate, it's probably better to speak to him on his own ground – he might be a little more forthcoming. We need him to admit that it was him Higgins was speaking to outside Court 18, and when he does, I want to know what was said between them. It's probably a red herring, but at least it might give us an insight into Martin's state of mind. Then we can spin by the CCJ to see Judge Henderson. He wouldn't want guards turning up at his house.'

'Do you think he's likely to talk to us about his tipstaff?'

'I just don't want to tread on his toes. He can be a prickly customer. This is a professional courtesy before we start questioning his family.'

Dr Ronan Reagan was less than welcoming. Fraser decided to let Ahern take the lead, fearing his intense dislike of the psychologist might prejudice the questioning.

'Thank you for making time in your busy schedule to speak to us.' Ahern was perched on the edge of his seat. Reagan swivelled his body away from Fraser, making obvious he returned his disdain.

'I just have a few questions to ask you concerning our investigation into the death of Detective Garda Martin Higgins,' Alan continued. 'I know you've spoken to my colleague.' He gestured at Fraser, but Reagan pointedly ignored him. 'I believe you know him?'

'Yes.' Reagan's answer was clipped, dismissive. 'I've already told your colleague that I cannot divulge details of my consultations with Detective Higgins.'

Ahern ignored the hostile tone. 'That's not why we are here. You spoke to him on Thursday 2 January, outside Court 18 in the CCJ.'

'Did I? I have no recollection of any meeting with Detective Higgins. I am frequently in the criminal and family courts to provide expert evidence,' Reagan said pompously. 'But I don't see how I can be of any assistance in your murder enquiry.'

'But you did know Martin Higgins?'

'I think you are well aware that he and his wife were clients of mine. And as I have said, I cannot discuss the content of our sessions. This is a waste of my time. I know nothing about the circumstances of his death. So unless there is anything else ...' His voice tailed off and he made to stand.

'It's not the counselling sessions we're interested in.' Fraser addressed Reagan and with a flick of his hand signalled for him to stay seated. Fraser pulled his seat closer to the desk and laid a folder on it. He took his time opening it, then pulled out a piece of paper, which he slid across the desk towards Reagan. 'This is a still taken from CCTV footage of the concourse outside Court 18.'

Reagan leaned over and looked at the picture in front of him. He shook his head and shrugged his shoulders. 'So?'

Fraser pointed at one of the figures. 'This is Martin Higgins. And the man in front of him is you.'

Reagan picked up the page and brought it closer to his face. 'That could be anyone.' He dropped the sheet of paper back onto the desk and made to push it back towards Fraser, but Fraser slapped his hand down over it.

'Dr Reagan. Look at the bag the man is holding. You have an identical bag. It's quite distinctive. If I ask Mrs Foster to come in, I'm sure she would recognise it. I would even go so far as to say that I doubt anyone else in the CCJ would have, or use, such an expensive accessory.'

Reagan sat back, a thunderous expression on his face. 'So?'

Fraser decided they had danced around the issue long enough. 'According to Garda Higgins's final movements on that day, you were the last person to have publicly spoken to him. We are keen to find out what Martin Higgins said to you. It may give us some fresh clues as to the reason for his murder. From the CCTV, his body language shows that he is agitated.'

Reagan's shoulders slumped. 'He said nothing he hadn't said before.' Fraser watched as Reagan seemed to decide what he should or could say. Eventually he let out a long breath. 'He called me a charlatan. He threatened to report me to the Medical Council. He blamed me for …' He drummed his fingers on the desk. 'His exact words were "not getting my wife to toe the line." A truly offensive man.'

Fraser and Ahern shared a look. 'And how did you respond to that?' Fraser asked.

'I said he was entitled to his opinion. I explained that there was a separate regulatory body for psychologists. I would give him their details if he wanted.' He looked directly at Fraser. 'I have nothing to hide. After that, Detective Higgins stormed off. That's as much as I can tell you.'

As the questioning continued, Reagan went on to make it clear that he had strong views on men who abuse women and that sometimes he despaired of the justice system, which he thought was weighted towards the men.

And he was quite vocal in his criticism of his friend Judge Henderson, whose judgments he thought were safe, rather than fair to the victim. Reagan was in the no smoke without fire camp, whereas, in his words, Henderson wanted cast-iron evidence before he would convict, although their views on the matter were in agreement behind closed doors.

When Fraser ran out of steam, Ahern took over the interview again. 'Dr Reagan, perhaps you can tell us where you went when you left Court 18 on that day?' He touched the picture on the desk.

Reagan placed both hands on his desk and pulled himself up out of his chair. 'I attended a meeting at the Royal College of Surgeons. I was presenting a research paper in the area of emotional abuse. Dr Maeve Price, my colleague in the clinic here, was there, as well as a roomful of psychiatrists and psychologists. They will all corroborate my presence.'

'Thank you, Doctor. We'll speak to her.'

Reagan smoothed down his jacket. It was a dismissive gesture Fraser chose to ignore. He made a show of flicking through the bundle of papers in his folder. 'This is another image from the CCJ that day.'

'This is preposterous,' Reagan spluttered. 'I have answered your questions about my … discourse with Detective Higgins.'

Fraser kept his eyes on the image. 'The man exiting Court 18, do you recognise him?'

The psychologist glanced at the figure Fraser was pointing at. 'He looks vaguely familiar.'

'Igor Henderson. Judge Henderson's cousin.'

Reagan looked disconcerted. 'His cousin? Why would I know him?' Realisation dawned. 'He's the tipstaff, isn't he?'

Fraser made no comment, merely slid the image back into his folder.

Reagan began edging around his desk, but Fraser and Ahern stayed seated.

'Before we leave, could you tell us where you were two weeks later, the weekend Dr Maguire died – from Friday, 17 January to Sunday, 19 January?'

'I was in Kinsale,' Reagan said as he took out his phone, showing them pictures of him standing at Charles Fort and at a restaurant by the harbour, stamped with the relevant dates. 'I'm sure I can dig out some receipts too.' Fraser tried to mask his disappointment that Reagan had alibis for the times of the deaths of Martin Higgins and Cillian Maguire.

Realistically, he couldn't see Reagan as a killer. *But I would love to have a reason to get a warrant to turn his office upside down and wipe that supercilious look off his face.*

Judge Gerard Henderson was likely to be a trickier customer, Fraser knew. He was loved and hated in equal measure by his staff, but the gardaí and those in the witness stand, and even the alleged victims, feared his wrath. He was not to be crossed.

Gardaí were rarely granted access to the judge's chambers, and Fraser thought this must be akin to an audience with the pope. The CCJ might be ultra-modern, but Judge Henderson had taken a different approach to decorating his personal space behind the scenes of his court. No expense had been spared. Judge Henderson, looking resplendent in his court garb, sat imperiously behind an ornate dark-wood desk. Fraser suspected his chair was on a raised plinth, as he appeared to be hovering in mid-air. The room felt entombed by the leather-bound books that filled the shelves on three walls. Henderson was old school and favoured a horsehair wig, but for this meeting it had been artfully discarded onto the desk in front of him, his only concession to the perceived informality of the discussion.

After the introductions, Fraser made his opening gambit. 'We are very grateful to you for agreeing to speak to us.' It was best to be deferential. 'You will be aware we are investigating the murder of one of our colleagues. I'm following several lines of enquiry.'

'I'm intrigued, Superintendent. Although, I have to admit this is rather unusual. Unless you consider me a suspect?' he said, with a look of mock horror.

Fraser smiled. The normally aloof persona possibly hid a sense of humour. 'I'm sure you'll let me know if I'm overstepping the mark.' The judge did not return his smile but Fraser detected a slight change in his attitude. 'This regards your tipstaff, Igor Henderson. We require some information on him. We believe he is your cousin?'

'I make no secret of that fact. It's perfectly within court rules to employ a relative. And he is perfectly able to perform that function.'

'I'm not questioning that.' The relationship between the judge and his tipstaff was common knowledge in the CCJ. It was just another example of acceptable nepotism in the circles the judge moved in. 'It's just that we would like to speak to him, but I wanted to inform you of our intention beforehand. Professional courtesy if you like.'

'I appreciate that. What can I tell you?'

'Whatever you are comfortable sharing. Maybe if you could tell us about your relationship with him outside of your professional capacity.'

The judge clasped his hands in front of him and stared off into the distance. 'Igor's mother was Russian, and significantly younger than my uncle when they married. Sadly, they died in a road traffic accident when Igor was only a child. He was badly injured, but survived. My mother was his closest living relative and so took him in. I was in my thirties and had long left home. I promised my mother I would look out for Igor after she died, and so I employed him as my tipstaff.' Fraser got the impression that Henderson fulfilled his quasi-parental role out of duty rather than love.

'And do you see much of him outside of work?' asked Fraser. 'He enjoys coming out with me on my boat on occasion, although I can't say that he's a proficient sailor,' said the judge, a note of derision entering his voice. 'Unfortunately, I cannot tell you where Igor is right now. I'm not his keeper. He left after court ended today.'

'If you would give me his contact details that would be helpful.'

'Certainly, Superintendent. Perhaps you might like to speak

to my sister, Aoife Foster, Igor's only other relative? They are very close. She was responsible for much of his care, as my mother was elderly when he came to live with them. I know Aoife is now away for the weekend, but she should be back by Sunday.'

Fraser was dumbfounded. He hadn't heard of any other relation – it wasn't even known if Henderson was or ever had been married. 'Sorry, Judge, can I just confirm – is your sister the same Aoife Foster who works as a receptionist at the psychiatric clinic at Rockroad Clinic?'

The judge looked surprised. 'Yes. She works for Dr Ronan Reagan and Dr Maeve Price.'

'And, Judge, you are familiar with Dr Reagan? Friendly?'

'I make it my business to know frequent visitors to my court. Professional visitors. And Dr Reagan is a frequent professional visitor.'

Fraser wasn't sure if that was intended as a criticism. 'I believe he is an advocate for women in abusive marriages.'

'Yes,' the judge replied curtly. 'I admit, I was not in favour of my sister working in his clinic. It troubles me, Superintendent. Aoife is far too trusting. She gets over-invested in Reagan's clients – the women, I mean. She thinks they need to be saved, and so she tries to befriend them. She sees herself in them, possibly.' He looked wistful, and then shook his head. 'To be honest, I think she is a little in Ronan's thrall.'

It was obvious Henderson didn't approve. Maybe he thought the women Aoife met at the clinic should be kept at arm's length. It was one thing to see that abused women got their day in court, another thing entirely to get too close. Fraser thought there was no fear of anyone getting too close to the judge. His sister obviously had more empathy for these women.

'There is one other thing you might be able to help us with,' Fraser said. 'Nothing to do with your family.' The judge's eyebrows shot up.

'Do you remember a Dr Maguire who applied to join your yacht club?'

Judge Henderson picked up a fountain pen and made to open a legal brief. 'I heard he died recently.' And that was that. The subject was closed.

Fraser was a little exasperated by the sudden end of the interview, but he didn't think that Henderson was a spiteful man, just a throwback to another era.

Fraser wasted no time sending a patrol car to check out the address Henderson had given them for his cousin Igor, but he wasn't at home. They didn't have too much else on him. He wasn't known to them, or really to his neighbours. The gardaí had spoken to as many of the people on his road as they could. 'Odd' was the adjective that crept up time and again.

Their only hope was Aoife Foster. Fraser thought it better not to mention Aoife's links with Judge Henderson and Igor to Terry. The last thing he wanted was for her to get involved.

He would get a couple of guards to call to Aoife's house, just in case Igor was there, but they would have to wait until she returned from her trip before they could have a chat with her.

38

Terry was in a bad mood. Being cooped up in Fraser's cottage in the arse end of north Dublin was not her idea of a fun Saturday morning. A coffee and a croissant at Il Valentino's, a walk down Grafton Street and a mooch around the shops was more her cup of tea. She was definitely a city girl. She had hoped Fraser would suss she was missing Bella and offer to take her out, but he seemed busy tapping away on his laptop in the living room. And she wasn't going to beg.

She phoned Michael from the bedroom. 'What are you up to?

Fancy meeting up for lunch in town?' she asked hopefully. 'Nah, I can't. Would love to, but I'm in the lab.'

'What are you doing working on a Saturday?'

'Alan had to go in, so I thought I might as well catch up on some work. Why don't you and John go out – make a romantic day of it?'

'I think he's busy and I don't want to seem desperate,' said Terry. 'Why did Alan have to go in anyway?' She was interested now – could this have something to do with any of the investigations she was working on?

'Not sure. I think they're ramping up the investigation into Higgins. You know me, I don't pry.'

'What are you insinuating?' Terry said in mock outrage. 'I'm not nosey! I just like to know what's going on.'

'And that's how you get yourself in bother, Tez. Just cool your jets. It can't be that bad being looked after by a hunky cop.'

'Mitts off. Anyway, we're not – we haven't … you know?' she added coyly.

'What's the issue? Is he not keen?'

'Thanks very much, Michael,' said Terry drily. 'For your information, I think he's very keen. I don't want to complicate matters.'

'God, you always make things complicated regardless. Are you sure you're not just pissed off because he won't tell you what's going on?'

'I don't need counselling from you. Never mind me anyway, what are you working on?'

'Working on that axe from your fire death. You guessed right – there were traces of blood on the blade. It had been wiped, but not very well. I'd bet my bottom dollar that the clown wiped it on his trackie bottoms and then threw it into the bushes. Anyway, I should have a profile later today.'

'Great. You will let me know, won't you?'

'Of course! So, what are you up to tomorrow?' asked Michael, but Terry could tell by the tone of his voice that he wasn't interested in the answer.

'Superintendent John Fraser has to go in, so I'll probably tag along. Sundays are a drag anyway. We could do a carvery.'

'Not a chance. Oh! Machine's beeping. I need to go.'

'That's your kettle. Do you think I zip up the back? Go back to your test tubes. I know when I'm not wanted.'

She returned to the living room and sighed as she sat on the sofa, picked up her phone and started scrolling through the news feed. She studiously ignored Fraser.

'Terry.' She looked up from her screen. 'I have to go out for an hour. When I come back, we could go for lunch?'

'I suppose so. If you've time.' She didn't want to sound too keen. It might give him ideas.

Fraser was enjoying the opportunity to spend time with Terry. This recent turn of events had accelerated their relationship to a stage that was not quite back to where it had been last year, but it was certainly getting there. He didn't want to force things, but a relaxing day together might be just what they both needed.

It turned out to be a pleasant afternoon in Skerries. They managed to get a table in Stoop Your Head and shared the battered cod strips and the tempura prawns, along with a couple of alcohol-free beers. After lunch, they wandered around the shops and stopped for the obligatory 99s.

When they got back to the house, Terry settled in front of the television, while Fraser spent an hour checking emails and getting updates from his team.

Dinner was a Chinese takeaway and a bottle of red. He wasn't sure who made the first move and he didn't care. He fell asleep eventually with Terry wrapped in his arms, and the next time he checked his phone it was 8.30 a.m. He was alone. He could smell her perfume on the pillow, but the bed beside him was cold. He had a fleeting sense of panic, trying to think what he had done or said that might have made her take off. Maybe she had decided that last night was a mistake.

As quietly as he could, he got up and pushed the bedroom door open. He cringed when it shut behind him with a bang.

'That you up?' Terry's voice rang out from the kitchen. 'Coffee's made. Toast?'

Fraser smiled and relaxed. But it wouldn't be for long.

After breakfast he sat at the dining table reading through reports. Terry was engrossed in something on her phone – he didn't ask what. He suddenly realised she was very quiet, and when he looked up, she was staring fixedly at him.

'What's the matter, Terry? You've got an odd look on your face.' He couldn't read her. He didn't know if he should be worried or not.

'Now ...' She sounded excited and that immediately put him on high alert. What had she done? 'Don't overreact,' she warned.

He had a sinking feeling. Terry got up from the sofa and walked over, phone in hand. 'You know the other day when Michael couldn't get hold of me?'

He noticed she didn't mention it was the day Bella had died. She still couldn't talk about Bella. 'Well, I had met Aisling O'Neill about her father's death. He died a couple of years ago and the Wicklow coroner asked me to review it. He's the one linked to Maguire by an unidentified DNA profile. Remember we told you about it?'

Fraser knew better than to interrupt.

She continued, 'He drowned in the bath and the local gardaí refused to consider anything but suicide. The coroner wasn't so sure.' Terry started walking back and forth across the room. 'To cut a long story short, Aisling said her mum and dad had gone for counselling.' Guess who the counsellor was?' She didn't wait for, or expect, a reply. 'Reagan!'

Fraser still wasn't sure where this was going.

'So on the way back from Wicklow, I dropped in to the Rockroad Clinic.' Terry cleared her throat and looked uncomfortable. 'And I happened to take a few photographs of Aoife's desk diaries. Look.'

Fraser started to scan the diary entries, incredulous. What part of don't interfere did she not understand? And what did this mean for his investigations? Part of him wanted to shout at her, part wanted to hug her. Because this might give him the leverage on Reagan he needed.

39

Terry was relieved that Fraser seemed to be taking her discovery seriously. She had to admit the photos weren't the best quality, but they were legible enough. She had simply wanted to confirm that Owen O'Neill had been one of Reagan's patients. He had been found dead in his bath in the summer of 2022. So Terry had started from January. In February, Owen and his wife had had an appointment. This had been highlighted by Aoife and a note added: *recommenced couples counselling.* The appointments had continued until June, when *DNA* – 'did not attend', Terry presumed – was written next to the appointment date. There was another note in the margin, in different-coloured ink, possibly added on a different date: *Mr O'Neill did not return calls* and a little symbol, like an asterisk, drawn next to it.

As Terry had looked at the pages she had managed to photograph, she had begun to see a pattern emerge. There were other couples who also fell by the wayside and some had Aoife's cryptic notes in the margins.

Aoife had written *successful* beside some names, neither party returning, and occasionally *divorced*. On very rare occasions, the male of the couple continued alone – usually it was the women who kept up their sessions with Reagan.

Terry had managed to get some of 2021 before Aoife had come back from lost property, so she had looked through, hoping to work out when the O'Neills had started counselling.

On 20 March 2021 she saw what might have been their first session. And her eyes had alighted on another familiar name, Tormey, which was interesting. The O'Neills had attended regularly until May 2021 – *Mr O'Neill cancelled (Mrs O'Neill says he refuses to attend)*. Again, that symbol. It would appear that Aoife had been keeping her own private record of the couples attending counselling.

She was idly following their progress when something had caught her attention, *Book Club*, and beside that, in her neat writing, a list: *Dr Price, Mrs O'Neill, Mrs Clarke, Mrs Brady and Mrs Tormey*. Bless her, Aoife had started her book club meetings on the first Thursday of the month.

That was when Terry had decided she needed to bring it to Fraser. There might be something there but she would need all the pages to see the whole picture and make connections.

She was surprised he hadn't read her the riot act now she had come clean about her undercover operation in the clinic. Instead, he had immediately tried to contact Reagan in the hope that he would co-operate and give up the office diaries voluntarily, but the call went straight to voicemail.

'Well, I tried,' Fraser said. 'I don't have time to track him down. And I doubt that the hospital will play ball. Guess I'll just have to get a warrant.' He smiled at Terry. 'I think I might just be about to upset Dr Reagan.'

Despite it being Sunday morning, he secured a warrant for the premises with the intention of retrieving the full set of desk diaries. She wondered what Aoife and Dr Reagan's reactions would be to this development.

Terry and Fraser arrived at Walter Scott House at the same time the guards returned with the diaries. She volunteered to trawl through them, which made more sense. Her strength was recognising patterns, and she knew who and what she was looking for. Terry decided she could work better in Fraser's office, as there was too much frenetic activity in the incident room and the OCRU office was wedged with boxes of case files. She couldn't be distracted when she was trying to concentrate. She needed space, and she needed peace and quiet.

Smiling to herself, she pulled the freshly seized Rockroad diaries out of the evidence bag and dropped them on the desk. Next to them she stacked her notebooks for the Higgins, Maguire, O'Neill and Tormey deaths. Each had some unusual features, ranging from relatively odd – O'Neill's head shaved – to the downright bizarre – Higgins's tongue hacked out. She still thought they could be linked, although so far a broken marriage was the only common denominator.

She decided to work back from the most recent death, Dr Cillian Maguire. He had been found dead three weeks earlier.

He and his wife led separate lives under the marital roof. The décor in Mrs Maguire's bedroom hadn't looked freshly done, so Terry took a gamble that the missus had left the marital bed at least a year before. If so, counselling would have been earlier. She opened the 2023 diary and began speed-reading page after page of unhappy marriages.

She was halfway through March 2023 when she came across the Higginses. Followed at the end of the month by the Maguires. All her ducks were lining up.

The Higginses had weekly sessions scheduled, but it seemed that Martin didn't take them as seriously as other couples. Aoife had written in the margin beside some of the appointments *Mr Higgins DNA*. So Martin couldn't be arsed to turn up to try and save his marriage. Terry would bet he used the job as his excuse – there would always be some case that required his urgent attention. On his third no-show, after *DNA*, Aoife had added *Mr Higgins ceased couples counselling*. The same symbol she had seen beside O'Neill's name. Did it just indicate defaulters? Terry flicked forward a week: Mrs Higgins continued her weekly sessions alone.

The Maguires' names cropped up again, but it was four weeks after their first joint appointment at the end of March before they had a second one. However, between times, Mrs Maguire seemed to attend weekly sessions alone. The next mention of Dr Maguire was at the end of May. There in Aoife's neat handwriting was *Contacted Dr Maguire, no wish to continue couples counselling*. What was it with these men? Mrs Maguire continued fortnightly sessions until the end of the year.

There wasn't anything to add to what she had already seen about Owen O'Neill. Started off well, faltered and gave up counselling. It was a pattern of sorts.

That left her with Tormey. She had noticed mention of him and his wife on 8 January 2021 when she was looking for Owen O'Neill's name. New year, new start to the marriage? But the new year's resolution faltered pretty quickly. The appointments were sporadic, and on 20 March, there was the final nail in the coffin: *Mr Tormey refuses further counselling.*

This looked like pretty compelling evidence to her. All four couples had been counselled by Dr Reagan, and all four men seemed to have binned him off. It was perhaps an overreaction, but had Dr Reagan been more than a little irked? Enough to take matters into his own hands?

Terry went on through the months, then in September there was an odd addition, a midweek spa day. The date was vaguely familiar. She opened her Tormey notebook: his body had found in his burnt-out shed on Wednesday, 8 September 2021 – the spa day.

She felt the hairs on the back of her neck rise. She grabbed the O'Neill notebook. Owen O'Neill was found dead in his bath after the weekend of 16 July 2022. She cross-checked with the Rockroad Clinic desk diary for the same weekend. *Powerscourt – wine tasting and fashion show.*

Terry's heart was racing. She knew Mrs Higgins had been at a book club the night Martin was killed – she had volunteered that information when first questioned, and Mrs Maguire had complained that her ex-husband's death had put a dampener on her spa weekend. Terry quickly scoured the dates of the

Higgins and Maguire deaths. There was the book club, and the spa weekend listed in Aoife's diary.

Well, well, well. How convenient. Tormey, O'Neill, Higgins and Maguire all died when their wives were attending functions. Arranged by Rockroad Clinic? Or by Aoife Foster?

Without delay, Fraser assembled DI Alan Ahern and DS Mary Healy in his office.

'Terry has been looking into links between Martin Higgins's death and the deaths of Dr Maguire and a couple of men from 2021 and 2022. Seems all four were clients of psychologist Dr Reagan out at Rockroad Clinic.'

Terry jumped in. 'Martin Higgins's body was found on Friday, 3 January, death presumed early hours that morning or late the night before. On the night of the second his wife was at her book club. It was a monthly book club, and it appears that it was organised by the receptionist for the psychiatric clinic at the Rockroad Clinic, Aoife Foster.

'Then we have Dr Cillian Maguire,' she continued. 'His body was found on Saturday, 18 January. His wife was at a spa weekend.'

'Organised by the Rockroad Clinic?' asked Mary incredulously.

'Yep.' Terry nodded.

'It might just be a coincidence?' Alan Ahern sounded less than convinced.

'Maybe, but Owen O'Neill was found in July 2022, the weekend his wife was attending a fashion show at Powerscourt Hotel. That outing was also organised by the Rockroad Clinic. And Emmett Tormey – the fire death I asked you about, Alan –

well, it seems his missus was enjoying a spa day when his shed went up in flames. Book clubs, spa days. Maybe Aoife was instructed to organise activities that would appeal to a certain type of woman attending the clinic?'

'Rich bitches, you mean?' A sneering voice came from behind them.

Four heads swivelled around. Bob Paterson was standing defiantly in the doorway. 'What? Don't tell me none of you were thinking the same. Have you seen what that chancer charges? Martin was having none of it. Reagan probably offed Martin because he told him to shove it,' he spat.

'Bob! Outside – now!' Fraser jumped to his feet and Bob backed out the door, arms outstretched, palms raised in surrender.

'Okay, boss. I'm not here to cause bother. I just wanted a word.' He turned and sneered at Terry. 'Got yourself a new guard dog, I see?'

'Out!' Fraser slammed the door behind them.

Terry, Alan and Mary sat in awkward silence for a few moments, trying in vain to hear what was being said behind the closed door.

'Are you all right, Doc?' said Mary, when the voices outside faded away. Fraser must have escorted Bob out of the building.

'Fine, Mary. What did he mean "new guard dog"? Did he mean Fraser?' She looked from Mary to Alan.

'He's probably trying to wind you up,' Alan replied. 'How did he know we were meeting today? Have you been talking to Paterson, Mary?'

'Yeah, I have,' said Mary. 'What's wrong with that? We were

working together on these cases. He asked me to update him while he was off. I didn't think there would be any problem keeping him in the loop.'

Terry put her head in her hands. She should have told Mary the truth, but she didn't want to face the wrath of Fraser or HR by breaking confidentiality.

'I don't know what you're both getting all worked up about. He's just been back home looking after his mam,' said Mary, looking askance at Terry and Alan.

The door burst open and a furious-looking Fraser strode in. 'Right. Where were we?'

Mary shot Ahern a defiant look. 'Maybe Bob's right – this all points to Reagan.'

Terry could feel the tension in the room. 'Forget Bob,' Fraser barked at Mary.

But she was not to be silenced. 'I don't know why Reagan would kill his clients, but it is very strange that the dates of the deaths coincide with the dates of outings that the clinic organised. He could know when they were coming up. So was he ensuring the wives had alibis and wouldn't be implicated?'

'I don't know, Mary. We can't assume anything. I'm just saying that the dates match.' Terry gave Fraser an apologetic smile. 'It's just a thought.'

'Thanks, Terry.' Fraser stood up. 'It's worth a look.'

Alan was shaking his head. 'It's all very odd though. Why would Reagan kill his patients? Bob's right, he makes a fortune out of them. And then there's—'

Fraser interrupted. 'This is all conjecture at the moment – linking four deaths, when we only know for certain that one was a murder.' He looked directly at Terry. 'You can't be sure of the others, can you, Terry?'

Terry shook her head. 'Apart from Higgins, there's a drowning, a fire death and a hanging. All with peculiarities, but you're right, John, it's just speculation at the moment. Nothing concrete.'

'And then there's another thing,' Ahern began again. 'Where do Henderson and his cousin Igor fit in? If at all. Just because Henderson and Reagan are friends of sorts, and Aoife Foster is Henderson's sister—'

'What? Aoife is Henderson's *sister*? The tipstaff's her cousin? How long have you known this?' Terry said to Fraser accusingly.

'Just since we spoke to Judge Henderson.'

He waited for Terry to kick off, but she sat quietly for a few minutes before she said, 'So, Reagan could have acted with them. I mean, the judge and Igor. And maybe they pressured Aoife into setting up the alibis. She could be easily manipulated. Her husband died in sad circumstances and she has that downtrodden look about her. No wonder she tries to make friends with the women she meets in the clinic.'

Fraser shook his head. 'What did you say to Mary about not assuming anything? Can we just stick to the facts?'

Mary rolled her eyes at Terry.

Fraser gave them both a warning look. 'Well, we're going to have to have a word with Aoife in any case. Mary, check out the wives' alibis for those deaths.' He pointed to the whiteboard. 'Speak to them and see what you can find out about these clubs and days out. Alan, bring Reagan back in – we need to hear what he has to say about this … theory. And get a couple of uniforms back round to Aoife Foster's house. Tell them to stay put until she appears, then bring her in.'

They both headed for the door.

'Wait, Alan, how did you get on with the CCTV? You said you were going to take another look.'

'Like you thought, Igor Henderson came out of the CCJ a few minutes after Higgins. Sorry, boss, but that's the last we have of either of them.'

Fraser tapped his pen on his desk. 'Can you check if we can access footage going back to the week before the Christmas break, specifically the Thursday? See if Higgins shows up. And find out the cases listed for that week.'

'Sure, boss. What have you got in mind?'

'Book club on Thursdays. Coincidence? Maybe our colleague had a long-standing appointment at Delaney Gardens, especially given the histology results showed he was in the habit of wearing his own handcuffs. This wasn't a random attack. Someone knew he was going to be there.'

Terry felt deflated. Tasks had been assigned and the others had dispersed. She had found a link between the deaths, but something else was niggling. She decided to take another look through the diaries. She flicked frantically through their pages until she found it: the same symbol she'd seen beside another man's name.

She raced over to the incident room, which was buzzing with activity and an energy that had been lacking as the Higgins investigation had stalled. Now there was a sense of purpose and anticipation in the air.

Terry dropped the 2025 diary in front of Fraser. He picked it up and looked up at her.

'You need to see this.' Leaning across, she opened it at a date a few weeks earlier. 'Tony Watson. He and his wife came into the clinic when I was waiting to see Maeve Price. Aoife was a bit off with him, and then Reagan came out and he was all over the wife. The next time I was in I had a wee peek at the diary to see who they were and I noticed this beside the name.' She pointed at the entry.

Fraser nodded. 'An asterisk.'

'I think that might be how he identifies the victims: Higgins, Maguire, Tormey and O'Neill all had the asterisk beside their names. It's the men who opt out of the counselling. There might be more men identified this way, but I haven't had time to do a thorough check – I was concentrating on the deaths we knew of. And then look at today's date.'

Fraser's eye was drawn to where Terry was pointing. 'Afternoon tea at the Westbury?'

Terry stabbed her finger at the page. 'And look who's on the list of who is going to be there. Sinead Watson. The wife of Mr Watson with the asterisk.'

Fraser looked pensive. 'That's a big leap.'

'You want to take a chance?' she asked.

Fraser didn't look fully convinced but lifted the handset of his desk phone and called Mary. 'Mary, I urgently need the address of a Tony and Sinead Watson. Terry's got some info for you. Is Alan with you? Tell him to send someone around there once you've got it – we need to find Tony Watson. Then get in here.'

Fraser brought the two detectives up to date when they came into his office. 'We also need someone at the Westbury to check if Sinead Watson is there and who's with her.'

'Leave that with me, boss. I can get Clodagh onto it.' Clodagh Rafferty was a crime scene officer Mary had taken under her wing. 'She lives nearby so I'll tell her to go home quickly and get dressed up a bit. She'd stick out like a sore thumb in cargo pants and a polo shirt.'

'Tell her she's just to check if Aoife Foster's group is there. Have you a photo of Sinead Watson? We need to know if she's with them. Clodagh is just to keep an eye on the group and let us know if they make a move to leave. She's not to approach them directly.'

As soon as Mary left, Fraser turned to Terry. 'Well done.'

She smiled back. 'If I'm right.' She had her fingers crossed behind her back.

40

Alan Ahern had been expecting a call from Dr Reagan. They had known he would not be happy when he heard that gardaí had raided his clinic. Ahern listened to his tirade then, when Reagan ran out of steam, dropped the bombshell that the doctor should immediately come into Walter Scott House. His offer of sending a squad car to pick up Reagan was declined.

Ronan Reagan arrived with his solicitor, Mr Colson-Brown, who looked put out at having to come in on a Sunday.

Fraser and Ahern sat down opposite Dr Reagan and Mr Colson-Brown, who made the opening gambit. 'My client wishes to co-operate fully with these enquiries, Detective Superintendent Fraser, but so far, I'm not sure what information Dr Reagan could give you regarding any of his patients. There is the small matter of *confidentiality*. He is an eminent psychologist and has successfully treated many patients, the details of which must remain confidential, unless you make a written request for them under the Data Protection Act.'

The doctor put his hand on the self-important solicitor's arm. 'Clients.'

Fraser ignored the solicitor and spoke directly to Reagan. 'Yes, Dr Reagan, we're interested in some of your clients.' He shot the solicitor a look and opened the brown envelope in front of him. He pulled out the diaries. 'Do you recognise these office diaries?'

'Of course.'

Fraser opened the top diary and started flicking through the pages.

'Not au fait with technology then?' Alan Ahern gave a derisive laugh.

Reagan bristled. 'I like to keep things simple. I don't trust technology. My clients expect confidentiality and there are … hackers that could get hold of their details. Mrs Foster maintains my appointment diary. But it's irrelevant what my thoughts are on these,' he pointed at the volumes on the table, 'as those diaries aren't for my appointments. They are the personal diaries of Mrs Foster. I wouldn't break her trust and read them.'

Fraser pushed the book across the table. 'Look at this entry.' Reagan picked up the diary, but before he could respond, Fraser pushed the next one across. 'And this entry.'

Reagan looked up. 'As I said, I'm not comfortable with this. These are Aoife's diaries. There may be entries that I have no business reading.'

'What exactly is your relationship with Mrs Foster? Is it purely professional?' Fraser and Reagan both looked stunned by Ahern's question. 'Just asking …'

Fraser kept his head down to hide a smirk.

Reagan spluttered in response, his face turning puce, 'It's utterly professional. I would not have a relationship with a colleague. We're not all having affairs, which is more than I can say for the likes of the gardaí.' He glared at Fraser.

Fraser decided to move back to safer territory. 'So tell me, Dr Reagan, how does the system work? How do you keep track of your appointments?'

'Like I said' – Reagan was exasperated – 'Aoife records the appointments in *my* diary.' Fraser and Ahern exchanged looks. 'It's kept in a locked drawer.' He sounded defensive.

'So you wouldn't have access to this diary?' asked Fraser, picking one up and dropping it back down onto the table in front of Reagan.

'Well, it sits on Aoife's desk.'

'You wouldn't add notes regarding the patients in it, then?' Fraser sat back and gave a small nod to Ahern.

'Any comments I make are in the client's file. Those files are kept in locked filing cabinets in my room. Only I have a key to those. And they are *clients*, Superintendent. They are not ill, only experiencing difficulties with a certain area of their life.'

'In their marriages?' Ahern looked quizzical. 'Well, yes. I specialise in couples counselling.'

'Successful, are you?' Ahern sounded, and looked, sceptical.

'It depends on what you define as success. Not all marriages are worth saving. I support people to make the right decision for them.'

'And if it doesn't work out, you're there to help the ladies pick up the pieces.' Ahern leaned across and picked up the diaries.

Reagan's face reddened and he made to stand. His solicitor pulled him down and gave him a disapproving look. He turned to Ahern. 'What are you insinuating, Detective Inspector?'

Reagan thumped the desk then, obviously riled. 'Support and counselling do not always happen within the confines of the clinic.' The solicitor glared at his client.

Fraser sat forward. 'Dr Reagan, four of your clients have died in, if not suspicious circumstances, unusual circumstances. Not exactly great PR for your practice.'

Mr Colson-Brown spoke directly to Fraser. 'Do you have any evidence to suggest my client was in any way responsible for these deaths? If not, then I assume Dr Reagan is free to leave.'

Fraser ignored the solicitor. 'Martin Higgins?'

'Higgins was a guard. I am sure there were many people who would wish to harm him. I am a psychologist and, where possible, I help resolve conflicts,' said Reagan pompously.

'What about Cillian Maguire?' Fraser maintained eye contact with Reagan.

'Judge Henderson told me about his suicide.'

'Suicide?' Fraser repeated with a distinct note of scepticism in his voice.

'He was a difficult client. I hadn't seen him in months.'

'But you knew about the allegations against him?'

'There had been rumours. He is, was, a disgrace to the medical profession if they are true.'

'So if those allegations are true, you're not upset he's dead.' Reagan paled.

Fraser picked up one of the diaries. 'What about today?'

The psychologist looked flummoxed. 'I don't understand.'

'Did you have something arranged?'

'Well, I was meeting a friend at the driving range, until you summoned me here.'

'Would that friend be Tony Watson?'

'Why would I meet Mr Watson?' Reagan looked genuinely confused. 'I'm meeting an old college friend, Colin Fitzpatrick. You can call him if you like. I'm happy to give you his number.'

Fraser stopped the interview about twenty minutes later. He didn't like Reagan, but his reactions seemed genuine. He seemed bewildered that they thought any of these deaths were not straightforward suicides or accidental. Apart from Higgins, of course. Could Fraser really imagine this weasel in front of him standing up to someone like Higgins and wrestling his gun from him? As for the others, Reagan had seen so many 'clients' over the years that three deaths among them were not a lot in the grand scheme of things.

Fraser would leave him to sweat, while he waited for someone to retrieve the appointment diaries from the locked drawer in Reagan's desk in the clinic. He had grudgingly handed over the key after a heated discussion with his solicitor. Fraser reassured him he was only interested in the diaries. For the time being.

'Any update?' Fraser addressed the incident room.

Mary looked up. 'Clodagh phoned in. Mrs Watson's having a high old time. Clodagh managed to bump into her, accidentally, in the toilet. She hasn't seen anything of Aoife Foster, though.'

Fraser felt uneasy. 'Henderson said he thought she was away for the weekend. If she's not at the Westbury, where the hell is she? We need to find her, and soon. Something about this is off.'

'Boss!' Ahern waved the desk-phone handset. 'The boys I sent over to Foster's house say she's still not there. They've spoken to the neighbours. One of them said she saw Foster go out this morning with her boyfriend. The description matches the odd cousin by the sounds of it.'

41

Michael was desperate to tell someone. He couldn't believe the DNA results. His first thought was to ring Terry, but he was worried he might say too much. It was better to call Alan – Tormey was originally his case, after all.

'Alan,' he said breathlessly down the phone.

'Sorry, Michael, we're on our way out. I can't talk now.'

'Look, I'll keep it short,' said Michael quickly, anxious to get all the words out before Alan hung up. 'I thought you'd want to know. I've got a result on the axe from that fire death. There were traces of blood and I got two profiles – the muppet wielding it must have cut themselves. Anyway, one is Tormey, and you'll never guess what?' Michael didn't wait for Alan to respond. 'The other one matches the unknown profile from the Maguire and O'Neill deaths.' He heard a car door slam.

'So the same person is involved in all three deaths? That's great work, Mikey. I'll pass that on to Fraser and the team.

Looks like we made the right call to have a closer look at Reagan. I need to go, though. I'll see you at the flat later.'

'Stay safe. And Alan, less of the Mikey, please.' He smiled when he heard Alan laughing.

The bottom line was that Terry was right: the murders, because this more or less confirmed they were murders, were linked. It still didn't mean Higgins's death was directly related – that was for Fraser's team to decide – but the axe had got Michael thinking.

He put his mobile on his desk and walked back to the lab. Higgins's Leatherman had been wiped, so no fingerprints, but it was no surprise that Higgins's DNA was all over it. Michael went over to the tray holding the evidence samples from the detective's murder and picked up the bag containing the knife. He checked the signatures on the label. His was after Alan Ahern's, as he had made sure he was there to receive the samples personally when Alan had brought them into the lab. Pathetic, wasn't it? But that was the past. Luckily, he could now see a future for the two of them.

He sighed and twisted the bag this way and that. Weaponry wasn't his thing, but he had to admit the Leatherman was a thing of beauty. He picked up an Allen key and set about dismantling the knife, intending to swab every nanometre.

As he worked, Michael's mind wandered. He had other worries – he'd got the results from Terry's necklace. But that would have to wait until later. It wasn't urgent, and it wasn't as if Terry was at risk, but it was going to turn her world upside down. He wished Monica hadn't agreed with the Scottish lab that the FSI would carry out the analyses on the necklace. Now he would have to be the bearer of this news.

It was just that it didn't make sense. He would give his friend George McLaughlin in Forensic Science Scotland a call. It would be good to have the input of another DNA expert. At any rate, he had promised to call George as soon as he had anything. George had mentioned that a partial fingerprint had been found on Jenny's necklace at the time of her murder, but there were no identical matches in the Scottish fingerprint database and they never identified any suspects. George had told him that the fingerprinters at the time had been cagey about any potential matches on their database. They said they had checked them out, but none of them were viable suspects. Michael wanted to see that original list of possible matches, even if at the time they were deemed not a close enough match.

After he finished swabbing it, he repackaged the Leatherman and returned it to the Higgins evidence tray.

He had had a thought about Jenny's results – there was one more loose end he needed to tidy up. Picking up her evidence tray, he looked down at the shiny Christmas paper Jenny's necklace had been wrapped in as he swiped a DNA swab across it. Monica would berate him if he didn't do a thorough job.

Terry felt like a bit of a spare part, which was something she rarely felt. The incident room was buzzing and everyone seemed to have a job to do except for her. It was with relief that she heard her phone beep with a message. Francis Foster file has come in. It's on your desk. The ever-efficient Mrs C had come through, even on a Sunday. Obviously prepping for the week ahead. Terry immediately ordered a taxi, and five minutes later she was on her way to the OSP.

She took the stairs up to the reception area two at a time and went straight into her office. The building was deserted, and it felt strange being there without Jimmy or Tomas to greet her. But there on top of the pile of files she had been working on was a purple folder. Francis Foster. Aoife's late husband.

Suddenly Terry felt very vulnerable – she needed to be around people. Dropping the file into her bag, she ordered another taxi. She had a weird sense of being watched, and she waited anxiously outside the mortuary, glancing over her shoulder to see if anyone was around. But no, she was definitely alone. Relieved, she climbed into the taxi and sped off back to the relative safety of WSH.

Things must have ramped up because by the time she got back – even though it had been less than forty minutes – the incident room was almost empty. She went into Fraser's office to use his fancy coffee machine and settled at his desk with Foster's file and a new notebook.

Inside the purple folder was all the information the coroner had gathered. There was a report in Spanish, which she put to the side. The coroner's own record was a mash-up of what she guessed was badly translated Spanish and the accounts from the golfing buddies Francis had been on holiday with, with a smattering of newspaper reports thrown in for good measure. The gist was that Francis Foster had been on a lads' golfing holiday, equal amounts golf and drinking. On the night of his death the group had enjoyed a very boozy dinner, followed by a trip to a local nightclub. After their return in the early hours of the following morning, they all went to their respective rooms. And none of the group saw or heard anything until the Spanish emergency services arrived the next day.

It would appear that somehow Francis Foster had done a header over the balcony. A post-mortem had been carried out in Spain, but only the cause of death had been translated: multiple injuries due to a fall from a height. Three storeys onto concrete would do that to you. It had been a closed-coffin affair, sealed in the Spanish mortuary and not opened until it arrived in the City Mortuary in Dublin.

The Spanish police were content this was a drunken accident. Foreigners falling off Spanish balconies was not an infrequent occurrence. Case closed. Even Frank's best pals didn't seem perturbed. No love lost, it seemed.

Strangely, it wasn't Aoife who had lobbied the coroner to investigate the death – it was her husband's mistress, Francesca Rossi, who had expressed concern. Aoife was described in the file as Foster's ex-wife. That was interesting. Maeve Price had alluded to Francis Foster as Aoife's husband, not her ex. Was Aoife in denial about the breakdown of her marriage?

Francesca Rossi had given a statement to the gardaí regarding her trip out to Murcia. She had gone as soon as she got word of his accident. She told the guards that she had been distraught, the Spanish policía wouldn't tell her anything, and Frank's so-called friends didn't seem too concerned by his death. Ms Rossi had stated she couldn't understand how Frank could fall over the wrought-iron railing of his balcony as it was chest-level high. The policía had told her that drunk British men did it all too frequently.

The coroner had agreed to look into it, which meant a post-mortem examination when the body returned to Ireland. Terry thought he might have been irked by the British comment.

Paul Hannah had carried out the post-mortem. He did what he could, given that one had already been carried out in Spain and the body didn't seem to have been embalmed well. Paul commented in the file that there was patchy decomposition.

Terry speed-read his report and nothing jumped out. The impact must have been massive: there didn't seem to be an intact bone in Foster's body.

There had been an inquest some months later. Luckily, Paul had attended and taken notes as the witnesses gave their evidence. Foster's cronies were quizzed by the coroner, but all were a bit hazy about the night, due to the drink taken. The coroner tried but eventually had to admit defeat. The facts were that Foster had been drinking and had fallen to his death. There was nothing to suggest this was any more than an accident, but the coroner agreed he had only limited information regarding the circumstances. An open verdict was returned. It was anyone's guess what happened that night, but alcohol and gravity are a dangerous mix.

However, Paul had added a note at the bottom of his post-mortem report: 'Woman (FR) asked coroner if valuables returned. Claddagh commitment ring missing. Informed coroner ring not on body. Injury to left little finger could have been caused by ring caught on something in fall.'

Terry looked back through the report. Paul had described

an irregular laceration on the left little finger and that the distal and middle phalanges, the small bones of the finger, were missing. *Avulsed* was the word he used – torn from the finger.

Terry sat back and finished her coffee while she googled *commitment ring*. 'A promise to commit for life.' What a load of codswallop. But that begged the question about the state of Aoife's marriage. It looked like she had been well and truly usurped by this other woman, Francesca. Poor Aoife.

42

There was no doubting it, Fraser agreed: Tony Watson was one lucky man. He was tucked up in ICU and was in a relatively stable condition. If it hadn't been for Terry, Mrs Watson would be organising a funeral.

The two detectives Fraser had sent over to check out Watson's house had obviously disturbed his attacker. David Duffy had only recently been made detective, but it looked like he would probably require counselling for a considerable period. His partner said it had been a veritable blood bath, and, for once, that was no exaggeration.

Mr Watson's right arm had been part severed with a hedge cutter. He had been left bleeding out while someone had set about doctoring the scene to make it look like a gardening-related accident. At the hospital, the doctors had found another cut across his chest. Watson had just missed having his chest sliced open. Which would have had a very different outcome.

They were doing scans and X-rays at the hospital. It looked as though he might have been knocked out and subdued before he was set about with the hedge cutter so the doctors wanted to ensure he didn't have a brain injury. Fraser had left instructions that as soon as he rallied, the gardaí stationed at the hospital were to contact him.

Fraser thought it was unlikely there was a single assailant. It certainly wasn't Reagan, who was still anxiously sitting in WSH with his solicitor. Aoife Foster and Igor Henderson were still missing. He had gardaí out scouring the city for them. It was only a matter of time before they were found.

He was relieved to see Terry sitting in his office in WSH. Alan Ahern and Mary Healy followed him in.

'The attack on Watson looks as if it was being set up as an accident,' Fraser said. 'Whoever attacked him didn't get a chance to complete the scene or finish him off.'

'But it's similar to Maguire, O'Neill and Tormey. Their deaths looked like something they weren't. It's a pattern.' Terry looked from Fraser to Ahern.

It was Alan who replied first. 'Michael called me earlier. He's confirmed the other deaths are linked by a DNA profile. He found blood on the blade and handle of the axe from the fire death: two profiles, Tormey's and A.N. Other, which matches the unknown from O'Neill and Maguire.'

'But nothing linking Higgins to them?' Fraser could tell Terry was miffed that Michael hadn't shared this with her. 'Maybe Higgins is different. The mutilation of his body was pretty gross.'

'A needle up your willy is no picnic either,' Mary chipped in.

Fraser raised his eyes to the ceiling. 'So we have three deaths with a common perpetrator and now an attack on another client of the Rockroad Clinic. Reagan was with us today, so he wasn't directly involved in Watson's attack.'

'But that doesn't mean he wasn't involved somehow, boss. It doesn't exonerate him. He could have planned it – he just doesn't like getting his hands dirty, so to speak.'

'True, Mary. We'll leave that hanging just now. What about the psychiatrist, Dr Price?'

Terry jumped in. 'When I spoke to her at the clinic, I got the impression that she and Reagan aren't too cosy. It seems they have a professional relationship only. And anyway, why would she kill his clients? I'm sure she's got some oddballs of her own she could take out if she was that way inclined.'

'Maybe, but she was with Sinead Watson at the Westbury, so we'll have to check her out.'

'What if the wives were all in on it?' said Mary. 'They could've arranged it, like some sort of ex-wives club?'

Fraser looked thoughtful. 'Wishful thinking. Mrs Watson was quite forthcoming when the guards took a statement from her at the hospital. They might be going through a tough patch, but she loves him and she's in total shock about what's happened to him.

'I've spoken to Judge Quigley and we've got warrants to search their houses – Aoife Foster's, Igor Henderson's and Reagan's' he continued. 'Alan, you take Henderson's, and can you organise a team to search Reagan's? He's definitely not off the hook. Mary, you come with me to Foster's.' Fraser threw his car keys to the detective.

Then he looked over at Terry, knowing she would be desperate to be part of the action. 'You can come too.' Terry jumped up, grinning with delight to be involved. 'That way I can keep an eye on you.' He gave her a knowing look.

Aoife Foster's home looked fairly ordinary, a detached red-brick in River Valley, Swords. The drive was empty. Mary was out of the car in a flash, intent on getting in first. Terry trailed behind, still a bit put out that Fraser had warned her on the journey over to not get in the way. He disappeared off, barking orders at the SOCOs.

Dressed in the obligatory white Tyvek coverall, with her hood up and mask on, Terry could move through the house like a ghostly presence. The hall was a trip hazard, being used as the dumping ground for the SOCOs' equipment, so she moved into the living room. It was bland and beige, although the furnishings looked expensive enough. It just lacked any personality or warmth.

Vinnie had set up his tripod in the kitchen and was busy photographing the contents of a large cardboard box on the kitchen table. Despite her disguise, he recognised Terry and waved her over. She peered into the box and began pulling the items out and setting them up to be photographed. There was a selection of knives, scissors, rolls of packing tape, coils of rope and wire, a claw hammer and a couple of screwdrivers.

Lying loose at the bottom were a handful of bullets and a selection of shotgun cartridges. Terry was no ballistics expert, but even she could tell the bullets were of different sizes and the cartridges contained a variety of shot. She doubted that Aoife Foster was a big-game hunter, but buckshot could do a lot of harm to the average human.

'Fraser needs to see this. She could be armed.'

Terry left Vinnie setting the ammunition up in an orderly row, with a scale alongside, in order to take photographs. She had a quick snoop through the kitchen cabinets – just the usual food, tableware and cookware. Kind of incongruous with the box full of weaponry, though. A calendar hung on the wall next to the back door. Dates were ringed, but there was nothing to indicate why. Terry whipped out her phone and photographed January and February.

Fraser and Mary had joined Vinnie at the kitchen table. Fraser was speaking to someone on the phone, likely Ahern, and Mary began assisting Vinnie with photographing what he had set out on the table. Terry squeezed past and back out into the hall and climbed the stairs. The SOCOs were busy downstairs and hadn't made it upstairs yet, so she decided to take a quick look around rather that get in their way. She sidled into the first room – a bedroom.

'Jeez!' She was taken aback. The only word to describe it was boudoir. She looked around at the very feminine frills and flounces, from curtains to drapes around the bed, which was piled with fluffy baby-pink cushions.

The next room was gloomy because the curtains were closed, so she switched on the ceiling light and was astounded for the second time in as many minutes. All she could do was stand at the door gaping, taking it all in. She had never seen anything like it. The room was set out as a shrine. Terry assumed the man dominating the photographs on a dresser was Aoife's dead husband.

On the wall was a huge portrait of a slightly overweight dark-haired man, rapidly going to seed but attempting to look suave. Terry's eyes were drawn to the straining buttons of his shirt. It never ceased to amaze her that men didn't seem to have the hang-ups about their bodies that women had.

There were many more images of the same man accompanied by a variety of similar-looking men, ruddy of face and portly of build. There was only one with Aoife. Bless her, she was grinning like a hyena, hanging on to his arm, wearing a dress that ensured not an inch of her body was on display.

Terry walked over to the bed. A tuxedo, shirt, bow tie and dress trousers were laid out. A pair of gleaming black patent shoes sat on the floor. On the nearest bedside table was a Longines watch and gold cufflinks. She walked around the bed to where another framed photograph sat on the other bedside table, with a few tealights scattered around. She did a double take: this photograph was of Dr Ronan Reagan. Then she noticed a large display cabinet in the corner and walked over to have a closer look.

On the top shelf, at eye level, was a plinth, centre stage, holding a gold wedding band. On the shelf beside it was a rather mangled-looking gold ring, which looked as if it was coated in dried dark material and attached to which was some dried-out, almost black mummified tissue. Multiple objects sat on the other shelves, including a ring, a belt, a gold tassel, little ring pouches, a brass key and a grey scarf.

A single book was on the bottom shelf. Terry was both

intrigued and slightly perplexed to see that it was DiMaio's *Forensic Pathology*. Aoife had never once expressed an interest in pathology to her when she saw her at the clinic.

Terry had to restrain herself from touching the artefacts and unfurling the scarf. Preservation of evidence was ingrained in her psyche. And she knew exactly what these were. Souvenirs of Aoife's crimes. She was desperate to search the little pouches – she would bet one contained a lock of Owen O'Neill's hair. And the stains visible on the scarf would surely turn out to be Higgins's blood. Terry wished she could check it to see if there was a bullet hole in it – that would confirm her theory it had been used to silence the gunshot.

She rushed out and leaned over the banister. 'Vinnie! Fraser!'

Vinnie's head appeared at the bottom of the stairs. 'What's up, Doc?'

'Hysterical. Just get up here,' she yelled. 'Now!'

Fraser's head popped up behind him. 'You've found something?' They both rushed up the stairs and entered the room, their eyes widening.

'It's Aoife's trophy cabinet,' she said, as the two stunned men took in the scene.

It was late when the teams got back to WSH. They had pulled the house apart looking for guns. All they found was a double-barrelled shotgun in the wardrobe in what was now dubbed the trophy room. Everyone was knackered and starving.

'I can't believe all that shit in her house.' Mary Healy sat on a desk, swinging her legs and munching on a chocolate digestive. 'Who would have thunk? She doesn't look the type.'

'Who ever does?' Terry sat beside her.

Ahern sighed. 'Igor's flat meanwhile was sparse in furnishings and personal belongings. There was some manky cat running about. The place was rank, stank of cat piss. I need a shower.' He dropped into a chair across from Terry. 'So do you still think she might have had something to do with Martin's death?'

Terry nodded. 'I wasn't sure, because it doesn't have the same patterns as the others, but now I think maybe she did. She had a collection of trophies, and in it was a grey scarf that looked like the one Higgins had in the CCTV from the court. We didn't touch anything. Someone from FSI will have to go out tomorrow morning to collect it all.'

'It was really creepy.' Mary shivered.

Ahern smiled over at Terry, then turned to Fraser. 'The lads got sweet FA at Reagan's. It looks like he keeps all his work at work. At the moment, it seems the doctor's clean. We've got nothing on him and all his alibis stack up.' Ahern sat quietly for a moment, deep in thought. 'Do you think Aoife could be the mastermind, boss? Igor Henderson the stooge, the muscle?'

'It's beginning to look that way. Her cousin doesn't strike me as having the wit to organise any of this.'

'Could her husband have been her first?' They all looked at Terry. 'He fell off a balcony during a golf weekend in Spain. Paul Hannah did a post-mortem on the body when it was repatriated. There's nothing definite that stands out. He died from the type of injuries you would expect in a fall from a height, but there was an inquest and his girlfriend, a Francesca

Rossi, asked about a ring he should have been wearing. It wasn't returned with the body, but I'm pretty sure I saw it in Aoife's cabinet. Maybe it was her first memento, and if it was, she had to have been in Spain to retrieve it, because the coffin was sealed after the post-mortem there and wasn't opened until it arrived in the City Mortuary in Dublin.' She grimaced. 'I think part of his finger is still attached to it.'

43

Fraser hadn't slept much. He had been in constant contact with the Emergency Response Unit through the night, ready to deploy them if there was any sniff of Aoife Foster and Igor Henderson. So far, nothing.

He had a quick shower and was sitting at the desk in his living room with a mug of coffee by 5.30 a.m., ready to make a few calls before heading into work. He was careful to speak quietly so as not to disturb Terry.

'Morning, Alan. I didn't wake you, did I?' he asked as Alan blearily answered his phone. Fraser could hear a kettle boiling in the background. He suspected his DI hadn't got much sleep either. 'A car picks up Judge Henderson for court at 9 a.m. I want to get to his house early. There's been no movement at his sister's or his cousin's homes overnight, but the judge might have heard from his sister. It's a long shot, but we don't have any other leads. We can't rule out the possibility that they've sought refuge in the judge's house. I doubt they'll have gone far if it was them at Watson's house yesterday. There've been no sightings of Foster's car.'

Fraser was taking no chances, so he waited until the Emergency Response lads were in place before he headed to the judge's house in Sandymount. As soon as he arrived, Fraser knew something was up.

He had been to the house before when collecting warrants, and it was well known that Henderson's pride and joy was a classic Jaguar, which he kept in a temperature-controlled garage. Apparently he only drove it on warm sunny days, which were a rare occurrence. But it was a grey, drizzly morning and the Jag was sitting in the drive, exposed to the elements.

When Alan pulled the unmarked car in to the kerb, a guard in full riot gear came over and bent down, resting his left arm on the roof, and peered into the car. 'Who's in charge?'

Fraser leaned across to reply. 'Detective Superintendent Fraser.'

'Morning, sir. Detective Sergeant Aitken. My men are in place. There's someone inside but the curtains are drawn, so we don't know who or how many.'

'Right. Have you checked the garage?'

'Blue Toyota Yaris, 2023, a hybrid. We ran the plate. It's registered to Aoife Foster.'

'Thanks. I'm worried that means Aoife Foster and Igor Henderson are inside the judge's house. They could be armed – ammunition was found at Foster's place. But we need to be careful how we handle this. Judge Henderson might be in danger, and we have to ensure his safety. Just be cautious.'

The sergeant pulled his cap down over his eyes. 'Are you sure the judge isn't involved?'

'I don't think so. But you're right. Best not to take chances. Though I'm speaking to the expert.' Fraser smiled at the burly officer.

'The crisis negotiator is due shortly so we'll leave it to her.' The DS gave Fraser a thumbs-up and sauntered back to his men.

The team was on tenterhooks waiting for the crisis negotiator to arrive, but they didn't have to wait too long. Fraser debriefed her and it was decided that he would call Judge Henderson first to establish what was going on inside the house.

Fraser pulled out his mobile. 'Let's go easy. I don't want to spook anyone. I don't think he'd respond well to public humiliation if we brought out the megaphone straightaway.'

He pressed a few buttons and let the phone ring. As soon as it was answered he put it on speakerphone. An angry female voice carried to Ahern and the negotiator standing on the opposite side of the road. 'Who is this?'

'Is that you, Aoife? I'm Detective Superintendent John Fraser. Can I speak to Judge Henderson?'

'No,' she said angrily.

'I just want to talk. I'm sure we can—' The call was cut.

Fraser retried the number. Nothing – it had been switched off. Time for Plan B. He took the megaphone. 'Aoife. I want to know if Judge Henderson, Igor or you need medical attention.' They all stared at the house waiting for some response.

The crisis negotiator came over. 'Do you want me to take over? She might respond to a woman.'

Fraser relinquished the megaphone. He had to agree – from what he now knew of her, Aoife Foster wasn't going to pay heed to any man.

Just then he heard raised voices emanating from the house.

'Aoife, put the gun down – stop this nonsense!' This was Judge Henderson. Fraser strained, but couldn't hear any reply.

'Now!' The judge's voice was strong and stern. He didn't sound afraid. He was used to his orders being obeyed. 'Igor! Unlock that door.' There was a moment's silence. 'You will never get away with this.'

Suddenly there was an almighty crash from inside, followed by a bang. The ERU leapt into action and the order was made to storm the house. Fraser and the rest took cover.

It unfolded quickly. The front and back doors of the house were rammed, and the ERU flooded in. All Fraser could hear was a lot of shouting and screaming. Fraser and Alan stood staring at the house until the noise and confusion faded. Shortly afterwards, a kicking and screeching Aoife was dragged out handcuffed, a defiant look on her face. There wasn't a single trace of the mild-mannered homely receptionist. An armed guard holding a double-barrelled shotgun followed behind. A bloody-nosed Igor Henderson stumbled out the door then, escorted by two guards. He didn't look as if there was any fight left in him.

After another few moments, Judge Henderson had still not appeared. Fraser sprinted up the path expecting the worst. As he reached the front door, he could hear the judge giving the ERU guys a hard time. Henderson spied Fraser and addressed him directly. 'This is all totally unnecessary,' he blustered. The judge was dressed in black monogrammed silk pyjamas and his hair was mussed. 'This guard is preventing me from getting dressed.'

Fraser looked back to where Alan Ahern was standing on the road and nodded towards the indignant judge. 'Alan. Take this from here. He's unhurt but the hall mirror didn't fare too well.'

44

Terry paced up and down Fraser's office in WSH, unable to relax while waiting for Fraser's return, with or without Aoife and Igor. She was idly flicking through Aoife's diaries again when her phone rang. She snatched it off the desk, hoping it was John with an update. Her heart sank when she saw her uncle Jim's name flash up on the screen. 'Hi, love,' he said cheerily. 'I'm off back to Glasgow today, but I need to give you the new keys to your flat.' Terry felt immediately guilty at her irritation towards him. He was only looking out for her, as ever. She had forgotten that he had offered to get her locks changed. Asking him to leave the keys with the building's security guard seemed a bit ungrateful. Maybe she could nip out and meet him in the pub, and then go over to the OSP. She needed company and distraction in any case.

She couldn't help but feel uneasy as she walked past security in WSH. These last few days had been unsettling to say the least. She checked over her shoulder and smiled at the guard at the barrier. Apart from a garda van idling near the gate, there was no one else around. Keeping her head down, she walked briskly over the Seán Heuston bridge and towards the CCJ building. She was finding it difficult to shake off this strange feeling of being followed.

Terry crossed at the lights outside the courts, scanning the street as she walked. When she pushed open the door into Nancy Hands, no one looked up. The lighting was subdued and despite it being just after twelve and the pub having only been open for ten minutes, quite a few folk were already settled with drinks. Big Jim was at a table over by the far wall, away from the bar. She gave a little wave.

'Hiya, Jim.' She bent and gave him a peck on the cheek. She noticed him looking intently at her.

'You look well, love.'

'Aye, right. Thanks for getting those locks changed. Let me know how much I owe you.'

'Ah, sure, it's no bother.' He pulled out her new set of keys, with a novelty skull key ring attached. 'Here you go. I checked that they all work.'

'I like the gothic humour.' She grinned, playing with the skull charm. He gave her a quick smile, before his expression turned serious. 'You'd be better steering clear for another while. There's a lot of dodgy characters hanging around. I could get some of the boys from the old days to keep an eye out. I don't want to have to tell your dad you're in a bit of trouble.'

'Don't you dare, Jim Malone! Dad worries enough about me

without you stirring it. And I don't need some retired guards cramping my style.' She gave him her best stern look.

'I'm only messing with you.' He toyed with his pint, not meeting her eyes. 'I was speaking to an old pal of mine, works out of the Hamilton office back home.'

The mention of Hamilton immediately had Terry on high alert. When her sister had been murdered, it had been decided that the main police station in Hamilton would take over the investigation because her dad had been a sergeant in the office in Wishaw. It would be a conflict of interest for him to handle the investigation. She looked at Jim warily, not trusting herself to speak. He didn't seem to notice.

'He was saying that your pal Michael was doing a bit of work on Jenny's case.' Jim looked straight at her. 'Your dad was asking if I'd heard anything new.'

'How did the guy in Hamilton know about Michael?' It sounded like there were leaks in every police force.

'Sandy, that's my pal – Norman Shaw's his real name, but we all called him Sandy.'

Terry was watching him carefully – was he trying to avoid answering her question? 'Was he about when Jenny was murdered?'

'Yeah, he was just a constable at the time. But I suppose we all have one case we can't quite forget. His nephew George is in forensics, and he knows your Michael from work.'

'Well, as far as I know there's nothing to hear. Michael hasn't finished with the neck—' As the words left her mouth, she felt her heart sink. She didn't want her dad or Jim to know what was going on in case it got their hopes up. It could all amount to nothing. But Big Jim didn't give any indication he had clocked what she had been about to say – his eyes were trained on the horse racing on the TV screen in the corner.

She quickly changed the subject. 'What time's your flight?' 'Are you desperate to get rid of me?' He beamed at her, taking a sip of his pint.

'No, no. I'm just busy with work and need to get back to it soon.' She gave him a wan smile.

Jim took out his phone. 'My flight's at three-ish, I think.' He looked down at the screen. 'Ah shite. The battery's gone. Can I borrow your phone to check my email?'

'Sure. Here.' She punched in her password and passed it over. 'I'll just nip to the toilet before I jump in a taxi to the OSP.'

Michael's hunch had paid off, or rather his perseverance with Higgins's knife had. Bingo! He had found the same DNA profile that had been recovered in the other deaths. Higgins, Tormey, O'Neill and Maguire were linked. But that wasn't all he had discovered.

Now, Michael left a message for John Fraser to call him. Even Alan wasn't picking up. As well as providing an update on the Higgins evidence, he was also in search of advice. He wasn't sure how to handle the DNA results from Jenny's case, and he wanted reassurance. Terry had just texted him to meet at her flat for a late lunch, which was odd. He thought she was still staying with Fraser. But he needed to sort this out, so he replied saying he would see her there in an hour or so. He was about to drop a bombshell on her that could make or break her. She might never speak to him again. What was that saying again about shooting the messenger?

He went back into the DNA lab. He just had to finalise the results from the paper Aileen had wrapped Jenny's necklace in. He wanted to make sure there were no weak links in the chain of forensic evidence, and this was the last analysis in this particular chain. In the next ten minutes he would have the information he needed to make sense of it all.

DNA could be a curse – it was about to open up a real can of worms for Terry's family. He had an answer to who killed Jenny O'Brien, but it wasn't the answer that Terry wanted. In a few minutes he would know for sure.

45

All in all, the potentially deadly siege had ended well. Nobody had died. No one had been injured. Aoife and Igor were in custody. Judge Henderson had treated his family exactly the same as he treated everyone in his court: with much disdain. They all still had to be questioned.

Ahern had been persuaded by Judge Henderson to drive him to the CCJ once he was suitably dressed. According to Alan, the judge was furious with his sister. Aoife and Igor had turned up in the middle of the night and let themselves in. The judge hadn't understood why, or what they had expected him to do. If they were guilty of any misdemeanours, he'd told Ahern – and them – he would be the first to report them to the gardaí, family or not.

Fraser had joined Ahern in the judge's room in the CCJ for a quick debrief, Henderson adamant he had cases he couldn't possibly cancel and promising to make a full statement in due course. Satisfied that the judge hadn't been involved in any wrongdoing, Fraser agreed it was a compromise he could live with.

Judge Henderson had been vocal about the incompetence of the gardaí in tracking down his sister and cousin. He told them he had woken up in the middle of the night when he heard the unmistakable growl of his Jaguar's engine. It had sounded like he was more upset about his car being left out in the rain than his sister and cousin being fugitives from the law.

'Aoife changed after she met Francis Foster,' he said quietly. 'I tried to warn her about him, but there was little I could do when she was so madly in love. I see it every day in my courtroom, men controlling women, wringing them out, reducing them to shells of their former selves. My sister … she used to be so bright, but she dimmed under his constant put-downs.'

He paused, shaking his head. 'I'll admit it. I was almost relieved when I heard that Francis was dead. I even told her it was what he deserved.' He sat quietly for a few seconds. 'Surely you don't think she had anything to do with it.'

Fraser nodded sympathetically. He could tell that the judge was stunned at this turn of events. 'We want to question Aoife and Igor in relation to several deaths but we will also look into Foster's death.'

'It's what some men do, men like Foster – ruin women's lives. And so many of them get away with it. Why are we surprised when women retaliate? Sometimes the law just isn't enough to protect them.' It was the first time Fraser had heard the judge question the law.

As Fraser stood to leave the room, Judge Henderson added, 'I'm sure that Igor was just doing whatever Aoife told him to do. He's trailed after her like a little puppy from the day he came to live with my mother. I can't condone what my sister did. What she's become.'

When Fraser returned to WSH there was no sign of Terry. He was surprised – he thought she would be eagerly awaiting news of the raid. He had had his phone on silent all morning while he was talking to Judge Henderson, and was sure that he'd at least have had several messages from her demanding an update. He fired her a quick text letting her know that Aoife and Igor were in custody, but could see that she wasn't online. He popped a pod into his coffee machine. With luck, he would finally be able to wrap up the murder of Martin Higgins: the scarf Terry had found was key to that. He could have done without another three murders and an attempted murder in the mix, but he was hopeful Aoife Foster would admit to killing them all. He could always threaten her with her brother. Problem was, were there more?

The upside was that he could now put all his focus into the investigation of the Hayeses and their sex-trafficking ring, which had been placed on the back-burner over the past couple of weeks. He would have to leave the fentanyl problem with the drugs unit. The Hayeses' connection with Terry still perplexed him. He didn't want to speculate, but he thought it all pointed to them tampering with her car and poisoning Bella. But why?

Fraser carried his mug over to his desk. Something Terry had said flashed in his mind. After her tyres were slashed, she said Bernice had mentioned Seamus Ward. Was Seamus Ward,

Lou's brother, the link? He pulled the keyboard nearer. He had to dig a bit, but eventually he found what he was looking for. Seamus had been shot dead while carrying out an armed robbery on the Bank of Ireland on St Stephen's Green in 1993. He skimmed through the information, but then something caught his eye. Two gardaí had responded, Sean Ó Briain and Seamus Malone. There was a tussle and Lou's brother was shot with his own weapon by one of the guards. It was subsequently concluded that the shooting was necessary and reasonable in the circumstances.

He had a sudden thought. Was it possible that Lou blamed these gardaí for her brother's death? Was this who she had a grudge against? He knew Terry's family had moved to Scotland in the mid-1990s. Were Sean Ó Briain and Don O'Brien one and the same? If so, Seamus Malone must be Jim Malone. Were they the ones in real danger? Or was Terry the target as a means of revenge? Either way, Fraser needed to find her immediately. He rang Michael. 'Is Terry at the OSP with you?'

'No, she's not,' replied Michael. 'Is something wrong? She texted me earlier to meet her at her flat for lunch, which I thought was a bit odd—' Michael didn't get a chance to finish his sentence. Fraser had cut the call. He frantically speed-dialled Alan, who answered on the first ring. 'Alan, get a car to meet me at Terry's flat. Tell them to stop her if she tries to go in. I'm on my way over. I'll be back in time to question Aoife Foster.'

Jim Malone knew it was a risk – Michael might not turn up – but he needed to scupper the investigation into Jenny's death.

At the time of the initial murder, the Scottish police had nothing they could pin on him, and he wasn't aware of any new evidence. George in the Scottish lab had been unusually tight-lipped with his uncle Sandy about what was going on, but that little shit Michael was involved somehow. Sandy had given him the name of a guard who could access the database for him – Bob Paterson, who turned out to be next to useless. He couldn't tell Jim if Michael had discovered anything new. So now he had to find out for himself, and if Michael had nothing on him, then he could make up some excuse and walk away. But if he had something, well … needs must. There would be nothing to link him with Michael's death. He had checked Terry's apartment block, and the only CCTV cameras were in the car park. There was no fancy security system to worry about either. He took his gun from the back pocket of his jeans and checked it was locked and loaded. When Bob had sold him the gun, he assured him that it would only be traced back to some scumbag. No, Jim would be in the clear if anything happened to Michael, and it would give him time to work out what to do next. Whatever happened, Anne Therese must never know that he was responsible for Jenny's death. Michael was just collateral damage. No loss.

All he had left was Anne Therese. He needed to watch out for her. He knew she was smart, but she didn't know this world – not the way he did. He was the only one who could protect her.

He checked the door was unlocked.

46

The midday sun temporarily blinded Terry when she walked out of Nancy Hands onto the street. It was with some relief that she had said her goodbyes to her uncle Jim earlier, giving him directions to the Aircoach that would take him to the airport. She had spent another fifteen minutes in the quiet, cosy booth of the pub responding to a couple of urgent email queries from Mrs Carey. Now she stood at the kerb, trying to flag down a taxi to go to the OSP, but to no avail. The rain started, light at first, but she could tell by the heavy grey clouds rolling in that it was going to get worse. She gave up and crossed the road and walked towards the Luas stop at Heuston. She might as well drop into her flat, check the keys worked and wait for the rain to pass.

As she stepped out of the lift onto her floor, Terry's phone vibrated in her pocket – Fraser – but she would call him when she was inside her flat. And a missed call from Michael. She was dying to get the full update, but not in a communal hallway.

She put her new key in the lock and tried to twist it. It wouldn't budge. She kicked the bottom of the door in frustration.

She tried the handle – the door opened. It hadn't been locked? She pulled it closed again – was someone in there? She slammed her hand against the door. 'Whoever is in there, I've called security.'

'Terry! It's me, Jim.'

Tentatively she pushed the door open.

'Christ, you near gave me a heart attack,' the man said. 'What are you doing here, Terry? You're not supposed to be here.'

Big Jim was red-faced and shaking.

'I've come to try out the new keys, but more to the point, what the hell are you doing in my flat? How did you get in? I've got the keys,' she said, holding them up.

Big Jim turned away from her and walked into the kitchen. He took a glass out of the cupboard above the sink and filled it with water. He drank half of it before he turned back to her. 'When I scooted off earlier, I realised I still had the spare key. I'd put it in my back pocket by accident. Sorry. I was going to put it through the letter box, but I thought I'd double-check that your flat was secure. I've left it on the table.'

Something about his demeanour was making her feel uneasy. She wanted to get rid of him. 'Oh. That's kind of you, but it's fine. Look, I just need to make a couple of calls. I'll only be a few minutes. You better get off. Head for the airport. You'll miss your flight otherwise.'

'I've plenty of time. I'll wait and come out with you. Your own personal bodyguard.'

She took a long look at him – it was the mention of

'bodyguard' that rang a bell. Where had she heard that recently? She dropped her bag and her door keys on the kitchen counter and went into her bedroom.

Sitting down on her bed, Terry started a message to Michael, saying she would be a bit delayed getting to the OSP. Then she heard an almighty crash. She rushed over to the bedroom door. 'Jim! Jim!' She pulled at the door but it wouldn't budge. She started to panic. 'Jim, are you okay? What's going on. I can't get out.'

She could hear Big Jim and another male voice shouting, but couldn't make out what was being said. She put her foot against the doorjamb to get more purchase and pulled the handle as hard as she could. A loud bang startled her and she let go, falling back onto the floor.

'Jim! What's going on?' Her hands were shaking – she needed to phone for help but couldn't seem to hit the numbers on her phone screen.

The door burst open. Big Jim grabbed her arm and pulled her to her feet. 'Move! Quick! Keep behind me.'

She held onto the back of his jacket and followed, blindly, along the hall towards the door.

'Watch your feet!'

Terry looked down. It took a moment to assimilate what she was seeing. Dark red blood spreading across her tiled floor. In her flat.

Jim grabbed her by the shoulders and shook her roughly. 'Stay put!'

Trembling, she watched as he crouched down. She saw feet, tracksuit bottoms. 'Who is it? What's happened to him?'

Jim kept his back to her – she realised he was rifling through the man's pockets.

'Fuck!'

'What? What, Jim? Tell me!'

He threw something on the ground, a bank card. 'Fuck, it's Liam Hayes. For a moment I thought it was that fucking double-crossing weasel Bob Paterson coming at me with a gun. I should never have trusted him. It had to be him who snitched to the Hayeses about me being in your flat.' Jim was seething, his mouth twisted into a hard grimace, his face flushed an ugly shade of puce. Terry had never seen him like this.

'Bob?' Terry was confused. 'What's Bob got to do with anything?' Suddenly, Bob's comment about having a new guard dog sprung to mind. Had he been talking about Big Jim?

'I don't understand, Uncle Jim,' Terry whispered, as if talking to herself. She was desperately trying to work things out in her head, make the connections, join the dots. 'What's anything got to do with Bob Paterson? How do you know him? And why is Liam Hayes lying covered in blood on my kitchen floor?' Terry glanced down at the prone body. 'Have you killed him?' she asked shakily.

'No. I got him in the leg. Just gave him a thump when he went down. We need to get out of here. He won't have come alone.' Jim bent down again – she couldn't see what he was up to.

He helped her stand then handed her something. Terry took it automatically then looked down at what was in her hand.

'You might need this. If they get me, just run.' She realised Jim had handed her Liam's gun.

Terry held it as if it was a grenade. 'No! I don't want this.'

'You sound just like Don.'

'What's my dad got to do with it?'

'He couldn't hack it. Didn't want to know when things got hairy. Why the fuck do you think you ended up in Scotland? It wasn't for the fucking weather.' He had never raised his voice to her before, never bad-mouthed her dad. Whoever this version of Jim was, she didn't like him very much. But what else could she do but follow his instructions? A prominent gang member was bleeding out on the floor of her flat, with more armed men potentially close by, all looking to cause her harm, it seemed.

She grabbed her bag. Jim grasped her shoulder tightly to prevent her sliding on the blood. He pushed her out of the flat then reached down and dragged Liam Hayes closer to the door, making it harder for someone to open it.

'Shouldn't we call someone?' Terry asked, breathless.

Jim grabbed her arm. 'We don't have time. Come on.' They ran along the corridor towards the lift.

47

Fraser rang Michael again on the way to Terry's flat. 'Has Terry mentioned to you if Jim Malone's been in touch with her in the last few days?'

'Not that I know of. Not since the day Bella died. I'm glad you called back – I need to speak to you about him. You need to find him and keep him away from Terry.'

Shit, Fraser thought to himself. Had his instincts been correct? Michael interrupted his thought, sounding breathless. 'I'm just in her apartment building. When she texted me earlier to meet for lunch, she asked me to bring Jenny's necklace. I emailed you the results on Higgins's Leatherman earlier. Have you seen them? Oh! Hang on.'

Fraser heard some sort of commotion in the background. He could hear Michael talking to someone: 'You're sure it was a young guy that knocked into you on the stairs? Not a big heavy guy?' Fraser couldn't hear the reply.

'Michael, I'm on my way,' he said. The call was cut abruptly. He didn't know if Michael had heard him.

'Shit!' he shouted. He called the ERU and turned on the siren on his unmarked garda car. The traffic along the quays was diabolical. 'Move out of the bloody way,' he shouted, gesturing angrily at the cars around him reluctant to let him get through. He frantically tried Michael's and Terry's numbers again and again. No response.

Fraser quelled the siren and flashing lights as he neared her apartment block. He had no idea who or what was waiting for him.

He drove up onto the pavement at the front of the building. His phone rang as he jogged towards the main entrance. He put it to his ear without checking caller ID.

'John, it's Michael. Where are you?'

'Out front.'

'Do you think Jim Malone could be looking for Terry? If he is, I think Terry could be in terrible danger,' he whispered urgently.

Fraser pushed open the door into the ground-floor area. 'Why do you think that? Have you seen her?'

'No. I'm outside her flat, but it's deadly quiet inside. I knocked and tried the door. It's not locked but I can't budge it. You don't think Malone's done something to her, do you?'

'Michael, stay calm. Just wait there for me.'

'But you don't understand, John. Jenny was killed by Terry's father.'

'What? Don O'Brien killed his own daughter? No!' He stood on the first stair and grabbed the banister. 'I don't believe that.'

'But that's just it. Terry's dad isn't Don, it's Jim Malone. Jim Malone killed Jenny.'

'Fuck!' Fraser pocketed his phone and bolted up the stairs, two at a time.

By the time he reached the third floor his breathing was ragged and his pulse was racing. His fear was so intense he thought he was going to vomit. He steadied himself against the wall as he caught his breath and looked along the corridor to Terry's flat. Michael was pushing at the door.

'It's unlocked but I can't get it open. There's someone moaning inside. I think they're hurt.'

'Where are your car keys?' snapped Big Jim, frantically jabbing at the button for the car-park level.

Terry was slumped in the corner of the lift. 'This is stupid. We're sitting ducks in here. We should have taken the stairs. Why are they here? What do they want with me? Why are they trying to kill me?' She could feel hysteria rising. Taking gulping breaths, she tried to stay in control.

'They won't expect us to take the lift.' He slapped the doors. 'That's our protection. These guys will be carrying.'

'You might have killed that man.'

'If I'd wanted to kill him, he would be dead. He's just a mammy's boy. Even she doesn't rate him. He's got guts, mind you. Stood his ground against me.'

Terry was aghast – Big Jim was unrepentant. Michael had always said he was a bit of a bully, but she hadn't pegged him as a killer. Who was this man?

'It's kill or be killed.' Big Jim pointed at the gun she still had clutched in her hand. She dropped it on the floor. 'Pick it up! You'll need it,' he barked at her.

Terry looked down at the gun, then back up at him. 'You have a gun too?'

'Yes, of course I bloody do. He didn't shoot himself, did he? Although I wouldn't be surprised if he did. If he had brains, he'd be dangerous,' muttered Big Jim as he went back to smashing the button. The lift shuddered into life and started descending.

'Were you going to kill me?'

Big Jim stood perfectly still, then turned and slid down the wall to sit beside her. 'No, of course not,' he said softly. 'I wouldn't harm a hair on your head. You weren't supposed to be here. It was supposed to be Michael.' He shook his head. 'That bastard Paterson must have set me up.'

Michael? Paterson? Terry couldn't think straight – what the hell was going on? Big Jim wanted Michael to be here, at her flat, and Bob Paterson was involved somehow.

She tried to stay calm. 'But you were prepared to kill someone?'

'No. I just wanted to talk. I needed to know what he knew.'

'Why would you need to talk to Liam Hayes?'

Big Jim's face contorted with anger. 'I don't want to talk to the Hayeses! Those fucking scumbags ran me and your dad out of the country.' Before Terry could ask what he was talking about, the lift stopped, and he bellowed, 'Get flat on the floor.' He positioned himself against the wall of the lift so he wouldn't be visible when the doors opened. Terry raised her head – he was to the side of the doors, gun in hand. Sliding her hand across the floor, she grabbed the gun she had dropped.

Once the doors were fully open, Big Jim stuck his head out and looked around.

'Where's your car?' he whispered.

'Near the security box.'

He pointed at her handbag. 'Take out your car keys.' Terry did as she was told, and Jim took her bag from her. He pulled her out of the lift. The doors began to slide shut, and he quickly slid her bag in place to keep them wedged open.

Big Jim put his finger to his lips and signalled with his hand for her to follow him, but keep her head down. He grabbed her hand and they ran over to the line of cars opposite the lift.

'Keys.' Terry's fingers were slippery with sweat as she hastily held out the keys to him. 'Stay!' he warned her as he moved in front of another car.

Terry tried to wedge herself under the van beside her and closed her eyes. How was this even happening? A hand grabbed her ankle and she froze. Another hand was clamped over her mouth.

'Shh!' Big Jim sat on the floor beside her. 'We can't move your car – it's blocked in by a black Merc. One of the gombeens is at the wheel. I'm guessing at least one other has gone up to your flat.'

'What about the security guard? Can't he help?'

Big Jim ran his right index finger across his throat. The colour drained from her face.

'Just do what I say.' Terry swallowed and nodded. Big Jim scooted along to the far end of the line of cars, away from the exit. He checked left and right and ran across to the next row. He dropped to his knees and waved her over. She held her breath and ran.

Fraser stood outside Terry's flat trying to catch his breath. He unholstered his gun. It wasn't ideal enlisting the help of a civilian in a situation like this, but if Terry was in danger, he didn't have time to wait for back-up. 'Ready?' he whispered. Michael nodded. Fraser gave him the thumbs-up.

'Gardaí! Stand back!' Fraser put his shoulder to the door and pushed, but it didn't budge. He put his back to it and Michael added his weight. They managed to get it open enough for Fraser to stick his head in. He saw a man on the floor, his balaclava concealing his identity. Fraser thought he could make out his chest moving up and down, and he could smell the familiar metallic scent of blood. There were no other sounds from the flat. 'Terry?' he shouted through the gap in the door. No answer. He pulled out his phone and dialled 999.

As soon as Fraser barked a request for an ambulance, he heard shouting from the stairwell. Shoving his phone back in his pocket, he and Michael redoubled their efforts and managed to open the door far enough to get inside. Just in time too. There was a loud thud as the door to the stairwell was flung open.

Fraser signalled to Michael to help him move the hall table up against the door.

'That should give us some time. Michael, check his pulse!' Fraser pointed to the man on the floor, then searched the flat for Terry in case she was hiding. Or worse.

When he returned to Michael, he simply shook his head. *Where is she? And who the fuck shot this guy?* 'How is he?' he asked.

'Not good,' Michael responded. He was pressing his jacket against the man's wound. 'He's lost a lot of blood.'

'Next question: who is he?' Fraser reached down and pulled up the balaclava covering the face of the man on the floor 'Shit, it's Liam Hayes.'

The Hayes crew had come here looking for someone – could it have been Jim Malone rather than Terry? Targeting Terry was a means to an end. Lou wanted retribution, to settle old scores – she wanted an eye for an eye. A Seamus for a Seamus. She wanted Seamus Malone dead – Big Jim. Terry was a pawn to flush him out, but she would do too. Lou must have had Malone on her radar, watching and waiting. He wasn't difficult to spot. Fraser would worry about that once Terry was safe.

He went into the living room and unlocked the door to the balcony. He looked over, there was no one around outside the building. Getting Michael's attention, Fraser mimed climbing over to him and the gingerly clambered over the railing and dropped onto the balcony below. He could hear voices from above in Terry's flat.

Michael landed beside him. 'There's two of them,' he said, as quietly as he could. Fraser heard the quiver in his voice.

Fraser flattened himself against the glass door into the flat below, praying it was empty. Last thing they needed was an irate householder rapping on it and shouting for them to get off their balcony.

He heard the door above being opened. Holding his breath, he put his arm across Michael and pushed him back against the glass. They listened.

'Fuck, Dean, get back in here. Liam's ma's gonna blame us. We need to get the fucker who shot him. Stop messin' about.'

'Well, you shouldn't have shot that guy in the car park.'

'Don't be putting this on me. That fuckin' guard, Bob or whatever his name is, said the security guy would be round the back.'

'Never trust a fuckin' guard. C'mere, watch the blood! Dec'll go mental if you bring that into his Merc. Come on.'

Fraser tried to assimilate what he was hearing. Were they talking about Bob Paterson? He was the only guard called Bob that he knew. What the hell had Paterson been up to? Was he the real rat, not Higgins? But he couldn't think about that now, not when Terry was in danger. He hoped she hadn't been anywhere close by when the security guard had been shot, but it seemed the most obvious place to look next.

As soon as it went quiet, Fraser went over the balcony to the next floor down and then dropped down to the ground. Keeping close to the building, he made his way around to the gate, which opened onto the road from the apartment block's garden. He heard the thud Michael made as he landed. Fraser ran around to the entrance to the underground car park.

The door between the car park and the stairwell flung open and rebounded noisily against the wall. Two balaclava- clad figures staggered out, breathing heavily, one doubled over, hands on his knees. Jim Malone put his finger to his mouth and motioned for Terry to keep close to him. He pointed over to a black jeep. It might afford more protection from a bullet than some of the vehicles.

As quietly as possible, they slunk around the cars. He hoped that the two thugs would assume that he and Terry would head for the exit. Terry sank down to the ground, leaning her back against the jeep. Jim rooted around in the pocket of his jeans and pulled out a pile of loose change. He flung it as far across the car park as he could. As the coins clattered against vehicles and the ground, there was a burst of gunfire.

Terry put her hands over her ears as the noise reverberated around the concrete walls.

Jim could see chunks of concrete splinter into the air.

'Over there,' one of the men shouted to the other. Terry shrank back.

Jim moved towards the front of the jeep to see in what direction they were heading. As he slowly raised his head and shoulders to scout the area, a shot rang out. He clutched his right shoulder and dropped to his knees. Another shot followed and the windscreen of the jeep shattered. He closed his eyes and tried to control his breathing. He felt Terry checking his arm. The pain was bad, and he couldn't move it. Why had he trusted Paterson to give him information about the investigation into Jenny's murder? He knew they had some evidence and that Michael held the key to it, but he should have been cleverer. Paterson had obviously told the Hayeses he was here. He should have known Lou would never let him live in peace.

Another bullet whistled by, striking the car alongside them.

Terry bent down and whispered in his ear, 'How many bullets have you got left?'

'Four, maybe five,' he whispered back, grimacing. Even speaking was painful.

She unfurled his fingers and took the gun from his hand, fingers trembling. She exchanged it for the gun he had retrieved from Liam Hayes and he took it in his left hand. 'Don't know how many he has left.' Jim nodded. It was exactly what he would have done in the circumstances.

He watched as she crawled along to the front bumper and positioned herself with her elbows on the ground. She looked back at him and attempted a smile, then took aim and fired: five shots. He heard a scream. She'd hit one of them. Shots came back fast and furious, the noise deafening, almost drowning out the sound of sirens.

The gunfire stopped as suddenly as it had started. 'Gardaí! Drop your weapons.' Fraser's voice echoed through the car park. 'Terry?' Big Jim heard Fraser call out.

His vision was hazy, but he could see terror crossed with relief on Terry's face. She crawled towards him and knelt beside him. She shouted back to Fraser. 'Big Jim has been shot. We need to help him.'

No, it was his responsibility to keep her safe. It was his job. He grabbed her and, wrapping his left arm around her, pinned her against the jeep. 'No! It's too dangerous.'

'Jim.' Terry tried to shake him off her. 'You're crushing me! Stop! Fraser's here to help us.' He heard the raw fear in her voice. She shouted out 'John!' drawing attention to them again.

'Keep your head down, Terry!' Jim saw the defiant look on her face. His voice softened. 'I won't let them kill you. You're all I've got.' He shielded her against the jeep with his body as more shots rang out. He raised his left arm and steadied his hand against the roof, trying to support the gun. He was finding it hard to focus, his vision blurry. He dropped the gun to the car roof and wrapped himself around Terry, strangled sobs heaving in his chest. Images of a woodland flitted across his mind, the open-mouthed silent scream of Jenny as his hands tightened around her neck. The feeling of her body growing limp as all the life drained out of her. If only she hadn't threatened to tell Don the truth. If only she would just shut up. 'I'm sorry,' he whispered into Terry's hair.

'I never meant for Jenny to die. Don'll never forgive me. You'll never forgive me.'

He could feel Terry squirming beneath him, trying to free herself.

More shots were directed towards them – he could hear them strike the surrounding vehicles. 'Sorry, so sorry,' he whispered, his voice ragged. 'I'm so sorry.' His whole body jolted as the bullet hit his head.

Terry heard more shots ring out. There was yelling. From Fraser, from Alan – she couldn't tell. Then footsteps, and Fraser's voice right beside her.

'Terry! Don't come out until I tell you.' She hoped that meant Fraser had things under control.

'Jim, you're suffocating me.' She tried to push him off, but he was impossible to budge. He let out a moan and slid away from her.

'Jim – Jim! Speak to me, Jim!' She grabbed him around the waist and he fell back on top of her. He began to slip down again, and his bloodied right hand ran through her hair, smearing blood over her face. They were both on the floor. Terry was crying. 'Jim! Jim!' She held onto her uncle. 'Jim, speak to me. Please.' She could tell he was slipping away.

She was aware that someone was close by. 'He's been shot. Help him. Call an ambulance.'

Terry felt someone grip her arms and pull her up. She tried to wriggle free, but they held tight. Then Alan's face appeared above her. Dazed, she looked around. Fraser was standing near the rear bumper of the jeep, a gun pointed at Jim.

'It's all right, Terry. You're safe now.' Alan tried to pull her away.

She struggled out of his grip. 'But I *was* safe. Big Jim looked after me.'

48

'**A**re you sure you want to do this?'

Terry nodded, not trusting herself to speak. They were sitting in Fraser's office in WSH.

She wiped away a rivulet of water from her forehead and swept her wet hair behind her ears. She had showered, washing every molecule of Jim Malone from her body. She changed into Mary's spare polo shirt and cargo trousers. Mary had even found a pair of boots to fit.

Now she was ready to hear the truth.

Fraser handed her a mug of coffee. She hunched over it, aware that they were all staring, waiting. She inhaled the comforting aroma of Nescafé. She would never drink anything else if she had a choice. It always transported her back to a time when they were a family. Whenever they got a new jar of coffee, her dad always let her drive a teaspoon through the foil covering the coffee granules. She never forgot the sudden release of that wonderful smell, even though she hated the taste back then.

Michael put his arm around her shoulders, drawing her in

for a reassuring hug. She disentangled herself and he moved away to give her space.

Fraser went over and locked the door and drew the blinds of the window looking into the incident room. He sat close by her.

The room felt claustrophobic. Fraser reached for her hand. She tugged it away and clasped her hands together on her lap. She needed to face this alone. She didn't want anyone sharing her pain.

She looked at Michael. He sniffed and wiped his eyes. 'Just the facts, Michael. That's all I want. From the beginning. I want you to go through your thought processes, step by step.'

Michael looked down at the report he had prepared and cleared his throat. 'You asked Aileen to send you Jenny's necklace. It had been returned to the family once the investigation into her death was complete.' He cocked his head. 'Right?'

'Right.'

'There were two DNA profiles recovered on the necklace, one female, one male.'

'Jenny and her killer.'

'That's assuming no one else handled it directly.' Michael nodded, making sure she was following what he was saying. 'It was still wrapped in a sealed evidence bag when it arrived in Ireland, a mini jiffy bag.'

'Yes. You saw it. Clear plastic about five centimetres squared. They weren't going to send it back in some big fuck-off brown paper bag, were they? It was only a wee necklace. I just wrapped tissue around it. I never opened it.'

'Right, so we'll go on the basis that it had not been handled after it was returned to the family.' He looked over at her.

'Uh huh! Go on.'

'Neither profile was on our DNA database. But the Irish database did throw up a close relative.'

'That would be me? Given that we're sisters? My DNA is on file for exclusion purposes. You know that's standard practice for everyone involved in murder investigations.'

'Well. The female profile from the necklace did match with you. But she, Jenny, was a half-sibling to you. You share a mother.' He stopped.

Terry looked at him, her jaw practically on the floor. 'Jenny was my *half-sister*? And the male profile from the necklace?'

'Is also a match to you, but not Jenny. The male profile is your father.'

Fraser leaned over. 'Are you sure you want to hear all this? After everything you've been through today?'

She ignored him and stared at Michael. 'And? I actually can't believe this.' She shook her head. 'My dad's not Jenny's father?'

'Correct. Your father, biological that is, handled Jenny's necklace. But does that necessarily identify him as the person who killed your half-sister?' Michael looked at her.

'Go on.' Terry needed Michael to spell it out. She couldn't think straight. This was all so surreal.

Michael nodded. 'There are other reasons for his DNA to be on the necklace.'

'Such as?' She looked over to Fraser, but he was giving nothing away. She returned her gaze to Michael. 'Come on, Mr Scientist, what do you make of this?' She didn't mean it to sound so sharp. She should bite her tongue – this wasn't Michael's fault.

'I double-checked all the results. It didn't make sense to

me either. But I had a thought. I swabbed the wrapping, the Christmas paper.'

'What has that to do with all this? We know only Aileen and Uncle Jim handled that. Remember we gloved up. I wouldn't take it from Jim. I got him to drop it on the table.'

Michael fixed his eyes on the papers on his knee. 'I extracted two profiles from the outside of the paper, one female, one male.'

'Aileen and Jim,' Terry said. 'So what?'

'Well, if you want me to stick to facts, Aileen's DNA is not in our database. I would require a sample from her to compare. But, yes. Let's assume the female profile is Aileen. The male profile from the same wrapping paper ...'

'Must have been Jim, Uncle Jim.' Terry gave Michael a half smile. That made sense. 'Go on.'

Michael looked nervous – he wouldn't make eye contact. 'Yes. But.' He looked over at Fraser, who was staring at Terry. 'I'm really sorry, Tez.'

Terry was bewildered. 'What?'

'The male profile from the wrapping matched the male profile on the necklace.' Michael kept his eyes on his report. 'The male who handled Jenny's necklace, handled the wrapping paper. And both obviously matched with you. A close match. Your father.'

Terry put her hands up to stop anyone saying anything. 'But you said you found Uncle Jim's DNA profile on the wrapping paper. He brought the package over from Glasgow. You were there when he gave it to me. And now you're saying his DNA was also found on Jenny's necklace and ...' She must have this wrong. 'Jim Malone. You're telling me DNA proves he is my biological father? Don's not my dad.' Her voice cracked. Slowly, realisation dawned. She looked at Michael wild-eyed. 'Jim Malone killed Jenny? Why? Why would he kill her?'

'I don't know. I only know he's your biological father. I've checked and rechecked.'

'I need a minute.' She walked out into the incident room.

Mary and Clodagh were sitting at one of the desks. Mary looked up. 'You okay, Doc?' Terry hurried past, blanking them. She reached the bathrooms just in time.

Afterwards, she wiped her mouth on a wad of toilet paper and flushed the toilet. She put down the lid and sat for a few minutes. This was all too much. Her uncle Jim was her father and he had died in her arms protecting her. Could he really have killed her sister? Slowly she remembered his quasi-confession in the car park. She had thought he was just delirious. And what about her dad, Don? This news could bring on another stroke.

Michael, Fraser and Alan were sitting where she had left them. 'Jim Malone is dead. Does anyone else, other than us four, know he killed Jenny?' She looked from one to the other.

Michael was looking at the floor. 'Michael?'

'Well, I wanted to be sure, so I contacted George MacLaughlin.'

'Your friend in Forensic Science Scotland?'

'Uh-huh. They recovered a partial print way back when the necklace was first examined. They never got a definite match, but George told me that they had some possibles.'

'And one of those was Jim Malone of Strathclyde Police?'

'It wasn't long after the fiasco when a policewoman was

wrongly accused of interfering in a murder investigation on the basis of an incorrect fingerprint identification.'

'So they hid it.'

'Well, I can't say that, but they didn't pursue it too vigorously. He must have been questioned at the time, but he was close to you all. They couldn't prove anything beyond reasonable doubt.'

'That old chestnut. And so he got away with murder. He killed my sister and got away with it. Did you share the DNA results with this George?'

'He's a scientist. He agrees with me. Your situation aside, all the DNA says is that at some time before Jenny's death Jim Malone touched that necklace. It doesn't tell us when, and the necklace has been kicking around for twenty years. George doesn't think the procurator fiscal would be interested in maybes.'

She spun round to Fraser. 'Are you going to do anything with this information?'

'He's dead,' he said gently. 'What would you want me to do?'

'Nothing,' she replied quietly. 'Dad never wanted me to keep digging. He lost one daughter and a wife – he doesn't deserve to lose me too.' She looked over at Michael. 'Anyone else?'

'No.' He looked as distraught as Terry felt. 'Are we okay, Tez?'

Terry nodded. She couldn't stop the tears. All of this needed to be contained. She could trust the people in this room. Scotland, she had no control over, but she hoped they didn't want another scandal on their hands.

She said, to no one in particular, 'My dad must never find out about any of this. Promise me.'

49

Terry refused to go back to Alan's flat with Michael for the night. Fraser and Ahern were staying on to question Aoife Foster and Igor Henderson. She said she would wait and go back with Fraser when he finished.

Her head was spinning. She should be celebrating that she'd found Jenny's killer. And that he was dead.

But it was just sinking in that her mother had had an affair with her dad's best friend, and she was the result of it. He then killed her sister and her mother took off. It was a complete mindfuck.

Her dad thought her mother had left because Jenny's death was too much to bear. But was it because she couldn't handle the situation with Jim Malone? Was it guilt? Or was it fear? What had Jim said to Terry in the car park? *'I never meant for her to die.'* Had Jenny found out about their mum and Jim and threatened to tell? Only two people knew the answer to that question, and they were both dead.

Terry had always thought she wasn't enough to compensate for Jenny – enough to keep her mother with them. Well, hadn't she done well without her? Terry and her dad, because Don was her dad, were a unit. Nothing, not even DNA, could ever change that. She just wished she'd told him she loved him more often. She would now.

Terry squeezed into the tiny room adjacent to the interview room to observe Foster and Henderson being interrogated. It was little more than a cupboard, and she and Mary were squashed up next to each other.

'You up to this, Terry?' Mary asked. 'You've had a shocker of a day.'

'I'll be fine, Mary.' She meant that. She would be fine. Soon. Mary set herself up in charge of the controls and twiddled with the volume, turning it right up. Terry shot her a look and she turned it down a fraction.

Igor Henderson had his back to them. He was slumped in the chair, his fingers drumming on the table. He looked around the room as Fraser did his introduction and twice had to be asked to identify himself for the recording.

After a while Terry zoned out, as he answered 'no comment' to every question. His solicitor sat stock still, her eyes on the table. Fraser carried on as if Henderson's answers were riveting and helpful, but it was clear that they weren't getting very far.

Suddenly, Fraser's attitude changed from Good Cop to Bad Cop. The look he threw Igor gave Terry goosebumps. She watched as he shuffled the papers in his hands.

'These are the reports from the forensic science DNA laboratory.' He looked up and gave Igor a cold smile. 'Cillian Maguire.' He placed a report on the table. 'Emmett Tormey.' He placed a sheet of paper on top of the first. 'And Owen O'Neill.' This report he let drop onto the others. He sat back, his eyes never leaving Igor's face.

Terry noticed he still had a sheet of paper in his hands. She watched as he slowly placed it on top of the others and smoothed it out. 'And Detective Garda Martin Higgins.' Fraser stared Igor down.

Terry looked at Mary, who shrugged.

'All four men dead. All four deaths linked by trace evidence. DNA.'

So she was right.

'We've taken a mouth swab from you, which will be sent to the forensic science lab. Will we find that it is your DNA that has been recovered during the investigations into these deaths?'

'No comment.'

Next, Fraser picked up an envelope and extracted an image.

Terry could see that Igor was now visibly shaking.

Fraser slid the image across the table. 'This is you coming out of Court 18.' He fished out a second one. 'And this is you leaving the CCJ building shortly afterwards.' With a flourish another image was produced. 'And this is you leaving the court on Thursday, 2 January.' Fraser smiled a genuine smile. 'Do you recognise this man?' He spread out the images and pointed to each in turn. 'For the record, I am pointing at the man Mr Henderson is following. A man that Mr Henderson followed out of the courts on eleven different occasions between 5 December 2024 and 2 January 2025.'

Mary thumped Terry's arm. 'Igor has been following Higgins. That's how he knew about Delaney Gardens.' She high-fived Terry. 'We got him, Doc.'

Fraser was oblivious to the celebration in the viewing room and continued his questioning. 'Is that what you did? Stalked your victims. Got to know their movements and habits.'

Igor glowered.

'Is there anything you would like to add, Igor?' Fraser said without any hint of sarcasm. Ahern beside him had picked up the file, ready to go.

'Aoife made me do it all.'

Everyone seemed startled by this. Particularly Igor's legal representative. Mary thumped the ledge in front of them. 'Now we've definitely got him.'

'God, he really is thick,' muttered Terry. 'He's just landed himself and Aoife right in it.'

The sound was muted and Fraser and Ahern left the room. The solicitor was very animated – they didn't need sound to know she wasn't happy with Igor's last-minute outburst.

'Another coffee?' asked Mary, stifling a yawn. 'I think it's going to be a long night.'

An hour or so later, Aoife Foster walked into the room with a middle-aged man dressed in a loud pinstriped suit that Terry reckoned had cost the price of a small car.

'Quentin Cuthbertson,' Mary whispered, despite the room

being soundproof. 'Rich prick lawyer. He's with some fancy-pants criminal firm. They only take on big-money or high-profile cases.'

That made sense, Terry thought. Judge Henderson would be behind that. He would be supporting his sister the only way he knew: using the might of the law. The best that money could buy.

But it was Aoife she was interested in. This version was a million miles away from Aoife the simpering receptionist, the woman fawning over her boss, the wannabe friend of other suffering souls. This was Aoife the manipulative mankiller, a woman scorned by her husband and out for revenge. She even sounded different. She had fooled them all.

Aoife was leaning back in her chair, arms folded defensively across her chest. Her eyes were flinty and she looked directly at Fraser, a smug grin on her face. She was dressed not dissimilar to Terry in her borrowed get-up. Very much an action woman, not a saccharine-sweet knitter.

Terry sat fascinated as Fraser probed and dissected Aoife's answers. It was akin to how she conducted a post-mortem: they knew the answer lay within, deep inside, and it was their job to reveal it. This was a masterclass in interrogation – on both sides. Aoife showed no remorse, no emotion, as Fraser questioned her. Terry wished she could be in the room, no barrier between them.

Fraser read the list. 'Dr Cillian Maguire, Emmett Tormey, Owen O'Neill, Detective Garda Martin Higgins. Do you recognise these names?'

Aoife shrugged and grinned inanely.

Fraser pushed one of the clinic's desk diaries across in front of her. 'Maguire!' He pointed to a page. 'O'Neill!'

She didn't look down, but replied in a flat voice, 'No comment.'

Fraser picked up another diary and made a show of flicking through the pages.

'That's *my* diary.' Aoife's eyes were blazing. She shifted in her seat and looked over to her lawyer. *A slight crack in the hard veneer*, thought Terry. He glared back at her, as if warning her not to stray from anything more than 'no comment'.

Fraser realised this was an opportunity to break her silence. He put the diary on the table between them. 'Tormey!' He didn't wait for a reply but dropped another diary on top. 'Watson. Tony Watson.' He stared at her. 'He's in ICU, but minus an arm. He should pull through. I'm sure he will be able to tell us about his weekend.' He sat back, increasing the space between them. 'You don't look too pleased to hear he survived the assault.'

Quentin Cuthbertson, who had been feigning indifference until a few moments earlier, realised the ramifications of this nugget of information and immediately and instinctively placed his hand in front of Aoife's chest as he leaned in towards Fraser. 'I need to discuss this with Mrs Foster.'

Ahern went through the usual spiel of halting the interview before he and Fraser left Aoife and her lawyer to slug it out. Fraser turned the sound off.

Terry and Mary watched, fascinated at the silent theatrics being played out in front of them in the interview room. Aoife seemed to be doing most of the talking. Mr Cuthbertson was looking decidedly uncomfortable, and a little scared of Aoife.

When Fraser and Ahern returned, sound was restored in the viewing room.

'My client wishes to co-operate fully.'

The words they all wanted to hear. Aoife had a brazen look on her face, not an iota of remorse.

Fraser opened a pink file that had been under the diaries and pulled out a photograph. Before he put it on the table, he glared directly at her. 'All the victims were clients of Dr Reagan. You wound your way into their lives in a very personal and manipulative way under the guise of being their wives' friend. Did the women complain about their husbands to you? O'Neill was vain. Tormey preferred pottering in his shed and playing golf than spending time with his wife. And Maguire, well' – Fraser clasped his hands together and placed them on the table – 'Mrs Maguire must have been embarrassed by the rumours of his sexual transgressions. And what about Martin Higgins?'

He slapped the photograph of the body of Martin Higgins, his gunshot wound clearly visible, down in front of Aoife. Mr Cuthbertson quickly looked away.

Terry leaned forward, trying to see the image. He placed another one on the table. This time, it was of Dr Maguire's prone naked body laid out on the chaise longue. Mr Cuthbertson sighed deeply and closed his eyes.

'This is Dr Maguire when he was found dead in his study. But then again, I'm sure you recognise him.'

Terry watched transfixed as Aoife smiled as she looked at the photograph. 'Mrs Maguire is a real lady. She deserves better than him. She has impeccable taste. Unfortunately, not in men.'

'Did you kill Dr Maguire, Aoife?'

Aoife looked up at Fraser. Her expression was one of perplexed amusement. 'Well. Yes.'

'Tell me about it?'

From her vantage point in the viewing room, Terry noticed a sly smile cross Aoife's face. 'Anne – Mrs Maguire – didn't know the half of what he got up to. He was a dirty old creep. It was just a shame she didn't find him. Then she would have known the true extent of his perversions,' she said with a snarl. She seemed to grow in stature with her rage. 'He was another example of entitlement. What is it you men call it? Having your cake and eating it. He expected his wife to turn a blind eye to his affairs and what he referred to as his minor peccadillos.' She smiled. 'I read Dr Reagan's notes.' Aoife suddenly looked worried. Terry thought it was a genuine moment of emotion. Surely she didn't think she stood a chance with the psychologist? 'I'd rather you didn't tell him that. He trusts me. I wouldn't want to disappoint him.' She stabbed a finger at the image before her. 'Did you see his collection of pornographic images of his patients? He stupidly had them in his desk drawer. He disgusted me. He deserved to die.'

'You doctored the scene. Made it look as if he hanged himself.' Fraser slapped his hand onto the desk. Terry and Mary jumped but Aoife didn't move a muscle.

'Chapter 8.' She looked as if she had just been congratulated on a job well done. 'He did put up a bit of resistance, but it was an opportunity to display his considerable talents.' This was said in a coquettish tone.

Terry was astounded. She looked to see how Fraser would react but he sat back, seemingly unperturbed.

In the viewing room, Mary leaned into Terry. 'What's she on about? Chapter 8?'

Terry was already scrolling on her phone. She turned it so Mary could see. 'It's a textbook she had on her shelf, DiMaio's *Forensic Pathology*. Chapter 8, Asphyxia, Sexual Asphyxia.'

'Fuck me!' Mary looked alarmed. 'She's a nutter.'

Fraser had moved on. 'You must have overcome him and set the scene. Was Mrs Maguire involved?'

Aoife thumped the table with a clenched fist. 'Why would you even think that? Those women were oblivious. They had no idea what I was prepared to do to keep them safe.'

'Very admirable, but you needed help. This wasn't a one-person job. Tell me about your cousin, Igor Henderson.'

Aoife scowled.

'You needed help and your cousin was a willing accomplice. Unfortunately, he was a little slapdash. He left his DNA behind at every scene. Pretty solid evidence, I'm sure the DPP will agree.'

'Whose idea was the needle in the penis?' Fraser went on. Mary smirked and gave Terry a dig in the ribs when they saw the lawyer pale. 'Who was responsible for the little extras?'

Aoife smiled. No need to say it. She clearly took pleasure in mutilating the men's bodies.

Another picture was placed over the first. Fraser sat back. 'This one is a real masterpiece. Detective Garda Martin Higgins.'

Aoife nodded in agreement. 'Chapter 7.'

Fraser looked puzzled. 'What does that mean?'

Aoife shrugged. Terry whispered to Mary, 'Sharp Injuries.

Mutilation. She's definitely murdering by the book – the forensic pathology book.'

'Why did you leave his body in Delaney Gardens?' Fraser put an aerial view on the table.

Aoife gave a hollow laugh. 'His home from home. He was very partial to a late-night dalliance with those ladies. He was a misogynistic bully. Who would blame one of the girls for seeking her revenge by shooting him with his own gun? Why not leave him there for all to see?' She gave him a sly smile. 'For his wife to see him in all his glory.' Her face closed down again. 'It was a case of two birds with one stone. Whoever was exploiting the young women in that apartment needed to get what was coming to them – both the punter and the pimps. Why shouldn't they take some heat?'

'How did you know about the brothel? That is what you're referring to? What's your connection with the Hayes family?'Aoife looked genuinely confused by Fraser's question. 'Who?' she asked, looking to her barrister for some sort of back-up for the first time. Cuthbertson avoided her gaze, his fountain pen scratching across the page as he furiously took notes.

Fraser seemed convinced she didn't know who the Hayeses were. He took a different tack. 'We have CCTV footage of your cousin Igor following Detective Higgins out of the criminal courts complex several times over the course of the month.' He leaned back. 'You see, I think that's how you operated. Igor Henderson got to know the potential victims' routines and then you set them up.'

Aoife stared back, giving nothing away.

'Maybe Igor was a patron of the brothel too? Had he seen Detective Higgins there?'

Aoife gave a harsh laugh. 'What? I doubt the punters have the chats while waiting to be serviced.'

'Did you wait outside and shoot him as he was leaving?'

'It was easy. He was too busy tucking in his shirt to realise what was happening until it was too late and Igor grabbed him and pinned him down. He was still high on something. Didn't put up much of a fight. "Don't shoot me!"' she mimicked in a whiny voice. 'That's how you treat bullies – stand up to them.'

'Why did you cut out his tongue?'

A look of disgust passed over Aoife's face. 'He recognised me from the clinic. He called me a frigid bitch, amongst other things, and laughed in my face. I grabbed his scarf, wrapped it around his mouth to shut him up and shot him. Igor said he shouldn't have said those things about me. So what can I say … karma's a bitch.' She looked at Fraser, appearing to expect validation, but he merely looked back at her blankly. He wasn't going to give her the reaction she so badly wanted.

Fraser passed the questioning over to Ahern then. Aoife didn't deny anything, but didn't offer up anything more. O'Neill warranted a 'Chapter 15', which Terry discovered was drowning, and Tormey was 'Chapter 13 – Fire Deaths'. Even when Ahern read out a list of objects recovered from her display cabinet, she offered no explanation for them. She merely shrugged when Ahern asked how she came upon the Claddagh ring they thought was her husband's. Terry hoped she was right that there was still a bit of dried-up tissue from the finger attached that might be useful for DNA.

Terry was amazed that Fraser had kept so calm but she knew he wasn't going to push anything, there would be plenty of time. He looked deep in thought while Ahern asked the final few questions. He would know the onus would be on Michael to process all the evidence and provide the guards with the ammunition to convict successfully. And there was no doubt about it, Aoife was going away for a long time.

Fraser made a show of gathering the diaries and the photographs and then, almost as an afterthought, he asked, 'Why, Aoife? I know these guys weren't what you would call decent men, but did they deserve to be murdered and mutilated?' Fraser sat back, looking at her. There was no accusation in his voice. It was a genuine enquiry.

Aoife looked directly at Fraser and sat up straight. 'I see it in their eyes. Women who have the same look I had before Francis's death. I loved him. I asked him to come to counselling with me. He scoffed at Dr Reagan, made fun of the sessions. Dr Reagan told me it wasn't working. He couldn't force him to change. Francis belittled me. Manipulated me. Trampled over my heart and made me feel worthless. And those men, they were the same. Even my brother couldn't help. Gerard may be a hotshot judge in court, but he says his hands are tied. He needs evidence to prove emotional abuse – witnesses, bank statements, emails, texts. I know the realities of court from Gerard. I know how stressful and tough it is. So I decided to take matters into my own hands.' Her tone was derisory. 'No one sees what goes on behind closed doors. But I know. I had access to their inner secrets. I saw these women, downtrodden and exhausted. The crap these awful men put them through is unbearable. I could help those women. Even if they didn't know they needed help.'

Terry watched, fascinated, as the solicitor tugged at Aoife's arm and whispered in her ear. Aoife pulled away and gave him a look of pure malevolence that made even Terry shrink back in her seat. 'Take your hands off me!' she spat at him.

Aoife tried to increase the space between her and her solicitor, but the chairs were riveted to the floor. She shuffled away from him in her seat. 'Gerard told me Francis got what he deserved, falling off that balcony. And so did those other men.' *Defiant to the end*, Terry thought.

'Did you kill your husband, Aoife?'

'That has nothing to do with you.'

Francis Foster's death covered Chapters 4 to 6: blunt force trauma and head injuries, one cause being a fall from a height. The interview was over, for now. Mary patted Terry's hand and left her alone in the viewing room. Terry sat in the quiet. It was unlikely they would ever get a blow-by-blow account of the murders from either Igor or Aoife. There was no doubt they had stalked their prey and then devised methods of killing their victims that would not raise suspicion. That was a deeply chilling thought on its own – the fact that they could be so cold-blooded and calculating.

She closed her eyes. The deaths played out in her mind.

O'Neill's drink had been spiked, and when he passed out, he was submerged in the deep-filled bath, his lungs filling with water until he drowned. She could only imagine Aoife's glee as she shaved his head.

As for Tormey, the fire had succeeded in concealing any injuries he'd sustained before death. Part of his skull was missing, and Terry thought he had probably been struck on the head, possibly with the axe, and knocked unconscious. At that point, his fingers were chopped off, the ring removed and pocketed by Aoife as a morbid souvenir, and he was locked into the burning shed. The fire had finished him off.

Maguire, well, he had been strangled, pure and simple. Then stripped and displayed before a needle was inserted deep into his penis. A punishment that fit the crime, Aoife no doubt believed. God alone knew if there were other victims out there.

Deep down, she suspected the guards all agreed with Aoife that these men were abusers and deserved to be punished. Perhaps Aoife's way was not the right way to settle your scores. But what do you do if the legitimate ways fail?

EX-GARDA KILLED IN SHOOT-OUT: Hero ex-garda Jim Malone foiled a murder attempt on Dr Terry O'Brien, state pathologist. Liam Hayes, son of Donal and Lou Hayes, was injured during the incident. Marcos Ferreira, a security guard from Rialto, Dublin, originally from Campos, Brazil, was killed in the ambush. Two men affiliated with the Hayes gang have been remanded in custody. Malone served as a member of An Garda Síochána until 1994. He moved to Scotland and joined Strathclyde Police Force, where he served for 10 years.

John Fraser sighed and threw the red-top into the bin.

Only a handful of people knew the truth. And it would remain that way.

There was still unfinished business. Terry had let him know what Malone had told her about Bob Paterson. Had he been blindsided by the Higgins murder into thinking Higgins was an informant when Bob was the rat all along? It was a dangerous game Bob had played, and it looked like he had lost. Fraser was sure he wasn't the only one out to get Bob. All Fraser knew right now was that police work never ended – there was still a case to prepare against Aoife and Igor, and a sex-trafficking ring to disassemble. He knew for sure Terry wouldn't rest until Mags, Chisom and the other girls had been found safe and well. The Hayeses had gone to ground, but like snitches, he knew it wouldn't be too long before they regrouped and resurfaced. He shrugged on his coat and closed the door of his office behind him. He smiled when he saw Terry, who was scrolling through her phone as she waited for him in the foyer. He slid his arm around her shoulders, and she grinned up at him. 'Ready?' he asked.

'Yep,' she replied, with a note of certainty in her voice. 'Let's go home.'

Epilogue

The churchyard in Balbriggan was packed with mourners. Terry huddled between Michael and Becs, both for moral support and to shield her from the freezing chill in the air. Her gaze was locked on the hearse as it came to a slow stop by the church steps. She gripped her friends' hands tight.

This was her second funeral in as many days. Bella's urn had been brought to the mortuary after she was cremated and she, Jimmy, Fraser and Tomas had scattered the ashes at Shelbourne Park. She wasn't sure it was entirely legal to do so, but Jimmy said Bella had always been happy there. Terry wasn't going to object. This, in contrast, was a grander affair.

Jim Malone had a huge family. She had a huge family. She suspected most didn't know him and had never met him, but this was Ireland – attending funerals was a national past-time. The press and even RTÉ had turned out. If the funeral had been in Glasgow, she suspected only a handful would have been there. Her dad had been Jim's best, and probably only, real friend. Jim had never married and had no children. Other than Terry.

She still didn't know if her dad knew anything. She hoped not.

Don appeared beside them. 'Ye holding up, hen?'

Terry smiled at him. He and Aileen had come over on the ferry and were going down to Cork to her auntie Bridie's for a few days after the funeral. He had been a bit maudlin at the wake the night before, but that was probably the whiskey. She had gone to the wake to support him, not Jim Malone.

They had all swapped stories of Big Jim. Her dad had met him on their first day in Templemore. They had only fallen out once, he told the group: when Big Jim had made a move on his girlfriend. He never stood a chance, her dad joked, but she saw the sadness in his eyes. Terry had feigned a headache and left.

'I'm fine, Dad. Get away on in, it's starting to rain. They've a seat saved for you at the front. I just need a minute.'

Becs and Michael squeezed her hands and followed him in. She watched them walk away. She still wasn't sure how she felt about her uncle Jim. One thing for sure, he would always be Uncle Jim.

Now she realised how much he had been in her life without her realising it. She remembered the fun and laughter in her home. Jim had always been a part of it. He had never been cross with her. Even when she accidentally drove into the gatepost at the side of the house when he was teaching her to drive.

She had wondered why he had never married. He'd had a few girlfriends, but nothing that lasted. Her dad said he was just an eternal bachelor – now she knew differently. Could her mother have been his only one true love?

He was what everyone described as a good man. And she knew better than most that good people were sometimes driven to do a bad thing. But she could never forgive him for killing her sister. It's hard to imagine any motive that would make killing a teenage girl understandable or that Terry would forgive him. Fraser appeared at her side. They were both scanning the faces of the people filing into the church, although not looking for the same person.

Terry had thought her mother might turn up, but her familiar face was nowhere to be seen. Surely, she wouldn't have changed that much. But Terry's memories had faded – maybe she wouldn't recognise her.

Fraser gave a signal to someone unseen, then put his arm around Terry's waist. She looked back over her left shoulder. There was only an old woman laying flowers on a grave. Terry turned her head towards the car park, but apart from a couple of guards lounging against a patrol car, it was empty. She didn't see the blonde figure sitting in a small black car outside the church gates.

Terry turned up the collar of her coat and smiled up at Fraser. Together they walked towards the church to pay their respects to the dead.

Acknowledgements

If you've got this far in the book, don't panic, I won't keep you much longer, but I just want you to know that I couldn't have written *Deadly Evidence* on my own.

Firstly, thanks to the multitalented Ciara Considine, publisher extraordinaire at Hatchette Ireland. I knew I would be in good hands the first time we met. I hope I have at least met your expectations.

If you, the reader, enjoyed this book, then it's down to Claire Pelly, my fantastic editor, who knocked me and the book into shape. Thank you, we both benefited from your input.

Thanks also to Stephen Riordan and Joanna Smyth at Hachette Ireland for their helpful input.

Of course, I cannot forget Faith O'Grady, my agent. It still sounds pretentious to claim to have an agent, but I really couldn't navigate this new world without her support. I'm not sure what she expected when she agreed to represent me, but it has been fun. For me anyway.

I am a reluctant self-promoter, which doesn't make life easy for Elaine Egan, Publicity Director, who has the unenviable task of dragging me around the country to meet all you lovely readers. I am humbled by the fact that you take time out of your busy lives to read my books and turn up to events. It is always a joy to chat to you; surprisingly, I realise, admittedly late in life, that the living are as interesting as the dead.

Lastly, thanks to my family, my husband Philip, and my darling children, Kieran and Sarah, my biggest supporters. Right back at you.

RAISING READERS
Books Build Bright Futures

Dear Reader,

We'd love your attention for one more page to tell you about
the crisis in children's reading, and what we can all do.

Studies have shown that reading for fun is the **single
biggest predictor of a child's future success** – more than
family circumstance, parents' educational background or
income. It improves academic results, mental health, wealth,
communication skills and ambition.

The number of children reading for fun is in rapid decline.
Young people have a lot of competition for their time, and a
worryingly high number do not have a single book at home.

Our business works extensively with schools, libraries and
literacy charities, but here are some ways we can all raise
more readers:

- Reading to children for just 10 minutes a day makes a
  difference
- Don't give up if your children aren't regular readers – there
  will be books for them!
- Visit bookshops and libraries to get recommendations
- Encourage them to listen to audiobooks
- Support school libraries
- Give books as gifts

Thank you for reading.
www.JoinRaisingReaders.com